MYSTIC OF THE ALPHA

THE ALPHA KING'S BREEDER
BOOK EIGHTEEN

BELLA MOONDRAGON

For Vickie. Thanks for reading.

CONTENTS

1

NOTHING BUT NIGHT AND ICE

Skye

THERE'RE ONLY TWO TYPES OF PEOPLE WHO WOULD EVER REMOTELY consider calling Lunaria home.

The wolves of the small towns and rural pack territories that dot the eternally icy, always dark frozen wasteland so far north of Crescent Falls that the sun only rises a few inches over the horizon for three months out of the year... and people like me—intellectuals. Researchers. Souls chasing the unexplainable with new scientific methods and theories even magic can't decipher. People who haven't been outside in weeks because the daily negative sixty-degree low is cold enough to freeze eyeballs in less than ten minutes. *Crazy people.* I digress.

I love it here. The darkness. The *stars*. The endless, flat landscape of ice against the wash of the aurora, painting the sky in shades of emerald and pale pink every night... and day, in reality. It's fall, a week before the official start of the semester, and already the sun has failed to rise for several days, barely poking above the horizon, giving off nothing more than what the locals call the "blue hour," where the normally dark sky turns an impressive midnight blue before fading back to black.

After four grueling years of my PhD studies and post-doctoral research, I've made it. I've done it. *I did it.* The small but sleek box of glass expanding around me is mine. The whiteboard? Mine. The empty bookshelves? Also mine. The slightly battered desk and ancient computer that will definitely need to be replaced? Mine, mine, *mine.*

I snap a few pictures of my empty office with my phone, grinning from ear to ear. The group chat with my parents fills with shots of my empty desk, the solid, slate-colored walls, the wall-to-wall white-board I'm aching to fill with the theoretical equations I've been working on during my free time all summer.

Floor-to-ceiling windows stretch toward the south, giving me all the light available during the blue hour–a true miracle of circum-stance seeing as this was the only empty office available in the physics department, and it's...

"All yours, huh?" Dad's smile is wide and rich over our video call as I spin the phone in a circle for him and Uncle Ryan to see. Silver-hide in all its autumn glory takes up the screen, but both men smile when I smooth my hand over the built-in bookshelf.

"Will you make sure Mom sees the pictures? She's been asking me for days when I'd get the keys, and I just got them today."

"I'm sure she's already showing your aunt and cousins," Dad replies with a soft, proud chuckle. "I love it. It's all very–"

"Straight lines and gray?" Uncle Ryan chips in with a hearty laugh. "How long until you see the sun again, Skye?"

I sink into the desk chair and swivel with a creak, adding a new chair to the mental list of things to request from the supply depart-ment. "I'll come back for Solstice, so not long. There's a bit of a break between classes then."

"How many classes are you teaching this semester?" Dad walks away from Ryan, and the scene in Silverhide shifts to rain clouds peeking over the valley and a group of muscular, sweaty men carrying harvesting tools while wolves pull carts of freshly harvested grain.

"Uh, two., All lectures. All graduate level." I smooth my hand over the gray surface of my desk before looking through the drawers to see if the last person who claimed this space left anything behind. I find a few old mints that crumble to dust in their plastic wrappings and a long-dry pen. "The rest of my time is just... research." Thank the Goddess. I was adjunct faculty during my postdoc and spent all of my time grading undergraduate papers on Physics 101 and answering asinine emails that normally went something like, *"Hey Dr. Abbot, I forgot that essay was due today. My fish back in Moonrise died :(Can I have an extension?? TYSM!!!"*

I rise and turn to the window, testing the glass against my fingertips. Compared to the icy landscape, the glass is warm and frost-free, offering a crystal clear view.

"So... how's everything going?" I ask, and Dad sighs heavily, our connection buffering for a few seconds. "Dad?"

"I'm still here. It's going fine. We're all headed to the festival grounds tomorrow."

A pang of guilt whispers through my chest. "I left a wedding gift back in Moonrise for Kieran. He told me his fiancée likes books, so I wrapped up a few of my favorites."

"They'll appreciate it. Kieran and Lyra's bookshelves in that little cabin he finished building this summer are empty as it stands. They'll be the most well-read wolves in the Emberfyll Pack–"

His image freezes mid-sentence.

"Dad? Dad? Shit." I hiss out a breath and hang up, setting my phone down. Maybe it was an act of the Goddess that the call dropped during an otherwise uncomfortable conversation. Kieran, my cousin, is getting married in a few days during the harvest festival. His is the first wedding of our generation, and I'm missing it. I have a valid excuse. I'm thousands of miles away and starting my new job, the job I fought tooth and nail for, but I know what the family thinks about my situation.

I turned twenty-eight last spring. I'm single, otherwise thriving, but have undoubtedly separated myself from the way of life set forth by my great-great-grandparents almost a century ago. I have magic in my veins. Real, unfathomable power. I've never questioned how to use it. I know who and what I am.

Unlike my family members, I'm desperate to understand *why*.

A resounding knock on the door is followed by a short, stout woman entering my office. I'm perched on the edge of my desk when she walks in, smiling at me, her hazel eyes crinkling. "Dr. Abbot! How are you liking it? If it's too cold in here, I can have maintenance check your thermostat. Dr. Kleinhowser liked to keep it near freezing. He was a local, you know, of Aurorium."

"I know," I say with a polite smile. "He was one of my professors during my master's program."

Maisie Robertson, faculty administrator, grips her clipboard with a grin bright enough to light the night sky–or morning sky, since it's not even 10:00 A.M.

"Well, settle in, take your time. Classes don't start until next Monday anyway. You know how to request supplies–"

"Yes."

"Oh, right, you were a postdoc!" She grins again, but it's a bit strained, her cheeks staining a deep pink. "Anyway, here." She passes me a flyer, still warm from the printer. "There's a little meet and greet tonight, nothing formal or mandatory, but it's strictly for the faculty. The advanced psychology department had a bit of funds leftover from a research grant last year and bought a margarita machine! They promised to bring it. Otherwise, there's going to be beer and wine for sure."

I nod along, resisting the urge to mumble under my breath about the fact that a department had leftover money from a grant, whereas I was scrambling for funds to replace dry-erase markers and ended up sketching equations on napkins with pencils I dug out of the trash bins in the physics lab's break room.

"I'll be there."

"Great! Oh, it's been so long since we've had someone so young on staff!" She practically hops out of the room, closing the door behind her.

Silence sweeps through the room, rattling the normally quiet voices that whisper along the shadowed outskirts of my mind. My bracelet barely holds them back anymore. They begin to chatter.

"Not now," I tell them, folding the flyer into a little crane and setting it on my desk.

THE OBSERVATORY IS A WIDE, CIRCULAR ROOM SET UP LIKE AN auditorium. A stage rests under the glass dome protecting observers from the elements, but otherwise, the sky is wide and open. I sink into a chair at the very back. It's dark, the stars are out and blinking, and it's only noon. This place? It's sacred to me—like a church where I pray, but instead of talking to the Goddess, I sit here and look up, trying to piece together the strange elements of my mind that make me who I am and determine what I see in my visions.

I use this place as a lecture hall sometimes. An exterior shield can be brought up over the dome itself, and projectors paint the night sky instead, giving students and staff alike a view of the far reaches of our universe.

But I like it best like this—open, quiet, watching comets whizz across the blanket of navy blue and shadow.

I lean back, my neck draped over the top of the scratchy fabric covering the chair, and almost miss the shadow moving several rows in front of me. A tall, lean man rises and gathers his belongings before moving toward the exit—probably a student using the space for a silent study session.

I close my eyes for a moment and let myself drift through my memories like turning pages of a book, letting my guilt over missing Kieran's wedding during the harvest festival wash over me in gentle, lapping waves until it fades. A hazy memory I hadn't thought of in years takes hold, bringing me back to my early twenties, when I'd first come to Lunaria on a tour with my parents to see the facilities and decided, for certain, that this is where I wanted to pursue my graduate studies.

It had been utter madness. I was considered a prodigy back at

Wellington, then at the University of Moonrise. When I transferred during my undergraduate studies, I was the star of the physics department, and Lunaria U *wanted me*. They even threw a welcome party for me and my parents, and I fell into bad habits I thought I'd kicked as a preteen, when the social aspect of life finally caught up to me and turned me inside out.

I have none of the grace and social butterfly gifts of my mom and granny, Leona. I favor my dad and his rigidity, his inability to fix his face to smile when appropriate. I am his daughter through and through, and while that ensured I'd heavily favor math and science, it also meant I spent a great deal of time alone, researching how to make friends and practicing facial expressions in the mirror until I had several trained masks I could wear at any given moment.

The party they'd thrown for me was overwhelming. All the questions, the praise…. My mask started to slip. I got confused about how I was supposed to talk, look, and behave. So, when the professor of advanced experimental physics turned his back, I ran, ducking into a utility closet in the hallway off the conference room full of people who demanded something from me I didn't know how to bend my body into being and… hid.

Tears blurred my vision. I kept rubbing them away, but more would come, and then it got hard to breathe.

A hand pressed on my shoulder, slightly cold, like the person had been outside recently or holding an iced drink.

"Take a few breaths. You're having a panic attack." His accent was strange. It wasn't anything I'd ever heard before. Deep and rolling like waves against a distant shore.

"Wh-who–"

"In, and out—like this," the deep male voice explained, but his image was so blurred by my tears I couldn't make out his face. He sounded young–probably a student, which only made it worse.

I tried to follow his direction but kept choking and wheezing, and all the while, he crouched, only a few inches from me, gripping my shoulder every time I inhaled.

"I don't think I can do this," I admitted through a torrent of tears. "I–I don't like–the fact–that I have to–"

"Talk to people?"

"I thought I could just–sit in a lecture hall, or the library, or–"

"You can. You're not the only socially-inept creature that's going to haunt these halls. Lunaria U is a hotbed for people like us."

Us.

That word… it changed everything.

He left before my vision cleared enough to dab my cheeks and go back to the party, but when I did, I noticed everyone in the room, save for a few administrators and my mom, were just like me. Their eyes didn't match the curve of their lips. Their expressions were strained, like an event like this was painful for them, and when my dad dropped me off for my first semester of my graduate program, and I thrust myself into a full student life, I actually fit in.

Everyone here is like me. Left-brained. Science-minded. Weirdos who like the dark and cold. People who can sit in the silence with each other and call it socializing.

It doesn't mean we don't have *fun*, however.

I leave the observatory and go home to get ready for the get-together. The door to my apartment slams shut while I'm dabbing my lips with deep burgundy lipstick, followed by grumbling and a low, insanely colorful curse. Abby, my roommate, a microbiologist doing her postdoc, strides past my bedroom, red in the face, and it's not from the cold.

"Hey? Are you okay?"

She backs up, tucking her platinum blonde, perfectly straight hair behind her ears, and glowers, brown eyes shining. "No, I'm not."

"What's up?"

"You know, I've come to realize that murder can't be all that bad if it benefits the common good."

2

WE'VE MET

Skye

I cock my head and laugh as Abby braces her hands on my doorframe. Her fair skin is flushed pink from the cold, which means she was likely outside, possibly in one of the "bubble labs" as we call them, where a few of the departments do their experiments on the ice. Or, more probable, in the terrifying ice labs beneath the surface, where tunnels of ancient ice go on for miles.

The gray slate walls behind her gleam in the pale light in the hallway of our apartment–which isn't much, but we have windows to the outside world, which is a privilege.

The student dormitories are in the tunnels weaving beneath the university where the sun never shines even in the summer, and the lights are specially made to give students who live there a minuscule amount of synthetic sunlight to aid the copious amounts of vitamin D supplements everyone keeps in their backpacks.

I landed an apartment in one of the towers two years ago. It was a miracle, an actual act of the Goddess, and no one can convince me otherwise. After spending the two previous years as a certified mole person, walking into a space with windows brought me to my knees, but then I met my roommate.

Angela.

A postdoctoral researcher in the psychology department who spent an entire year using me as her test subject, subjecting me to often mean, nefarious forms of psychological torture in the name of the humanities.

When she left to take her place as an administrator, in the torture department in Hell, for all I know, I actually wept with joy—and then I met Abby.

"Murder?"

"How do you kill someone without anyone knowing?" Abby leans into my room. She smells like an astringent cleaning solution and the soap that makes her hands crack so badly we block out a night once a week to soak them in warm milk, cover them in the thickest lotion we can find, and force her to wear socks on her hands until morning.

"Uh, you don't? Who do you want to murder? Toby? I thought you guys were dating again."

She licks her cold-chapped lips, dark eyes narrowing to cat-like slits. "Not Toby. Dr. Scarlett is on my shit list, and I'd love to see him bleed out on the ice. I'm sure his blood would be black, given that he's a fucking demon!" She groans and pushes off the doorframe, flopping face down on my bed. "I hate him. He's making my life fucking miserable."

"Just go to the dean—"

"He's not a postdoc," she groans into the comforter. "He's a professor, like you. All fancy, tenured, and untouchable. He also just so happens to be my lab director." She turns her head to the side to look at me. I stare at her, the name not registering. She rolls her eyes. "You wouldn't know him because he's in the biology department, and unlike your heated lecture halls and labs within the towers, his labs are outside, *under* the ice."

"I see." I swivel in my desk chair to face her, closing the compact mirror I used to do my makeup in my palm.

"I have one more year of postdoctoral research, Skye. Then I'm moving back to where it's warm. I'll go into industry if I have to, researching fucking dolphins for all I care, as long as I don't have to work with him ever again. I swear I will."

Abby is from Maatua, and for reasons only a career academic could possibly understand, didn't leave Lunaria when she graduated with her PhD last year and go into "industry" or the real world, using her skills at a mainland lab or one of the marine labs in Maatua that offered her the world, which she refused.

She'd stayed for Toby, but she'll never admit it. Not even to me.

"I think you'd love industry," I coax, but she frowns at me.

"I'd love to publish my research, but Dr. Scarlett is part of it and has been giving me hell about my current sea ice theories. I've been a mile under the ice since this summer, digging with my bare hands." She flexes her fingers. "Must have been nice getting tenure and taking the summer off."

"Don't turn your anger on me." I tsk, and she rises on her elbows, narrowing her eyes while scanning my face.

"Are you wearing makeup?"

"A little." I blush under her scrutiny. "Why? Does it look bad? Is it too much?"

"You look like a living person for once."

"Amazing what a little bronzer will do," I huff, giving her my back and fumbling in my makeup bag for the ancient tube of mascara I bought six years ago, which is long expired, but desperate times call for desperate measures.

"Do you have a date?" Her excitement rings through the room, bouncing off the floor-to-ceiling windows overlooking campus, a maze of sparkling, glass towers and skybridges connecting the different departments, labs, and common spaces.

"No." I laugh, swiping the mascara across my lashes. "There's a little 'start of the semester' party for the professors tonight. I feel like I have to go."

"Ah, I see. A little gathering to decide how to torture the students this year, huh?"

"Just the undergraduates." I smirk, catching her eyes, and she grins back. "Speaking of which, you'll have an entire pool of new students to seduce into working as lab assistants. Maybe instead of murdering your research director, you can pawn his wrath onto someone else?" My phone buzzes, alerting me to the time. "Shit, I have to go. How do I look?"

I turn back to her, but her eyelids flutter, and she slumps into an exhausted, utterly limp kind of sleep. Fair enough. I suppose letting her borrow my bed means I have free rein over her well-stocked closet.

My normally smart, academia-leaning style isn't much more than a thick sweater and black leggings, but based on the flyer, this is a more formal affair. I flick through Abby's options and find a black cocktail dress that isn't too short and drape it over my body, completing the look with a pair of her knee-high black leather boots.

My usual black wool coat is next, and that's it. I'm ready. Ready to step into a new chapter of my life as a professor and research director.

Which means mingling with people from the other departments isn't something I can avoid anymore.

The maze of skybridges connecting the LU towers is mostly empty. It's late evening, and any students who've arrived early for the start of the semester or postdoctoral researchers who remained to continue their research in the icy recesses of the north are the only people around, likely congregating in the common spaces surrounding the library at the heart of campus, a spiraling glass structure that creates a midpoint in the center of the four towers, where all the skybridges eventually lead.

It took a while to mentally map this campus when I was a new student. The crystalline towers are massive, and the spider's web of skybridges took days to figure out, and don't even get me started on the tunnels that run underground in the ice, connecting everything at ground level. Dad has visited more than anyone as it stands, and I doubt it has much to do with me, his favorite and only daughter. He has a thing for architecture, and we've spent days roaming the glass hallways while he inspected every impossible curve and sharp angle.

I reach the library, digging the flyer out of my pocket. It's still in the shape of a crane. I carefully unfold it to check the room number while I step into an elevator bound for the commons closer to ground level, scanning the page instead of my surroundings.

I slam into a hard body.

The elevator doors close behind us, and my stomach flip-flops as it drops with speed.

A tall, lean, but broad-shouldered, man clutches my arm for a moment, my vision filled entirely with the fibers of his forest green sweater, before letting me go and stepping back.

"Sorry," I murmur, slowly looking up at him, taking in his dark jeans and black leather jacket over his sweater, then... *him.*

The handsome stranger just nods curtly before rolling his eyes to the door at my back. He's in his early thirties, clean-shaven, with fair skin and dark, glossy hair. Black hair, actually, with a blue tinge I so rarely see in nature. But on second glance, I think it's just the heavy fluorescent light reflecting off his sharp, ocean blue eyes giving off that startling color. I find him familiar in a way I can't place.

He slowly looks down at me, catching me staring boldly. "Are you new here?"

"Me? No. No, I–sorry, I guess I'm not used to sharing elevators yet. It's been a quiet week." I step to the side to give him more space, but his gaze follows my progress to the transparent wall. I should say something, right? He's probably a graduate student or new postdoctoral researcher. I haven't seen him around before. It's my duty, I suppose, as a tenured professor to be amiable and social with students and researchers when the circumstance calls for it.

I open my mouth with nothing to say, but the light cuts out as the elevator breaches the surface of the ice and dives down into the tunnels.

"Scared of the dark?" he asks as the elevator slows.

It's an odd question. I shiver under the weight of the darkness and his presence. "Uh, no."

"Hm. Could have fooled me. Your heart's racing."

His scent is everywhere. Cool and clean. Like the ice all around us—with a hint of laundry detergent. But when he steps closer, the underlying masculine tone hits me, and it's warm, cozy, spiced with a gentle, non-overbearing cologne. Something woodsy and simple.

"Do you live in the dorms?" I ask, my voice hitching against my will.

"I haven't for a long time." The doors open wide, revealing a hallway of concrete broken up by several open spaces for lounging and gathering. I step out, but unfortunately, the stranger follows, walking a few feet behind me while I navigate the hallway as it branches, following it to the right.

And… he's still behind me. Still matching the cadence of my steps. It takes all of my strength to resist the urge to look at him over my shoulder. I, naturally, pick up my pace as the room assigned to the party comes into view. Voices and music drift into the hallway, and at this point, I can't help it.

I have always been, and likely will always be, a firm follower of the rules.

"This is a private event for tenured staff," I bite out, whirling to face the stranger.

He smirks as he strides past me, his arm brushing my shoulder. "I'm aware."

"What—"

"Dr. Scarlett!" I slowly turn back to the door as Dr. Gerralde, a professor in my department and one of my advisors during my graduate days, beams up at the stranger, his green eyes crinkling with surprise.

My eyes, on the other hand, narrow at the mention of Abby's demonic research director.

Dr. Gerralde continues. "I didn't realize you'd be coming, but I'm so glad you're here. I heard a rumor that you're looking for someone from the physics department to help with your research in the biology department. I wanted to pick your brain as to who you were thinking, but you're a hard man to pin down."

I step into the room. It's dizzying. The music is suddenly too loud, and the voices screech against the concrete walls. I can't look away from the tall, sweater-clad man as Dr. Gerralde claps him on the upper arm and motions to me.

"Ah! Skye, my dear! Alex, this is who I wanted you to meet. Dr. Abbot was one of my..." His words drown in the endless sea of sound and bodies. I'm suddenly trapped in my head, unable to move, my body doing that thing where it ceases to function.

Alex–Dr. Scarlett–turns to me ever so slowly, ocean blue eyes meeting mine. He tilts his head in a weak, half-assed silent acknowledgment of my presence. "We've met," he says to Dr. Gerralde, thoroughly, *bitingly* uninterested, then side-steps through the crowd, falling out of sight.

3

GET RID OF ME

Skye

DR. SCARLETT, ALSO KNOWN AS ALEX, MOVES INTO THE CROWD, BUT that doesn't stop me from unintentionally catching his tall, imposing figure in my peripheral vision. He's taller than everyone here, and his hair is, in fact, so black it's nearly blue–absorbing every fractal of light in the room like a black hole.

Dr. Gerralde turns to me, pushing his glasses up the bridge of his nose with a short, sharp chuckle. "Whenever I think the physics department is full of antisocial weirdos, I am reminded that the biology department might actually be worse off than we are in that regard."

"He's far too young to be a department head," I rush out, but then quickly reel myself back in and clear my throat.

"Not a department head–yet. Although, I know the university president has him pegged as the future dean of the biology department as long as he doesn't go into industry. He's a professor, and he has been for a few years now. He is leading his own lab, though."

I'm not sure why I want to know, but I ask, "What kind of biologist is he?"

"Paleomicrobiology is his specialty."

I think of the ice labs buried deep under our feet. There're dozens of them now, all connected by tunnels of gleaming blue ice, all being used for research into the medical sciences and history, mostly. Biologists and researchers are easy to spot around campus because they proudly wear their neon yellow thermals under whatever regular clothes they have on hand after leaving their labs and returning to the surface. I've turned entire loads of laundry yellow by accidentally washing Abby's thermals with my clothes.

Dr. Gerralde steps closer, leaning in to say, "I wanted the two of you to meet. I was going to put together a little meeting, but like I said, he's impossible. I'm shocked he's here tonight."

An impossible asshole? Abby would say so, seeing as this is the same man who torments her and calls her research garbage. I keep those thoughts to myself, for now. "Why would I need to meet with Dr. Scarlett? We're in different departments."

"He has been doing some impressive research in those ice labs. He got a grant three years ago from the Alpha King of Celestoria, enough to fund his labs for the next decade if he's frugal."

A decade? Impossible. "Seriously? What kind of research–"

"He's looking for what the biologists call the Goddess Particle." He arches a brow and gives me a knowing smirk.

"Oh, good grief."

"My sentiments exactly. But we are theoretical physicists, you and I. I know how you feel about such a particle, and I can take a guess and say you know how I feel about it, as well."

"It doesn't exist. We've proven that time and time again in our own lab." My throat thickens around the admission. I'm not proud of my failures there. Everyone in the sciences here is looking for the same thing–the answer to everything. The powers, the magic, the one missing puzzle piece that the private benefactors who fund our search need to know–for their own gain, I suppose.

Everyone wants a piece of the magic my family has naturally.

I'd like to find that puzzle piece, if only to keep it hidden a little longer.

Not in a selfish way. At least, I've been telling myself that for years. I just know firsthand what it's like to have unfathomable magic at my fingertips, and it's so dangerous. So life-altering. So wrong, honestly.

But these days, research into what is popularly called the Goddess Particle is about more than greed.

"Tell that to Dr. Scarlett, who, by the way, has been looking for a physicist to help with his research, and you are the lucky victim."

"Do not sacrifice me for the good of the department, I beg you!"

Dr. Gerralde laughs at my dramatics and claps me on the shoulder, but I'm not laughing. I'm looking right at Alex, who's looking *right at me*, his icy blue stare sucking the warmth right out of the room.

I do my best to keep my expression painfully neutral. I can play nice with other departments. I understand the politics on campus and the undercurrent of disdain between the sciences, of course. Biologists don't like physicists like me, especially. I'm a theorist. It's literally my job to question everything I see, and my theories then get turned into experiments carried out by more experimental physicists.

Not biologists. They're the warriors of the sciences, especially those who work in the ice labs. It's a dangerous job.

I've never been beneath the surface of the ice. My lecture halls and office are always a balmy sixty-five degrees. This man? He's hardened. Vicious. The amount of funding it takes to keep those ice labs running is exceedingly expensive, and I know, based on Abby's constant complaining, more of their experiments go wrong than any other department, but their research is crucial.

It's a well-known fact across the Allied Kingdoms that once, decades ago, there was a cure for everything. Every ailment. Any injury. Anything that hurt could be resolved.

Because of my great-great-great-grandmother's tears.

My great-aunt Misty's healing gifts can't touch what Isla's could. Her children never carried the gifts... not as much as their mother and great-grandmother, anyway.

And my dad? He doesn't heal. We don't *heal*. We change the Goddess's own will. Our powers are… a sleight of hand.

Cheating death when it's not our call to make.

While witches have the ability to create healing potions, and some have healing powers, it's not enough. Not enough to mass-produce, at least. So that's what those insane biologists are looking for in those labs—remnants of ancient magic from a time when gods and goddesses supposedly walked among us—more so than they do now.

I would know, seeing as I'm one of them.

Instead of the ice, I like to look up for the answers to the questions that have been plaguing me since girlhood, however.

Dr. Gerralde is swept into another conversation. Eventually, there's a blended margarita in my hand. Eventually, I finish half of it and decide there's nowhere else I'd rather be than in my own apartment, but when I sneak out of the party, I can still feel Dr. Scarlett's gaze on the back of my neck, tingling.

When I get home, Abby's thermals are drying out over the radiator, and she's sitting on the couch in nothing but a sports bra and her underwear.

"Back so soon?"

I flex my jaw, chuckling in disbelief as I shrug out of my coat and drape it over the kitchen island. "I met Dr. Scarlett."

"I bet he was a joy to talk to." She grits her teeth and shakes her head like I've ruined her night just by mentioning his name.

"We didn't really talk." Just stared at each other, and he was so… frustratingly familiar.

I sit on the couch with Abby while she goes on and on about Dr. Scarlett and how much she loathes the man, but my mind slips into the recesses, my powers, while muted by the bracelet, guiding me into a darkness of my own making.

I used to come here so often. When I was a child, this place—the observatory—took up so many of my dreams. I had a friend here. I never knew his name, but he was little like me. Childish and playful, like I used to be. We'd play checkers on a board that randomly appeared one day, and I'd tell him everything about myself.

Now, the vision in my mind is tainted by crackling ice and the smell of blood.

I haven't seen that little boy for many years.

I wonder if he thinks about me as much as I've thought about him over the years. We never really had a chance to say goodbye before the heavens plucked the thread that bound our dreams together.

"Skye?"

I groggily open my eyes to see Abby standing in front of me, dressed in her thermals again. "Sorry, I fell asleep. You're going back to the lab? It's midnight."

She shrugs. "Speaking of Dr. Scarlett... that bastard never sleeps, which means the lab is open all the Goddess-damned time... and I have some work to do." She pulls a beanie over her head and slips a pair of gray sweatpants over her thermals. "Did you find out if you're getting a new place? Don't all professors get their own condo or something?"

"The Pillars?" I smooth my hand down my face. When did I fall asleep? Sometimes, I don't even notice the pull of my powers until it's too late. I make a mental note to reach out to Posey for a new charm— or two... or three. "I haven't heard, but I'm sure I will." I think of The Pillars, which is a neighborhood on the outskirts of campus that was built in a semicircle atop glass columns jutting out of the ice. It's like a moon that hugs the campus with a view of Aurorium, the closest big city to LU.

"Well, I really hope you don't. I don't want a new roommate." She winks at me and leaves me alone in the chilly silence, and after a moment, I go to my room to sleep for a few hours.

The rest of the week is simple and easy—nearly laid back. I finalize my syllabi. I make my new office mine with pictures of my family and a few plants that can't live without the purple UV lights that turn the gray glass box into what Abby calls a rave, but I digress. I spend time in the physics lab and the observatory, working on my search and mapping the far off galaxy I've made my life's work. I fall into what I hope is a new routine, and it feels great. Like everything is going exactly how it should be, which is just the way I like it.

It's a frigid Friday afternoon, three days before the official start of the semester, when Abby and I walk through the skybridges to the commissary because we're out of cereal when I run into Maisie, the physics department's administrator. I've successfully avoided her for the past several days and dodged several emails related to department social functions, but my good luck can only last so long.

Abby tosses two boxes of cereal into our basket while Maisie goes on and on, apologizing profusely about her lack of haste in rehoming me, essentially.

"It's a two-bedroom, one bath, pretty standard," she explains with a self-deprecating sigh. "Seeing as you're single, I figured it would be enough space?"

"Uh, yeah, it's plenty, but–"

"She'll take it," Abby cuts in, rolling her eyes and snatching a third box from the shelf.

"Great! I'll have the keys sent to your office once the cleaning crew is done."

Maisie disappears into the crowd of students returning from summer break and shopping to fill their mini-refrigerator. I throw a sharp look at Abby.

"What? You're a professor now, Skye! And leading a lab. You're entitled to this. It's part of the job! Plus, I'll have a new cool place to hang out. I heard each condo in The Pillars has its own washer and dryer units. No more digging for coins in our coat pockets and couch cushions!"

I scoff, pivoting to face her. "You're using me for your own convenience."

"This is a promotion for both of us. I'm your best friend, Skye. What's mine is yours, and I have very little. You're about to have an actual house."

"I'm fine with our apartment!"

"You're not a postdoc anymore!"

"It shouldn't matter! You just told me you didn't want me to move out–"

A shadow falls over us as two men brush past–one being Dr. Scarlett, who doesn't even glance down at me until Toby pulls him to a rough stop.

Dr. Scarlett looks just as surprised to see me as I am to see him.

4

WARNING!

Alex

BITTER COFFEE SCENTS THE AIR AS TOBY SLIDES TWO PAPER CUPS FULL
of ink-colored liquid across the counter. I grab one while he pours a
copious amount of sugar in his cup and wait for him to finish with
the carafe of cream.

It's Friday, and normally I'm in the lab, but today I needed to make
myself available to sign for a supply delivery coming from Aurorium,
and Toby took that as an opportunity to turn my down-time into an
entire event.

We used to be roommates back when I lived in the dungeon-like
dormitory beneath the ice. Unlike everyone else, I loved it down
there–the darkness of it all. The shuddering pipes and crackling ice
against feet of concrete felt like home, but when I was offered an
apartment after I graduated with my master's and planned to pursue a
PhD, I took it, mostly because Toby begged for me to take it–and to
take him with me when I finally breached the surface. So I did.

We don't live together now, but for whatever reason, I'm leaning against the counter in the campus coffee shop while he flips through a grocery list he made on his phone.

"We need hand soap and towels for the lab…. Do you think the commissary is going to have any in-season vegetables?" He brings his coffee cup to his lips.

"I highly doubt it."

He frowns and rolls his eyes to the windows behind us. It's well into the afternoon and pitch black, long past the mere minutes of blue hour, or civil twilight, we get a day this far north. "Meat? The hunting here has sucked lately."

"Your guess is as good as mine."

He growls. "You've never been a fun person to take grocery shopping."

"Why not take Abby with you then?" I resist the urge to remind him he's technically holding me against my will, but if I say that out loud, he'll just smile, tease me, maybe even turn this into a whole thing and bring up my strange dietary habits from our time as under-grads, when I wouldn't come near the pizza and the blended and fried raw garbage he called chicken nuggets. He only recently switched to real food.

"Abby is honestly worse of a shopping companion than you. She buys everything on a whim. It's chaos. Meanwhile, you spend an atro-cious amount of time reading the labels on everything and not even buying anything. What do you eat these days, huh? Your precious black coffee and what, protein bars?"

"It's a well-balanced meal."

"You're insane, Alex."

"The best scientists are."

He huffs a laugh and sips his coffee then turns back to the counter to pour more sugar into his cup. I wince, shaking my head and biting my tongue against the flurry of warnings that come to mind about glucose and its effects on wolves like Toby, but then he claps the plastic lid back on his cup and says, "Ready for shopping?"

I reluctantly nod, falling into step with him. The little cafe near the commons connects to the library by a glass bridge, but we bypass the archways leading into LU's massive library and head to the elevators. The commissary is perched just a story above ice level and serves as a quick stop for things like toiletries and groceries for the students who live in the dorms beneath the ground, as well as the graduate-level students, researchers, and professors above.

I rarely come here. I watch Toby scan the shelves as he moves through the tight, crowded aisles. Even after over a decade in Lunaria, in the Allied Kingdoms, all of this still feels foreign to me. I follow along as Toby does his shopping.

"Oh, cereal!" Toby steers his cart, which is full of soap and whatever decent looking meat and vegetables he could get his hands on around a sharp corner, and I stop short.

Skye Abbot is tucked against one of the shelves. She nods along to whatever Maisie, the insufferable faculty administrator, is gesturing about. Skye's eyes are slightly glazed over and remain that way when Maisie walks away, but then she blinks, and those violet irises sharpen on Abby, who's arguing with her about something.

I step into the aisle to follow Toby, each step calculated and determined to squeeze past her without being noticed.

I met her before the party the other night, but she doesn't remember. I suppose it's best if it stays that way.

But when Toby's hand grips my forearm and drags me to a stop, I'm forced to face them. Face her. The one person I told myself I'd avoid like the plague.

She's... not just a shifter. It's evident in her scent, the way she carries herself and the sharpening of those eyes when her gaze locks on mine and narrows into a glare.

There're other kinds of shifters, or at least, there used to be, according to what I've learned during my decade in the Kingdoms. Perhaps she's a... cat shifter? If those exist? She moves like one, especially as she slowly follows my fingers to pry Toby's grip from my thermal shirt.

"Babe," Toby beams, but Abby, like usual, snarls at him.

SKYE

AFTER YEARS OF NOT ONCE SEEING THE MAN AROUND CAMPUS, ALL OF A sudden he's in front of me all the time. He's here now, turning to us as Abby snaps at Toby, who looks like being under Abby's wrath is exactly where he wants to be at any given moment.

I've never seen someone more in love. Abby, on the other hand, is still on the fence about her feelings. That, or she thoroughly enjoys torturing the poor man every second of every day.

"You were really about to just walk right by me and not say anything?" Abby snaps, gripping the basket like a weapon. "Asshole!"

"Babe, I literally just talked to you on the phone!"

"You could have said you were coming to the commissary. We could have come together!"

"I didn't know I was going to be up here until we ran out of hand soap in the lab washroom," he grumbles. His rich, light brown hair is slicked back from wearing a beanie most of the time. His hazel eyes briefly meet mine, and he nods, murmuring, "Hey, Skye."

"Hey, Toby." I give him a quick, apologetic smile. Abby can be... a lot. But he knows that. They've been playing this game for years.

They're mates. Fated mates. Their dynamic is strange, to say the least.

Dr. Scarlett is just standing here, watching the scene play out, his expression totally unreadable. He catches me staring but says nothing, just arches a brow while Abby continues to rail into Toby for the simple fact that they ran into each other in public.

"This day couldn't get any worse," Abby huffs, shoving the basket into my unready arms. I drop it, and Dr. Scarlett catches it before it hits the ground, handing it back to me without a single word.

"What else is going on because this can't just be about me shopping!" Toby grips Abby's shoulder. "Come on, Abigail."

"Skye just got her fancy professor condo, so she has to move out–"

"I haven't decided—"

"You don't get to decide! I knew it was going to happen. There's never been enough apartments for the postdocs. You know that!" She's pouting now, a trick I know all too well. Toby can't help but melt at the sight of her puppy dog expression.

I roll my eyes, accidentally catching Dr. Scarlett's gaze, and this time he smiles... a bit. No teeth, but he's obviously enjoying the show. The slight curve of his lips softens his features to something almost... handsome. Maybe even a little warm and approachable, but barely.

"Babe, that's great news!"

"What? Skye is moving out, and that's great news to you? Fuck you, Toby!"

He shakes her. "I'm supposed to be getting a new roommate, but we can room together now!"

Dr. Scarlett and I both wait in shockingly companionable silence for Abby's reaction, which is likely to be explosive.

She wipes her eyes, which are dry, and looks at our sorry group, then realizes her arch nemesis is standing there, looking down at her.

"What are *you* doing here?"

"Picking up supplies for the lab," Dr. Scarlett deadpans so dryly it makes the temperature in the commissary drop by ten degrees.

"You know what, Skye? You'll be neighbors," Toby cuts in, looking between me and Dr. Scarlett. "Alex lives in The Pillars."

Great. Just super. "Again, I literally just found out there's a place opening up, so—"

Dr. Scarlett's watch beeps aggressively. Toby stiffens, leaning in to see the alert lighting up the doctor's wrist.

"Shit. Uh, Abby, I'm gonna call you late—"

"Don't bother!" Abby snaps, but Toby presses a rushed kiss to her forehead that she doesn't fight and hustles down the aisle with *Alex*.

I stare at the way Alex's muscles shift under the fabric of his thermal shirt and dark jeans, the former of which aren't bright yellow. No, they're deep navy blue and tight enough to show off the broadness of his chest and shoulders.

"Ew," Abby scowls.

"What?"

"Why are you looking at Dr. Scarlett like that?"

"Like what?" I hiss, my cheeks flaring with heat.

"Toby thinks he's the Goddess's gift to the world, and I don't get it. Sure, he's a looker, but he's also a fucking demon, Skye!"

"I wasn't–I wasn't checking him out!" I whisper-snarl, glancing around to make sure we weren't overheard.

"Sure. Babe, I saw it."

"Maybe it's a good thing I'm being forced to move out."

She rolls her eyes and drapes an arm over my shoulder. "Would it be too soon to move in with Toby?"

"You've known you were mates for five years and have been fighting just as long."

"It's foreplay." She shrugs, laughing when I make a gagging noise that has her smiling from ear to ear. "I guess we should get some cardboard boxes while we're here, huh?"

Abby turns back to the shelves to browse the meager selection of granola bars. I take a shallow breath and turn to look down the aisle, unsure if the prickling on the back of my neck is just nerves or my powers making it very clear I'm being watched.

Alex is looking right at me, unabashedly, like he isn't bothered in the slightest that I just caught him staring.

I do a very dumb thing. At least, I might look back on this moment and think it was the stupidest, most ridiculous event in my entire life thus far... I smile at him. Just the smallest upward tilt of my lips, and at first, his reaction edges on outright confusion.

He blinks, reaches up to scrub the back of his neck, and gives me a similar kind of smile that's quickly erased when Toby, standing at one of the checkout lanes, motions for Alex's wallet.

Alex pays for... all of it. Toby's groceries and the soap.

"What are you looking at? Oh, my Goddess, Skye!"

I quickly look away and meet Abby's eyes just as she cackles.

"What? I–I wasn't–"

"Do you think he's hot?"

"Al–Dr. Scarlett?"

"Obviously! Who else?"

"I don't know how to answer that question."

"Oh, girl," she murmurs, roping her arm around mine. "Look, date anyone else. I really don't care if you bring home a date with four sets of eyes and six fingers on each hand because that would be way easier to digest than you having the hots for the man making my life so much harder than it needs to be."

I glance back at the checkout line in time to see Toby and Alex disappear from view into the nearest skybridge and finally feel like I can breathe. "He seems nice enough."

"You haven't been in his lab."

"I–I might be consulting with the biology department soon. I'm not sure–"

A crackle of static splits the air before an announcement blares over the intercom.

"Good afternoon, Lunaria University. This is a campus-wide weather warning. I repeat, this is a campus-wide weather warning. All outdoor spaces, including the bubble labs, will shut down at 5:00 P.M. this evening because of inclement weather. All outdoor spaces, including surface-level labs, exterior access for shifting purposes, and exterior access to ice roads will close at 5:00 P.M. because of–"

"Jeez. I wonder what the hell that's about?" Abby blinks up at the ceiling like the owner of the dry, monotone female voice who's been haunting us since undergrad is hanging from the rafters.

"Winds of 100 miles an hour expected until Saturday at 6:00 P.M.," she drones on.

"Great," I whisper, clutching the basket a little closer. "Our windows are going to be flexing and popping all night."

"With a high temperature of negative sixty and wind chills of negative 90."

"I've made up my mind," Abby rushes out, laughing nervously. "I'm going into industry."

"Will the ice labs be closed tomorrow, too?"

"Oh, absolutely not!" She lets out another signature cackle and nearly brings herself to tears. "It's a whole other world down there, and Dr. Scarlett doesn't listen to a Goddess-damned thing the university's emergency alert system says. Never. But the good news is we can still go out tomorrow night. Right? Right?" She nudges my shoulder three times until I give her a stiff nod.

But my mind wanders, my powers simmering, still on high alert. Because of him? Why?

5

COLD AS ICE

Alex

TOBY GRUNTS WITH EFFORT AS WE MOVE THE PATCH IN PLACE. IT'S nothing more than a sheet of steel to frame one of the smaller tunnel entrances in the lab, creating an archway leading down into the glacial, blue-tinged darkness below.

"Shit!" Toby huffs.

"Just hold it in place a moment longer," I say through gritted teeth, my gloved hands slipping over the metal while trying to get a good grip. The whirling screech of the drill echoes all around us as I drive several screws through the steel and into the ice. Sensors secured to the tunnel are supposed to catch cracks before they spread, and so far, none of the sensors are going off.

"One more," I rush out, breathless, and send the last screw through the metal. Toby eases the pressure before letting go entirely, his hands falling to his knees in an attempt to catch his breath.

Puffs of cold mist leave my mouth while I examine my work and check the sensors.

"Well," Toby remarks, chuckling, "good thing the dean doesn't know about this."

"He wouldn't care. He hasn't been down here in six years, and I doubt a tunnel collapsing would make a difference on that front. Who'd it fall on?" I ask, smoothing my gloves over the metal.

Toby shrugs. "Some idiot engineering graduate student testing drills down in the ice core storage area." He points down the incline into the darkness. "He's fine. Spooked him, is all. He thought the whole tunnel was collapsing."

As much as I hate having engineers in my lab, they do have the tools we need to expand the tunnels and drive drills deep into the ice to collect samples. I tolerate them as much as they tolerate my presence–because I have a habit of watching their every move. One fuckup and the entire tunnel system is coming down, and this is *my* lab. *My* research. *My* lab assistants and students. I've made sure everyone knows that.

I chew my lower lip in thought while gathering our tools and following Toby up into the main area of the lab, which is at least thirty degrees warmer than the ice-core tunnels.

A wide, circular room of ice expands around us, the ceiling just high enough that Toby, also a tall man like me, can walk comfortably without having to crouch. Several more ice tunnels branch off the main lab. I hold a single class here at the graduate level. Otherwise my lectures are upstairs, past the ice, in the sparkling glass towers. This space is used primarily for research on the ice, and I mean to keep it that way, even if the occasional curious onlooker from another department begs for the key code to the elevator.

It's Saturday, which means the lab is mostly empty of graduate students, research assistants, and postdocs, but a few mingle in their bright yellow thermals and insulated bibs around microscopes or at workstations made of pure ice.

I don't speak to any of them. I rarely do. I have a reputation to uphold, of course. A totally unintentional reputation.

Some people call me a demon. A monster. A fucking dick.

I just don't like being wrong.

I don't like others fucking up and not living up to their full potential, either.

Toby, thankfully, has never fallen into that category.

"Did Garret get those blood samples from Aurorium that I requested?" I ask Toby before he reaches the exterior door of the lab.

He punches a few buttons to activate the elevator and turns to me, nodding, pulling off his beanie to run his fingers through his flattened hair. His cheeks are dusted red from the cold. "They're in the specimen fridge, top left shelf. Hey–" The elevator door opens, and he holds it while stepping in. "What're you doing tonight?"

"Me? Why?"

"I'm taking Abby to the club for a few drinks to try to get on her good side again now that the weather warning has passed and the terminal reopened. You should come. Skye's coming, too, from what Abby said."

"Why would I ever go to a nightclub with my postdocs, let alone another professor?"

Toby doesn't react to the dead, dry tone of my voice. He shrugs, smirking. "Don't ya get lonely, Alex?"

"Never. Not once."

He steps into the elevator, which is nothing more than a janky metal tube, and disappears through the layers of ancient ice, where he'll pop out on the surface in the washroom, going through all the mandatory sterilization steps everyone who steps foot in this lab must do before entering and leaving.

Meanwhile, I go to the specimen fridge, doing my best to block the sound of Dr. Skye Abbot's name from my head.

I've known who she is for years. It was hard not to hear about the double-major-physics-prodigy the physics department was worshipping like a deity day in and day out. Her admittance to her PhD program came with money and royal family connections, something the other departments, including mine, could only dream about. It left a bitter taste on my tongue, to say the least.

At first, I figured that's all she was–a princess with the money and connections to get her into such a prestigious institution without so much as batting an eyelash.

That's not what she is. Not really. Not at all.

Skye Abbot is a freak of nature. She's impossible, actually. I still don't want to believe she was able to swing two PhD programs, but she did. One in theoretical physics and the other in observational astrophysics, which is where she shines. I've seen her work only because I find the observatory a warm and quiet place to sit... not because I've ever been interested in the stars and heavens.

I like concrete evidence, not speculation.

Which is why I hate theorists.

Which is why I have to hate her.

Which is why I will not go out tonight, even if Toby is the closest thing to a friend I've had since I was a child.

Which is also why I have to ignore her thick, dark brown hair and those strange, oddly familiar violet eyes that betray every rule of nature and biology–just like I attempted to do yesterday at the commissary. She's beautiful for a shifter. She has a whimsical type of beauty that I want to study because there's something about her that doesn't make sense and hasn't since the moment I first saw her, first touched her.

That was years ago. She doesn't remember. She thought we were meeting for the first time in that elevator, when she had the gall to assume I was a student here and not a leading researcher in the biology department.

I know very little about her personally. She's a princess–I know that much. She's Toby's mate's best friend and long-time roommate. I know she's related to the royal family of Crescent Falls in some way but graduated with her master's from the University of Moonrise, for some reason. I've never been to either place. I never read up on royal gossip or the news, for that matter. My life is here. On this campus. In this lab. Buried in this maze of ice older than anything else in our strange, magical world.

And it will always be that way unless I find what I've been looking for.

I pull the box of blood samples–little glass vials and sterile bags this time, an interesting mix–from the fridge and sort them until the few remaining lab assistants and students who have nothing better to do than try to look busy around me to win my favor, leave. Then, I tuck four of the samples in my bag and head out, shutting off the lights and checking the sensors one last time before the elevator doors creak shut behind me, and the ice closes in on all sides.

The blood is ice cold when I finally reach The Pillars. The skybridge wraps around half of campus with a view of nearby Aurorium, which is far enough away that it's just a tangle of flickering light against the ice and stars beyond. The Pillar houses are boxes of glass that line the outside of the skybridge. I walk past a dozen front doors before reaching mine, press the key into the lock, and close myself into a familiar–but practically bare–space.

I tuck the blood samples into the empty fridge, change out of my thermals, and put on something comfortable before opening my laptop on the couch and prepping myself for a night of finalizing syllabi and going through postdoc applications. That's when my watch alerts me to a new sensor reading at the lab.

"Fuck," I murmur, dragging a hand down my face, and repeat the process several more times before changing back into my cold-weather gear.

It's an endless cycle. I made myself a bed made of ice, and I'll sleep in it, so to speak. But on my way back to the lab to figure out which sensor is malfunctioning or which ice-tunnel core is on the verge of collapse, I see her.

Abby and Skye are walking along a skybridge below mine, both bundled in thick coats and hats. They disappear at the end of the skybridge and reappear in a glass elevator that whizzes down into the ice.

Below campus, there's a series of interlocking tunnels that link the dormitories and the tunnels leading into Aurorium. High-speed rail trains cart students back and forth from the city to campus a few times a day. At ground level, there's an entrance to the ice for shifter students dead-set on trying to shift outside in the elements. Beyond that, there's nothing here in Lunaria but a wash of ice and pitch black darkness.

It's not a bad setup for someone like me.

"Dr. Scarlett!"

Dr. James Kanten, the dean of the biology department, waves and jogs in my direction, meeting me halfway across the skybridge. Shit. I try to avoid the man at all costs. He's a doctor, sure, but he spent most of his postgraduate years working in industry before stepping back into academia, and even then, he has spent little time in a real lab.

I don't think he's ever been to my ice lab. He prefers to stay at ground level, in what we call the "bubble labs," which are constantly being battered by wind and ice storms—if he's in a lab at all.

"James." I nod in greeting, hoping he's just jogging past, but he stops and turns to me, panting a bit while checking his watch.

"Going back to the lab at this hour on a Saturday? I figured you'd be joining the droves headed to Aurorium for a little fun before the semester starts."

"We have several malfunctioning sensors." I hold his gaze, hoping he's reading between the lines and remembering the six emails I've sent to him personally about our dire need for new sensors. A tunnel collapse would not only kill whoever was inside, but it would erase years' worth of research and cost the university a fortune. New tunnels would have to be drilled, new ice cores dug. He knows it, too. He just doesn't give a shit.

"Better get on that," he says with a breathless smile, and he continues on his run.

I lick my lips, scowling after him, my tongue catching on my pointed incisors. I make a mental note to shave them down a bit when I have the chance. "Bastard."

It's well past 4:00 in the morning when I finally get back to my apartment and shed my thermals for the second time. I linger by the fridge for several minutes before pulling out one of the samples and reading the contents.

Animal blood. Reindeer. Clean. A healthy animal. No diseases or injuries to speak of, which means no antibiotics to worry about. The lab uses these samples for experiments, and Aurorium keeps us stocked.

No one notices when a few go missing.

No one has noticed for the past decade.

I open the vial and tilt the contents into my mouth.

It's not enough, but… it'll do.

For now.

6

BLOOD EVERYWHERE

Skye

ABBY CLUTCHES MY ARM, TREMBLING, HER BREATH COMING IN FRIGID puffs of white mist. The subway station is nearly frantic with bodies stuffed into heavy winter gear, everyone waiting for the evening train from Aurorium to arrive and offload anyone returning to campus after a day spent running errands in the city.

We'll board that train and head straight to the snug, ice-coated city, and it can't come soon enough. Even under the fluorescent glow of lights that supposedly radiate like the sun, giving the students who live in the dorms below the surface a minuscule amount of their daily dose of vitamin D, it's freezing. The grates above our heads spill out hot air, but it's barely enough against the constant, bone-aching chill.

When the train's lights finally breach the darkness, the entire gathered crowd sighs in relief, and within minutes, shuffling and squeezing, we're standing at the back of the train, arm in arm, watching the university platform fade into the shadows.

"Goddess, I'm so glad we don't live down here anymore," Abby says, her teeth still chattering slightly despite her heavy, fur-lined parka.

I scan her face for a moment, tilting my head as I take in her little details. "I always forget you're half witch."

She huffs a laugh, her dark eyes absorbing the flickering track lights running the length of the train car. "I blame my father whole-heartedly for falling in love with a witch, but you've seen my mom. She's a smoke show. It's a damn shame I didn't inherit my dad's warm, wolfish genetics."

"You need to shift more. It'll help, you know, keeping the wolf inside of you more active."

"What will help me is a stiff drink and a hot club," she retorts, grimacing as the train jerks to a stop and steam hisses, fogging the windows. Other passengers jostle toward the exits, everyone murmuring excitedly about their plans for the night. Aurorium is the closest any of us can be to the modern world and its entertainment. Concerts, bars, restaurants–Aurorium has it all, two-thirds of its economy driven by bored, overworked students and faculty of Lunaria's pride and joy–its university.

Aurorium isn't the capital of Lunaria, however. The Alpha King and his flock live further south, in Northstar, which is a sharp contrast to Aurorium's ever dark, ever ice-coated exterior. Northstar is mountainous with frost-bitten trees and two real seasons–winter, and "break-up," when the lake and river ice melt for a few months, which counts as their summer.

While Northstar is lovely, nothing will ever be more beautiful than Aurorium in my opinion.

The aurora the city is named for dances above our heads as we hurry out of the tunnel and up a steep, winding staircase to ground-level, where the city glimmers all around us in a wash of neon light. The buildings are tall here and cloistered together, which keeps the streets shockingly warm–a solid zero degrees compared to the icy tundra beyond, where negative sixty to eighty degree days are commonplace.

Most of the people who call this place home stay in their wolf forms when traveling through the streets, and it's no wonder. It's cold. Bitter cold. Even in the summer.

Smaller towns and even villages spread out against the ice. Nomadic packs still live here, moving from place to place, staying in their wolf forms more often than not while hunting reindeer and seals, but they're much closer to the northern coast. Here, in Aurorium, we're settled over what was once an ancient ocean that's been frozen for thousands of years.

I often wonder what would happen if someone like Abby, Toby, or even Alex–Dr. Scarlett–drilled deep enough.

"I am absolutely frozen solid!" Abby shouts before bustling through the front doors of the nightclub I hate but she adores. Noise immediately rattles my senses. It feels like we're being blasted by a hairdryer that's been in use for too long. Abby helps me out of my parka and stuffs it in a locker with hers before taking my hand and dragging me through the arctic entrance leading to the club, and when we breach the interior, noise screeches into my head, rattling my powers to the point of pain.

I choke it down like I always do because it's temporary. Once the bass of the throbbing EDM music registers in my head, my powers quiet, thrumming to the music like the blood being driven by every beat of my heart.

Abby takes the lead, as is usual when she manages to drag me off campus. She orders me a drink, finds us a booth, and gives me a few minutes to get my bearings again. She's never questioned why I am the way I am, so I haven't told her the truth–that I'm a freak who can see into the future, a strange, unearthly being of mist who can teleport wherever I want, and that I have visions of… stuff I can't explain.

I suppose she thinks I'm like her in some way–a hybrid. There are so many of us now, anyway. Witches and shifters can be mates, but it's rarer than a wolf-to-wolf bond, for sure. Or, more likely, she's used to people like me–people who have a hard time in loud places or crowded, closed rooms and prefer solitude to having a large social circle.

I'm coming back to reality when Toby slides into the booth beside me, bracing his hands on the table and grinning from ear to ear. He's several beers deep, judging by the slur of his words and the looseness of his posture, but thankfully, instead of starting another fight, Abby blushes and smiles back at him.

"So are you guys mates again or what?" I ask over the rim of a bright, fruity cocktail that tastes like synthetic pineapple and something else I can't place–but it's awfully sour. My nose crinkles on impact.

Abby rolls her neck and fixes me with a look I know all too well. "We've *been* mates. Pissing me off is just Toby's kink."

"I love it," he agrees, and I take a deeper gulp of my drink.

"There's something seriously wrong with both of you."

He leans back, legs splayed, perfectly comfortable encroaching on my space. "It's Lunaria. Everyone here is crazy. Fuck, I'll be getting out soon, I think. Another year or two, when Abby is finally ready to throw in the towel, we'll be living large in Maatua."

Abby scoffs at him, leaning forward. "Oh, is that our plan now?"

"You know I talk to your dad every day. He keeps me updated on all the games and royal gossip." He shrugs like casually chatting with an Alpha, let alone his on-and-off again mate's father, is a totally normal thing. "He's got a house lined up for us and everything, and Abby has that job waiting for her at the marina." He arches a brow in Abby's direction in a challenge to argue.

"And what will you do without your precious Alex, huh? What will you do without him? He'll never leave the lab. He'll die down there in a tomb he builds himself within the ice, I'd bet my life on it. And he'd deserve it."

"You're always so hard on him," Toby protests.

"He's unnecessarily hard on me!"

I angle my body until I'm facing Toby, blocking out Abby's heated scowl. "Are you friends with Dr. Scarlett?"

"Yeah, I mean, I consider him a good friend. I doubt he shares the sentiment."

"Because he's a fucking dickhead!" Abby shouts over the music.

"What makes you think that?" I ask Toby, leaning in. I don't know why I care, but Alex... if I can call him that... he's an enigma. He's also the driving force behind Abby and Toby's department. I've heard his name spoken for years in a variety of ways. He's an artist. A savant. A prodigy. He's also mean and strict, far more than any of the other most hated professors on campus.

People either worship the ground he walks on or loathe him.

And I'm sharing a table with two people on opposite sides of the spectrum in terms of their feelings about him.

"Alex has always been cool. I like him, regardless of what Abby says. He's a damn good scientist, but I get it. He can be really hard on his postdocs."

"He was never hard on you," Abby retorts, and Toby smiles softly, heaving a breath.

"I don't know. He tried. I like fucking with him a bit, trying to get him to laugh—and he does, on occasion. He's like every other freak of nature who takes tenure and decides to call this hellhole home. That's all. He's not a social guy."

I edge closer to him, dropping my voice while Abby's distracted by a group of women she knows from campus who stop at our table. "What is he like?"

Toby smiles to himself again, silently chuckling while looking down at his cold-roughened hands. "You know, he recently asked the same thing about you."

"What–"

"We're going to dance now!" Abby commands, grabbing Toby's hand. He obeys in a heartbeat, and I watch them go, swirling my nearly empty drink in a circle. Abby already knows I'm going to dip out without saying goodbye. She knows I can handle maybe an hour of this noise and crowd before I crawl back into my hole of quiet solitude, and when she turns to look over her shoulder at me, winking, I take it as a silent understanding that I won't see her for the rest of the night because she's going home with Toby, and I'm free.

The cold bite in the air is a welcome relief from the heat of the club. I stand on the curb, zipping my parka up to my chin and tucking the fur liner of my hood around my ears, watching a group of wolves stroll by. It's easy to spot the locals. Their fur is far thicker, and they're smaller but denser wolves than I'm used to seeing in places like Moonrise and Crescent Falls. They're definitely more acclimated to the elements here, that's for sure.

I shiver, tucking my gloved hands into my pockets, and duck my head against the breeze, but I catch a shadow leaning against a lamp-post on the other side of the street, a man smoking a cigarette, smoke bleeding against the cool puffs of mist rolling off his tongue.

Sharp, nearly-red eyes meet mine and hold, but his face is almost totally cast in shadow.

I used to talk to strangers as a kid. I used to tell random old ladies at the park about how long they had to live. I used to scare away potential playmates with my recounting of my rather dark, grisly visions and dreams.

I've learned it's better to keep my head down and bite my tongue, even if the aura flooding off this man is making my skin crawl, like death is following his every move, his every smoke-tainted breath.

The subway stairs come into view under the glare of hazy neon lights as I trek across the ice. No one drives here unless it's off-road vehicles with chains and stubs embedded in the tires. Instead, wolves drag carts on skis, and people crunch over the ice in spiked boots, so the worn, weather-stripped steps are a welcome contrast to the slick street above when I breach the tunnel and come to a sudden halt.

A small crowd is already gathering to catch the next train back to campus, but it's not the usual scene of students carrying grocery bags and cases of beer they can't buy on campus. The benches are empty, and warriors in both human and wolf form are keeping the crowd back from something I can't see but can taste. Death. I can smell it. My bracelet warms against my skin in warning.

"What's going on?" I ask a group of young students to my left, likely undergrads. Young. So young. Maybe my brothers' age. Freshmen.

"They have the whole waiting area taped off. Won't let anyone through. We were told to wait here for the train," one of the guys says, tucking his girlfriend closer as she shivers from the cold.

I rise on my toes to try to look over the crowd, but train lights cast a haze over the area as it pulls into the station.

"If you're getting on, do it now!" one of the warriors shouts, motioning sternly toward the first car.

I follow the crowd, trying to catch a glimpse of the scene and...

"Goddess above," someone murmurs as I'm jostled, my feet refusing to move.

Blood coats the platform. Dark, sizzling blood. Still warm enough to send mist snaking through the air. It's... everywhere, sprayed across the concrete wall, a bench, and the ground, where a black tarp covers what I know is a body.

"Get on if you're going to Lunaria U!" a warrior shouts at me, motioning wildly. "Now!"

I side-step onto the train just as the doors shut, and the train jerks into motion. The bloody scene fades until the platform is nothing but a speck of light resembling a star–then darkness.

7

WHAT DID YOU SEE?

Skye

ABBY SLOUCHES IN ONE OF THE FIRM, SLIGHTLY WORN ARMCHAIRS IN MY office, picking fluff from the seams while I hurriedly answer several emails. She tilts her head, watching me like a hawk, her bright, nearly-white blonde hair falling over her shoulder in a platinum sheet.

I glance at her, huffing a breath, and ask, "What?"

"You're freaking out."

I slowly close my laptop, sliding my hands over its outer shell. "I am not."

"You are. I can see all the arteries in your neck. You're going to give yourself wrinkles scowling like that. You'll be fine, Skye. Jeez, you've lectured before!"

"Not at the graduate level." Even the mention of it has my chest tightening to the point of pain. Abby ignores my comment and takes several seconds to swivel side to side in the chair, readjusting her position, the shiny yellow fabric of her parka crinkling with every move she makes. The sound gnaws at my nerves, and she knows it.

I roll my lower lip between my teeth and let it go with a pop. "Can

49

I ask why you're here? Is it just to annoy me? It's the first day of the semester, and I'm very busy."

She shrugs, fishing a chocolate bar out of the pocket of her parka and taking a bite. Her yellow thermals beneath contrast sharply with the slate gray walls and darkened glass windows. Outside, a windstorm is absolutely hammering the icy plains beyond. "You guys have way better snacks in your faculty lounge than the biology department."

I instinctively reach into the pocket of my cardigan, finding it empty. She smirks, tossing my badge back to me.

"When did you–"

Her watch beeps several times, and she grunts a curse around a mouthful of chocolate, then proceeds to stuff the rest of the bar in her mouth and wipe her chocolate smeared fingers on her insulated pants. My brows are nearly to my forehead by the time she's done, and she smirks, salutes me, and walks out like hanging out in my very professional office and stealing my badge to get access to the good snacks is going to be her new thing.

"Bye, then!" I call after her, rushing around my desk to the door, which she left wide open, but when I reach the threshold, she's gone, and a pair of voices fills the normally silent corridor.

"I've been going department to department asking if anyone has heard anything about it."

I slowly peek to the left. Alex's voice drifts to me before he comes into view, startling in full lab attire. No, he doesn't wear a starched white coat and goggles, but he is decked out in heavy winter gear, his parka unzipped and dark thermals underneath. He swipes his beanie from his head and runs his fingers through his hair, damp with perspiration, his expression shadowed with frustration.

"What exactly happened?" It's Dr. Gerralde. He's standing just outside his office door, stepping closer to Alex. "All we've heard is there was an assault in the subway in Aurorium."

My heart thumps, quiets, then restarts at the scene I've been trying to scrape from my prefrontal cortex since Saturday night. All of that blood. The tarp. The obvious body beneath it.

Alex sighs, bracing his hand flat against the wall, essentially boxing Dr. Gerralde in. His lips part, but then he stills and slowly turns to look in my direction.

He straightens and moves with an unnatural stillness I'm just now noticing–a way that makes my heart quicken with alarm.

"Excuse me for a moment," he says to my colleague and takes a step in my direction.

Alarm bells skitter through my skull. I spin back into my office and yank the door closed, but he catches it, slides inside, and shuts it.

"Hey!" I retreat until my back hits the window with a thud. "You can't just–"

He turns the lock, his brows raised in challenge. My heart begins to race for an entirely different reason. Fear? Maybe. That's what I should be feeling. Overwhelming curiosity about his intentions? Definitely.

It's the slightly panicked look in his sharp, ocean blue eyes that gives me pause. "What happened in Aurorium? What have you heard?" I ask.

"You were there. You tell me." He shrugs out of his coat and tosses it onto the chair Abby recently vacated, like he plans to stay for a while. His muscles fill the thermal shirt to a T, and for a moment, the thudding in my heart turns into a quiver.

He pauses, his eyes dipping from my face to my chest, before he chuckles and smiles to himself.

"What?"

"Your heart is doing weird things."

"How–you know what? Get out of my office. You can't just barge in here!"

"What were you doing in Aurorium?"

"I went to a club with Abby, but you know that, seeing as Toby invited you. He told me."

"I'm sure he did."

I take two cautious steps away from the window. Tension seeps between us like molten lava. I'm sure it's pure electricity causing my hackles to rise. I've been lucky. I can readily admit that. My journey through academics has been fair and simple. I haven't had many run-ins with egotistical maniacs, even in my field of study.

Alex is the exception, and we've said maybe thirty words to each other in the few days I've been able to put a face to the name.

"Are you accusing me of something?"

"I'm just asking. There're rumors beginning to swirl in my department, and I need to put an end to it before it gets out of hand."

"Sure," I retort, mimicking his skeptical expression even though my feelings betray everything about the slight rise of my brows. Something about him makes me... vicious. I'm not sure how else to describe it. Viciously angry? Intrigued? Whatever it is, it's giving me the confidence–no, desire–to look him directly in the eyes and say, "Kindly fuck off, Dr. Scarlett."

"I'm asking a simple question."

"I answered it. Simply. Get out."

"I have lab materials stuck in Aurorium because the Alpha shut the terminal down for the next two days. I'd like an explanation, and seeing as you were in Aurorium Saturday night and came back to campus early–"

I take a step away from the window, narrowing my eyes to slits. "Are you stalking me?"

"Why would I waste the time? We live in a glass box, Skye."

"Dr. Abbot–"

"*Skye.* We live in a glass box. I see everything. *You* see everything. All I'm asking is for the truth before I lose my fucking shit on the supply department responsible for the shipment one of my studies is riding on."

This man is insane. There's no way around it.

"First of all, you'll call me Dr. Abbot. I'm not your student. I'm not even your colleague. You and I simply exist in the same place and time."

He arches a brow, which... enrages me.

"Secondly, I don't give a shit about your supply request being late. Send runners." I look him up and down, my gaze sweeping over his tall, well-built frame and catching on the smooth muscles filling his thermal top before I can stop myself. I rein myself in and shake my head. "In fact, you can easily just shift and run to Aurorium—"

"If I had the ability, I would have been there and back by now."

Oh. *Oh.* "You're—you're not a shifter?"

"I am absolutely not a shifter, no."

To say I'm perplexed would be the least of it. A witch, perhaps? Male witches, otherwise known as wizards, or sometimes warlocks, aren't common, seeing as the traits pass from mother to daughter, so on and so forth, but they do exist. I've never met one, but there's a first time for everything, I suppose.

I find myself glancing at his smooth, rounded ears anyway just to confirm he's not fae.

"Can I help you?" he asks sternly.

"What are you, then?"

"That's an exceedingly rude thing to ask someone, Dr. Abbot. Should I ask the same of you?"

"Why are you in my office?" I step around my desk and ease into the chair. "Are you here to interrogate me?"

"I am, seeing as you were in the terminal that night. What did you see? That's all I need to know."

"Why? Because of your supplies?"

"Because I lecture at both the undergraduate and graduate level, and I have eighteen-year-old students, and *their parents* are blowing up my email inbox asking if they're safe and why their only connection to the modern world has been cut off. I have students who live in the underground dorms only a few miles of tracks away from where whatever happened, happened." His tone is as sharp as a knife.

I grit my teeth, feeling suddenly guilty. In my defense, he did come in with his metaphorical hackles raised. "Someone died; that was obvious."

"How?"

"How? How am I supposed to know? I was herded onto the train, and that was that. I didn't see much. Just…Just—"

"Just what?" He edges toward my desk, arms crossed over his broad chest. He's so still. I find myself looking closely at him against my will again, drawn to him, like those strange powers inside of me I try so hard to keep dormant are clawing to touch him, to study him like I study the stars just beyond the frosted windows. I wait for his chest to rise and fall. Seconds pass. More. *More.* He just stares at me, waiting, like the time I'm wasting doesn't matter to him in the slightest.

Odd.

When he finally takes a breath, I reply, "Blood. A lot of it. Everywhere. On the terminal walls, the ground, the benches." My lungs strain as I suck down air and continue, the memory burning through my brain like acid. "It was fresh, still steaming."

"And the body?"

"Dead, obviously, and covered by a tarp. That's all I know. There were warriors everywhere."

He nods once and turns to snatch his jacket off the chair. "Was that so hard?"

"You are as much of an asshole as everyone says you are."

His smirk is as sweet as honey. "I'm not that bad when you get to know me."

"Well, seeing as I won't be getting to know you, that doesn't matter. Please exit my office, Dr. Scarlett."

"Severe as always," he murmurs under his breath, turning for the door.

"Excuse me?"

He folds his parka over the crook of his arm and turns on his heel to face my desk. He apparently took my reply as an invitation to stay, and now I'm seething, doing my absolute best not to show it.

Praying my eyes don't light from within. Goddess, that would be the last thing I need right now.

I clutch my opposite wrist on impulse, letting the old charms pinch my skin, and feel them warming in warning.

"Do you know that you and I have a similar reputation here, Dr. Abbot?"

"That's impossible."

"You're a theoretical physicist underneath all your advanced studies and titles, so you know nothing is impossible. Far from it." He sinks onto the armrest of the chair, all sharp lines and space, like the room is suddenly smaller with him in it.

"People like me. No one likes you."

"People are just as terrified of you as they are of me. I don't see it as a bad thing in the slightest. I'd rather be feared than loved."

"I'd rather be respected than feared." The charms warm to the point that my skin begins to tingle. I ignore it–the warning bells and prickling skin. His eyes are undoing me at the seams. I'm not sure how to describe it, but with his stillness, it's like looking into a calm pool of crystal clear water so deep I can see the bottom but could never reach it without losing my breath.

Not without drowning.

Just an endless, breathless cycle.

"You're a prodigy in your field of study. So am I. One day, you'll be the head of your department, and so will I. Everyone knows it." He leans forward, casual, rolling his lower lip between his teeth and letting it go slowly. "Our students worship the ground we walk on regardless of how they feel about us personally."

"Your students think you're a monster."

"Untrue. And mean, I might add." He chuckles, straightening. "The only person I know who hates me like you're describing is Abby, and her reasons are strictly personal."

"Abby told me you're preventing her from publishing her research–"

"Abby doesn't know what she wants," he retorts with sudden heat. "She's a brilliant biologist, but her heart's not in it, and she knows it, and I remind her of it every single day. She can publish her sea ice research when she actually has something substantial to publish, which she does not." He rises, and I realize with the mention of Abby I've hit a nerve.

Does he... like her? In a...

He rolls his eyes to the ceiling. "Do not look at me like that."

"Like what? What–"

"There is nothing between Abby and me. She doesn't like me

because I'm forcing her to actually use the brain she was blessed with, and I don't like her because of how she treats my friend."

"Oh."

"Oh," he parrots, shrugging into his parka.

"I–I didn't know you and Toby were *that* close."

"I don't make friends easily, and he forced the subject when we were roommates during my undergrad. I've grown to appreciate his company."

That statement settles like lead at the base of my spine. I watch him pull his beanie over his thick black hair, his eyes never leaving mine. If he dropped his strange accent and lifted his voice, those words would have been... mine. Something I would say. Something I've said before... or at least thought.

"Thank you for your time, Dr. Abbot."

I rise as he reaches the door. "I never gave you my time in the first place. You took it."

"Unfortunately, you'll have to get used to that, seeing as Dr. Gerralde has pawned you off to my department as a consultant."

"I don't know anything about paleomicrobiology. I don't see how I could possibly be of use to you."

"Then, it's a good thing I do." His mouth pulls up into what appears to be an actual smile, and I flinch, caught off guard by the sincerity of it, the slightly teasing glint in his sharp eyes. The smile evaporates in an instant, like he didn't mean for me to see it, and he says, "Good luck this evening."

I find it suddenly hard to swallow. "I've lectured before. I doubt I'll need it."

"Graduates are a different breed. If you thought you were loved by your students, you'll know you're not before long."

He pulls open the door, but I'm already edging around my desk. "What do you mean by that?"

With a sigh, his hand curled around the doorknob, he replies, "Like I said, it's better to be feared than loved. Undergraduates are infants away from their mothers for the first time. They'll do and believe anything. Graduates have been through the academic meat-grinder and think they know what to expect… and if I know anything about you, Skye, you're about to unravel everything they thought they knew about space, or whatever the hell you physicists study for no reason at all. They're going to challenge you."

"What? Hey!"

He pulls the door closed behind him when he leaves.

8

YOU'RE WRONG

Skye

"It went fine," I say on a breath, moving toward the back row of the empty observatory. It's well past midnight, and if anyone is going to be awake in the odd hours of early morning, it's Posey, whose soft, disbelieving chuckle rings through my ear.

"You sound like you hated it."

I sink into a familiar chair covered with scratchy, well-worn fabric and prop my laptop on my knees. "I don't hate lecturing. It just felt odd, I guess. My previous lectures were all at the undergraduate level... physics 101, you know? The definition of matter versus now having to explain to a room full of physicists who lean more toward experimental physics why we'll never fully understand the physical confines of our own universe."

"You could always come home. The temple in Moonrise would move mountains to have you within their ranks."

I click a few buttons on a controller, and the ceiling erupts in a sea of distant stars. "You sound just like Mom."

"No one would blame you for being unhappy, Skye. You've been living in the dark for years."

"It's not about the dark. I like the dark. It's quiet here. Actually, you're the only other person in our family who I think would thrive in this place."

Aris's laugh from the far side of whatever room they're sharing in Veiled Valley creeps through the phone, and I frown. "Hi, Uncle Aris."

"He's barely listening. Juliette had a nightmare and is currently on his lap trying to manipulate her way into staying up with us tonight," Posey says with an obvious smile.

I miss them. Everyone. My entire family. They're all so settled down south and moving forward with their lives. I feel like I'm stuck in time here in Lunaria while the rest of the world continues without me.

But this is what I chose.

For a reason.

"Are you still joining the family for Solstice this year?" Posey asks.

I click a few more buttons to zoom in on a particular galaxy and tuck the remote between my thigh and the seat. "Planning on it. I'm getting a new place here. My own condo, it sounds like. I–"

The door to the observatory opens, spilling a ray of light across the thin, worn carpet. A shadow moves through the dark then stops in the halo of a floor-level sconce, body angled toward mine.

A flash of recognition tightens my throat. "I'll call you later."

"Send us pictures of your apartment!"

"I will." I quickly hang up. I've always found it rude when people take phone calls or scroll on their phones in the observatory, and I also don't want Alex overhearing any type of conversation with my family, regardless of how innocent the conversation is.

I'm a royal. I know there're people who think I've gotten as far as I have in academia because of my social status, who my father is, and how far his wealth can stretch. But they're wrong.

Alex slowly walks up the ramp to the back row and shuffles down the aisle. I tuck my laptop closer to my lap to try to look busy, but I'm not even logged in yet, and when the blue-hued laptop light reflects against his eyes, I know I'm caught.

"Do you know what time it is?"

"One in the morning."

He hums to himself as he sits beside me, a single empty seat between us, and slouches, closing his eyes for a moment. He's dressed in his heavy snow pants and a dark thermal top like he just left the lab, and his hair is slightly damp, dark curls clinging to his temples.

I wait for him to say something, anything, but he simply... sits there. Silent.

"Were you looking for me?"

"No."

"Why are you here?"

He opens one eye to a slit to meet my gaze. "I come here often. It's quiet. A nice warm place to decompress after an entire day under the ice." He shifts his weight to get more comfortable and practically folds in on himself like he's planning on sleeping here.

"Don't you have a condo in The Pillars where you can decompress?"

"Are you always this territorial over what you believe is your space, or is this about me?"

"You," I answer honestly, looking away from his face to punch my credentials into the university interface. Pages full of live images from the telescope across campus pop into view, and Alex leans in, the stars reflected on his irises.

"Can I ask you something?"

"Shoot," he replies, still fixated on the slowly rotating images.

"Why does everyone else in the biology department wear those ugly yellow thermals and you get dark ones?"

The corner of his mouth ticks into a wry smile before falling flat again. "They serve a purpose. Safety. Yellow is easy to see under the ice. If anyone gets trapped, we can find them quicker, at least in theory."

"Morbid."

"Entirely."

"But you wear black?"

"Technically, mine are dark navy."

My eyes roll to the ceiling, and I take a breath to stop myself from snapping at him. "So you don't care about whether anyone can see you under the ice?"

He leans his head back against the top of the chair, his eyes on the ceiling, on the depictions of the same stars dancing across my laptop. "I'm the director of the ice lab. It doesn't matter if anyone can see me. If someone needs to be rescued, I'll be the one going into whatever hell swallowed them first." His tone is level, without so much as a teasing glint to his words. He's serious. Based on his tone, this is something he's thought about often.

I... might have been very wrong about him.

"You feel responsible for everyone who works in your lab."

"Of course. I am." He meets my eyes.

"But they choose to be there."

"It's different for you, Skye. This is your lab. The observatory, the telescope, the physics research center with its whiteboard and electronics. You don't dig beneath the ice. It's different down there. It's not even just the ice that can kill you. The elements, the darkness, the lack of sound... it drives people insane."

I lean toward him. "Are you insane?"

"Anyone who chooses to remain here on tenure is insane. I believe the psychology department recently published a study about it."

Now, the corner of my mouth ticks up into a smile. He searches my gaze for a moment, really looking at me. "Why are your eyes that color?"

"Violet? It's a family trait."

"It's not a naturally occurring color in any species."

"Well, tell that to my father and grandmother."

I lean in again, deciding to give him a taste of his own medicine. He narrows his eyes in suspicion, his lips parted in a weak smile.

"You have rather pronounced cuspids for someone who says they aren't a shifter."

He arches a brow. "It's a family trait."

"Mhmm..."

He leans closer, his arms folded over his chest. "Are we doing this?"

"Doing what?"

"Arguing. Seeing how far we can get under each other's skin?"

"I wouldn't call it arguing. I don't know you very well, but I'm sure if you continue stalking me and taking up space in my territory, I'll find reasons to argue with you, sure."

His thorough inspection of my face, like he's trying to decipher every emotion and fleeting feeling shining behind my eyes, ends when he hooks his foot around one of the folding tables fixed to the back of each chair in the row in front of us and drags it toward him. He makes quick work of setting it up and pivoting it between us–a little desk, so to speak–and motions for me to set my laptop on it.

"I don't need a surface–"

"I want to know what you're working on."

"Why?"

"Everyone with tenure has a passion project. Otherwise, they would have never agreed to stay."

"Oh? And what's yours?"

"The Goddess Particle, but you already knew that."

I clutch the sides of my laptop. "You know it doesn't exist, right? Not in one singular way."

"Nothing exists unless it's proven."

I set my laptop down and turn in my chair to face him with a sigh. "This is why you need a physicist to consult on your research, isn't it? What exactly have you found down there in the ice? What are you really looking for?"

He eyes me for a moment before he shrugs a shoulder, turning his attention back to the ceiling, where the stars continue to shine. "We find a lot down there, actually. Every new layer we drill opens up an entirely new world that often forces us to scrap what we thought we knew about time, ancient kingdoms, and animals.... Things like you and me. I'm looking for pieces of DNA specifically. LU is one of the only institutes with access to a sample of Queen Isla's tears–her magic. It was sequenced and studied long before I came here, and since I've been in Lunaria, I've been looking for what, if anything, gave her that kind of magic. That *power*. We can't find any traces of it in the falls where she supposedly emerged able to heal. Her powers weren't embedded in her DNA, either. But, you likely already know that, seeing as you're directly related to her."

"She was my father's great-grandmother. It's not like I ever knew her." I feel suddenly uneasy under his direct attention. While it's common knowledge that I'm related to the royal family, I've never been open about my direct line. I find it easier to keep it that way– fewer questions, less concern over my privileges here at Lunaria U.

"Don't worry, I won't tell anyone," he teases, but I bristle.

"It's not a secret. It never has been. Are you going to ask me for a blood sample, or something, to test against what you already have?"

"No. It wouldn't be necessary. There's nothing in her DNA that would even remotely help me find what I'm looking for–nor yours, I assume."

"What exactly are you looking for, then?"

He thinks about it for a moment and then replies, "Most of my funding comes from territories and cities looking for better healing options. Some are worried magic is waning, especially with witches and shifters living so comfortably together and interbreeding. Even our modern healing and witch magic isn't what it could be, or what people think it used to be like, which is why I have the money to drill into the ice. I'm looking for ancient DNA, diseases, and power markers. For the magic that once existed, so we can somehow replicate it again."

A flicker of memory drifts through my head. Me, here, in the very observatory, but in a vision. I was just a little girl when I first had dreams about this place, and for whatever reason, Alex's words threaten to pull me back into the dreamworld. My bracelet warms in warning that a vision is close at hand, but I ignore it, tucking my hands between my thighs.

"Meanwhile," he says on a breath, "you physicists are more interested in far-off places that have no bearing on what's happening here, now, in our world."

"That's not true!"

"Then what, exactly, are you researching right now, Skye?"

"I study the origin of magic." He rolls his eyes. I scoff. "How is that any different than what you're doing?"

"The origin of magic is going to be found here–buried."

"I don't think that's correct. Look." I press the remote, and the ceiling of the observatory shifts, stars blurring at the speed of light, replaced by the far off galaxy I've been studying for the past... oh, gods, four years? "This is the Cerridwen Galaxy. My... life's work." I don't mean to choke on the words, but I look up, and even though I've seen this same map of the stars hundreds of times before, it always takes my breath away. "We didn't have the technology to look this far into space until very recently–within the last decade. It's a marvel, honestly, and even then, it took an incredible amount of research and theorizing to put this map of that galaxy together."

I press the remote again, zooming in to a bundle of stars like nerves settled in a body–a soul. "These stars are incredibly important to witches in particular. This nest of light? That's the Cauldron constellation. The witches believe their ancestors, the first witches, used this cauldron to spread magic all over our world. Before, it was just a faint tangle of starlight only visible in certain places during certain times of the year, but now I found it for them."

Alex looks up in silence. I glance at him, trying to catch any glimmer of emotion behind his eyes.

"These stars are the Moon Lake, which is exactly what it sounds like. Four of the seven planetary structures are, in fact, moons. Big ones. I believe they used to orbit around something here, but now they're freely orbiting objects locked in place by this star, and that star, and they dance, reflecting light like lanterns on a lake."

"And what do the witches use that for?"

"Well, it's hard to explain, and I haven't figured out why yet, but the only time this constellation in particular is visible is in the weeks leading up to the sacred lunar eclipse. It's a massive deal in Moonrise, trust me." I click the remote three more times, zooming in and out. "During the lead up to the lunar eclipse, witch magic wanes severely. Some believe it's directly tied to the moon, but I can't find a rational reason for that to be true… so far. So I'm studying it."

"You made this?"

I take a much-needed breath. "I did. It's rendered images. The real images we have from our telescope still don't reach this far, but based on what I have seen, this is what this galaxy would look like. I've done the math. It's a large place. Several life-giving stars, for sure. Hundreds of planets and thousands of moons, but–this is where it all comes from. I'm certain."

"Where what comes from?"

"The magic. The visions. Think of it this way." I click off the simulation, and the ceiling turns black, the only light coming from the sconces that line the outer shell of the room. I turn my laptop to face him, to show him the equations and alphanumerical sentences I know he won't understand, but in my brain, it's a novel. It's poetry. An ancient language I'm trying to crack.

"Witches and mystics use the stars to strengthen their magic. Mystics use them to read prophecies and decipher visions and dreams. Witches who have lunar magic, or their magic favors specific cycles of the moon and the seasons, can strengthen spells based on the position of the constellations in our skies. Before, it was tricky. It didn't always work. Spells fell flat. Visions tangled. I'm giving them something better, something concrete. Science is the backbone of magic. Magic isn't something tangible. At least, not in a way that we can understand–yet."

"There are many who would disagree with you."

"So be it. They can't prove me wrong." I hold his gaze, waiting for him to argue otherwise.

But he leans in, his hands braced on the table between us, his words ghosting through my hair. "What are you actually looking for, Skye?"

"Exotic matter," I reply pointedly. He stares at me for several seconds and then sighs. "Magic. It's one and the same."

"I want you to come see my lab tomorrow."

"Why?"

"So I can prove you wrong."

9

BARGING IN

Alex

WALLS OF ICE REFLECT AN ICY BLUE, TURNING THE SCRATCH PAPER littered over my metal desk a hazy cerulean. My gloved hands steadily manage a pen after years of practice, but many of my lab assistants and postdocs still grumble about my nearly unintelligible handwriting.

In my defense, I had to learn an entirely new written language in my early twenties.

I shift my weight on the stool beneath me and brace my elbows on the desk. Behind me, the main area of the lab is alive with murmurs, the hum of lab equipment and heaters, and the crunch of threaded boots over the sleek floor of ice.

I look back down at my notes. They're nothing major, just personal commentary on a recent discovery in a core of ice brought up from nearly two miles below the surface—the deepest we've ever been able to drill without something going wrong. The chemical makeup wasn't anything unexpected—water, of course. A few traces of the same glassy, dust-like sediment we found in another core a few feet above this one. Toby and I are both under the assumption the sediment might be the result of an ancient volcanic eruption, but seeing as the leading geologists reside in sunny Tarsian, it's now my job to compile all the data on the samples and send it to the University of Tarsian. Maybe we'll have an answer in a few months for this... single thing.

I take off my beanie and run my fingers through my hair before slipping it back over my head and hunching, continuing to scribble my notes on the core.

A flash of hazy memory soaks into my mind—a gray, rain-soaked morning. My mother leaning over me to guide my small, childlike hands. Learning how to write with a fountain pen–Father's favorite. Practicing the neat, looping, interconnected scrawl so common back home.

It's so different here.

"Dr. Scarlett?"

I turn my head to the mousy-pitched voice of Laney—a lab assistant, and the only undergraduate I've allowed within my ranks in the past five years. She's pre-med, and why she wanted to be in my lab is still a mystery to me, but she's brilliant and spends a good deal of time volunteering at the university's clinic upstairs, which often benefits me.

"Yes?"

"I hate to bother you–"

"Fuck, man!" Toby's voice rings out through the lab as he appears with two graduate researchers at his sides, all three dressed in their heavy yellow parkas and thermals as they breach the plastic curtains separating the main lab from the ice tunnels.

I rise so abruptly, the stool clatters to the ground. My brain ceases to function. My only thought is: *What's wrong?* My eyes sweep them for injuries, for blood, for the telltale signs and sounds of the tunnels beginning to cave in, but they're in one piece. I look up at the ice ceiling. No cracks. The silence in the lab is so thick that nothing could penetrate it. Everyone turns to look at us, holding their breath.

"We found something," Toby says, eyes wide.

"What?" I ask sharply, my chest straining with mingled relief and unease.

Toby glances at his fellow scientists excitedly, then continues, "Core thirteen hit something big, Dr. Scarlett."

"A natural formation? Rock?" I ask, my normally slow heart rate skyrocketing into space.

"No," Toby grins. "Bones."

"Uhm, Dr. Scarlett?"

I motion for Laney to shut up. I'll apologize later. She shrinks back, pale, twiddling her fingers and glancing at the elevator to the surface while I approach Toby. "You're sure?"

"Almost positive. We were able to pull up the core but didn't even scrape the surface of the fossil. There's about four inches of ice on top of it still. We can see it on the drill's camera, bright and clear, though."

"We'll wreck a drill getting through both ice and bone," one of the other scientists says.

I nod, gritting my teeth in thought. "Have Abby analyze the ice core you brought up. Do you still have cameras on it?"

"We're going to drop one down."

"We need to drill around it to widen the section of ice, so four more cores in each direction." I scratch my head, pondering the logistics. "Get Mark from engineering down here and have him and his guys help. I want this done right and the fossil as intact as possible until we know what it is for sure."

"Dr. Scarlett?" Laney's nervous voice tries to rip through the conversation but falls flat.

"Take core twelve and fourteen offline and bring them back up to the surface. We're going to need the space," I add.

"It's a half-mile down from our deepest tunnel," Toby says, pulling a map of the tunnels from his pocket. He points to a spot on the spider-web-like map. "We can tunnel further down, open the area up to give us more space to work with the fossil closely. The ice is in great shape. It will only take a few weeks."

"Once we confirm it is a fossil and exactly what it is, that sounds like a plan," I reply, but Laney grabs the sleeve of my coat and tugs, just as the elevator doors open, spilling hot, unsterile air into the lab.

Chaos turns the normally quiet space into a vacuum of sound. Four armed Aurorium warriors step into the lab while my lab assistant and postdocs struggle to pull plastic sheets over their research specimens and core slides.

"GET OUT!" I shout, shoving Toby, and unfortunately, Laney, out of the way to block the warriors from leaving the elevator.

"Are you Dr. Scarlett?"

"I am, and you're contaminating my lab! Out!" I shove the leader of the group into the elevator so hard he falls back against his comrades. My fist slams against the button that shuts the doors. "Everyone, sterilization protocol. Now!" I watch the elevator rocket to the surface, disappearing in a blur of metal against glass. "Gather your things. No one can return until it's done."

"How long?" Toby asks, but his eyes are on the elevator shaft.

"An hour, tops." I curse under my breath and glance at the ventilation system. This entire ecosystem within the ice is so fragile. New germs can ruin months, if not years, of research. Excess heat can ruin the integrity of not only the tunnels but the lab itself. Microfibers from the clothing of four warriors who barged in here without going through the proper sterilization process and entering in their day-to-day clothes?

It could have been enough to tarnish everything these students and researchers have been working for their entire careers.

Toby starts herding people to the elevator the second it returns. I punch an alarm on the wall that sends a buzz of noise into the tunnels, and within five minutes, five more scientists breach the plastic sheet of the tunnel entrance, looking dazed and concerned. Toby and I shout commands, trying to keep everyone calm, but several postdocs are crying over the future of their slides and potions while I try to explain that the worst-case scenario is that they have to start over, which only leads to more tears and hyperventilating.

Laney, however, looks nearly gray with dread as she creeps toward me like the little mouse she reminds me of.

I frown at her, then work my expression into something I hope is reassuring, and say, "I'm sorry for shoving you."

"Um, I tried to tell you, but the dean called down and said warriors from Aurorium are here to talk to you. I didn't think he'd just send them down."

"Oh," I manage to gut out as anger rips through my body. "I see." That fucking idiot. He's likely the one who let them onto the elevator without going through the proper steps. "Great. Thank you, Laney. Please go with everyone else."

She nods but looks like she's ready to curl into the fetal position as she scampers to the elevator, where the last of the group is huddled, ready to board.

Toby and I hang back until the elevator departs, leaving us alone.

"Well, that's everyone. I know you want to, but don't kill the dean. You'll go to prison, and I'll be stuck here forever in your place."

I rein in my anger and nod, but my tongue slides along my incisors. They're hot, ready to sink into someone's–preferably the dean's–flesh... and tear.

Once I've had a second to cool down, I step into the elevator with Toby. Seconds tick by, and then we're in the sterilization room, going through the motions. I punch in my credentials on a screen beside the elevator and approve the chain of events that sucks all the oxygen from the lab and pumps it full of clean, sterilized air once again.

We can only hope the damage was minimal.

The second we step out of the airlock, the warriors approach, livid. The dean of my department, of course, has made himself scarce.

There's a lot I could say to them–a lot more I could threaten, but I choose to keep quiet, even when Toby shouts his protest against one of the warriors grabbing me roughly by the arm and escorting me down the hallway and into a conference room. The door shuts with an echoing snap. Everything is concrete and plastic down here in the levels beneath the surface, but the fluorescent lighting highlights the broad, roughened man sitting at the head of the conference table. He's dressed for the weather in a black parka, but there's something about his aura that tells me he's important.

Shifters are like that. Some simply bleed energy–an undercurrent of violence–without even realizing it. They're what we call Alphas, but this man isn't quite *that* important.

"You're Dr. Scarlett?" he asks in a deep, rolling voice.

"I sure as fuck hope so," I grind out, clipping back my anger before it can boom through the room. I shake the warrior off my arm and grip the top of a chair, arching a brow at the man at the table. "Your warriors may have very well ruined years' worth of research in my lab."

He just stares at me, drinking me in, unperturbed. "I'm Ash Wilcox, Beta of the Aurora Pack of Aurorium. My Alpha's territory encompasses the city itself."

Should I bow? Nod my head? Probably.

Instead, I remain silent and still.

He continues. "I'm under the assumption that you're a biologist."

Again, I return the favor and keep my eyes locked on his. He takes a shallow breath and rises, tucking his hands behind his back. I tower over him by a foot when he comes near and stops a chair's length between us and nods to his warriors, dismissing them from the room. When it's just us, he pulls a bundle from his inner jacket and hands it to me. It's heavy.

Before I can ask what it is, he says, "I'm sure you're aware that there was a rather brutal attack on a civilian of Aurorium last weekend."

"I am."

"There's been another, further out, on the ice. We believed the first might have been a contained situation–a falling out, given that the victim was someone on our radar who'd recently been banished from our pack but was refusing to leave. However, this second attack was different."

I open the bundle and feel for the contents—a file, some loose plastic bags. I pull one of the bags out and find a blood-soaked strip of fabric, then I meet the Beta's eyes.

"The university has the technology needed to run tests."

"On what?" I ask, not sure if this man is going to be able to tell me what I need to know. "Are you looking for DNA?"

"The body—we haven't been able to identify it. There wasn't much left."

"Ah." So DNA. "I have a few students in my department who work in the clinic and can make a genetic profile—"

"It's imperative this is done swiftly and discreetly. We don't want to cause public worry."

I purse my lips as the door to the conference room opens, and warriors file back in, leaving the door open in their wake with a view of the hallway. I lower my voice to ask, "Was this a murder or an animal attack?" There are, occasionally, polar bears that wander close to the city—real animals, not shifters, as far as I know.

"We're not sure. That's for you to find out. Good day, Dr. Scarlett."

I grit my teeth as the Beta leaves, followed by his warriors, and start looking through the bundle, when another presence steps into the conference room.

"What was that about?" Skye asks.

"What are you doing down here?" Tiredly, I meet her eyes. She's dressed warmly in a thick sweater and fleece pants that completely swallow her figure. I'm not sure why I notice, but it feels criminal.

"You're giving me a tour of the lab, remember?"

"Oh, shit." I close my eyes for a moment. "About that."

10

COMFORTABLE

Skye

"You didn't have to do this." I cup my hands around the warm paper coffee cup and meet Alex's eyes. "I can buy a coffee."

"I invited you to my lab and wasn't able to follow through."

"We can reschedule. It's not like you're going to find the Goddess particle tomorrow and turn me obsolete."

He frowns at me, taking my little jab at face value. He's smart. I mean, of course he is. He's a paleomicrobiologist, for Goddess' sake. But he's also sharp and cunning, able to read my often confusing facial expressions like an open book. "I don't like going against my word."

Random lines of chatter take up the space between us in the little open cafe near the library. "You had a perfectly acceptable reason." I risk a small smile, which he inspects, but then his sharp expression falters, the lines of worry between his brows smoothing, making him look far younger than usual.

I can't help myself when I ask, "How old are you?"

He inhales, wraps his hand around the coffee he hasn't so much as sipped, and replies, "Thirty-three."

"I thought you were older than that."

"Because I look like it?" he asks a bit wryly, but his tone is still strained.

I chuckle, and it's a natural sound, not forced–for once. "No, I mean, you're heading a lab."

"You're also young to be leading a lab, which you do."

"I'm twenty-eight. I wouldn't consider that especially young."

"You're still very young. I don't know why you don't think so."

"Well, seeing as most of the women in my family are mated and settled down by the time they're twenty-five, I do feel rather old and unsettled sometimes."

A beat of silence settles over the round white table separating us. He leans back in his chair, but again, doesn't touch his coffee. The coffee he paid for. The coffee growing tepid with each minute that passes. He watches the ebb and flow of the crowd for a few moments, and the silence between us is surprisingly comforting. He's not giving me any need to carry on a conversation neither of us cares about. I've found that a lot of the time I'm roped into long, sometimes unending conversations about my experiments and studies. I don't like talking about what I do. It's complicated, and I hate the glazed look in people's eyes when I've gone too far.

I have only a handful of people in my life that I can truly talk to, who know me. My family. Abby.... Well, I suppose that's it. Even when I was young, I had few friends who really knew what the inside of my mind was like. That little boy from my visions? He knew. We used to talk all the time.

"How are you related to the royal family?" he asks.

The question catches me off guard. I glance at him before looking down at my coffee cup. He's not looking at me. He's more invested in something out on the ice–a group of wolves sprinting around several stories below us in the frigid cold.

"Do you really want to know, or are you asking because you think I'm only where I am because of my ties?"

"I actually want to know. I'm curious." He meets my gaze, all blue eyes and sharp lines. His accent is so strange, and sometimes I find myself caught up on the way he rolls his vowels and bites each consonant. I've never heard it before, even in Eastonia, where the dialect changes rapidly as one moves from Veiled Valley through Moonrise and into the Roguelands, the Deadlands, and Tarsian. Even Crescent City has a dialect–sharper, quicker.

His is... foreign. I suppose, if I tell him the truth, he owes me an answer to a question as well. It's only fair.

"My father is Prince Blake of Crescent Falls. He was the heir to my grandfather, Sydney's, throne... of Crescent Falls. Grandpa Sydney is the Alpha King of that kingdom." I twist my coffee cup in a circle before picking it up and taking a sip. "My mom..." I smile, hit directly in the chest by a pang of homesickness I pray doesn't show on my face. "She's a violinist. She's brilliant. I didn't inherit any of her gifts of music. I'm more like my dad."

"Why is he no longer in line for the throne?"

"He chose not to be." But oh, there's so much more to it than that. His powers, my powers, the danger of us, of what he could have been. It's so complicated. And it's not the time or place to explain this to Alex, who still feels like a stranger to me.

Even if his presence is doing weird things to my brain and body.

"But you're from Moonrise."

"I am. Kind of. I grew up there. Why is that not making sense to you?"

His smile is soft and secret, like he doesn't know the corners of his mouth are lifting just a touch. "I've never been to either place, and I can't pretend that I keep up with the royal family in any way. There have been rumors you're somehow attached to the Firestone Queen."

"Yeah, Maeve. She's technically a cousin, if we're being strict about genealogical lines, but I've always considered her more like an aunt. I spent a great deal of time with her and her mate, Soren. My dad is her second in command–almost like a king when she's traveling or dealing with kingdom business outside of Moonrise. But he's also an architect. He loves it. It's his calling. I think, if he'd been given the choice to choose to be–" I cut myself off before the word "normal" slips off my tongue and shut my mouth tight.

Alex tilts his head, scanning my face like he's reading between the lines and realizing I had more to say, but then he looks up over the top of my head and winces.

I have a single second to turn around before Maisie floats into view, beaming at us in pleasant surprise.

"Well! It just tickles me pink to see two professors from rival departments getting along! The two of you have just made my day!"

"Maisie," Alex says gruffly in greeting.

She ignores him, turning to me instead. "I have great news. Your condo in The Pillars is ready! I have the keys in my pocket! Do you have time to go see it right now? I'm supposed to give you a full tour of the condo and the neighborhood. Oh, and Alex, you'll be her neighbor! You should come as well!"

He shakes his head. "I'm well-versed in the community and layout of the condos, seeing as I've lived there for years–"

"Oh, don't be silly. Everyone is always so curious about everyone else's living spaces. Come on, both of you! It'll be fun! I never get to have two professors at once."

Maisie, oblivious to the connotation behind her words, smiles and motions for us to stand, but I catch Alex's eyes, and he looks just as startled as I do.

But then, he smiles at me, and I give him a pitiful smile in return.

A few minutes later, standing in front of a set of wide, frosted glass double doors, four stories above the surface of the ice, I find myself beside Alex, who has become Maisie's stunt double, essentially. "See how Dr. Scarlett just has to scan his badge here? That's all you have to do, and you'll have full access to the neighborhood. See?"

Alex grits his teeth in annoyance and fishes his badge out of his jacket, which he wears on a lanyard around his neck. He presses the badge to the scanner and stares hard at Maisie in the process, who hasn't noticed how annoyed he is in the slightest. The doors slide open, revealing a wide hallway of glass with a view of the ice on one side and the campus on the other.

"There's a small lounge here with a gym, which has a steam room and sauna, but the steam room is currently out of commission. Maintenance is working on it!" Maisie hops down the hallway. I keep pace with Alex, who has a long gait but is unhurried.

"This is the grocery store," she says excitedly, motioning to an archway with a single room of well-stocked shelves and coolers, and a bored-looking attendant slumped over the checkout counter with his laptop open. He gives Maisie the most half-assed smile I've ever seen, but again, Maisie has only two emotional functions—glee, and super glee.

"Josh is normally here during the day. He's a psych graduate student! You'll love him!"

Alex makes a low grunt in reply, tucking his hands inside his pockets, and the tour continues.

After the grocery store, the hallway widens even further, curving into the half-moon shape The Pillars are known for, and the condos come into view. It's a strange kind of architecture—two- to three-story condos suspended on thick pillars of glass, their front entrances connected to the hallway-like-skybridge. Most of the front doors are decorated in some way. Some doors even have potted plants and doormats. And beyond, and above? The aurora dances and weaves between the stars, and the campus around us gleams like a beacon of light against a wash of darkness so thick, so unending, it's like being in space.

Like I'm close enough to the stars that I can touch them.

"This is where Dr. Scarlett lives," Maisie says, motioning to a door with no decorations and a simple black doormat.

Alex just stares at Maisie, one brow arched in silent challenge, like Maisie half expects him to open his door and give me a tour of his personal space, but she moves on.

"And this is you," she says with a beaming smile, four doors down and across the hallway. "There's a keypad, and you'll have to change the code. I sent you an email this morning with instructions on how to do it, but for now, it's just four zeros. Go ahead!"

I glance at Alex. He shrugs, and I punch in the numbers.

A rush of warm, clean air greets us. The condo is wide at the base, with a nice kitchen with an island, a living room with a view of the icy landscape and stars, and a staircase leading to a loft. I step into the center of the living room, which is furnished tastefully.

"Upstairs is the smaller bedroom, right off the loft. Down this hallway is the main bedroom and bathroom. If you need anything big, like a TV or new furniture, you'll need to talk to the supply department." Maisie's phone rings. She giggles, excusing herself, and steps outside the condo, shutting the door behind her.

Alex moves through the kitchen, his fingertips dusting over the smooth countertop.

I'm grateful he's here. This is hitting me in full force, to say the least.

"I've never lived on my own before," I admit thickly. "I've always had a roommate."

"You might enjoy the privacy. It's nice sometimes." He sighs heavily and comes to stand at my side at the window, to look out over the view. "You have a much better view than I do. I have the campus side."

We stand in silence for what feels like several minutes, and again, it's comfortable. Almost warm.

Then, he says, "There's a private elevator at the end of the hallway that has access to the underground areas of campus. It also stops at the surface, and there's a warming room with outdoor access for shifting."

I can't remember the last time I even felt the urge to shift since I arrived back on campus. I had all summer to frolic in the sun.

"Thank you for doing this with me."

"It's not a big deal."

"It is to me. I like Maisie, but she can be…"

"Very annoying?"

"She's just so happy all the time. It's like the darkness doesn't affect her in the slightest," I laugh, and he smiles, his eyes gleaming like I've never seen them before. "So… what happened today in your lab?"

His smile vanishes, and he straightens, looking suddenly peeved to the highest degree. "I need to go settle some things down there." He turns toward the door, but then stops, adding, "If you'd like some help moving your belongings… just let me know."

"That's very kind of you."

Something big shifts between us when he meets my eyes again. I don't have a name for it. I'm not sure there is a name for this—a sudden, brutal, mutual trust.

"Enjoy your new view," he says and leaves.

Leaves me wondering what this strange feeling is in his wake.

11

OUT OF CONTROL

Skye

ABBY SLIDES DOWN THE BANISTER OF THE STAIRCASE IN MY NEW HOUSE, gaping at the view beyond the floor-to-ceiling windows. Toby managed to get the electric fireplace up and running after an hour of trial and error with the little remote we found in one of the kitchen drawers, and now the house downstairs is borderline too toasty warm, but both of them left the lab to help me move, and now I get why.

An hour later, we're across campus in the apartment towers where all the graduates and postdocs live… where I lived until this morning, when I packed up the rest of my things into boxes, and went back for more of my things. "This apartment is the best Toby and I can get, for sure," Abby says with a rough sigh. "We talked about it for a while, but I think we're making the right decision. It's quieter this high up compared to Toby's place, and I would have to move!"

"Pivot to the left! Pivot! PIVOT!" I grunt, and she disappears from view for several seconds while I shove my mattress through my old bedroom door, bracing all of my strength against it.

While the new condo came with a bed, the mattress is terrible, and I'm not leaving the specially ordered, high-end mattress my parents sent me last year behind. It cost a fortune to ship it here, for one.

It's going to take all Goddess-damned day to get it across campus at this rate.

"Wait! I'm squished!" Abby shouts, breathlessly, while banging on the side of the mattress.

I let go and drop my hands onto my knees, panting. "There's no way we're going to be able to do this. How are we going to get it into the elevator?"

"Well," she replies, rising on her toes to peek at me over the top of the mattress where she's trapped in the corner of our hallway. "How'd it get up here in the first place?"

"I don't even remember. It was delivered."

A sharp knock on the door rings out before two sets of booted footsteps and two familiar male voices fill our apartment, which doesn't take much. Compared to my new condo, this place is only half the size but with a lot more twists and turns–too snug for the amount of people and the mattress. I might have to saw it in half to release Abby from the tight corner we wedged her into.

"Wow. What have you guys done?" Toby laughs heartily as he scans the hallway. I have just enough room to push up onto my toes and peek around the doorframe, spotting him and… Alex, of course, lingering a few feet away.

Alex sighs heavily and scans the mattress, then the hallway, then meets my eyes and gives me that look. The look with a slightly raised brow punctuated by clear… annoyance?

Yeah. Maybe it's weird I've been looking at him this closely. It's especially weird now that he knows I've been watching him because his eyes narrow and that arch of his brow deepens.

I clear my throat, duck back into my room, and let the blush threatening to erupt all over my body spread like wildfire across my cheeks in private instead.

Meanwhile, Toby makes quick work of simply pulling Abby over the top of the mattress by her armpits and depositing her on the other side. I'm still trapped in my room, and therefore, have to stand here like an idiot listening to both men criticize us for not waiting for them to help.

"Well, I didn't know you were bringing him!" Abby argues somewhere out of sight. "We thought we'd at least get it off its frame and into the hallway...."

"Just move, okay? We've got this."

I step back as the men shove the mattress back inside my room. I'm damn near pinched against the windows when Alex comes inside... my space. My room. The one place on campus I could privately be myself. It's mostly empty now, but there are traces of me here. The plants I refuse to move until my new condo is ready. The two boxes of rocks and crystals I can't carry across campus by myself. A few books that didn't make it into the boxes. Pictures still taped to the wall.

He scans the room, briefly catching my gaze, and drops into a gruff, highly scientific plan of action with Toby about the best way to get the mattress out.

Less than five minutes later, they have the mattress safely outside the apartment on a dolly.

I feel like an idiot. I'm a physicist. Apparently, my skills and understanding in the subject of matter, even in terms of moving a mattress, have their limitations.

"Is that everything?" Toby asks in the service elevator—a much wider space than the elevators we normally use.

Abby and I glance down at the scattered boxes and potted plants and nod, but I meet her gaze and feel a little sad, to be honest. We walk side by side, dragging a cart full of my things into my new condo, in silence, but that silence is deafening.

While the guys swap the mattresses, taking the other one to storage, I sit in the loft with Abby, carefully taking out each of my rocks and setting them along the wall. I'll organize them later, maybe move a few to my office on campus. Abby's going through my books, bleeding silent melancholy.

"It feels kind of weird, doesn't it?" she asks. "We've been roommates for so long and… like, I love Toby, and he's moving in and it's where our relationship was always headed despite my efforts to pump the brakes, but… I don't like the idea that you and I had a deadline on our relationship."

"We don't have a deadline on our relationship!" I almost laugh, but Abby looks so sad. The furrow between her brows and the deep set of her glistening eyes is new to me. It sets me off, to say the least. My bracelet warms. I want to reach out and touch her, to catch a glimpse of the inside of her mind, what she's feeling, but she doesn't know I can do that. If I didn't have the bracelet, I wouldn't even need to touch her to see her inner thoughts. "You'll always be my friend. When I reset the code to my door, you'll be the first to know. We'll still hang out all the time."

"Abby!" Toby calls from below. She rises, dusting off her leggings.

"Dinner in the cafeteria tonight?" Abby asks me, and I nod, then watch her maneuver down the stairs and out the door, but Toby and Alex linger in conversation for a moment.

I gather a box of rocks and carry it back downstairs just as Toby crosses the threshold, roping an arm over Abby's shoulders, and leaves. Alex turns to me, watching me shift the box from hip to hip.

"Where are you going with that?" he asks.

"My office. I want to move some plants there, too. I don't have a lecture today, so I figured I'd get this done since I need to spend the rest of the week in my lab."

He eyes me skeptically for a moment. "Is that a box full of rocks?"

I hug the box impulsively, my instincts to hoard and hide my precious collection taking over control. "What of it?"

"You're a strange creature, Dr. Abbot."

I throw him a glare, but the amusement shining behind his eyes is palpable. There's a strange note of incompatibility between us that's hard to ignore and takes up every pocket of my mind now that I've gotten to know him a little better, at least at surface level. Maybe it's because he's not a shifter. Again, I don't know any wizards, but that has to be the reason for this feeling settling into my bones as he takes the box out of my hands and holds it like it doesn't weigh a hundred pounds.

I like him. Maybe against my better judgment. I've been on dates before. I've shared a few kisses, although I've never really dabbled in *attraction*. I know how that sounds. It's not that I don't find people attractive. I just need more than that to actually like someone. To trust them. To lean toward them.

"Where'd you go?" he asks.

I blink and then meet his gaze. How long have I been standing here trying to reconcile the fact I find Alex incredibly attractive in some weird, exotic way? It's like I want to study him. I want to find out who he is on a mathematical level just to understand the concept of *him*.

Maybe I'm just insane and lonely. I have no idea.

"I just have a lot to carry upstairs. I'm debating the best way to do it."

"You grabbing that potted plant and following me to the elevator seems like the best course of action."

"You don't have to continue helping me. I'm sure you have a lot of other, more important things you could be doing."

He steps into the hallway, where other front doors come into view under the faint glow of artificial lights that dim like a sunset and brighten like a sunrise, depending on the time of day. Now, they're fading. It's late afternoon already.

"I actually have something tied up in the lab and have a free evening. I'll help. You can owe me."

"Owe you?" I follow him out into the hallway after picking up the sickly Monstera plant I've been trying to keep alive for four years. It hates it here in Lunaria, but I don't have the heart to let it succumb to its natural end just yet. It was a gift from Maeve, anyway. She asks about it every time we talk.

"I may need your help with something that has nothing to do with the university at all."

"Oh?"

Twenty minutes and nearly two miles of walking from one side of campus to the other, and several staircases and two elevators later, we're stepping into my office while he wraps up the story about how the Beta of Aurora, the pack that resides within Aurorium, came to him seeking help.

He sets the box of rocks on my desk. "I've analyzed the samples, but there's nothing abnormal about the DNA profiles I found. Trace elements of exotic material, maybe, but my lab assistants are working on that as it stands."

"So you're tasked with finding the killer?"

"No, just doing the math for them. I try to stay out of pack business like everyone else on campus." He picks up a rock and examines it. Meanwhile, my heart leaps into my throat like I'm a child again and someone is touching my things–putting them down where they don't belong.

I lunge toward him and take the rock. It startles him, and he lets go of a disbelieving laugh. "What is going on with you?"

"These are just very important to me." My voice wobbles. I grit my teeth. I sound so ridiculous.

He eyes me like I'm about to bite his hand off as he reaches into the box, arching a brow. When I don't move to stop him right away, he pulls out another rock.

"It's a–"

"A botryoidal chalcedony?" he says before I can finish. "It's a rather nice one, too. I like the color variation." He turns the geode over in his palm to inspect its bumpy surface. "Where did you find it?"

I blush. I can't help it, not when he seems genuinely interested. People are rarely interested. "The lakeshore in Moonrise. They're all over the place there."

"So this is your personal collection?"

"Yeah. I…. It's weird, but, yeah, I've collected a *few* rocks."

"There's at least two hundred crystals and geodes in here." He corrects me with a wry grin that deepens my blush.

"Do you want to see my favorite?" I enthusiastically reach into the box, fingers grasping for the chunk of raw kyanite, but my bracelet snags on the pointed tip of a hunk of quartz.

It happens in a split second. One moment, I'm here, in my office, my feet grounded and Alex standing a hair's breadth away, and then the bracelet clasp snaps like a length of thin thread. My powers roar to their full potential without warning.

The room fades in a blink, replaced by whirling sound and darkness. Voices and visions strangle my senses. I fight for control, but it's useless. I haven't taken the bracelet off like this in years. The reserves of my powers stored in the charms flood back into my body like a tidal wave, and the moon and stars pull me into the depths, head over heels.

A sharp ache ripples through the voices screaming through my mind. A sudden snap quiets everything–every sound, every color, every distorted vision.

I'm on the ice.

And I'm not alone.

A hooded figure stands only yards away, the wind beating against a dark cloak, his face hidden by shadows. Crimson red eyes hold mine.

"Run!"

12

———————

MYSTIC'S OUT OF THE BAG

Skye

"RUN!"

I open my eyes to my office, to glittering starlight shimmering through the floor-to-ceiling windows. My hand is resting around… a rock. The kyanite, right. I curl my fingers around it and lift it out, but my hand trembles like the small stone weighs a ton.

I'm still trapped between the realms–the real world and the land of visions driven by the same stars I've been studying for years.

I feel weak, like I've expended most of my magic. It happens so quickly for me.

I close my eyes and take several deep breaths to ground myself but bite back a gasp when someone moves, their shadow stretching across the floor.

Alex.

His eyes are narrowed to slits. He scans my face, posturing defensively, his shoulders squared and spine tight–ready to lunge, if he must.

What did he see?

"What the fuck was that?" he asks sternly, in a whisper, glancing at the door behind me, which is, thankfully, closed. "Skye? What the fuck–"

"I'm a mystic," I whisper back.

He blinks at me, his brow furrowed tightly. "A what?"

"A mystic. A seer. Whatever–whatever you want to call it."

"I don't know what that is." His hands, tightly curled into fists, relax. He comes to stand in front of me and leans down close enough to inspect my eyes, and with a cringe, I notice the shadows falling over the planes of his chiseled cheekbones have a faint violet glow to them.

"Your eyes are insane right now. Are you on drugs?"

"What? No–" I snap back to reality with a gasp. "Alex!"

He grabs my face, pinching my cheeks between his thumb and forefinger, and turns my head from side to side slowly, inspecting me like a specimen he just pulled from the ice, or however that works. I let him. I sink into his touch because it's been so long, I think, since anyone other than Abby has come this close to me, and those voices are still humming, still knocking me sideways, still haunting the darkest, deepest recesses of my mind, and I start to slip back... into it....

"What's happening to you?" Alex's voice, deeply flavored with concern, pulls me back to reality. He's gripping my shoulders now, and we're nearly nose to nose in the quiet, private sanctuary of my office. I reach up with arms like lead but can't bring myself to grip his forearms for the support I desperately need as my body regenerates the magic I depleted.

"My bracelet," I murmur as new, fresh voices screech through my head in warning. Another vision funnels into view, splitting my mind into fractals. I groan and double over, but Alex presses against my shoulders, holding me upright.

"Skye, I want to take you to the clinic. Something's not right."

"My... bracelet. It's in the box. P-please. Please."

"Why–"

"Please?" My vision goes black. I'm suddenly back on the ice, but the landscape is far more detailed than it was before. I'm closer to the city of Aurorium this time, lingering in the vision long enough to make out the hazy fluorescent glow of the buildings in the distance. The smell of copper is so thick I choke on it. Mist rises around my legs like white snakes, and below, the ice is stained red. A thick, bloody, crimson red that melts the ice. Fresh and hot–

"Skye! Skye, Gods, look at me–"

There's another body on the ice. A young woman, I think, judging by the thickness and length of her hair, but I can't make out the color because of the blood. It's everywhere. There's so much of it.

"Is this what you're talking about? Your bracelet?"

A shadow rises over the body–cloaked in black. Red eyes meet mine and hold.

"Skye?"

"*Run.*"

Cool metal wraps around my wrist, and I'm yanked back to reality in a split second, the vision fading into pockets of icy haze that dissipate as my office rolls back into startling focus. I'm on my knees. Alex kneels in front of me, gripping my fingers, his eyes holding mine a vivid, almost unreal blue against a wash of gray plaster–a far cry from the glowing, violent red I'd just witnessed.

"How many attacks have there been in Aurorium? Just one?" I ask, dizzy and breathless.

"Skye, what happened?" He looks down at my wrist and pulls my hand up between us to inspect the charms. They glow violet, just like my eyes, the little alchemy derived gems swirling with my magic as the excess drains into the magical storage bins that Posey created with her magic.

"My magic just got a little intense. I don't practice very often."

"What are you talking about? I thought you were a shifter?"

"I am, but I'm more–more than that. My dad–just give me a second."

He lets go of my hands. I bring them to my face, closing my eyes against the room and trying to piece together what I saw.

"Why did you ask about the attack in Aurorium?" he asks, his voice cool and steady but tinged with concern I can taste. I feel bad for him. Mystics are rare outside of Moonrise–at least, well-developed, trained mystics like myself. But even then, only witches with specific powers or shifters with acute senses of smell would be able to pick them out of a crowd. I'm different. I'm something else in the same magical class. There're only three of us that we know of. Me, my dad, and my grandma Sarah. My great-grandpa Isaac and Grandpa Sydney do have the power of sight, but it's not like me and Dad. How can I possibly explain all of this to Alex?

"Skye? Step out of your head for a second and talk to me, please."

"I'm sorry I scared you."

"You fucking did," he admits, his teeth bared when I peek through my fingers. "Explain."

"I see things. Visions. It's–Goddess, I don't even know where to begin, but ever since I was a little girl, I've had an uncanny ability to see into people's minds and into the future, if I willed it. I'm trained—well. My father is like me, but far more powerful, and he…" I lick my lips. "I can see the future. I get visions from the stars–prophecies. I can look into and manipulate people's minds." I finally look at him. "I'm very good at it."

He just stares at me with his lips slightly parted.

"I wear this charm bracelet because it keeps a good bit of my powers contained, so I'm not flooded with images and sounds all the time. I can still use my powers, but this prevents what just happened. It was an accident."

He's still staring at me, not even blinking.

"And I had a vision."

"Okay…" he says slowly, not leaving my gaze. "About?"

"You don't believe me."

"I saw your eyes turn bright purple and roll back in your head, Skye. I'll believe anything."

I swallow hard. "I had a vision of someone dying. Someone being murdered near Aurorium." I reach for the details, but they're already hazy, falling away. "Out on the ice."

He nods, chewing his lower lip in thought, and I notice, not for the first time, his longer than normal incisors. They glint in the dimmed fluorescent glow of the lights dotted across my office ceiling. "There was an attack in the subway terminal and another one, out on the ice. My lab, like I said, has been creating a genetic profile on the victim because—"

"It was a woman," I rush out, holding his perplexed gaze. "It was a woman, for sure."

"We know that. But we only found traces of her genetic profile. If her attacker, person or beast, left any traces—"

"It wasn't a beast. It was a man. His eyes were—were red." I wince as the last details fade out of focus entirely and dissolve into pieces I can no longer use.

Alex goes so still, I'm not sure he's breathing. "Did you say red eyes?"

I nod. He narrows his eyes to slits.

"You're sure?"

"I know it sounds crazy."

"It's not. Thank you for telling me." His tone is suddenly gruff and clipped. He rises and extends a hand to me to help me up, and I accept it.

But we stand for a moment facing each other in silence. He's looking at a blank spot on the wall above my head, deep in thought.

"Red eyes aren't naturally occurring, so this is probably a clue, right?" I offer.

"I'm not investigating anything. I'm just giving the Beta insight on the person who died so they can fully identify her," he says in a murmur like he's not totally aware he's speaking.

"Um, perhaps the attacker is someone like you?"

He looks down at me, his expression hard, damn-near chilled. "Like me?"

My entire body aches to take a step away from him, those same fight-or-flight feelings driving my wolf, as weak and as happy being dormant as she is, into restlessness. "Um, a wizard?"

He blinks, and it's the first time he's moved since rising. "A wizard?"

"You told me you weren't a shifter, so I assumed—"

"I see." He runs his hand through his hair, and his expression softens. "Maybe you're right." He seems to come back to focus then, tucking his hands in his pockets and examining my face closely. "Are you feeling okay?"

"I'm fine. I just feel stupid."

"Why?"

I shake my head, giving him an incredulous smile. "Because I should have more control. I should have been able to rein myself in. I could have hurt someone. Hurt you, had I touched you."

"I was touching you," he says, and the air between us thins. My heart leaps for no reason other than I'm imaging it–him standing here, watching me go insane, all violet light and unfathomable power… and he held me through it without a thought for his own safety or wellbeing, without knowing what was happening to me, and what I could have inadvertently done to him. "Innocently, of course," he adds, and his cheeks color–going ruddy, but in a deeper, almost blue-hued way that I'm not anticipating.

I should ask him about wizards. Maybe not now. Now doesn't seem like an appropriate time to get nosey about his powers, but one day. One day I'll ask.

"I have to be the one who wants to cause harm. I can touch you like this." I grab his arm. He doesn't even flinch. "Or like this." I let him go and reach up, sliding my fingertips over his forehead to tuck a lock of his thick, black hair behind his ear. He's cold, and no wonder. I probably scared the daylight out of him. "I have to will my magic to do my bidding. I can't hurt you unless–"

"Unless you want to?" There's that wry smile again, and I feel so, so much better.

I let my hand fall to my side and step back to the desk, to the box of rocks. "I'm sorry for scaring you. I'll ensure it won't happen again."

"You mentioned you can see the future? Do your powers have any bearing on your reasonings for becoming an astrophysicist?"

I pick up a few of the crystals and set them on my desk. "Of course. I want to know why I am the way I am and… make sense of it. Like I said, my dad had, and still has, a hell of a time with his gifts, and they're so similar to mine. Worse, I think, to handle. He's never had a special bracelet to keep them in check." He just pushed everyone away. I didn't know he was my dad until I was seven years old, and even then, I had only weeks with him before he tore himself away for a while.

I close my eyes against that terrible summer from my childhood memories and reach blindly into the box again, careful of my bracelet this time, but less careful about my skin.

A jagged geode edge slices through my thumb. "Oh, shit!"

I draw my hand back and curl it into a fist, turning to Alex with a wobbly smile, but he's completely across the room all of a sudden, his back flat against the wall.

"Alex?"

"I have to go," he says under his breath. Then, he yanks the door open so violently it nearly comes off its hinges, and darts away.

"Alex?" I call out as blood drips between my fingers.

13

───────

A STRANGER

Alex

I'M RARELY IN MY OFFICE IN THE SPIRES ABOVE THE ICE BUT WAS FORCED to make an exception today. After my lecture this afternoon, I had a meeting with a few of the other biology professors, which the dean did not attend, and found myself in the gray confines of this dusty little box of a room, which is home to bound copies of the research I've done over the years.

Laney blinks up at me expectantly while I look over the lab report on the blood samples the Beta asked for.

"Interesting. Was this confirmed?" I ask, pointing to a line of text.

She nods, so owlish I wonder if she's even breathing. She can't be more than twenty, and even then, she looks more like a terrified, socially awkward twelve-year-old girl in the blue scrubs the clinic volunteers have to wear during their clinicals. "It's a foreign substance, but there was a lot of it in the second sample–the one we weren't able to pull a profile from. It's foreign in nature, possibly an animal?"

"An animal on illicit drugs?" I arch a brow, and she cowers. Poor thing. She's brilliant, but I can already tell this girl is on an academic track. She'd never make it in industry. Yeah, the quiet, secluded nature of academia will lure her in and get her hooked by the time she's done with her master's degree.

"Abby tested it against all the animal profiles we have in the lab, and every match was negative. Whatever killed this woman wasn't like us but isn't an animal commonly seen in Aurorium, either."

I heave a breath and lean back in my chair with the results in my hands, skeptically eyeing the young researcher. "This is a massive amount of foreign substances in both samples."

Laney shuffles her feet. "Trace in the victim's, but the attacker's… yeah. We just don't have anything to test it against. If we knew what it was, that might explain why we've had such a hard time making it match genetically to everything we've tested it against."

"This is enough to give to the Beta. It's all he asked us to do, and we've done it to the best of our ability."

"But we… we have a second profile. The attacker–"

"And their profile is incomplete because we don't have enough information, and that's okay." A knock sounds on the door, and I rise. Laney glances in the direction of the exit but remains, nervously twiddling her thumbs. "Laney, is there anything else–"

"Are we safe?"

"Yes," I tell her, even though my stomach twists as she looks up at me with those doe eyes. "This campus is incredibly safe."

I edge toward the door, opening it wide, and Laney gathers her things and shuffles toward me just as Skye steps into my office.

I haven't seen her for two days, which is probably for the best after what happened.

"Oh, sorry, I didn't think you'd even be here, but I had to–" She steps out of Laney's way with a smile.

I wait until Laney turns the corner in the hallway before grabbing her wrist and dragging her over the threshold, shutting and locking the door behind us.

"Hey!" Skye laughs, her eyes alight in a different way than they were in her office in the spire I can see clearly from the view beyond the windows.

"Are you feeling well?" I ask.

She rubs her wrist, brows furrowing. "I am. Are you? You nearly tossed me across the room."

"I'm sorry. I'm also sorry for running out of your office like I did."

She looks down at her hands. "I suppose that was kind of weird, Alex. In your defense, I definitely freaked you out."

"You didn't. Not–not with the magic thing." I lean my weight against the door. "Look, I have a thing."

"A thing?" She narrows her eyes.

"About blood."

"Oh." She glances at the bandage on her thumb, the same bandage I've been trying not to stare at since I let her into my office. "But... you're a biologist? That would be like me being afraid of... the dark. Or heights."

I kick off the door and move closer to her. "Are you making fun of me, Dr. Abbot?"

"Uh, yes, I am." She laughs, and it's... magical. A sound that abruptly rewires something ancient and tangled in my brain. Her smile is like honey, and I realize with a start that I've never seen it. This is a first, something I don't think she does very often, and I'm the one to witness it–at my expense. "You have a thing about blood. Yet, you work as a biologist. You have to handle blood samples all the time."

"I'm a paleomicrobiologist," I correct tartly, taking another step toward her. "I study genetics in the minuscule samples of flora and fauna we're able to find in the ice. And blood samples don't bother me. It's the... act of bleeding that..." Heat blooms through my body as her cheeks flush. Her blush is a soft pink, like a rose petal. I bet her skin is just as warm as she looks.

I resist the urge to take another step toward her while alarm bells ping through my skull. This isn't right. This warmth I feel in her presence. I can't allow it.

"People bleeding in your presence grosses you out?"

"Something like that."

"Well, I'll try not to do it again."

I hold her gaze for several seconds and only look away when she blinks, breaking what I'm sure is a spell.

I'm not a weak man. I've spent the last decade and a half fighting for what I have now, and that meant keeping everyone at arm's length. For their safety and mine.

I haven't felt, nor wanted, to be this close to someone before. There wasn't room for it. When Skye brushes her arm against mine, stepping past me toward the door, I fight the urge to turn into her touch.

This isn't the way of my kind. It's why everything about her has always felt so confusing, from the moment I met her in that supply closet years ago and touched her then, felt her warmth as she shattered into muffled sobs. I was used to the strict nature of shifters–all senses and heat. Skye was less open, more guarded, keeping those normally outward parts of herself, her kind, tucked away and twisted in an iron embrace.

But now, in my office, she's open. Smiling. Teasing me.

"I came to ask if I could have a tour of your lab, finally, but you seem rather busy." She motions to my messy desk and my laptop open to the lecture I was writing when Laney dropped by with the lab results. "Anyway, I have to meet up with Abby." She checks her watch and unlocks the door but hesitates before opening it.

"Another time," I tell her with a hint of regret. "Anytime, actually. Later tonight the lab will be empty and..." Being alone with her is probably a bad idea, especially with how tired I am. The past few days have been insanely busy. I've been operating outside the parameters of my carefully crafted schedule. I run my fingers through my hair as a wave of hunger and fatigue bites through my body.

Skye opens the door just a crack, bursting our bubble of privacy. "Actually, I'm going out with Abby tonight. I have a few errands I need to run in Aurorium."

"I see."

"But... tomorrow?"

Tomorrow is Saturday, right? What's wrong with my head? "Yes. Tomorrow. I'll meet up with you in the morning and give you the full tour."

Her smile sinks into my chest, turning to heat, then hunger I struggle to contain. I don't breathe again until the door shuts behind her, locking me into a hell of my own making.

I sink behind my desk and pick up my phone. Toby answers on the first ring.

"I need you to call your contact in Aurorium."

<hr>

SKYE

I SMOOTH MY HANDS OVER THE FLUFFY FABRIC OF A SWEATER IN A SMALL boutique in Aurorium. Abby hums beside me, impressed with the velvety soft red fabric, and gives me a nudge with her shoulder when I begin to set it back down on the table. "No, you have to buy that. Red is such a good color on you!"

"It's very red," I argue, but I fidget with the sweater. "Like blood."

"Oh, please, it's exactly the kind of thing you'd wear. Buy it! Stretch those new tenured dollars, Skye. You deserve it!" She nudges me again and wanders off to continue browsing. I drape the sweater over my arm and move toward the counter, where a shop associate promptly accepts my money, and within minutes, we're out on the street again with several shopping bags each, wincing against a flurry of ice flecks being picked up by the ever-present breeze.

"Lockers?" Abby asks, tilting her head toward the entrance of the subway, only two shops away.

"Yeah. I'm done shopping. Do we need to go anywhere else or...?" I can already tell by the look on Abby's face that she has no plans to take the train back to campus after this. She's staying out, which means I owe her one drink at her favorite club, like usual.

I roll my eyes to the haze of neon light reflecting against the ice crystals fluttering through the air and meet her gaze. "Fine. One drink."

She squeals and shuffles in her parka to loop her arm around mine, and then we're off, carefully picking our way across the frozen street to the subway, where lockers lining the cavernous wall will store our things until we're ready to board the train home.

"Let's just share," she says, stuffing her bags in front of mine.

"Only because I actually remembered to bring a padlock," I counter, and she sticks her tongue out at me.

I scoff. She slams the locker into a closed position and extends her hand to accept the padlock in question, but a shadow moves behind us and comes to a graceful stop.

Prickles of unease ripple over my skin as a tall, lanky man in a hood turns to us, his face cast in shadow. I can only see the outline of a sharp jaw and a wide, full mouth before he asks, "Are you students at Lunaria?"

Abby, ever the social butterfly, whips around to face him. "What's it to you?" she asks in a near snarl.

"I'm trying to catch the next train to campus. I missed the last one."

She narrows her eyes, craning her neck to look up into the shadow of his hood, but a group of people push past us, hustling toward the platform.

The man just stands there, still as a statue. All shadows and a strange kind of stillness I find oddly familiar.

For a moment, my brain short-circuits, and I almost say Alex's name, but this man... his voice is different. Rougher. With a thick, clipped accent similar to Alex's but less practiced.

"Are you a new student?" I ask, stepping closer to Abby. She turns to put the lock in place.

"No," he replies, turning his head to look right at me. "I'm looking for someone. An old friend."

The train arriving from campus speeds into view, sending a gust of air and a screech of metal through the subway. The crowd waiting for the train hustles forward, forcing us to step back and the man to turn away, but he turns, just briefly, to look at us again.

Under the flow of the subway's fluorescent lights, his teeth illuminate, reflected like shards of silver against the shadows covering the upper half of his face.

I rear back.

Abby clutches my arm as the train's horn blares, tugging me back toward the stairs. "Come on! It's freezing down here, and Toby said he's already at the club. How lucky is that!"

"Did you–did you see that guy's teeth?"

"What?" she asks, but a crowd departs the train, and the stranger is lost to a sea of bodies.

14

LIGHT AS A FEATHER

Skye

THE STREET OUTSIDE ABBY'S FAVORITE NIGHTCLUB IS WASHED IN SHADES of hazy blue and green. It's a frigid night, and we're both bundled to the chin as we approach, slipping through the heavy front door and into the long hallway lined with lockers. Abby skips ahead to pay the cover charge while I open and shut lockers to find an empty one.

My twin brothers visited Aurorium and the university last year in the dead of winter, just after Solstice. Having grown up in Moonrise, they were shocked by the idea of having to shed layers every time they stepped into a store or restaurant, but after years of this, I've grown used to it. Wearing thick boots in a club? That still feels weird, but when it's negative forty, there's no way around it.

My bracelet snags on my parka sleeve. Adrenaline rushes to my fingertips, prickling like little needles. I force myself to take a breath, overcome by the memory of the bracelet coming unclasped in my office a few days ago, and slowly untangle it before taking off the parka and stuffing it into an empty locker.

The heat in the hallway floods over my body, seeping through my sweater. I shiver. It feels nice–so good, actually, after a full evening running from one store to the next gathering all the random, specialty grocery and toiletry items I need for my new condo. My fingers are chilled to the bone even after wearing gloves for the past three hours, and when Abby returns, she notices how I'm pinching my skin, trying to bring feeling back into my body.

She eyes me for a moment before taking a deep breath. Her dainty features crinkle. She frowns at me, shuffling as she pulls her arms through the sleeves of her parka. "Can I ask you something?"

"Of course." I pull my hat off my head and begin unraveling the tight braid I wore underneath.

"Have you been hanging out with Dr. Scarlett?"

My hair falls in loose tendrils over my shoulder. I brush them back, trying to smooth the static electricity causing the pieces to stick to the fibers of my dark blue sweater. "Define hanging out."

"You know what I mean, Skye. Are you guys, like, a thing?"

"A thing?" I try to sound shocked she'd even ask, but I'm not sure how to arrange my expression to match my tone. I doubt I look shocked. We have been hanging out, if I can call it that. I did go to his office this afternoon, knowing how unlikely it was he'd be there, but he was, like I was pulled in by a magnet. I wanted to see him. I've been thinking about him. He's been taking up little pockets of my mind that had otherwise remained untouched.

"Do you like him?" Abby asks, leaning her shoulder against the locker.

"Abby–"

"Look, I just want to know."

"I know how you feel about him." I hold her gaze. I don't want to hurt her. Her hatred toward Alex is well-known, but the more I get to know him, the less I understand why she feels so strongly about him in the negative. But then it clicks. I see it first in her eyes, the slight glossiness, the little wrinkle between her eyebrows. "Are you jealous of his relationship with Toby?"

She blushes and tries to laugh, but it's half-hearted. "No. It's not like that."

"Then what is it like?"

"You go first. He's been around so much. He helped you move, Skye. He carried your mattress across campus!"

"We needed his help, and you know it!"

"I just need to know whether my best friend has a thing for my research director or not, okay?" She crosses her arms under her chest and fixes me with a sharp look.

I bristle, relax, and take a deep breath before replying, "I'm not going to lie. I like him. I find him… handsome."

"Handsome?"

"He's hot. You've even said so."

"I didn't think he was your type."

"Do I even have a type? I've been on, maybe, six dates in total since I moved here."

"Is he nice to you?" Her voice falters, and she looks down at the toes of her boots.

"Yes, Abby, he is. He thinks highly of you, too, you know. He thinks you're kind of lazy in the lab, but you already know that's actually the case."

She tries to glare but huffs, rolling her eyes to the ceiling. "I hate the ice lab."

"I think you make that perfectly clear." I step closer to her as another group enters the hallway. "I'm going to be helping in his lab for a bit, I think. He needs a consultant from my department, and we have been seeing more of each other lately, but it's not like you're insinuating."

"Oh, really? Because he looks at you like he wants to eat you."

I blink several times, too stunned to speak. "He does not."

"Oh, my dear, sweet Skye, you have no idea, do you?"

"No idea of what?"

"Abby? Oh, hey! I thought you guys were going to get here like an hour ago!" Toby's voice rings out from the main entrance of the inner sanctum of the club.

Abby angles her body toward him to wave, but I step closer to her, spurred into action by something I can only call delusion. "Why do you ask?"

"About Alex?"

I nod, gripping her forearm enough to hold her attention.

"Because he talks about you all the time to Toby, and Dr. Scarlett rarely talks at all." Her dark gaze cuts through me like a blade, awakening something new, something foreign. Something that feels a lot like want.

She whirls out of my grip and practically floats over to Toby, who bends to kiss her forehead before they disappear through the door into the club proper, leaving me standing like an idiot against the lockers.

I've always confused curiosity with true feeling. I blame my dad for that. He loves Mom, of course, but never, not once, has he been open with me about how deep that love runs between them. Mom did her best to explain it–that Dad loves her to the point of obsession. That to him, she's the moon, the stars–his entire world in one soul, one body, and there's nothing he wouldn't do for her.

But Mom's a full shifter. Shifters feel things so heavily, so physically compared to… what I am. What my dad is.

Maybe that's why there's been this disconnect between my rational mind and my feelings for my entire life. As a mystic, I see things too deeply and read too sharply between the lines. I've read the curve of Alex's smile and the way he leans toward me during conversations. I've studied how his hands move when he reaches for me. I've tried to rationalize the feeling of his touch and the way I warmed from within, waking up to his eyes, his face, after having that terrible vision in my office. I don't know how to process this strange feeling. There's no equation I can use to work this out. Nothing I can study. Nothing I can research.

I have a crush, I think. That's what Abby would call it. It sounds so simple putting it that way.

Simple–and stupid.

I scrub my cold cheeks and take another deep breath before marching into the club to perform the ritual I've been following for years–find our table, drink a single cocktail, and wait for Abby to release me back to my cave of solitude, where I'll crumble under the weight of my feelings for the one man on campus who has tangled the loose threads in my mind so heavily I've found it hard to think of much else.

But the club rushes toward me, and everything feels off. The colors are sharper than I remember. It's louder, but the music doesn't rile my powers aggressively like it normally does. In fact, I feel like I'm moving in slow motion toward our usual table, taking breath after breath, each inhalation causing my heart rate to jump. The music thrums over my skin, settling me, melding with my powers and calming them in a way that makes me feel suddenly light as air.

It's not the usual screeching of voices I hear when I'm overstimulated. No. I feel....

I look around, feeling hot, my sweater sticking to my skin. I'm wedged in our usual booth–alone. Abby's on the dance floor. I can see her through a haze of bodies–all color and light. I blink, trying to clear my hazy vision. What's happening to me?

I check my bracelet, wondering if this is a vision, but it's still on. I pull my sweater over my head. I'm only wearing a pale gray camisole underneath, and the air against my bare skin feels like the Goddess's kingdom.

I slide out of the booth with a relieved sigh, swaying as I move toward the bodies dancing to music I can barely hear over my pounding heart. I feel drunk. I feel... good. I feel... heavy. Even my powers are bogged down, subdued. Or spent. I have no idea how I end up in the center of the dance floor, closed in by other bodies, other lifelines that stretch like little golden threads toward the ceiling. I normally can't see that unless I want to, unless I summon my powers to show me the tapestry beyond the stars, but here it is, stretched across the ceiling, and it's... glorious.

I know something is wrong, but I don't feel anything other than heat and bliss. My body moves on its own volition, swaying and writhing to the music. I lift my arms in the air and close my eyes and just... feel. Feel everything. Feel nothing. My overactive brain quiets until I'm nothing but instinct and feeling, and when I open my eyes again, there he is.

Alex is standing on the outskirts of the dance floor wearing dark jeans and a white T-shirt. His hair is ruffled, and he looks... damn good. Undone, unburdened, loose.

His bright blue eyes hold my gaze so intensely I feel it in my stomach, which tightens with a fresh, bright wash of heat when he slowly narrows his eyes at me, taking me in.

It's just me and him. The rest of the club fades. I stop dancing to look at him, and it feels like time is moving at the speed of light around us while we remain trapped in a vacuum where everything is slow and heavy.

He takes a step toward me, and the club rushes back into focus. The music throbs through my ears, and my body moves to it. I can't resist. I surrender, even as he moves in my direction, parting other dancers and side-stepping through the crowd to where I am.

He says nothing when he reaches me. His hands are cool against my heated skin when he caresses my cheeks and forces me to look up at him.

I want to melt into his touch. He smells divine. The fabric of his shirt is so soft. The feeling of his hands on me and his proximity is entirely intoxicating.

"Dance with me," I murmur, but the words feel garbled, and I'm not sure I've even said them out loud.

He tilts my chin up, looking down at me with narrowed, inquisitive eyes. "Your eyes–"

I rise up on my toes until our mouths are only centimeters apart, mouthing his name before pressing my lips to his.

He doesn't pull away.

I think... I might have pulled away, because now I'm looking up at him again, and he's arching a brow, utterly concerned as the world starts to spin, and the colors and sounds around me funnel into a kaleidoscope of color.

"Skye? Hey, something isn't right. What have you had to drink?"

Darkness sweeps over me, dragging me into the depths.

I sit up, holding myself up by the elbows as a living room almost exactly like mine comes into startling focus. Everything is off, all turned around. The staircase leading to the loft is on the opposite side of the room, as well as the kitchen. The colors are wrong, and none of my rocks, crystals, or plants are here, either. I lean back and palm my face, trying to scrub the heavy feeling from my eyes and brain, but then I peek through my fingers at *Alex*.

I forgot he was here… in his own house.

I'm in his condo.

Not mine.

How did I end up here? What happened last night?

He leans forward, resting his elbows on his knees, to inspect me. I jerk back. The look of concern drawing his brows together makes me feel awful, to say the least. I must have blacked out. How much did I drink last night? Actually, what time is it? I was just in the club. I can still hear the music, feel the heat on my skin.

I part my lips to ask what happened, but all that leaves my tongue is a groan.

"Here. Drink this." He extends a glass of water, but it takes me a moment to get my fingers to flex. I finally manage it and take several greedy gulps, wincing at the slightly sweet and salty taste. Electrolytes? Probably. I suppose I should thank him. "How do you feel?"

"Um–I don't know. Bad? What happened? How'd I get here?"

"You don't remember?" He arches a brow.

"No? Should I? What time is it?"

"Just after six in the morning."

"The *morning*?"

15

STARDUST

Skye

ALEX NODS, LOOKING THOROUGHLY CONCERNED WHILE I SPIRAL INTO oblivion. "Skye–"

"Did we...?" I look down at my clothes, voice shaking, and see that I'm wearing the same outfit I wore out last night, much to my relief. It was a stupid question, but I've already asked it.

"We did not," he confirms with a soft wince. "Do you remember anything from the club last night?"

"Barely. Was I drugged? I don't drink that much. I don't think I even had a drink last night at all. I remember walking in and...." My memory is strangely hazy. I take several gulps of water and try to hand the glass back, but Alex shakes his head.

"Finish it. It has electrolytes in it."

"I didn't drink–"

"It doesn't matter. You're going to feel like hell if you're dehydrated. You're a shifter, remember? You metabolize like a slug."

I frown, the rim of the glass pressed against my lower lip. He's not wrong, but it's still a mean, but very true, thing to say. "Was I drugged? Why do I feel like this?" My bracelet is warm against my skin, like I've been using my powers. In fact, the numbness in my hands is beginning to feel familiar–that cold, frosty bite when I've overdone it, stretching my powers too far and too thin, but the last time I did that, I was a kid. I would remember using my powers. I know it. Everything right now just feels wrong.

"No, not explicitly."

"Explicitly? What?"

"Drugged. It wasn't on purpose."

"What are you talking about?" I take another drink to appease him and set the cup down on the glass coffee table, but my hands are unsteady, trembling, and I miss the coaster, and it falls over on its side, spilling.

Alex silently rises and walks into the kitchen, a blur of movement in the darkness. Beyond the windows, it's another bitter cold, impossibly dark morning, the stars on full display. My last concrete memories were admiring those same stars while walking into the club and putting my parka in a locker. Then everything fades, like sand through my fingers.

"Have you ever heard of something called Stardust?" he asks, returning with a towel to mop up the spill.

I sink into the cushions of the couch that smells like him. "No."

I catch his gaze. That concerned look eats away at me. It's familiar, like I've seen that exact expression shading the sharp angles of his face recently, and then it hits me.

"Oh, gods!"

Alex chuckles as he sits back down beside me. "It's all coming back now, isn't it?"

"We kissed!"

"Um, no." He leans back against the cushions. "*You* kissed *me*."

"You–you didn't pull away!" I turn to look at him and find him smiling again as he massages his temples. He looks tired, like he hasn't slept all night. Like he was sitting right here, making sure I didn't keel over. "How did you get me back here?"

"Well, you were lucid enough to walk out of the club and begged me to take you home, so I did. I had to carry you onto the train."

I bury my face in my hands and groan with embarrassment.

Loving my reaction and continuing the torment, he explains, "You did walk here, to the condo, from the terminal, but you couldn't tell me the code to your door. It locked me out after twelve tries of the random chains of numbers you gave me, which you thought were hilarious, most of them being strings of 69 or, my favorite, 8008135."

"*What?*"

"Well, the version of you I met last night had the mind of a thirteen-year-old boy, because that string of numbers looks like 'boobies' on a calculator."

I gape at him. My cheeks singe red under the weight of my embarrassment, but he's loving this. He stretches his arms behind him to cup the back of his head with a sigh and says, "Anyway, I obviously couldn't get you into your condo, and I wasn't going to leave you on your doormat, so I brought you here and spent the night making sure you didn't slip into a coma."

"How did…. I don't do drugs, Alex."

"I know."

"Then how?" I find it hard to swallow. I'm itchy and cold, like I can feel the poison in my veins. I pull the blanket draped over my legs up to my chest, tempted to cover my face with it. "Oh, my Goddess, is Abby okay?"

"She's totally fine, and she's with Toby. They're both okay. Neither were affected. I've been texting him updates all morning. Abby is likely still drunk and will be horribly hungover when she wakes up."

Silence settles between us for several seconds before he rises again and paces to the windows, his hands tucked in the pockets of his jeans. When he turns around to face me again, he looks more serious, and I sit up a little straighter. "You had an odd reaction. I'm curious about that."

"I don't even know what I took."

"You didn't take anything. Not on purpose."

"I don't understand what you're saying." I wish my brain would just function normally for a single second.

He rolls his lower lip between his teeth and says, "Stardust is a highly illegal substance with hallucinogenic and euphoric properties. A normal person would have been–"

"Tripping balls?"

"Where did a princess learn a phrase like that?"

"I have two younger brothers." This time I pull the blanket up to cover my face, but lower it when Alex remains quiet for the space of several heartbeats. He's still watching me with that slightly enthused expression that makes my skin tingle in unfamiliar ways. "How did I get it? I don't remember. I barely remember anything. I remember dancing and… you."

"I know. I saw you on the dance floor. You were… not yourself." His eyes are suddenly intense.

I shiver involuntarily at the heat of the memory now barreling through my mind. The moment I placed my hands on his chest was real. The feeling of his shirt. The slow thump of his heart. He smelled incredible, like heat and sex and everything soft and delicious.

"What were you doing at the club?" I ask, tearing myself out of the memory at the moment I rose on my toes to kiss him. He has to know I'm thinking about it. My skin is on fire, and it has to show on my face.

He also has an uncanny ability to sense these changes–the skipping of my heart, the flushed sensation sweeping through me–like no one I've ever known. He's brought it up multiple times.

"I was there to find what you ended up ingesting, and that's why I said you didn't do it on purpose. It was in the air last night. Someone brought it to the club, maybe spilled it on a table, on the floor, something like that. Just a little bit can cause a slightly euphoric high, but nothing anyone would really notice. Dosed appropriately, it can be a wild ride, but you weren't exposed to nearly enough for that. However, your eyes? They were glowing like I've never seen. Not like in your office, either. This was different. I was there to try to collect Stardust and ended up finding you." He looks suddenly guilty. "Toby has a contact in Aurorium who can get us whatever we need–lab supplies, blood samples, you name it, without having to go through the university chain of command."

"Drugs?"

"Yeah." His jaw flexes. "I was tasked with testing the blood samples from the murder in the terminal two weeks ago. We found something else in both samples, something synthetic–a drug, we thought. Stardust was the most likely because it's so prevalent here, and I needed some to test to rule it out, and something went awry that night, obviously, because the sample we went to pick up ended up on the floor of the club, and… in you." He sighs, running his fingers through his hair before pacing back to the couch. "I feel responsible. *I am* responsible, and I'm sorry."

"It's not a big deal if I don't die." I try to laugh, to sound teasing, but the words spill and strain against the tip of my tongue. "I'm going to be okay, right? I didn't–I didn't hurt anyone, did I?"

"No, you just danced. You were happy. I think you had a good time."

I sit up a little straighter, scoffing, "A good time? I've never done drugs in my life, and I barely drink alcohol, Alex. I could have seriously hurt myself or someone else!"

"You were more inclined to kiss someone, that someone being me." The glint of his teeth in the starlight when he smiles makes me slip off the couch and onto wobbling legs.

"Well, it was the drugs. I kissed you under duress!"

"Felt like it," he murmurs, smiling softly. "Please, sit down before you fall over."

"What happens now?" The blush wreaking havoc on my face spreads over my skin like wildfire when I heed his warning and ease back onto his couch, hating every second of surrender, but he's right. I'm like a baby deer.

"You sleep it off. Drink water. Eat something. You'll be fine in a few hours."

"Have you slept? You look exhausted."

"I haven't. I don't need it." He gets to his feet.

"You look–"

Alex gives me his back and walks to the kitchen. He scribbles something on a piece of paper and folds it neatly before pivoting back in my direction. "Would you be willing to have your blood drawn?"

"My blood? Why?"

"I don't have a sample of Stardust anymore, but I do have you, and judging by the way your eyes are still glowing and you're panicking, you still have it in your system. I would have gone directly to the Beta to acquire samples of the drug except for the red tape, and I need to get this taken care of as soon as I can. There are other things my lab should be focused on." He extends the paper, which turns out to be a slip to the clinic with instructions for a lab tech. I clutch it with shaky fingers and read his neat, quick handwriting.

"But… no one can know I have this in my system. I could lose my job!"

"No one will know. The samples will go directly to my lab, and I'll destroy them personally when I'm done."

"You're so confident."

"Do you think this is the first time the biology department has had to go to illegal lengths to get their hands on samples like this?" He leans his weight on the kitchen island, brow arched in challenge.

I don't doubt it. Judging by the look on his face, I'm sure he's had to ask for worse and has secrets buried under the ice.

I lean back against the cushions, surrendering, letting the ebb and flow of whatever Stardust is left work through my sluggish shifter system.

"What is Stardust, exactly?"

His eyes catch on a moonbeam stretching over the kitchen island. "It's kind of hard to explain."

"Try. You owe me, seeing as your idiotic idea to buy illicit contraband put me in this position."

"It's… space material."

"It's what?" I blink, wondering if I heard him incorrectly.

"Meteorites. Ground up, mixed with herbs I'm not totally sure about, but that's the gist of it."

"You're joking." I clutch my bracelet, which has several charms made of a single meteorite I found as a child.

"I'm serious. And if you're willing to help, I might be able to pull specifics out of your blood sample if you go to the clinic."

"Why can't you just take my blood here? I know you can get your hands on the supplies you need. The clinic is right next door to the biology department."

He hangs his head, shoulders going rigid. "I—no."

"Oh, yeah, you're squeamish." I rise shakily, fighting a wave of dizziness that threatens to take me to the floor. "Fine. I'll do it. But only because I'm curious about how the hell people are grinding up meteorites and turning them into party drugs. I'm sure my Aunt Maeve will want to know all about this." I also need to know about this. Badly. No wonder I feel like my insides are turned inside out.

"I'm sure she would." He watches me cross the room, hyperaware of every step I take across the carpet to where he left my boots by the door. "Are you feeling all right?"

"As good as I can." I huff a breath while forcing my feet into the boots with a hand braced on the wall. "I'll get my blood drawn, okay? But if my department finds out, and I lose my job, I'm coming for your neck."

Alex's eyes darken a shade, turning from ocean blue to the deepest cerulean I've ever witnessed.

16

WHAT ARE YOU?

Skye

A LAB ASSISTANT, A YOUNG WOMAN IN HER EARLY TWENTIES BY MY estimation, makes quick work of the blood draw, but I still feel queasy and unsteady while wrapped in a blanket in the clinic lobby, silently munching on a bag of the stalest oatmeal raisin cookies in the Allied Kingdoms.

Alex dutifully escorted me here, choosing the quickest path through campus. This early on a Saturday morning, the chances of running into anyone we knew were slim, and luck was in our favor, because we didn't pass another soul. Now, it's closing in on 9:00 A.M., and my unintentionally wild night has caught up to me in droves. My stomach is in knots, and I feel like I haven't slept in years. I assured him I could get home on my own, and he left, which should make me feel better, but it doesn't.

"Dr. Scarlett said you're not feeling well," the lab assistant says, returning to my side. "I have some basic medicine here. We keep healing tonics in stock as well, if that's more your vibe."

"I'm–I'm fine, just dehydrated," I lie, smiling up at her. She's familiar, which I hadn't realized until now. Blonde and mousy, just like she was in Alex's office. I believe this is Laney, if I'm remembering her name correctly. I wonder if she's aware of his scheme when I notice the smaller cooler in her hand, which definitely has several samples of my blood resting within.

I wonder how often he has to do things like this, and that thought follows me back across campus, strengthened by a fully caffeinated, overly sugary can of soda and another bag of stale cookies–peanut butter this time.

Thankfully, my brain is somewhat back in working order when I punch in the code to my condo, the four zeros I never changed upon moving in, and slip inside, wincing at the memory of the mess I was the night before. Sixty-nine? Boobies spelled in numerals? *Kill me. Goddess, strike me where I stand. I've seen and done enough!*

I dig my dead phone out of my coat pocket, plug it into a charger, and change into a tank top and silky pajama pants before slumping on the couch. I don't bother to turn on a light. Starlight shimmers across the ceiling like water reflecting on glass waves of light. Glimmers and streams of that perfect, spellbinding magic, I wish I could just reach out and touch it. I want to know….

A rapid, thundering knock echoes through my eardrums. I swear the whole couch vibrates against the thrum of sound. I clutch the cushions, utterly disoriented by the hardest, darkest sleep of my life, thinking for a moment that this is it–all those rumors about major shifts in the sea ice are real, and the whole campus is crumbling into that ancient, mysterious ocean miles beneath us–but the second round of knocks has me flying off the couch in a tangle of blankets. How long have I been asleep?

Someone is dead. For sure. Abby and Toby broke up for real this time. I'm getting fired and escorted off campus by warriors and–

"Alex?"

Alex shoves his way through the door and paces to the windows, repeatedly running his fingers through his hair while I shut the door and lock it firmly. I whirl, my heart hammering to the point I can't catch my breath.

"Alex, are you okay?"

"You–" He points at me, eyes wide. He laughs sharply, which startles me, my heart leaping into my throat. "What *are* you?"

He looks deranged and slightly terrifying as he paces toward me but stops short, waving at me, then pacing back the way he came. I glance at the clock on the stove. I slept for hours. A whole day passed. It's night again. I scrub my hand over my face and peek at him through my fingers, noticing his unkempt state, his wild hair and the sudden sharpening of all his features. "Alex?"

"Your blood is like... nothing I've ever seen. It's–*you*–I've been looking *everywhere* for *you*."

I push off the door and edge a few steps in his direction. He braces a hand against the window, turning to face the night, the elements, the burst of aurora painting the sky in shades of green and the deepest purple. "What are you talking about?"

"You *are* stardust. You are made of it. I've never seen anything like it." He turns to face me, and it's like the Goddess has reached down and slapped me over the head. I reel back, my entire body recoiling in shock. I fight the natural impulse to shift and run away, the shifter side of me clawing for release, begging me to *run for my life* against something so unnatural, so damning, I... can't help but stand still and study Alex in all of his glory.

His very secret glory.

Fangs.

He has *fangs*. I hadn't noticed before. Sure, he had what I thought were mildly pronounced canines, which isn't totally uncommon, especially when surrounded by shifters, but he told me he wasn't a shifter.

And I don't know any witches or wizards with fangs.

He keeps them well hidden, never fully smiling, always so careful how his mouth moves, his stillness.

"What are *you*?" I counter, my voice hard and booming. My powers rile under the yoke of my bracelet in warning, warming my skin.

He bows his head.

"Alex?" I take a single step closer, but he holds out a hand to stop me.

"You have it in your blood."

"What do I have in my blood? Stardust? I feel like that's been well established–"

"More–more than that. It's there. I saw it. I've been looking for it for so long. And here you are, right here, the answer to–to everything." He tries to straighten but loses his balance, knocking his shoulder against the window. He hisses in pain, his fangs catching the starlight. Shadows play over the faint notches where he's... shaved them down.

Multiple times.

My fight-or-flight feeling ebbs into heartbreak as the aurora's glow spills through the window, highlighting his body. His pale skin. The gauntness of his face, the sunkenness of his eyes. He looked tired before–this morning–but I'd thought it was just from staying up all night guarding me, ensuring I was okay.

It's not.

I know in my heart it's not.

He's *starving*.

I should be frozen in fear. I'm not. I can't believe this is real, that he's real. All those stories from my childhood, all the lore, the myths....

I know what he is without needing to ask. I don't need confirmation. Every silent question I've had about him I refused to voice becomes startlingly clear–the cold pallor of his skin, his secretive behavior, why I haven't seen him eat, or drink, or sleep.

His aversion to blood has nothing to do with squeamishness.

"I've only heard stories about your kind," I whisper.

He shuffles forward, unable to stand up straight, and tries to grip the railing of the staircase but misses, falling to his knees. "You don't know what you're talking about."

"My family has several historians. Arthur–he's different. We're not sure what he is but he... he's been around a long time. He talks about your kind like you existed once, but not anymore. Not for a long, long time. My aunt Misty has seen–"

"Skye–" He motions for me to step away when I edge toward him. He's on his hands and knees trying to push himself upright, but he can't. He eases onto his side, then sits up, his back against the wall. "Don't."

"What do you need?"

"Don't ask me that. Just back up."

"Tell me what's wrong with you!"

His eyes are so dark and so endlessly blue, sharper than usual. Predatory, like there's only one thing on his mind, and it's survival, but he won't act.

He's so controlled. I wonder how he's survived all these years, but I suppose I already know.

"It's true that sunlight hurts you, isn't it? That's why you chose Lunaria, Aurorium specifically."

"Stay away from me."

"You're always in your lab, and it doesn't really affect you temper-ature-wise, does it? You're immune. It doesn't faze you."

"It–it does–"

"You take blood samples from the lab–"

"Stop!"

"You're a *vampire.*"

He holds my gaze for several achingly long seconds. I can practi-cally see the gears behind his eyes while he tries to come up with an excuse and more lies.

I edge closer, and he bares those fangs at me. I recoil, my skin prickling with gooseflesh, those shifter sensibilities screaming that being in his proximity is a very, very bad idea.

But the other side of me? The powers that make me what I am–a mystic?

Oh, my Goddess, this is amazing. He's amazing. He has no lifeline. No thread in the tapestry. He just exists. How is that possible?

"Back up," he warns, gritting his teeth. His nostrils flare as I crouch to inspect him at a closer angle. "Skye, get away from me."

"How long has it been since you've had any blood?"

He chokes a laugh. "You don't know what you're talking about."

"That's what you need right now, isn't it? Blood? How do you get it here? The blood samples from the clinic?"

He searches my gaze, stunned, I think, that I'm not screaming in fear. I reach out to touch him, and he moves away, grunting against what I think might be serious pain all over his body. "Don't touch me."

"What will happen if I do?"

"You're insane," he growls. "You have no idea how much danger you're in."

I've had enough. He's hurting, starving, likely disintegrating right before my eyes, and I know he won't be able to answer any of the million questions taking up every pocket of my mind until he's lucid.

And full.

I slam the palm of my hand against his forehead. He shouts but quiets instantly against the pull of my powers. My bracelet vibrates violently and heats to the point of pain against my skin in warning, but I push past the barriers of the charms and sink into his mind.

I don't pry even though I want to. Desperately. It's all there, but different than being in the mind of a witch or shifter. He sees more in… feeling than images, I think. Everything is color, and right now, the dominant color is red. Red fury. Red concern. Red hunger. Red heat when I push deeper, and he can feel me all around him. It takes him several seconds to submit, and then his mind quiets, and when I pull my hand back, he's slack against the wall, eyes open but unseeing.

I gently shut his eyelids and step back to admire my work and… him.

ALEX

I WAKE UP TO THE FEELING OF MY ARMS STRETCHED ABOVE MY HEAD. My fingers tingle as I open my eyes to slits, and Skye's living room comes into view. For a moment, I think the worst. The shadow in front of me is her body drained of blood, but it's not.

She moves closer to check the belt holding my wrists together above my head, bound to the railing of the staircase. Her scent hits me like a punch to the gut–warm and soft. Delicious, just like the sound of her heartbeat filling every space in my mind.

"Good evening," she says softly.

I test the strength of the belt, finding it secure enough to hold me captive for a while, at least. Smart girl.

"What are you doing?"

"How do I go about getting whatever blood samples I can find for you to munch on?"

I shut my eyes but feel her kneeling in front of me, eye to eye. "You can't. I'm out. They were supposed to come in that late shipment from Aurorium, but they sat warm for too long. I couldn't... I've been busy with the Beta's investigation. I didn't order more." I open my eyes enough to see her fully–her curious, unafraid eyes staring back at me expectantly. "You can't tell anyone."

"So I'm right? You're a vampire?"

I nod. My body feels feather-light and numb. I can't do much other than accept whatever she planned, which I don't think is killing me, unfortunately. She's going to torment me first, with questions, which is worse.

"How many others are there like you?"

"None here."

"Where are you from? Where are your people from?"

I take a breath, wincing. I can't undo this. Once she knows, she knows. "I'm from a kingdom called Scarlett Thunder."

"I've never heard of it."

"You wouldn't have. They don't know this place–the Allied King-doms–exists. We're cut off by a mountain range and a sea, and a few thousand miles of plains and rivers after that."

She rocks back on her heels, her hair falling over her shoulder as she inspects me like a research specimen. "You're immortal, right?"

"I can die. I'm dying right now, just slowly. Immortal to me just means a few centuries of life if I'm careful not to get killed or starve—"

She cuts me off with another question. "How old are you?"

"I'm still thirty-three."

"In vampire years?"

"Thirty-three. I was born thirty-three years ago."

She seems disappointed by my answer, which I would find amusing in any other circumstance, but my vision starts to fade, replaced by primal instinct. Her scent gets sharper. The vein in her neck pulses, and it's the only thing I can focus on. I imagine sinking my fangs into her skin. Tasting her. Holding her soft weight against my chest while I drink my fill and…

"You need to leave," I whisper. "I'm not—not safe to be around."

"You haven't had blood in weeks, have you? How long does it take to—"

"To kill me like this? Weeks, which it's been. You're right."

"Why didn't you just… use my blood samples?"

I barely have the energy to laugh. It comes out as a grunt. "I don't feed on people. Not anymore. Not for over a decade."

"The whole time you've been here in Lunaria—"

"Animals. The blood samples we get from Aurorium are always from animals—sheep and reindeer, mostly. I… I can't answer any more questions."

"You don't feel well?"

"Obviously," I growl, but then I bite it back. "Listen. Toby can… he can help. You just have to be very discreet, okay? The clinic might have blood samples. Maybe. I'm not sure, but Toby has access—he doesn't know what I am."

Her scent overwhelms my senses, and I jerk forward against the restraints when she leans toward me, her bare wrist less than an inch from my mouth.

I close my eyes. "Please don't."

"You need this."

"You have no idea what you're offering."

"It's just blood. I can make more."

"I could kill you," I explain, keeping my eyes firmly shut. If I see her, see her offering herself like this, as a fucking feeder? I'll snap. I won't be able to control myself.

"Well, you're restrained, so unless you're strong enough in this state to get free, I think I'll be fine."

"I won't risk it–"

"Also–" She reaches for me, running her fingers through my hair. It's such a... gentle, loving touch, and I lean into it on instinct. It's been so long since I've been... touched. Like this. But then a sharp pinch rips through my brain. I cry out as my senses fade, and my body jerks. I feel her then, in my head, like she's gripping the part of me that makes me into this monster, like she has it by the metaphorical balls. "I can just do this. You can't hurt me."

She lets me go. My head falls forward. It takes several long seconds to regain my composure, and when I do, she is still there, holding out her wrist.

"Do it. I want to know what it feels like."

"You're insane."

She presses her skin against my mouth, and I lose any sense of myself to the feeling, and taste, of *her*.

17

THE PULL

Skye

WHEN I WAS A LITTLE GIRL, I HAD THESE AMAZING DREAMS ALMOST every night. I could have gone anywhere in the dream realm, coasting on ribbons of thoughts and memories that didn't belong to me, but one place felt like home more than others. One place with scratchy chairs, sconces lighting the floor, and otherwise, darkness.

I still don't know why I used to have dreams about the observatory on the campus where I now work as a professor. I don't know why that little, nameless boy haunted those dreams. His memory is starting to fade with every year that passes, but I know one thing for certain.

I am meant to be here.

Not because of my brain.

Not because of my advancements in physics and the world of science as a whole.

Not because of my map of distant stars that witches will one day use to strengthen their magic.

No, it's because of *this*. Gods, I feel it in my bones the second I press my bare wrist to Alex's lips.

His eyes meet mine, unsure, maybe even a little scared. How long did he say it's been since he's done this? A decade? Longer?

There's so much I need to know. So much he can tell me about a magical species we thought was extinct, and yet, he's here, closing his eyes, sighing deeply against my skin before dragging his fangs over the little blue veins thrumming with blood beneath my skin.

It's no more than a pinch, like getting a shot. Like having my blood drawn. I barely feel it when he sinks his fangs through my skin and holds there, arms straining against the belt keeping him locked to the staircase for my protection and his, I believe. His body angles toward mine, his chest rising and falling with the deepest breath I've ever heard him take, and then he… sucks.

"Oh," I rush out, kneeling between his legs. The pull is insane. The suction. The warmth of it? I can't even put what this feels like into words. He takes a single swallow and holds again, struggling. He unlatches, panting a bit, his tongue pressed to the two deep, crimson fang marks marring my wrist.

For a moment, my skin heats with sudden fear, but not because of him. "Do I… taste bad?"

He opens his eyes, pupils dilated to little black specks. "No. You taste unreal."

"Is that a good thing?"

He holds my gaze. He doesn't so much as blink. Doesn't so much as breathe.

"Alex, take more."

"No." His eyes are intense–bright and honed on my face like he's fighting to remain calm in his body and to not let his mind and vampiric instincts take over–much like a shifter would, I suppose. We can't be all that different at our cores.

"Please. You need it. I can tell you need it."

"You don't know anything about me, Skye. Nor my kind. Nor what someone–something–like me is capable of. I could kill you before you realized what was happening. I feel like–as long as it's been since I've tasted–" He draws in a breath, mouthing, "fuck it," and aggressively clamps down on my wrist again.

I nearly lurch back. The breath that leaves my lungs is long and narrow–a whoosh of surprise, and interestingly enough, pleasure. This feels good. Warm. Calming. *Heavy.* Each pull feels delicious and makes my heart race, which makes Alex groan like he can feel it, that change of pressure. I lean toward him until we're chest to chest, my body heavier than it's ever felt and warmer than I thought possible. He takes a pull of my blood, then another, and another, each deep and lingering.

The room begins to darken, shadows creeping where they shouldn't. I feel sleepy. It sneaks up on me in bright tingles that stretch from my wrist to my shoulder. I press my cheek to the crook of his shoulder and find him shockingly warm and wonderfully solid.

Another smooth, deep groan radiates through his chest, and then he lets me go. My arm falls limp by my side, but I remain glued to him, listening to the faint thump of his heart–so much slower than mine.

His body is slack, unmoving. I'm too dizzy to look up at him to ensure he's not asleep, and instead, keep my cheek pressed to his chest for several minutes in silence.

Finally, he whispers, much calmer and smoother than before, "Give me your wrist again."

I obey for some strange reason, physically preparing myself to be drained to the last drop, but when I turn in his lap–because there's no hiding that is where I've ended up–and extend my wrist to his lips, he just... holds my gaze and drags his tongue across the two deep gashes in my skin, and the wounds pull together, completely healed.

I marvel at it for a moment before meeting his gaze again. His skin is different–brighter, less sallow and gray. He's almost peachy in the shadows, and with a sense of pride, I realize it's because of me. My blood.

"You can untie me now, if you want to."

"Are you sure?"

He nods, and I rise, trembling a bit. My legs tingle painfully, either from lack of blood or sitting in one position for so long, but I deftly unfasten the belt, and he removes his wrists from the tangle of leather that kept him bound. Likely, he could've just broken through the restraint now that he's eaten, but this is better. He doesn't rise right away. He leans back against the wall and stays splayed out on the floor like this is just as overwhelming for his body as it is for mine.

"You need to eat something," he says, his voice low and deep. "Immediately."

"What should I eat?" I move toward the kitchen, steadying myself on pieces of furniture until I reach the kitchen island.

"Salt and sugar. You'll feel better quicker that way. Back home, feeders are well taken care of and have a very finely tuned diet."

"Feeders?" I open the fridge and find a container of yogurt, some granola, and a sports drink I was saving for Abby because I know she likes them.

"It's what we call the people–shifters–who offer themselves to us. For blood, of course."

"They do that willingly?" I can imagine why. I quickly make a bowl of yogurt, quietly wondering why that felt *so* good, while he remains against the wall. I can feel him watching me, and I know, before I can fix my confused and flushed expression, that he knows exactly what I'm thinking about.

"We can't do that again."

I lick my lips. They tingle, just like my whole body is tingling, trying to make sense of the loss and the lack of a wound. My powers are equally rattled, and I notice Alex has a faint glow to his eyes that he didn't have before.

"You have Stardust in your system now," I say, and he smiles softly.

"Barely enough to have a reaction. It's been almost a day. I think this is just you." He examines his hand before forming a fist.

"Why can't we do that again?" I take a bite of yogurt and settle on the couch, putting what I hope is a comfortable amount of distance between us, even though I think he might be the one who wants the distance the most based on the conflicted look in his eyes.

"I'm sure it'll make sense when you're done asking me the billion questions I'm certain you have."

"Are you willing to answer?"

"Are you going to tell anyone?"

"What would happen to you if I did?"

He eyes me for a moment longer, then rises, carefully making his way over to the couch, where he sits, a single cushion between us. "Keep eating."

I take another bite.

"I doubt many people would believe you, for one."

"I think you're right." I take another bite and then another. The food takes an immediate effect, and the tingles begin to wane.

Before I ask my first question, Alex explains, "I believe I'm the only one here. I've never come across another vampire during my entire decade here. Not one."

"You said you have shifters where you come from?"

"Yes. Witches, too. Actually, quite a bit of both. But witches cannot be feeders."

"Why not?"

"Because they can turn into what I am." He meets my eyes. I'm mid-drink and pause, perplexed.

"Wait! Vampires aren't born this way? You're made?"

"Some. Um." He leans back, looking tired but still bright and warm. I can feel his warmth even with a bit of distance between us. "I was born a vampire. I have parents. Born vampires are different from those who are turned. Genetically, biologically different as well."

"How so?"

"You know I've never had to explain this to anyone," he replies swiftly, chuckling a bit. "I don't really know where to begin."

"Alex?"

"Yeah?" His voice is hoarse, tinged with the guilt I know is wracking his body as his gaze falls to my wrist, where a deep, black and purple bruise has formed in the shape of his mouth. He closes his eyes and looks away.

"I trust you. I like you. I think you're a brilliant scientist. I hate to admit it, but after we met, and while trying to reconcile the version of you Abby gave me and the you I know, I read your studies and publications. Your work is incredible. I don't care that you're a vampire. You can't hurt me."

"I can."

"You can't. I won't let you. I will also keep your secret. It's none of my business, and you're right. I don't know what would happen to you if people found out. Your kind is legendary here, in the Allied Kingdoms. Vampires are supposed to be monsters who hunt at night in cold blood, who can shift into bats and control minds."

His smile is soft and slightly self-deprecating. "I cannot turn into a bat, and it sounds like you're the one who can control minds."

I give him a similar smile. "I can't control minds, but I can break them. If I want to, of course. I've never had the need." I spoon another bite of yogurt into my mouth. Alex watches me, his eyes dipping from mine to my neck. "I'm likely more dangerous than you."

He's still hungry. I can feel the way his eyes graze over my neck. It's been so long since he's had blood like this, I'm sure. Blood that's warm and readily available.

"Why can't you feed off of me again?" I ask because out of the million questions I have for him, this is the one plaguing my mind the most.

"Because it's better to have options. There's less risk of a bond that way."

"A bond? Like a mate?"

"Not... entirely," he says, but he doesn't seem convinced. He takes a breath and leans forward, surrendering to the line of conversation even though he's obviously uncomfortable with it. "Feeding off someone multiple times messes with a vampire, and I'm sure, a feeder. I am not saying you're a feeder. I don't think of you that way."

"Isn't being a feeder a good thing?"

"I suppose, but Skye, I really don't know how to tell you about this."

"Try."

I set my yogurt down and turn to him, both of our knees drawn against our chests, our socked toes touching under the single pillow between us. He searches my face, then finally sighs and says, resigned, "Shifters are territorial beasts. They covet what they believe belongs to them, especially in terms of mates. I know shifters. I have shifters in my family, if you can believe it, and one day I'll explain how that works, but the reason I cannot let you offer yourself to me again is because vampires are worse than shifters. I already like you," he admits, breathless, and it catches me off guard. "I don't want to use you. This could easily turn into something neither of us is capable of managing. It's dangerous, Skye."

"But I offered–"

"A few more times like this and my body and mind will start thinking of you as something I own. Like a mate, but different. If you think shifters are territorial, you have no idea what a vampire can be like."

"You're saying you'd see me as a mate?"

"Pretty much. And since you haven't found your mate yet, and if that happens, especially here, I'm better when I'm weak, when I haven't eaten in a while. Now... I'm a serious threat. It's just in my nature. Vampires sometimes have prolonged relationships with their feeders, and it's often sexual."

I feel it in the pit of my stomach–that warm, liquid heat. It's only a memory now, but it was there when I pressed against him. It was the most intimate moment of my life so far. Alex watches my face, scans my eyes to read the conflicted expression I'm sure is painting starlit shadows under my eyes and across my cheeks.

"You're feeling things that you shouldn't," he says, "and I'll feel things that I shouldn't. That's why we can't do it again."

"Maybe just... once more."

"No."

I take another drink, frowning. "For research purposes."

"No, Skye. We can't." But he looks at my neck again and takes a deep, deep breath before biting back his tongue. "I need to lie down for a moment. I'm going back to my place."

"Just lie down here. It's fine. I have to go check on Abby anyway." I rise, knowing a dismissal when I hear one. He makes no move to follow, and before I even slide my feet into a pair of slippers, his head is resting back on the couch, eyes closed.

I forgot to ask if vampires sleep.

18

KILLER

Alex

Vampires generally don't need sleep.

By sleep, I mean the deep, vulnerable kind that allows dreams to fade into focus and a body to go slack. Vamp kids, sure. They sleep all the time, but once our biological clock starts to slow, once necessary things like sleep make less of a difference in our overall performance, we generally don't do it.

A light rest? Sure. I've needed one of those for a long, long time, which is why, when I open my eyes after an hour on Skye's couch to find her sitting on the coffee table in front of me, our knees touching, her eyes open wide and full of so much excitement she's trembling, I wish on whatever gods are listening that I could, in fact, just shut my eyes and let the entire world fade to black, even just for a few more hours.

She's gripping a notebook for dear life, her eyes holding on mine expectantly.

"What time is it?" I ask. Deciding not to move an inch and pretending to be in some kind of blood coma might work in my favor when it comes to the mountain of questions I know she's compiled in the notebook.

"I have no idea. But–"

"How long have you been here staring at me while I slept?"

"Half an hour." She blinks for what might be the first time in that long.

My chest rises and falls. I close my eyes in surrender, feeling warmer and more whole than I have in years… but hungry. So fucking hungry. Her scent is everywhere–strongest here, where I can still taste her on my tongue. Her proximity sends warning sirens through my skull, but I already know that telling her this, having to explain in depth the ins and outs of what I am, is only going to make it worse for me.

"I made a list," she begins, flipping open the notebook and clicking a pen. I keep my eyes closed, groaning, and she flips page after page.

"Would it be easier to just kill me and flay me open in a lab? I'm sure we can rent a room in the psych department quite easily, seeing as they never use their labs." I open my eyes to slits. She blinks at me and then flips back a few pages and presses her pen to a page.

"Why? Are we different on the inside?"

"Oh, my gods."

"What? I just want to know."

"Why?"

"Because you're a vampire, Alex. You're one of a kind."

Oh, she has *no idea*. "There are thousands of vampires. Hundreds of thousands, I'm sure, where I'm from. I'm the only one here, and that's a good thing."

"Can you tell me why?"

"Why what?" I finally sit up and lean forward until there are only inches between our noses. She doesn't balk, doesn't lean away, bristle, or lock up in fear. She just stares so intently, I feel like she's trying to look inside me for the answers to her questions.

Maybe she already is.

"I want to go first," I say in a near whisper. Beyond the frosted glass windows to our left, the aurora is dancing across the sky, painting her living room in a deep green haze. "Are you looking into my head right now?"

"No, you'd feel it."

"How do I know you're not lying–AH!" I rear back the second her fingertips graze my forehead, sending a charge of what I can only describe as white-hot electricity shooting through the ridges of my gray matter.

"That's what it feels like, and honestly, I can't read your thoughts or even see your memories. I tried."

"What? You did?"

She nods, grinning like this is the most exciting thing she's ever experienced. "When I tied you up earlier, remember? It's fascinating, really. Your mind is full of color instead of images. It's like every memory, every thought, is wrapped in... gift paper. *Emotion. Color.* I've never seen anything like it."

"How many heads have you looked into, Skye?"

"Not many. Not on purpose, at least. But–"

"You know what?" I rise, and she follows immediately, refusing to let me pass. "We're not doing this. I'm a vampire. That's already been established." I motion toward her notebook, clutched in her hands like a weapon. "I can answer every question in that little notebook of yours, but every answer will only lead to a new question, and I can't do this right now."

"Because you want to bite me again?"

I grit my teeth. If I breathe in, I'll smell her, damn near taste her again, and it's too much. She's too much.

She tilts her head to the side, leaving one side of her beautiful, smooth neck exposed. Fuck. Fuck her! Fuck me for giving in, for running back here when I saw her blood sample lit up under the lights of a finely tuned microscope. I knew I was fading. I should have left my lab and gone straight to Aurorium, bought the bloodiest steak I could find at their terrible grocery store, and sucked it dry in the bathroom in the subway terminal before confronting her about what I found that swirls inside of her like glitter–like the stars themselves drift in her veins.

"Can I ask you just one thing?" She edges a half step closer. It's as far as she can go. We're already touching, but now we're flush together, her notebook wedged between us.

"No."

"Why are you even here? What's the reason for putting yourself through this for so long?"

"That's two questions."

"I just don't understand. Lunaria? I get that. It's dark here practically all the time, especially this time of year. But you rely on blood samples to survive, and you must be so lonely. You're the only one like you. Why stay?"

"That's three."

"And if you're immortal, which, by all accounts–"

"Skye," I growl in warning.

"You can't stay here forever. You don't age, right?" She steps away to open her notebook, pen at the ready. "Or do you? Slowly? Because you look like you're in your thirties, and if that's the case, I mean, what are your strengths? What magic do you have that keeps you like this? What can you do?"

I grab her by the shoulders and twist until she's facing the couch, her back flush against my abdomen. I press a hand flat over her stomach, my other hand braced around her throat, fingers curled.

It happens in a single second–far too quick for her to react. "That's my strength," I rasp against the outer shell of her ear. She takes a shallow breath, her chest rattling. "I can kill you before you even know what's happening. I am quicker than a shifter could ever dream of being. I am silent on my feet, Skye. You might be able to subdue me with a single touch, but you'd have to catch me first, and you can't."

She drops her notebook. Her pulse under my fingers thrums, skyrocketing. The scent of her blood changes, shifting from the sharp, metallic hint of fear to something deeper, headier. I inhale, my mouth pressed against her hair. "I am a walking promise of death, and I'm one of the good ones. I can control myself and my natural urges. But you–just hearing your voice? I'm starving. I've been starving since I met you."

She lets go of a breathy sigh. I tighten my fingers around her throat. She doesn't stop me when I dip my head to press my lips against the side of her neck. She turns away, giving me fuller access, and it feels like someone has reached into my chest and fisted my heart.

We're on dangerous ground. She knows it. I've explained it thoroughly. She's seen the bloodlust in my eyes and how hard I've worked to control it–what I've had to do to keep this a secret.

"I'm not going to hurt you," I assure her, my mouth against her skin, my voice low and smooth. "But I could. You need to understand that. I need you to listen closely to what I have to say." My fangs lengthen against my will. "I am dangerous. It doesn't matter if you can stop me. It doesn't matter that you're powerful in your own right and have the particle I've spent a decade searching for in your blood–like you're made of it. I am still a vampire. My biological objectives are to drain and kill."

"I understand," she whispers, but her voice hitches, and not with fear. "But I want–I want to do it again."

"Why?" My voice rasps like a blade is being pressed against my vocal cords.

"I just–I just want to. I want to know what it feels like if you… bite me on the neck."

"Everything you're feeling right now–"

"I don't care about that," she rushes out. "You're starving. The first time wasn't enough. I can feel it, Alex, for Goddess' sake. Your hands are freezing!"

I move to step away from her, letting go of her neck, but she grabs my wrist, keeping my hand flexed against her stomach, the thin sweater the only thing separating my touch from her skin.

"Take more," she whispers, her eyes closed and lips slightly parted. She's standing perfectly still, and her heart rate slows, returning to its normal, rhythmic thrum. "I'm offering it to you willingly. I'll be fine. You can't hurt me."

"I can. I've just explained that to you. I can hurt you. I can kill you."

"But you won't because you don't *want* to. I'm offering, Alex. Please, just–I need to know–"

In a split second, I have her back on the couch, straddling my lap. She huffs in surprise but settles, thigh muscles rigid, her arms wrapped around my neck and those big, violet eyes locked on mine.

I dip my head to her neck, and she arches back, giving me better, fuller access, and hums a moan that vibrates over my tongue when I lick a line to the perfect spot, and bite.

She gasps, rocking forward, and leans into my body, writhing as I take pull after pull. I tighten my grip, my hands falling to her waist, and tug her as close as possible until our hips are flush.

"Oh, my Goddess," she moans, sighing as she runs her fingers up the back of my head and into my hair. It's euphoric–her touch, her taste, the way she moves against me.

I bite harder, and she hisses, grinding, forcing me to still against the urge to meet her movement by movement. It's too much for her. This can't continue. It can't happen again, but for now? It feels unreal.

"Fuck, Skye," I grunt, releasing my bite. I lick the wound I left, but the bruise forming won't fade for several days. I need to be more careful next time, softer, more gentle. No, there's no need because this–*won't happen again.*

She shivers, rolling her neck to look down at me, the tips of our noses touching. "I don't understand why it feels this good. I still don't get it."

"Is that what's bothering you?" I ease back against the cushions, satiated and relaxed in a way I haven't been in years. She remains seated on my lap, her hair falling around her face. She's flushed pink, and her eyes are sharper and darker than I've ever seen them, a far cry from when they'd glowed with what I can only describe as madness only a day before. It makes her look mortal. Innocent.

Like a feeder.

My guilt ties into knots I'll never be able to unwind.

"What is this?" she whispers, more to herself than to me, and reaches up to palm the bruise on her neck.

"Just a bruise."

"No, this." She presses a hand to my chest. "Why do you bond with people you feed from?"

"Well, you're my first, so I can't really say for sure."

"You've never done this before?" Her brows knit with confusion.

"I've never bitten anyone to feed, no. There's another reason vampires bite, and why we have fangs."

She searches my eyes. I wait for it to click, and it does.

"You killed someone."

"I did, yes."

"Is that why you're here? So far from home?"

Memories I've spent the last ten years letting fade trickle back into existence, but she remains, taking up the entire field of my vision. I'd expect an omission like that to ruin whatever trust we've built, but she continues to stare and waits for my answer.

"I am home here," I answer quietly, my voice barely above a whisper. "I can show you. Let's go to my lab."

19

DOWN WE GO

Skye

"Chin up."

I tilt my chin, my vision taken up by the serious but strangely devoted look painting shadows across the planes of Alex's face as he zips me into a bright yellow parka, all the way to the neck. He's careful, far more gentle when touching me than he was only half an hour ago, when I was breathless on his lap, and he sucked a bruise so deep I can still feel it throbbing. He'll barely meet my eyes as it stands. In all honesty, I can barely meet his. Whatever that was felt... less like I was offering him the sustenance he desperately needed and more like something totally, completely, out of control and overtly sexual.

I flush with heat just thinking about it, a small, involuntary squeak leaving my lips when he grips my fingers and reaches above my head to dig through a bin of gloves. We're chest to chest, and he smells... amazing. Like everything male, dangerous, and delicious. Like things I can't possibly place because this is the first time I've ever wanted–

"These should fit."

I stuff my hands into the gloves and stand there, rigid, worried if I so much as open my mouth to breathe, I'll say something I'll deeply regret.

Beneath the parka, I'm wearing the same yellow thermals I'm intimately familiar with but have never tried on. They're soft but thick and don't have much stretch–specially made to store heat and wick sweat away–according to Alex's thorough explanation only moments ago. He stuffs a beanie over my hair, mumbles a curse when he accidentally covers my eyes, and adjusts the hat just a bit.

"Is it really that cold down there?" I ask when he steps away, and his proximity is no longer turning my mind to molten mush. I blink into the sharply bright fluorescent lights of the dressing room, where neon yellow parkas hang along the wall, and lockers are mostly ajar, stuffed with thick, heavily-treaded boots and other winter gear.

"It can be, especially in the tunnels. Here, put your foot on my knee." He kneels and I obey, watching with interest as he secures cleats to my boot. "The other." I use his shoulder to maintain my balance while he secures the other cleat. Then, he rises, inspecting me from head to toe with a wry smirk.

"What?" I murmur, shuffling in what feels like an extra 30 pounds of clothing.

"Nothing," he replies, but that smirk doesn't fade. His gaze drops to my neck for just a moment, long enough I can see the gears turning behind his eyes. I think he might feel guilty about what happened. He shouldn't. I wish he'd believe me when I tell him so, but Alex doesn't seem like the kind of man who easily changes his mind.

The thermals and parka expertly cover the dark bruise on my neck, and I'm not in pain. In fact, I feel good. Great. Awake and alive in a way I haven't felt in years–maybe ever.

He takes my gloved hand and opens a metal door leading into a second room. This room is empty save for the doors to the elevator and a few racks for gear and coats, I presume, but it's 4:00 A.M., and based on how quiet it was when we left my condo and traveled down to the surface level of campus, we might be the only people in his lab this morning.

"Ready?"

I nod, and he slams his fist against a large red button on the wall. I startle as cold, dry air bursts from the ceiling, settling like mist around my feet. The mist snakes around us while the button blinks red. Alex is unperturbed. He moves the fabric of his coat away from his wrist to read his watch and then meets my eyes again. "It's okay to breathe it in. It's not going to hurt you or your lungs."

"What does it do?" I ask, lifting my arm to watch the mist curl and hang from the fabric of my sleeve before fading.

"Disinfects everything. It's a safety measure to keep not only the lab safe and clean, but to also prevent germs from traveling from one place to another. We'll go through the process again when we leave." The button turns green, and he pulls a lever on the door of the elevator to open it. It's a snug fit in all of our gear, but the walls are transparent, and when it starts to move, the walls turn from a thick, concrete gray to varying shades of blue.

It's like being underwater. The pressure changes. My ears pop. I press a gloved hand to the glass as the ice shifts color again and again, fading from the brightest to the deepest shades of blue that remind me of Alex's eyes. Thirty seconds later, the elevator comes to a rough, shuttering stop, and the doors crank out, revealing a wide, round room made entirely of ice.

The smell is hard to describe. It's clean in a cold kind of way, with hints of soap and the same disinfectant clinging to my clothes. I shuffle out of the elevator behind Alex, unsteady in the cleats. It takes me several steps for my body to catch up with the cling and drag of the metal picks, but it feels wholly unnatural, even when I get used to it. Alex, however, moves like this weighted feeling is normal.

Like he doesn't know anything else.

"This is the main part of the lab, or central, as we call it. Uh, over here–" He motions toward a row of metal tables lined with vinyl arranged against an icy wall. "Are the microscopes and a few chem stations. My lab assistants have their own workspaces and can experiment down here to their hearts' content as long as I've signed off on it."

"So they don't accidentally blow up the lab?"

Alex chuckles. Low and deep. I whip my head up to look into his face, having never heard that easy laugh before. He doesn't notice and instead walks toward the other side of the lab, where several thick plastic drapes house containment stations. "I'm not worried about them blowing things up down here. Something getting loose? Ancient infectious material? Yes. That's a concern." He pulls a drape back and motions for me to follow him into what I quickly realize is another room carved out of the ice. Several large glass structures funnel from the floor to the ceiling, and within, a variety of flora rest on little shelves.

"What are these?" I ask, perplexed. I press my fingertips to the glass to peer at the scraps of what look like fossilized plants.

"Ancient seaweed," he sighs. "Very exciting." I frown up at him, and he chuckles again. "Normally, the ice cores we drill are just that–ice. Occasionally, those cores contain fragments of sediment, and in cases like these, plant material. If we're lucky, we'll find a frozen specimen containing mammalian proteins, but that happens so rarely I honestly can't remember the last time it happened."

A metallic crack echoes from the main part of the lab before a whoosh of air, and soft, sleepy voices travel in our direction. Alex catches my gaze before turning to the voices, edging out of the containment room to part the drapes, and I turn to the trio of young lab assistants funneling in wearing their yellow gear. He turns back to me, tilting his head in a motion to follow, and I do, but I notice the lingering gaze of his students when he bends a knee to check on my cleats before turning me into another set of heavy plastic drapes.

At first, the shift from the bright light of the lab to a claustrophobic kind of darkness riles my powers. Then, just as Alex cranks a lever, and the tunnel fills with crackling, flickering blue light, the drastic change in temperature makes my bracelet heat in warning.

I hang back when he takes two steps into the tunnel and stops to look back at me.

"How deep are we underground?" I ask, reaching out to smooth my hand over the tunnel wall. It's high and wide enough to fit three grown men side-by-side with room to spare, and it's smooth to the touch—the deepest, clearest blue I've ever seen.

"Only about a hundred yards below the surface in the main lab, but our deepest tunnel is a mile under the ice."

"A mile?!"

"Unfortunately, yes. That tunnel isn't often in use, and for good reason. It's highly unstable that deep under the ice. The pressure, as you can imagine, is insane. We have special equipment we use to travel down that far on foot, but our main drills are stationed closer to the surface. Half a mile down, at the most."

I have no idea where we're going, but I'm at his mercy as we traverse into the depths. Alex talks for the entire walk, telling me about the drills they use to pull ice samples from miles below the surface, the discoveries they've found recently, and the work they do in the main lab. It strikes me how similar our fields of study are when we reach a fork, and he angles us toward the left, where the tunnel widens to reveal a room of sorts. The entire room vibrates gently, and sensors fixed to the wall blink in rhythm while Alex walks ahead to check a screen attached to a strange kind of mechanical box. Numbers flash on the screen, followed by a grainy image as he taps away, the electric green hue reflected in his eyes.

He searches back in time for the answers to his questions, traveling further than anyone has been willing to go, further than anyone has thought to have gone, and I... look up. I look far, far away for answers to those very same questions.

"This is an ice core, right?"

"Well, technically it's a drill arm, but yes." He straightens to look at me, frost beginning to coat his lashes and wisps of dark curls escaping from his beanie. "It's cutting away a sample from the ice—a core, we call them. That's why the room feels like it's vibrating. In a few days, we'll bring it to the surface for further study. This one is special."

"Why?"

He licks his lips, his eyes still holding mine intently. "Abby is going to be the one to tell us, actually. But we may have stumbled upon something big. An animal, likely. But based on the footage we have from when the drill hit, we think it might be more than that."

I step toward him, noting the hesitancy in his voice.

"Tell me about it."

"I don't know what we're looking at yet."

"A sea monster? An ancient whale?"

He sucks his teeth and smiles down at his boots. He's doing his best to hide an excited smile. "I don't think so."

"What do you think it is?"

"A village."

"What?"

He leans against the wall, and I do the same, facing him, watching and listening to the steadily beeping sensors and the soft hum of the drills turning in slow rotations yards and yards below us. "I think this is likely the biggest find of my career, if we're right," he admits. "I'm trying not to think about it, and the Beta of Aurorium's task definitely came at the right time to keep my mind off it, but yeah. A village. A settlement of some kind. We know the ocean here is roughly two miles deep, and we're as close to the bottom as we've ever been able to drill. We're scraping the bottom at this point, I believe, and our last few cores pulled from this tunnel in particular have produced sediment samples... iron-rich. Samples of coal. Foreign fibers and the like. Fur."

"Fur?"

"A few minuscule hairs, but yeah. It could be a fluke. It could be core contamination despite our best efforts." He crosses his arms over his chest, his coat crinkling with the movement. "Abby is the best at this. I'd hoped, when I met her during her graduate program, she'd start to lean into paleomicrobiology. It's rare form for biologists, though. We're the ones who find these things, who know where to look, what these samples could be, and then other scientists take over. She wanted the action of the process of discovery once that sample was already in her hand, not the thrill of the chase."

I smooth my hand over the ice again, noticing hairline cracks throughout the wall.

"Anyway, she'll run her tests, and we'll know for sure what we're looking at in a few weeks' time."

I form a fist against the ice before my hand falls to my side. "Alex?"

"Yeah?"

"What exactly did you find in my blood?"

Silence hangs between us for at least a minute. We watch each other, eyes holding fast, like we're both looking inward, reaching for something we can't ask or say.

I've questioned the hows and whys of my powers my entire life. My father has, too; I know that for a fact. But it's never seemed to matter. Many people in my family favor the idea that our powers are simply a gift, something divined from the Goddess, something passed down from Isla when she emerged from those falls in Maatua with the magical ability to heal and the gift of light.

Others have been questioning the origins for decades and why powers on my side of the family are waning while Ella and Ryatt's family line has only grown in power.

Alex purses his lips and sighs, giving me a slightly defeated look. His lips part in what I hope is an answer to literally any of the million questions I have when a sharp, echoing alarm sounds from deep within the tunnel system.

He grits his teeth and kicks off the wall, grabbing my arm, but I barely feel it through the thick layers of fabric. "Another time. I promise."

20

IT'S A BOND

Skye

I ADJUST THE THICK SCARF WORN AROUND MY NECK AND SQUARE MY shoulders, careful of every movement I make while Abby picks at the plate of food on the tray in front of her. The cafeteria around us is quiet at this hour, full of students snacking in silent solitude over laptops and stacks of books, and professors and postdocs finding scraps worth of a meal after a long day of research and lectures.

My last lecture of the day wrapped up less than an hour ago without the drama or fanfare I expected. Most of my lectures are math-heavy, which seriously irks my more experimentally leaning students. I spent the entire lecture with my back turned to the podium, making sure my scarf and turtleneck stayed in place, ignoring the groans and murmuring behind me. Now, the bruise is hard to ignore. It pinches with every move I make, and the scarf is definitely overkill. I'm sweating under the weight of it.

"What's up with you?" Abby asks, looking just as uncomfortable and as exhausted as I am.

I look up from my barely touched food. I'm bone tired. The kind

159

of tired threatening to pull me under with every moment of silence and stillness that passes. I didn't sleep after returning from Alex's lab yesterday morning. I spent the entire day puttering around my condo, trying to rationalize what happened over the weekend and come to terms with what he is, and what we'd done, until my thoughts became so tangled I had no choice but to revert back to pouring what little energy I had left into my lab and the equations and formulas always plaguing my thoughts.

But it's Monday. I haven't heard from or seen Alex since yesterday morning. Not a glimpse. Not a whisper.

I shouldn't be worried about it. The thought of him shouldn't be hanging heavy on my mind when I have a billion other things I need to focus on.

"Skye?"

"Yeah?" I stab at a grape, but it rolls to the opposite side of my plate.

"What's up with you? You've been weird lately."

"I just have a lot on my mind—"

"Dr. Alex Scarlett, by chance?" She arches a brow and leans back with her arms crossed.

"Abby." I rest my hands on the table.

"Look, I know you guys hung out this weekend."

Hanging out is barely half of it. I suck in a breath and settle myself before saying, "Abby, I love you. You're my best friend." It's the truth. When I went to check on her Saturday night, she'd been couch-bound, nursing what Toby told me was likely the worst hangover of her life. Toby knew I'd been with Alex but didn't seem that perplexed about the fact that Alex took me home from the club, and based on our brief conversation, he was under the impression I'd finally let loose and gotten absolutely hammered—not spaced out on literal space dust.

"I know I am, Skye." We hold each other's gaze as tension bubbles between us. "That's not the point."

"Then, what is your issue with me and Alex?"

"Nothing. I don't have an issue with it. You've just been weird since it started." My lips part to argue nothing has started, even though I know that's far from the truth, but she pushes forward. "I don't want this to come off in the wrong way, but you don't date. I've seen you talk to maybe three guys in the entire time I've known you, and even then, you've hardly done anything about it when they showed they were interested in you. You rarely even date."

"Alex is not interested in me like that."

"Are you kidding me?" She braces her hands on the table and hisses under her breath. "Skye, Toby and I have been talking about this for two weeks. Alex is… obsessed."

"He is absolutely not obsessed," I retort, but my voice cracks. I imagine his lips pressed against my neck and the way his hand felt firm against the flat of my stomach as he held me still while he drank me in. I shiver, resisting the urge to touch my neck where the bruise refuses to fade, a lingering reminder of what we did. What I wanted him to do. *How desperately I wanted to do more.*

How I haven't heard from him since he quickly ushered me out of the lab.

"Have you hooked up?"

"Abby!"

"I'm talking about sex, Skye. Have you slept with Alex?"

I launch out of my chair and lean over the table. "There are other people here, Abby, please!"

"You have!"

"We haven't. That's not what this is. He's a friend. A–a colleague. You know that."

"He looks at you like he wants to consume you, Skye. He's head over heels."

I sink back into my seat. *Goddess, if she only knew.*

"He's not." My voice falls flat. Confusion rockets through my system. He's not. He's not into me like that. I'm probably the only person who knows his secret, and now he's forced to trust me. Trust is a very specific level of intimacy. That's all this is.

My skin prickles with a sudden sense of knowing, a truth so deep it hurts. I like Alex. Maybe more than I should. Far more than what's appropriate. This is also the second time Abby's brought this up, so she's onto me. Toby is the only other person Alex has let get close.

How much can we trust them with this?

I adjust my scarf, eyeing Abby, and decide she might be the only person in the world I can say this to. "I enjoy his company. I think he's brilliant. I think we have similarities that I am struggling to rationalize, and I would like to spend more time with him."

"So you have a crush?" She chuckles a bit around a bite of spaghetti. "You can just say you like him. You don't have to be so robotic about it."

I bite my tongue several times before finding the right words to convey my feelings, which, likely, will still fall flat. "I'm in a complicated situation with him because I can't tell if he feels the same way." *Because he's a fucking vampire and I don't know!*

"You could just tell him you like him?"

I imagine his hands squeezing my hips while his fangs sank deep into the side of my neck.

"I don't think he'd believe me."

He told me straight that everything I'd felt in that moment wasn't real. That in that situation, him feeding on me, everything I felt, everything I thought, was essentially an illusion. At least that's how I interpreted it. I don't know enough about his kind to even start making assumptions, but he was clear on one thing—a situation like this can create a bond.

I can't trust the way I'm feeling now, can I?

Abby clears her throat and shoves her tray to the side, bracing her elbows on the table. "You know how I feel about Alex, but he has let up on me a bit ever since he set his sights on you. Being your best friend, and if I'm being honest, only friend, has its perks. So, I approve. What's our plan here?"

"What are you talking about, Abby?"

"Our game plan? You getting in Alex's pants?"

"I am twenty-eight years old," I remind her, but she rolls her eyes to the ceiling and laughs sharply.

"You're practically a virgin."

"I am not! You were there... kind of." My voice shudders as the memory of the first few weeks of our friendship comes barreling back to me in hazy, drunken memories I've long tried to forget, which are also, honestly, the reason I only have one drink when Abby wants to go out.

"I was there to pick up the pieces," she retorts, her face stained pink like she's holding back another laugh, "after you lost your virginity to Carl Cooper, and he found his mate at that same party two hours later!"

"That was an absolute disaster," I murmur, my face dropping into my hand like I can shield myself from the conversation, but Abby has a point. I had one wild night. One true college experience, but it didn't come until I was a graduate student, long after most people had found their mates and settled down with kids in tow. Things like that happened to me often. I'd crush on someone. We'd make it past that awkward getting to know you stage–maybe share a kiss, a touch–and then they'd find their person, their mate, like being with me was some kind of fucked up good luck charm.

Like I'm the Goddess's Matchmaker.

Like She gave me this odd gift, if I can call it that, in exchange for never placing a mate in my lifeline, my tether in the tapestry a single, frayed thread.

Abby met Toby shortly after that night. I didn't have a hand in it, but watching her storm into my room at our old apartment, announcing she found her mate, almost felt like a slap to the face. It had been Abby and me for three months at that point. She was mine. The only person who really understood me. The only person I trusted, even if I still continued to keep secrets from her about my family and my powers. But I like Toby. He's a good man, and he's good for Abby. They fit together like a puzzle piece, filling in the voids of their personalities to a T.

I'm jagged and uneven in comparison.

The next day, during my final lecture of the week, my students file into the observatory instead of the dedicated lecture halls in the physics department. I spend two hours in the dark showing them a map of the stars—my stars. The galaxies I created based on concrete evidence and mathematics, proven by the telescopes Lunaria U is most famous for. My greatest work.

Toward the end of the lecture, I notice I have an extra student tonight.

It's been three entire days since I've spoken to or seen Alex, but now he's sitting in the back row, cast in shadow, watching as I motion to the constellations dancing over our heads, and he watches carefully, his eyes never once leaving mine.

He doesn't rise when the lecture ends, and my students file out. The observatory falls into silence and dims as the presentation fades, and the ceiling cover rolls back, revealing the real night sky, the twinkling stars and overwhelming aurora writhing in pillars of red and purple light.

I go to him like I'm drawn in, like he's reeling me in like a fish. I wonder if this feeling of submission is my choice or something he's doing to me, part of his vampiric profile, I suppose.

"You're in my seat," I whisper, and he stands, towering over me, maintaining a proximity that makes me slightly dizzy when I catch his scent. He's in his dark thermals and smells like ice and the lab—like discoveries. Like science. Like everything I love.

He settles into the next chair, and I sit beside him, soaking in several minutes of companionable silence.

"I wasn't avoiding you," he says, like the distance of the last few days has also been weighing on his mind. "We had a few issues in the lab that needed to be sorted."

"I didn't think you were." I did. I really did. Now, I feel like a forlorn teenage girl sitting next to the guy who's totally out of my league.

He rolls his lower lip between his teeth, his fangs catching the light of the aurora for a split second. "I should have reached out. Let you know."

"It's fine. It's not like this meant anything more than it did."

"Can I see it?"

I meet his eyes, and his gaze drops to my neck, to the scarf. Something warm and greedy bubbles up inside of me before I can stop it, and I reach up, loosening the fabric until it falls over my chest.

His fingers are tepid but not icy when he touches my skin, his thumb swiping over the fading bruise. That same guilt I noticed in his eyes the morning he made the mark returns and cuts through me like a knife. I pull away.

I want to ask if he wants more.

But I already know the answer.

I hate that he'll say no.

"Do you understand why we can't do this again?" he says, his voice low, slightly scratchy.

"You've made it clear."

"I don't think I have."

I look down at my hands, feeling overwhelmingly like I'm being scolded for something.

"I don't want to use you. I respect you, Skye. You are more to me than just a feeder," he says, and I look up at him, catching his gaze.

"I'm never going to understand this," I admit. "This feeling. I don't get it. I don't get why I keep thinking about it."

"It's–"

"A bond, I know." I rise, choking back a retort so sharp I wonder if it'll cut my throat. "I'm sure there are other things we should be talking about, anyway. My blood sample, for one. I'd like to see the slides, to try to make sense of what you saw."

"Skye." He looks so defeated. So tired. His lips part, then close like he's also struggling to just say what he wants to say.

"I have work to do," I lie and leave before I start begging on my knees for him to touch me again because I think that's what I want the most.

Lonely. Pathetic. Unwanted. Those feelings funnel into a storm that causes the charms on my bracelet to warm and ignite.

He reaches out to stop me, to grab my wrist, but I move out of his way and leave.

STACKED

Skye

A NETWORK OF SKYBRIDGES AND ELEVATORS LEADS TO A HANDFUL OF warming rooms and airlocks directly on the surface of the ice. The main one is quite large and houses a row of lockers, as well as changing rooms for men and women, and separate outdoor entrances for both. I hang my coat in a locker, fiddling with my padlock, then walk into the women's changing room, where steam creeps across the floor, and several shower nooks spray warm, wet air, the entire space almost suffocated with humidity. I change out of my clothes and fold my pants and sweater neatly before donning the robe I brought from my condo. It took me an hour to find it, seeing as I've barely started the process of organizing my clothing after moving into my new place, but now it's almost midnight, and I knew I wasn't going to be able to sleep until I burned off some energy.

It's a balmy negative sixty when I shove open the door to the airlock and close it with a crunch behind me. Wind rattles the thick, frosted glass room as I drape my robe on a hook and roll my neck and wrists, debating letting the bracelet stay behind as well, but the timer on the clock above the door begins to beep in warning that the doors to a frozen wasteland are about to open.

"Wait! Oh, my Goddess, Katrina! Hurry up! It's about to open!"

I whirl, covering my exposed skin as two women scurry out of the door leading back into the women's locker room, both equally as bare as I am. My shift happens almost involuntarily, my body bending into my wolf form before they can catch a glimpse of me in all my naked glory, and I suppose that's a blessing, seeing as my neck is still tinged a soft greenish yellow where Alex bit me and changed my entire outlook on life.

I try not to think of him and his obvious rejection because I sound insane. I'm aware of it. The sudden, overwhelming obsession–the feeling I want to chase. I've been ruminating over it for days now, basking in the memories during his absence while I let my mind do what it does best–put a mathematical stamp of approval on my feelings. I've deduced one thing. Just one, minimal, oversimplified reason that my mind and body craves Alex–a vampire. Wolves and vampires have one thing in common–we bite. Hard. Biting for pleasure? That's definitely a shifter thing, and so, here I am, wanting to be bitten again. Overthinking it. Confusing his bite with something else.

The doors to the ice crunch open before the second woman is ready. She screeches from the blast of bone-cracking cold air, giggling frantically before her body blurs into her wolf form, and the three of us wait until the doors open wide enough to allow us to pass through. It's pitch black beyond the ever-present glow of the campus above, which creates a halo of silver, fluorescent light for nearly a half-mile all around campus, and while the other wolves sprint into the wind, weaving under the glassy pillars holding the university off the ground, I step out into the frigid, icy wasteland and slowly turn toward a pocket of darkness.

I want a real run tonight. Something quick and aggressive that makes my heart thunder. I've been so far gone in my mind that I can't think properly anymore, and it has been weeks, at least, since I've shifted. I take off in a sprint, my paws aching at first at the cold bite of the windblown ice, but after a few minutes spent skirting around the back side of campus, my paws begin to numb, and the warm rush of my blood heats my body like a built-in furnace. As I move into the shadows, I see the Pillars and my condo rising like glass spires against a blanket of starlight in the distance. It's easy to forget how beautiful this campus is, especially after weeks spent inside under the glow of fake light and gray walls. Out here, every building looks like it was carved out of the very ice beneath my feet, glimmering against the ribbons of aurora dancing vertically above my head in columns of green and the deepest purple.

I only run into another group of wolves once I've traveled three miles away from campus, our bodies shrouded in wind-beaten moonlight, separated by gusts that pick up ice crystals. I'm coated in frost when I come to a rough stop as a group of eight wolves cuts past me at a slow, almost casual pace, several of them dragging sleds packed with rolled furs and tents.

They don't even look at me. We can't mind-link. Their leader follows behind the group, his dense but strong wolf frame so different from the shifters I know back home in Moonrise. The nomadic wolves here, even the males, are smaller than me. Their leader passes me, stopping for a few seconds to eye me skeptically, trying to sense whether I'm a threat, and then moves on.

I linger for a few minutes, watching the stars blink, listening to the crunch of footsteps and sleds being dragged over the ice. For a moment, I feel a little disoriented and have a sneaking sense that I'm being watched, but when I look at the pack of nomadic wolves–hunters, I presume–their leader is no longer watching me. None of them are.

I'm alone. Like usual. Like I like it. Or at least, I used to–until Alex's presence made me start to question everything I thought I wanted. Everything I thought I knew.

A vicious gust of wind rips through me like I'm made of paper and effectively numbs my brain, whisking those thoughts away.

I often wonder what it would be like to even spend a single night on the ice with only the protection of tents, furs, and my wolf to keep me warm, but after standing still for several minutes watching the wolves disappear into the icy gusts, I realize why I've never attempted that.

My joints are locked up from the cold, and my sleek, almost-black coat is stiff with frost when I arrive back at the airlock. I leap onto my hind legs to slam my front paws against the wide rubber button beside the door to start the countdown, and a minute later, the doors crunch open, and I slip inside, shivering. Warm air blasts the second the doors shut behind me, thawing me from the bones out, and I shift back to my human form, drape my robe over my shoulders, and sit in the sauna until I'm dizzy enough to fall asleep.

The next day is the same. I lecture. I sit in the lab and pore over my equations. I use the telescope. I put in a maintenance request for said telescope and look over my equations again, finding my brain muddier than it's ever been. My neck loses the pinch of pain left in Alex's wake, and the bruise fades to the point that I can wear a crew-neck sweater again without raising suspicions. I shift, I come home, and I lie in bed wondering what the hell is wrong with me.

It's almost 10:00 at night. Alex watched my lecture in the observatory, and now I'm in the library, of all places, high in the stacks on the sixth floor, where the bookshelves create little nooks in a maze-like layout. Seating is scarce, making it one of the quieter spots in the library. It's also where students come to fool around, which I remember when I round a corner and find a couple in a public location and a compromising position. I backtrack before they can see me.

Unfortunately, every volume on advanced calculus, statistics, and logarithms is found up here.

And, unfortunately, so are many of the more technical volumes pertaining to chemistry.

Alex turns from the shelf and spots me before I've noticed the tall shadow stretching across the beaten, fraying carpet belongs to him. He slides the book he was eyeing back onto the shelf, catching me by the arm when I try to slide past him. "Wait."

I jerk to a stop, but he doesn't let me go. All around us, the library is buzzing with distant sounds: clicking keys on a laptop, the ever humming metal whirl of the furnace, soft voices not so far away, but still. We're not alone. He has to know that. If he's… wanting me for… blood….

Gods, I want to stop thinking about this. I shrug out of his hold, yanking my arm free, and meet his eyes in the dim shadows of the stacks. "What, Alex?"

"You left before I could talk to you," he says, his voice a low whisper and dripping with accusation.

"I think you've said enough for me to understand that we can't do this."

His jaw flexes, and frustration lights his blue eyes. They're brighter in the dark. I've noticed it before, but every moment I spend in his presence is now a reminder of what he is instead of wondering why he's so different. In the shadows, he's almost unnerving. A promise of death. A promise of a long life spent being a killing, blood-sucking machine. His fangs glimmer in the soft light slipping between volumes of books at our side when he looks down at me, catching his lower lip between his teeth.

The movement is like being dropped into a warm pool. I feel oddly boneless but tear my gaze away from his. Prickles of heat skitter over my skin, regardless.

"I don't want to," he begins in a hiss, barely audible, leaning down to brush the words over the top of my ear, "use you as a feeder because I care about you, okay?"

I turn ever so slightly to look at him, at his eyes, now glinting with flecks of what I can only describe as anger.

"You've said that already," I retort in the same tone, trying desperately to keep a handle on my feelings.

"You're not getting it."

"Then enlighten me–"

He presses me against the bookshelves. I huff in surprise, but the sound is stolen by his mouth on mine, and he's kissing me.

He pulls away, breathless after nothing more than an aggressive peck. I'm a champion of the unexpected. At least, I thought I was. I study astrophysics, for Goddess' sake. Everything is unexpected and constantly changing–always. I'm proven wrong more often than not.

I'm being proved wrong right now.

"Stop thinking so hard," he says under his breath, and I meet his eyes.

"Excuse me?"

"You heard me."

"Alex–"

He kisses me again, and it's very different from the last time. He bears his weight into my body, my back flush with the shelves, books rattling with the impact, and I float into a blissful, foreign kind of brainlessness that has my arms weaving around his shoulders and my fingers pressing down into the taut muscles I've been thinking about for days–weeks, if I'm honest.

"Turn off your mind for a fucking minute," he says against my lips.

I pull away to look up at him. "What are you saying?"

"You're overthinking everything. You're not hearing me."

"I–"

"I don't want to use you again," he says sternly, and then he's picking me up, his hands warm and splayed wide under my ass, pressing me against the stacks, "because I like you, Skye. I'd like to explore that without the fact that I'm a fucking vampire getting in the way of it."

We're nose to nose now. His lips brush mine, but he's breathing heavily, like he's ready to snap. Like he's been pacing for days, frustrated and angry–with me or himself. Probably both.

"I knew the second you started fussing about me feeding on you again that this would happen, and you'd be obsessed, and I'd feel like I was taking advantage of you, and now all I can think about is you, and Skye, you have no idea how much you're on my mind. It's impossible."

A liquid kind of heat melts down my spine. My breath quivers when I try to take a much-needed breath, but his lips brush mine again, leaving me wanting.

"There are so many reasons for me to stop this," he whispers, his voice deeper and hungrier than I've ever heard it. "This can't happen between us, but fuck, I want it to happen."

My heart threatens to burst out of my chest when he dips his head to press his lips against my neck, inhaling deeply.

"I want you for other things," he says against my skin. "But I want you willing and not under the haze of being a feeder. I can't have both."

My brain is useless. I need a full factory reset to feel even remotely normal at this point.

His tongue slides over my neck, and I grip his shoulders for dear life. Fireworks of pleasure burrow deep in my belly, and I can't take it.

"Please," I murmur when his mouth meets mine again. "I want both–"

"Dr. Scarlett?" A voice rings out a few stacks over that I don't recognize. "Shit. I swore I saw him up here."

Alex slowly, carefully, sets me down but doesn't pull away. His mouth grazes my forehead in what I think is a kiss, something small, tender, and silently apologetic.

Two undergrad students I recognize from my Physics 101 class during the spring semester step into the light at the end of the aisle, and Alex moves like the wind, like the speed of sound, turning to block me from view.

One moment, my heart is beating out of control, and the next?

I really hate coming back to my senses.

This was too public. Now I have even more questions, more confusing thoughts to unravel. I linger behind Alex, pretending to pick through the volumes of books on chemistry I doubt I'll ever need to review, until the students walk away with the promise that Alex will join them to discuss some scientific principle they're struggling with, and Alex turns back to me.

"We'll talk later," he says, and when I meet his eyes, I see hints of the same doubts I'm currently feeling.

I watch him walk away. He hesitates at the end of the aisle, running his fingers through his hair. He's struggling, too. I can sense that. The tension between us is thick enough a knife wouldn't be able to slice through it, and I know, without a shadow of a doubt, this might not be possible for us.

He's a vampire. I'm a shifter, and most importantly, a mystic.

But if we're just having sex? Could that be a bubble of delusion we can stay in, getting what we both want, what we haven't been able to voice?

Or is this something more?

He doesn't knock on my door later.

He doesn't show up at all.

The only presence that graces me is an email sent at 2:00 A.M. to all staff and facility regarding an emergency meeting at 6:00 A.M. sharp.

22

DEAD AND DRAINED

Skye

THE LECTURE HALL IN THE PSYCHOLOGY DEPARTMENT IS BIG ENOUGH TO hold every single faculty member and the entire university administration in one place at one time.

But I've never seen everyone gathered like this before, and the undercurrent in the room is so thick with unease I can taste it. Dr. Gerralde parts the aisle where I'm seated, sidestepping in my direction, and his pale face and uneasy eyes make my heart leap when I rise to my feet.

"Sit down," he says under his breath.

"What's going on?" I ease back into my seat. Everyone else is tittering nervously as well. Murmured conversations lift to the ceiling, but the podium remains empty.

"The president is meeting with the board and the deans as we speak," he says under his breath, glancing around the room before leaning in to continue. "A student is dead."

"What?"

The door to the lecture hall bursts open before I can process the impossible news I just heard. An echo claps through the crowd in its wake, abruptly quieting every conversation. The president of the university, a tall, regal shifter woman in her late fifties, steps up to the podium as the doors slam shut behind the deans of the departments—everyone but the dean of the Biology department, James Kanten.

"Good morning. You're all wondering what the meaning of this is," President Allaway says gravely, her gray eyes creased and desperately serious. It's so quiet, I can hear Dr. Gerralde's heart beating beside me. "Late last night…." She takes a deep breath, closing her eyes for a moment, and backtracks, "You'll notice a presence of Aurorium warriors on campus today. All lectures, classes, and study halls are canceled for the remainder of the week."

Shocked voices lift, turning into a thunderous murmur that President Allaway lets spread for several seconds before waving for silence again. She steadies herself and continues, "Last night, an undergraduate student was found dead in the clinic."

Another wave of voices rises in shock, louder this time.

"Please—please, everyone," Allaway urges.

"Was the student ill?" someone shouts, and more murmurs rise, pulling through the crowd like a wave crashing against a distant shore.

"No, the student was assaulted. Murdered." Her eyes shine as she grips the podium. "As I said, Aurorium guards are here to investigate. Students and postdocs are being notified of the lockdown—"

"Lockdown?"

It's pointless. Allaway tries to rein in the crowd as panicked professors and faculty rise from their seats and start shouting questions, talking over each other. I stand, but only to look around. Alex isn't here. In fact, the entire biology department is missing.

A feeling of dread sweeps over me. Abby and Toby are postdocs. Allaway mentioned a student's death. They're safe. But if she called us here to tell us the details, it's a lost cause now.

Dr. Gerralde tugs my arm, pulling me with him down the aisle and up the stairs to the upper entrance, where he closes us into a hallway and the noise from the lecture fades to an electric hum.

I whirl on him. "What do you know? What's this about a lockdown?"

He waves his hand in surrender, then adjusts his plaid button-up shirt like his collar is too tight. "I don't know whether what I've heard is confirmed to be the truth."

"I don't care." The door opens, letting out a group of professors who walk past us, murmuring rapidly to each other before falling out of sight. "Dr. Gerralde—"

"The student was a volunteer at the clinic, from what I heard. Investigators from the ruling pack in Aurorium are here and swarmed the biology department late last night."

That would explain why I never saw Alex again. A flash of guilt tears through me, and then we're interrupted again by another group of professors and faculty.

Dr. Gerralde scratches his head and steps toward me. "Skye, listen. The student was one of Dr. Scarlett's. She split her time between the clinic and his lab. I heard, but can't confirm, that she was *brutally* killed."

"How?" My voice holds steady despite the thundering of my heart.

He bites his lip, baring his upper teeth. "She was found in the clinic... with bite marks all over her body. It's bizarre, but she was, apparently, completely drained of her blood. I don't know if it's true—"

I'm already halfway down the hallway, running and weaving between the bodies leaving the lecture hall. There's only one under-graduate student I can think of that Alex works with regularly, only one student that young who has access to the clinic. One person spending time with a vampire without realizing it.

My heart is in my throat when I pop out of the psych department's tower into a skybridge, then my heart tumbles into the pit of my stomach when guards come into view, blocking access to the elevators.

I move with the crowd across the wider, main skybridge connecting us back to the library and cafeteria. Guards are every-where, some of them in wolf form, patrolling.

I cut to the left, taking a narrowing skybridge toward the biology department tower, slinking past a guard directing a group of nervous students to use the elevators in the library to access their dorms beneath campus and explaining that the department towers are now under restricted access.

Murmurs of worry and confusion fill the air. My mind reels over what needs to be done. The emails I need to send to my students alerting them to canceled lectures. The phone calls I need to make to my family, who will no doubt hear the news as soon as tonight, maybe earlier if the Alpha King of Lunaria is roped in. I reach the skybridge to the biology tower and find a thick tangle of guards arguing with a crowd of students demanding access, but the crowd is a blessing in disguise.

The service elevator is unguarded.

I scan my badge. The doors open. I slide inside and slam the button to close the door. The doors begin to close right as a guard notices me and shouts, but he's too late.

Silence sweeps through the elevator. I slam the button to the floor where Alex's office is located. If he's not there, I'll risk going down to the lab, which I'm sure has been cleared out for hours now. And I'll—I don't know. I don't know what I'll do.

He couldn't have done this. He wouldn't have, but if not him, then who?

I flex my fingers, my powers riling and warming my skin, and the doors open.

A hallway identical to the corridor outside my office expands before me, the lights dimmed and the glow of the aurora casts hues of green across the shallow blue carpet. Several doors stand ajar, offices empty, and an unnerving quiet envelops the hallway. I walk toward Alex's office, my breath caught in my lungs, and turn to his door, which is shut tight.

I don't knock. I turn the knob, and the seams pop, the door opening silently, the amber light of a lamp in the corner of the room spilling over the toes of my boots.

He's standing near the window with a cellphone pressed to his ear.

He braces a hand against the glass and hangs his head, mumbling something that sounds a lot like, "Please, let me know if there's anything your family needs," and brings the phone away from his ear. The screen goes dark, but he remains facing the window.

I close the door behind me and slide the lock into place. He flips the phone over in his hand a few times before sliding it into his pocket, his reflection in the glass hazy and dappled with starlight, but his expression is clear.

"It was Laney, wasn't it?"

He sighs heavily and slowly turns around.

I edge away from the door, my heart refusing to beat as I take in his appearance, looking for that warm glow he had after feeding on me.

He scans my face, deciphering my expression like my inner thoughts are loud and clear, spread across my cheekbones like text.

"Are you going to ask if I did it, or is there another reason why you're here?" he asks so coldly that the temperature in the room drops by ten degrees.

"No." My voice breaks, and his eyes sharpen, a look of dread so deep it guts me, turning his eyes an icy blue. It's a trick of my mind, I'm sure. A play on light. But still, hurt floods off him, drowning the space between us. "But a vampire did it. Right?"

He turns to the side to hide the expression carving lines of stress across his face. "You need to return to The Pillars and stay there."

"Alex–"

"Did you hear me, Skye? Have you listened to a goddamn thing I've said the past week since you found out my dirty little secret?" The vitriol in his voice has frost spreading across the glass behind him. "I understand your curiosity. Trust me. I was standing where you stood once. Desperate for answers to every question I've ever had. I stood there and faced a man who paved a forward trajectory for me, making me his heir–head of the biology research department. Me, a stupid fucking kid who killed someone and ran to prevent another bloody, useless war, stood there with forged papers in my hands. A fake name. A fake background." He scrubs his hand over his face and into his hair. "I have worked my ass off to stand where I stand right now," he snarls, but not at me. Tears glisten in his eyes when he meets my gaze. "And so did she, but Laney deserved to be here, and I was supposed to keep her safe."

Questions swim through my head, but my body propels me forward. I take a single step toward him, and he bares his fangs, holding out a hand in a motion to stop.

"This isn't your fault," I cry out, my voice shattering.

"Tell me, Dr. Abbot, how another vampire being in Lunaria isn't my fault?"

I shake my head. "I–I don't understand–"

"They're here for me, whoever they are. They're here for *me*. Laney was leaving the clinic to return to the lab last night when she was attacked by someone looking for *me*."

"You can't be sure."

"Who else leaves bite marks?"

"I don't know anything about vampires or your people because you won't tell me anything!" I shout, and his arms drop to his sides. "I don't know anything because you won't tell me. You're treating me and my feelings for you like I'm a fucking child! You're a vampire. I kept you from starving, Alex. I have never once even acted like I am afraid of you. I trusted you, and you should trust me. I want to know these things because I–I want to know you, not because you're a vampire. I want to know *you*."

He stares at me, dumbfounded, I think, by the force of my voice.

"I want to know about *you*," I repeat, suddenly desperate. "And you won't let me."

"You want to know me?" He seethes, stalking away from the window. "The kind of monster who just drained a twenty-year-old girl just for being in the wrong place at the wrong time? I just spoke with her father, Skye. I found out that he and his mate lost their only child and found out the news through a fucking email from my dean. A vampire did this, yes, because we are *predators*. When we are hungry, our first and only instinct is to eat–nothing else matters. We kill blindly and without remorse. You want to know about what I am?

I'll barely age from this point forward. My time here, everything I've built–" He waves a hand toward his desk and the framed diplomas and publications resting in frames along the walls. "I have another decade, maybe, before people start to notice, and then it's over for me. And you–"

"What about me?" I snarl, and he takes another step toward me, then another. "Huh? What about me? Me, who you kissed last night in the library after giving me the cold shoulder for days–"

"I wasn't–"

"What else could it have been, Alex? You don't trust me. You see me as a bright-eyed, eager child looking for answers to the very questions you won't answer."

"We are not compatible," he says sternly, and the distance between us feels like a gaping void–a sudden drop-off neither of us can escape.

"We aren't compatible, or you're just afraid of what you are?"

His phone rings in his pocket. He ignores it, but the sound slices through his office like a death knell.

"I've been wondering what I did wrong," I admit, shaking my head. "I know I'm different, that my brain and emotions don't mesh–I know that. It's because I see too much and understand very little. I'm a mystic, for fuck's sake. That's what I am, and I've never once been afraid of it. You can bite, sure. You can kill someone if you lose control. I can level entire cities if I will it. I can turn your mind inside out without even touching you. I can take away your name and the memories of your childhood. I can manipulate death and bend it to my liking, and yet," I hiss, my eyes filling with hot, bitter tears, "I never let that get in the way of how I was starting to feel for you."

He exhales deeply, nostrils flaring.

"You think you're some monster. Maybe you are. Maybe you saw something in those blood samples Laney took from me that scared you, and I'm the dumbass here. But I think you're just a weak man. I think you're scared. I think you're standing here blaming yourself for the death of your student. I think you've spent a decade hiding because you're ashamed of something you've never had to open up about, and now I'm forcing it. Am I wrong?"

His phone rings again. He closes his eyes, refusing to answer me.

"I'm sorry, Alex," I say, sucking back my emotions, pulling up that practiced mask of neutrality I learned from my father, a master of his craft. "Laney didn't deserve to die. And I don't deserve... this." I motion to my chest. "You said it's a bond from being fed on. Maybe you're right, and what I was starting to feel wasn't real. Or, maybe you're wrong, and we just fucking liked each other."

"Skye."

His phone rings a third time. He looks at me, and I look at him. Two scientists searching for the same answers to almost identical questions... for the same reason. Immovable. Stubborn. Stupid. The works.

I turn for the door.

"Wait."

2 3

—————

THAT'S NOT MY NAME

Alex

SKYE DOESN'T TURN AROUND. I SLIDE MY PHONE FREE FROM MY POCKET, noticing the three missed calls from Toby and the dozen other notifications from my horrified colleagues, but I ignore them, taking three steps and setting my phone on my desk.

I look at Skye, taking in the way her hair shimmers in the lamplight when she turns to watch me move. Her eyes gleam like polished amethyst, swirling with power so different from mine.

She's right. I've been weak. I've kept myself weak. I've kept her at arm's length even though everything I want is right in front of me, and for the first time in my life, I considered risking someone's safety to have something for myself.

"I haven't been honest with you."

"I know," she snarls—trying to look furious. But tears shine along her lower lashes.

"I understand this is confusing. It is for me, too. And I hate that you feel like I'm gaslighting you about how I feel, but I'm looking at this through the lens of... I want you. I like you. I respect you, and I

183

know, firsthand, how difficult an interspecies relationship can be because I've seen it be both successful and devastating."

She reaches up to wipe her tears, her eyes brighter than before now that I'm finally submitting to what she wants. Skye is like me in that way—she needs to know everything to understand her own feelings and convictions. We both need hard evidence to move forward. Our brains are wired to seek answers before jumping into something with both feet. The constant war between our emotions and instincts versus our need to rationalize our feelings and actions is... unfortunately unique for what we are.

It makes her a horrible shifter.

It makes me an even worse vampire.

"My name isn't Alex. Not officially." I lean my leg against my desk, crossing my arms over my chest. "I am called that back home, by my parents, but...." I take a breath. "When I came here, I had to forge papers to enroll at the university. I'm sure you deduced that."

More interested, she slowly turns to fully face me, edging toward one of the armchairs situated in front of my desk.

"Scarlett Thunder is the name of my kingdom. My parents still rule. My father is a king, and my mother—my name is Kieran Alexander, Prince of Scarlet Thunder."

"Kieran?"

"*Kieran*," I say, fixing her pronunciation of the name, but the way she said it is off, her accent harder and sharper.

The corner of her mouth twitches. "You say it so differently. I have a cousin named Kieran, but it sounds like Keer-an," she says, meeting my eyes, her voice softer and calmer than before. "You say it like... Ky-ren."

"Our languages are actually shockingly similar," I reply, feeling like some of the tension is actually lifting. "It didn't take me long to learn it. Weeks, honestly."

She perches on the arm of the chair and watches me expectantly, waiting for me to continue. I suck in a breath.

"My mother named me, and my father hated the name, so they

started calling me Alex. My grandfather, Lex, went by our last name, so it felt fitting. No one calls me Kieran, so don't start."

Her cheeks redden, but her soft smile works through my body, untangling some of the grief, making it hard to focus.

I angle my body toward hers. "I've never had to explain this before."

"Take your time."

She's not going to leave until I've explained everything, truly. She's like a persistent little owl with those big eyes and statuesque expression, soaking every word I say in like a sponge.

"I mentioned there were two distinct types of vampires. I was born a vampire. So was my father. The woman I call mother... she was turned. She was turned against her will."

Shadows creep over Skye's face, painting lines of grief under her eyes.

I clear my throat, looking down at my hands as my fingers curl into fists against my thighs. "She was a witch before she turned. She was very young–nineteen or twenty. She can't remember. But vampires stormed her village on the day of her wedding. They killed her entire family, her entire village. And she and her twin sister were spared for some sick, twisted reason, and turned against their will. That was... over two hundred years ago."

Skye makes a small, surprised noise.

I kick off my desk and begin to pace. "You want to know the difference between us, so I'll say this much. Born vampires are very similar to shifters and witches, and whatever else haunts our shared, but separated, worlds. We can have children. We age, but differently. Turned vampires are cursed to a long life, but they're sterile. They cannot have children. There's a wide variety of biological differences between born vampires and turned vampires, and it comes down to the fact that turned vampires are simply just... dead."

"And you're not?"

"No, I am very much alive."

"But... your mother had you?"

"No." Memories of my early childhood bleed into later years, when I started to unravel the truth about my parents and their story–how hard they had to fight for not only me, but just to be together. Two different species aligned by love. "I don't know my birth mother. She died when I was born, but she was a born vampire, like my father. They didn't know each other. My father was supposed to marry the princess of another kingdom but was in love with my mother and had been for years at that point, forsaking all others, but she knew they couldn't be together. He needed heirs. She couldn't give that to him. But my father had a drunken night, and I was the result. My mother, Emelda, raised me and loved me as her own. She has always wanted to be a mother. She was robbed of so much when she was turned, and I have dedicated my life to finding a cure. To… bringing her back to life. Still a vampire, maybe, but like me and my dad. Giving her a chance to have a child that's part of her and part of him, something I can never be."

I go on to explain how I trained in apothecary medicine in my kingdom; how I had the freedom to have my own practice shortly before I had to go, but I leave those details for another time. It's such a complicated web to weave.

"And you came here?"

"I did, but I had no idea that Lunaria had a place like this. I spent a year in Aurorium, making connections, gathering forged paperwork and giving myself a fake background I could use to gain entrance to the university. I was young, in my early twenties, and easily passed for an undergraduate student, and when I was able to enroll, everything changed for me. I had access to the tech I needed to actually find a cure, but it's been a decade. I moved through the motions. I've been in every lab, run every test, but my mother isn't here. They don't know where I am, and I've been gone for over ten years now. I chose to specialize in paleomicrobiology because I deduced I'd find the answers to my questions in a world that no longer exists, and I've come close. I get close to a conclusion, and something changes, new evidence reveals itself, and I fall back again. But then I met you. Then I saw the very particle I was looking for in your blood, like you're made of it, but that's the thing. It's not something I can use to cure my mother. It's not something I can bottle and sell to the masses. It's your magic, Skye, and it cannot be replicated."

Silence spreads through the room. My phone has been buzzing repeatedly, a constant reminder of the situation at hand.

But this feels more important.

"I don't know how to move forward with you because my time here is limited, especially now," I admit. "This goes beyond me being a vampire."

"Because Laney died?"

I look down at my hands. "I am at fault."

"Unless you killed her–"

"It was not me, but based on what I've heard, this was a vampire's work. And if I'm honest, I've had suspicions about the two other murders in and around Aurorium."

"Why didn't you say anything?"

"Because this falls back on me."

"I can help you," she cuts in, rising. "I can find this person. I just need–I could try to look into Laney's mind and find out who attacked her."

"She's dead, Skye."

"But–"

"I do not want you involved."

"Why? Why not?" she says in a near shout, and that electric tension soars once again. "I've been honest about who I am and what I can do."

"And I have been clear about the dangers involved!" I square my shoulders, my tone bitter and stern. "I killed someone very, very important a decade ago and ran to protect my family. I killed someone to prevent a war, and I knew, eventually, that would catch up with me, and if there is a vampire here, he or she is hunting me, Skye, and anyone in their way is collateral, including you. I don't care that you have powers and can protect yourself. Vampires are designed to hunt and kill, more so than shifters. A vampire will always be two steps ahead, and I need you to look me in the eyes and hear me when I say I cannot involve you, which means this–" I wave a hand between us. "This cannot happen unless you understand the consequences. This is what I want. I want you. I want to sit and talk to you about everything and nothing. I want to sit in the observatory and listen to you lecture. I want to bring you to my lab and show you everything I've ever touched and researched. I want you however I can have you, but I refuse to use you as a feeder, and I refuse to put you in the middle of what could end up in a fucking war."

She narrows her eyes, biting back another argument I won't hear. I refuse. Skye isn't used to people drawing hard lines in the sand. I assume people tiptoe around her, ever cautious, and now? With me standing up and putting a firm boundary in place?

She doesn't like it. Not one bit.

"I kissed you because I wanted to and because it was all I've been thinking about for days. Weeks, if I'm being totally honest. I kissed you because it's what I needed. Now, I'm telling you–firmly–that you are not going to get involved in what happens next. Laney is my problem. I will find who did this to her and end it. I do not need your help."

"You do."

"I do not."

We stare at each other, glaring in the glow of the lamplight.

"Have I made myself clear?" I ask in a tone I normally reserve for my students.

She scoffs. "Don't ever use that tone with me again."

"Skye," I warn, edging toward her, "I am not going to allow you–"

"I don't need your fucking permission. The entire campus is locked down. Someone died. Your student died in a vicious attack, and if, on the off chance, someone starts putting the pieces together and what you are gets out, you're the prime suspect. If–" She closes the distance between us, pointing her finger directly into my chest. "If my family finds out about this, and I'm sure they will, there will be an investigation, and my aunt Maeve will find out that vampires are in Lunaria, and you can't escape that, and I can't save you from it. I'm helping!"

"No!"

"You can't stop me!"

"Enough! You are not a part of this because if I lose you–if I'm responsible for your death–I will have to live with that for the rest of my long, unending life, and I can't."

She rears back, startled by the raw emotion woven through my words. She searches my eyes and softens a bit but steps away from me toward the door in what I hope is defeat.

I hate doing this to her. She's brave but naive. She has no idea what this situation could become.

"How are you going to get blood if the campus is locked down?" she asks in a tone that's meant to sting, and honestly, it does.

"Not from you."

She rolls her eyes, furious. "You're being so fucking stupid."

"So be it. Knowing you're safe and uninvolved is enough."

"Fuck you, Alex."

I look away, and she slips through the door, slamming it so hard it rattles.

24

TIME TO TELL HIM THE TRUTH

Alex

"The dean isn't coming," says Dr. Michelle Ambrose, one of my colleagues, as she twists her rings around her fingers and glances at the door of the lecture hall where we've all gathered under my direction. "I sent him an email an hour ago. I've sent him twelve emails today alone," she continues, sniffling. "Laney was one of mine. She's in my lecture class. She's–" She closes her eyes, her pale, gray-blonde hair falling over her face as she bows her head.

I look around the room at the eight seats filled by professors and the rows behind them filled further with the administrators from the biology department, our postdocs, student teachers, and assistants. Several graduate-level students came, but it's the young students in the back, shrouded by shadows of confusion and grief, that tie my stomach in knots.

I've been pacing as the department filed in, stuck in my own head, torn between thoughts of Skye and our argument, her points, which, if I'm being honest, were correct, and this.

The safety of my colleagues and students against an unseen threat I know all too well.

I sink onto the edge of the stage, my back to the podium, and look everyone in the eyes, one by one. My voice carries through the silence, hushing any lingering murmurs. "I don't have words to describe what happened, but I'm going to be honest. Laney Graves was murdered—here, on campus. So far, the warriors from Aurorium have swept the biology department and clinic for any evidence of who her attacker was, but they have come up short. They believe whoever did this is no longer on campus, but warriors will remain." I look up into the back rows at the undergraduates, some of them so young and childlike it makes me want to scream, maybe find Kanten and give him the beating that's been brewing for years now. "I've emailed everyone's parents in the undergraduate program. The campus will shut down for at least the next week. Your parents are asking about your safety, and I've been advised to say you're perfectly safe here, but I'm going to level with you. I don't know that for sure. Heed the commands of your RAs. Stick together in groups. Stay in the dorms if possible, and if you're traveling up to the surface, take two or three friends with you."

My colleagues murmur, most of them glassy-eyed as they nod their agreement and turn to face their students, whispering assurances.

I catch Toby and Abby sitting in the middle rows, and Toby nods at me in solidarity.

I roll my lower lip between my teeth, continuing, "If anyone in this department has concerns, bring them to me," I say firmly. "I will ensure everyone is kept in the loop. Students at all levels–keep your phones on and your emails refreshed, and be on the lookout for correspondence from us. All lectures, labs, and assignments this week are obviously canceled, but your professors and I will meet to discuss our plans going forward."

"Was–was Laney aware?" a small, feminine voice pipes up from the crowd. I search the rows and find a dark-haired young woman with tear-stained cheeks. Friends on either side of her comfort her while she trembles. "Was she in pain, or was it quick?"

My chest convulses. I've seen the official report, which won't be made public to the students. I know how she died, how her throat was ripped out, and she was drained. "I believe it was very quick. I don't think she felt much."

The young woman bursts into tears. The entire room murmurs, bodies shuffling as someone passes a box of tissues up the rows into the back.

I'm not sure what else to say, but people begin to rise and gather in small groups, and after a few minutes of talking and plotting plans of immediate action with fellow professors and lab directors, Toby reaches my side, closely followed by Abby.

He pulls me aside. "Are you okay?"

"No," I answer honestly, shaking my head. "The dean was supposed to be here. This is the last straw. I can't continue to allow him to ignore his own department. I should have done something to oust him early." I tuck my hands into my pockets and watch the crowd begin to file out of the lecture hall. It's a basic room, open to all departments, small and seldom used, but it's one of the only public spaces open right now on campus, other than the cafeteria, which is swarmed by warriors as it stands. "I'm going to talk to him if I can find him."

"He's definitely hiding with his tail between his legs. I wouldn't be surprised if we find out that he left campus altogether to take one of his lengthy vacations," Toby murmurs, but I catch Abby's eyes. She's staring at me so intently, like she's seeing me for the first time, which is an odd feeling.

I nearly ask if there's something I can help her with, but she leans in, grabbing my wrist. "Have you seen Skye today?"

"I have. We spoke in my office an hour ago."

"She hasn't returned my calls."

I glance at Toby, who shrugs, but I'm more concerned about the fact that Abby, who loathes me, is now touching me, clutching my arm like I'm an anchor. "She's very upset."

"This entire situation is upsetting," Toby says to calm his mate's nerves.

But I cut in, "She's upset with me. We argued."

Toby and Abby look at me, puzzled, and Abby's hand drops from my wrist. "What? What do you mean you argued?"

Toby glances at Abby before tilting his head toward the exit. "Let's talk for a minute, yeah?"

Abby tries to follow, but he stops her, angling her away from the door with a quiet promise that he'll fill her in later, and I know I'm in for a conversation about feelings, emotions, and relationships I've never had to have.

Abby scoffs, but the door to the lecture hall shuts in front of her. Toby and I weave down a snug hallway, stopping for a moment to talk to colleagues and answer questions about our dean making it clear he has no interest in the welfare of his department, and eventually reach the center of campus, where the skybridges stretch in a six-point star off the library.

A group of warriors catches us, but we show our badges and are allowed entrance to the hallway leading to The Pillars.

Toby doesn't say a word until we reach the entrance, then he stops me, tugging me to the side before I have a chance to swipe my badge.

"What's going on with you and Skye? Seriously, man."

"Out of all the things we need to discuss, this is what you've settled on as the top priority?"

"Abby is up my ass about it," he admits, leaning his shoulder against the wall while eyeing a group of professors from another department as they walk toward the entrance to the gated neighborhood and scan their badges. He waits until they're safely out of earshot and asks, "Are you guys dating?"

"No."

"Is that where you're headed?"

"I don't think that's your business–"

"Goddess, Alex, I can't do this with you anymore. You're a freaking robot when it comes to your emotions, and yeah, that makes some sense given that you're a scientist, but still. You can like her. You can want to be with her, to spend time with her, without having to be so far up your own ass that you miss your shot."

I blink, and he grunts a laugh.

"You know what Abby said to Skye? The same fucking thing. You're so similar–you and her. Everything has to have a mathematical solution tagged to the end of it for either of you to give it your time. I know you like her. I see it in your eyes. They light up whenever her name is mentioned."

"She's technically a princess, for one," I cut in, crossing my arms over my chest.

"That doesn't matter, dude. Come on. Just admit it. You like her. Ask her on a date–"

"We're past that. It–it didn't even come to that. This is more complicated than I can explain."

"Then what the fuck is going on? Because you're both being weird."

I grab him by the arm, scan my badge, and yank him into the hallway right as the doors open. He shrugs out of my hold and follows as I stalk down the hallway, which angles to the left in a half-moon shape.

"Alex!"

"I need to talk to you privately. No one can overhear."

"I don't get what this has to do with what I'm trying to clear up for you."

"That's exactly what I'm going to do. Clear things up." I stop and whirl on him.

He raises his hands in surrender. "Look, I get that the past day has been hell. Trust me, we're all in pieces over losing Laney. Okay? I'm just trying to support you here. You don't date. I've never once seen you with another woman, another partner–anyone. No one."

"It's not about that."

"Then what is it about?"

"Can I trust you to keep a secret?"

"What kind of question is that, Alex? I thought we were friends!" He gives me a slightly shocked but overwhelmingly incredulous look. "In fact, I think I might be the only person who actually knows you."

"You don't know me like you think you do." My voice hangs low between us, rough around the edges.

Toby catches the glint of unease in my voice, his expression twisting into confusion and concern. "What do you mean?"

This is it, isn't it? I start coming clean? Give myself a little bit more room to be what I am, freeing up space to allow Skye and all her questions and assumptions to fill that space instead? It's too much pressure for her to be the only one who knows. Based on the conversation we had only a few hours ago, I know that she didn't come to my office thinking I'd killed my own student, though.

She was afraid for me. She was worried about my secret getting out—and carrying that burden on her shoulders alone. There's nothing I can say to her that'll ever change her mind, that's clear.

But if Toby knows, maybe that will soften the situation enough for me to get through to her. Plus, Toby is going to come in handy if, or more likely, when this other vampire shows his or her face.

"I'm not a shifter," I tell him, and he rolls his eyes.

"I know. We've been friends for a decade."

"I'm not a wizard, either."

Toby narrows his eyes in confusion. "Wh–"

I lick my lips and glance around, thankful we're alone. "Just come into my condo real quick. We need to talk."

"Is everything okay, Alex?" His gaze cuts from mine to look over my shoulder. He straightens, pulling closer to the wall, and I turn my head as Skye walks down the hallway and stops at her front door. Her phone buzzes, and she lifts it to her ear while she fumbles with the door code.

"Dad, I know what you're going to ask, but I'm fine, really. Warriors from–" She cuts herself off abruptly, her face going so white it looks like she's about to faint.

I turn toward her, and her eyes meet mine across the distance between us. "Skye? Hey, what's wrong?" I shout, my voice pinging from door to door as it travels down the hallway in her direction.

Her phone drops from her hand, and she sucks in a breath, her hand plastered to her chest like it's hard to breathe.

"Shit, Skye?" Toby says sharply, but I'm already running, watching her suck in another breath, then another, growing paler and paler by the second, but then I notice the glow on her wrist.

I grab Toby by the shirt and yank him back just as her eyes light from within, and a gentle gust of pure energy erupts right in front of us, tinged with violet mist flaked with stardust.

"What the fuck?" Toby exclaims, stepping into the place where Skye just stood, but now it's only empty, metallic-tasting air.

I crouch and pick up her phone.

ISLA IS WAITING

Skye

It's raining in Maatua. Pouring, actually. Rain pelts the familiar metal roof while I stand on the porch, my fingers curled around the handle but frozen in time. I can already feel the vacuum-like sensation of doom hanging heavy in the air when I take a deep breath and pull. The humidity dries out, turning the air warm–but it's just as heavy–as the door closes on a phantom wind behind me.

Voices speak in muffled tones in the kitchen just down the hallway in front of me. A tea kettle whines against soft voices I recognize without seeing the faces they belong to. My mom. My aunt Brie. Aviva and Cole. Lexa and Nora. Other cousins and family friends.

I look up at the ceiling, where the wide, open living room bleeds into a lofted hallway, and the upstairs bedrooms are cast in rainy shadows pouring from the skylights.

One door is open.

"Sweetheart."

I look straight ahead and find my mom in the kitchen archway. She bunches a rag in her hands before walking out of sight and returning again, looking worn and thin, dark circles ringing her large, deep blue eyes.

I remain frozen in the front hallway, my heart pounding in a slow, heavy rhythm against my ribcage as she says, "Your dad's upstairs."

She has no reason to explain what's happening. I can feel it in the air. A shift in the timeline. A fraying lifeline in the tapestry. *An end.*

I silently, robotically, turn to the stairs and climb.

Six people linger in the shadows, painting my great-grandfather Isaac and great-grandmother Maddy's bedroom in shades of black and rich blue. Misty sits at her bedside, leaning forward at the waist as she holds her mother's hand tight, whispering words I doubt I'm meant to hear. Ella smooths Maddy's hair away from her face, tucking the long, pearly white locks behind her ears.

Maddy remains as still as death—because that's what this is.

Maddy was… incredibly beautiful when she was young. The thick, dark wine-red hair she passed down through the generations is still strong. Both of my brothers have it. I have it, even if mine is much darker than Maddy's ever was. She's beautiful still, her head resting on a silken pillow, her eyes open to glassy slits, and her chest rising in slow, shallow breaths.

"Do you remember," Ella whispers, a tear gliding down her cheek, "when we first met? You'd never seen a washing machine before. Hannah and I thought—we thought that was the funniest thing." She shakes her head, tears flying. "I still think of us as that young. I'm so surprised every time I look in the mirror."

Movement in the far corner of the room catches my attention. Uncle Ryan and my Grandfather Sydney are standing by the windows in silence, watching Ella fawn over their mother. Watching their sister stroke their mother's limp hand.

But it's my great-grandfather Isaac who's sucking the light out of the room. He's sitting in a chair in the corner, his eyes open but withdrawn as he stares at the bed where his mate *is dying*.

It hits me at once. I turn back to Maddy, my chest so tight I can't relax my lungs enough to take a breath, and reach for the clasp of my bracelet.

But then I catch my dad's eyes.

"Don't," he says into my mind, his voice level, calm. *"She's not hurting anymore."*

"We can stop this. You can—"

"It's her time. This is what she wanted, Skye."

I tear away from his gaze and look back down at Maddy. Oh, there're so many pictures of our family that she's taken over the years. She was the kind of mother who kept every piece of art, every little note that her kids made. There're dozens of albums scattered throughout the castle in Crescent Falls and here, in Maatua, of our side of the family throughout the decades. So many memories. Four generations of memories… because she *kept them*. She was the heart of the family. A normal shifter. No power to speak of. The friend. The lover. The mate. *The Luna.*

The one who baked cookies every single day when her grandchildren and great-grandchildren came to visit. The one who wrote letters and always answered a call on the first ring.

I notice the faint glow of Misty's powers under Maddy's skin, but I already know she's not trying to heal her. She's keeping her comfortable. That's all.

I had no idea Maddy was sick.

I scrub my hands against my cheeks, finding them wet with tears.

"Hannah is going to meet you there," Ella says, her voice cracking so painfully Ryatt takes a tentative step away from the wall toward his mate, but he stills when she continues, "Cosette, too. And Artyom and Cassian. My parents… Goddess." She grips Maddy's hand, sniffling. "It'll be a party. Ryatt and I… we'll take care of things here for you. We'll take care of Isaac. I promise, Maddy. You can go whenever you're ready." Ella turns her head so no one can see the pained grimace shattering her beautiful, ethereal face.

Ryatt closes his hand over her shoulder, bowing his head as she silently sobs.

But I'm looking at my great-grandfather, and he's looking at *me*.

"Skye," Dad says into my mind in warning, but my bracelet slips off my wrist, and I curl it into my fist. Yet, the voices constantly dancing

through my head remain quiet—nothing more than a gentle hum, even as the room begins to fade, and the tapestry opens wide for me.

I've never looked into the lifelines of my family members. It was a promise I made to myself when I was old enough to understand that my powers weren't gifts at all. They're a burden I carry. Knowledge damning enough to turn me inside out. I make an exception today that I swear I'll never make again.

Isaac's lifeline is *so long*. He has to know, doesn't he? That he'll live on without his mate for another decade, at least? He's like Ryatt, Ella, and all the other powerful, magical people in this family. He was blessed with a long life but cursed to live it without her.

I shake my head as my tears trickle like a leaky faucet. It's unfair. *He* thinks it's unfair. I try not to read his mind, to see inside, to look at the sensitive memories he's slipping through like a book, but his mate is dying, and he's showing *me. Begging me to look. To understand.*

"Skye, get out of his head," Dad warns, but I can't help it. I want to see. I want to know what it felt like for him during that first war when he was ready to fall on his sword to ensure she was safe and had a future, even if he wasn't in it with her. I want to know what it felt like when he readied for battle that next time, when he kissed her goodbye and told her he wasn't coming home without their daughter—the daughter now squeezing her hand and silently crying, her tears wetting the mattress beside her mother's arm.

I want to know what it felt like to be in love... and to have someone love you so much they'd let you go.

I want to know what he wants me to *do now*.

"Skye!" Dad hisses out loud, but Grandpa Isaac turns his gaze away from mine to look at Maddy. He doesn't rise. He's already said his goodbyes. He's been saying them for two months, when they returned from Kieran's wedding and Maddy finally admitted how tired she was. I listen to the promises she made him keep while my heart cracks and threatens to shatter.

We've built such a beautiful life. I regret nothing. It's my time. I can feel it. Can't you?

That was the problem. He couldn't feel it. His age barely has an effect on his body. But he was watching his mate, his wife, the mother of his three children, slip through his fingers, a constant reminder of how different he is, and how fragile she'd become over the years.

He was born with breath in his lungs because of the Diamond of Faith. He would have died—should have died—but the Goddess intervened.

And She won't intervene now.

But I can.

He knows that.

He *wants* that.

"Isla?"

I blink back tears and look at Maddy. Her voice rings through the room. She's staring at the ceiling, her white hair falling over her shoulders like a halo of pearly satin. Her lips part again, and the last sound she makes is a deep, relaxed breath, tinged with Isaac's name. *I'll wait for you. I'll be here when you're ready to rest.* Her inner thoughts dissolve in my mind, floating away against a blanket of stars only I can see.

I press my fist against my chest to keep my heart from shattering as the room bursts into a strange kind of silent chaos. Misty sucks back a wail of dismay and shudders so violently that the bed shakes. Ryan and my grandfather Sydney close in around the bed while Ryatt wraps an arm around Ella's chest and pulls her close while she sobs.

I've never seen her cry before.

I choke on the sob that erupts from my throat without warning. The voices in my head grow so loud I can't drown them out. Dad is standing on the other side of the room, torn between going to the bed where his grandmother just took her last breath and *stopping me.*

I look at Isaac through a torrent of tears. He's still in that chair, still looking at his mate, but his eyes are dry and set in grim determination when he turns his head to look at me.

"Do it," he says so softly I could have easily missed it, losing those two words—his last—to the aether.

It's like plucking an apple off a tree. Like throwing a pebble into a body of water and losing sight of it. A flick of the finger. Yanking a thread from a sweater. It's easy. So easy.

And I do it. I pluck my blood's thread from the tapestry.

It's silent and painless. A secret he wants me to keep.

And then he's just… gone.

Isaac's eyes remain open and locked on mine as the light fades from him. He stills, his body finally relaxing, like he's just fallen asleep.

Somewhere, in a place I haven't been able to find regardless of my powers or my research, I imagine he's taking Maddy's hand and guiding her home. He's seeing his parents again and reuniting with friends, and he's with her. He tried to promise he'd go with her, but he knew he couldn't, not without help.

"Dad?" Misty wipes her tears on the back of her hand and looks at the chair in the corner. "Dad? D-Dad, are you okay? Dad!"

I shake my head, trying to focus on the sudden shift–the bodies, the blur of movement and sound as shocked, raised voices cut through my dimming powers and the room comes back into focus.

I gasp out a breath, a jolt of cold spreading up my spine, and look from the bed to Isaac, where Ryan is shaking his shoulder and calling out for him, his expression falling with every second his father doesn't answer.

But then I look at Ryatt, who's still holding Ella. His violet eyes hold mine with an intensity that slices me into pieces… but *he knows*.

And he's… thankful.

Dad grabs my shoulder and yanks me out of the room. The hallway is a mess of bodies. Mom shouts his name, but he barrels through the sea of concerned family members who are running up the stairs and into the room to see why Misty was yelling.

My fault. My fault. I didn't think. I let my powers act. I didn't–I don't regret it. He wanted it.

I did it. I did it.

Dad closes us into a bathroom. It's a snug fit. My back hits the pedestal sink with a crunch, and he's still holding my arm, digging into the pocket of the jacket I never had a chance to take off. "Where's the bracelet? You need to put it back on."

The charms cut into my fists when I squeeze with all my strength. "No."

We lock eyes. His swirl with magic that I feel in my veins. Magic he gave me. Magic we were both cursed with. "Skye, what have you done?"

"What you couldn't do even though you knew he wanted you to do it," I gut out, my eyes watering so violently his image blurs. "He asked you, didn't he? And you–said–no."

He takes a shattered breath, his grip loosening. "You shouldn't have."

He lets me go, and I pull inward, letting my powers explode, letting them drag me back to where I need to be, even if I can't voice it. The bracelet slips from my fingers, disappearing into the void, forever lost.

I gasp in pain and heartbreak when the world funnels back into view. The air is familiar–dry and synthetically warm. It's dark, like always. The stars are bright and flickering beyond the ceiling-height windows....

Of Alex's condo.

He's standing a few feet away, dressed for bed, his eyes wide. He drops the glass of water he was holding, and it shatters on the ground between us.

I take several hard breaths, my lungs refusing to function, and choke, "I didn't know vampires needed to drink water."

His lips part, his brow furrows, and I see the look of concern that flashes behind his eyes as he reaches for me....

I shatter, falling to my knees, and sob.

2 6

BLEEDING AND BARE

Skye

"Don't move."

I suck in a sob and blink back tears. Alex crouches in front of me, his hands on my upper arms to steady me. I'm still kneeling when his apartment comes into full focus. I never gave it much thought when I woke up here in a drug-induced haze, but it's a masculine, nearly identical layout to mine. He's not fussy about his decor. Small knick-knacks rest on shelves, with more books than I have rocks, which is a feat, but that's it.

His scent is everywhere–clean and reassuring–familiar and... comforting. More comforting than I deserve.

Strands of my hair stick to my tear-dampened cheeks. My eyes feel heavy and sore from crying. I stare at the space between us, at the shards of sharp glass reflecting the light of the aurora spilling through the windows and the soft amber haze of a floor lamp in the corner of the room, but then the glass darkens, turning inky and sticky with an oozing crimson liquid my mind doesn't immediately comprehend.

207

"I'm going to pick you up," Alex says cautiously, tucking two fingers under my cheek to force me to look up directly into his eyes.

"I can walk to the door. I don't know why I–"

"You're bleeding. You dropped onto your knees directly into a pile of glass."

I nod because it's all I can do. My throat is thick, and my lungs contract. I hold back a whimper of embarrassment, guilt, and a myriad of other tangled emotions fighting for dominance. Alex's hand ghosts down my arm before dropping to grip the curve of my waist, and all the while, he keeps his eyes on mine, steadying me. Maybe steadying himself, too.

"I'm sorry," I mouth, but he shakes his head. His eyes don't darken with bloodlust. His grip isn't overly tight when he hooks his arm around me and swiftly hauls me upright.

"Wrap your legs around my waist."

Bright pain slices through my knee the second I move my right leg into position. My sharp inhale is broken by a hiss, then fresh tears spill down my face. A small shard of glass is lodged just below my knee, glimmering in the lamplight, then the light in the snug hallway off his kitchen, but Alex doesn't say a word. He silently opens the door to his bedroom on the first floor and carefully deposits me on the edge of his bed.

"My mattress isn't nearly as expensive as yours," he says somewhat wryly. Then, he kneels again to inspect the wound.

I roll my head back and look up at the ceiling in a half-assed attempt to dry my tears. "You're right. It's not."

"Perks of being a princess."

Princess. Grandpa Isaac calls me that. *Called me that.* My stomach pitches, tightening so much that a small, desperate sound is forced from my throat. Despair clouds my senses so sharply that I shudder with more sobs that just won't stop.

Alex ignores it, which is the only reason I'm not totally falling to pieces.

"I'm going to pull it out. It's not deep."

"Okay," I squeak, my leg jerking up reflexively, but his hand on my calf prevents me from kneeing him in the face when he yanks the glass from my leg. He examines the shard for a second before rising and tossing it in a wastebasket near the door. Then, he grabs a shirt from a stack of clothing folded on top of his dresser and presses it on the wound. But he looks around like he's missing something, and I notice the sharp line of thought furrowing his brow, his body rigid with tension.

"I'm sorry. I know you have a thing about blood."

His eyes meet mine so quickly that I jump a little. "I think we've established the real reason."

"Do you have a bandage? I can just wrap it up and leave."

He looks down at my jeans with a sigh. They're soaked with blood from the knee down. I glance down once, then cringe and fix my gaze on the ceiling again.

"You need to take these off."

"Okay." I reach for the button, but my hands shake. My fingers are damp and slippery from repeatedly wiping my tears away, so I fumble. I don't look down when he sighs heavily, and his fingers grip mine. He moves my hand out of the way and undresses me.

It's innocent. At least, it should be, given the circumstances. I sliced myself open in front of a vampire, who's now whispering quiet reassurances about his totally innocent intentions as he slides my jeans off and down my legs, one of which is smeared with blood that won't stop coming.

He rises, takes one look at the jeans, tosses them in the trash can with the glass that maimed me, and leaves.

That's probably it. He's going to pace his living room while fighting his totally rational vampiric tendencies. I'm going to be the reason he goes absolutely insane with bloodlust and–

Alex returns to the room with a first aid kit and a fresh glass of water. For me.

"This isn't going to feel good." He kneels, handing me the water and setting the first aid kit on my thigh.

I huff a laugh that goes against everything I'm currently feeling. "Why would a vampire have a first aid kit?"

"It came with the place. I'm sure you have one, too, likely tucked in the cabinet in your bathroom. You should check. They come in handy, I'm sure."

He digs through the kit, thumbing through different-sized bandages and setting a roll of gauze and antibacterial ointment on the bed beside my leg.

"I heal quickly." I force myself to swallow past the knot in my throat.

"You're also a bleeder, more so than others," he replies, like it's a totally casual thing to say.

I risk a glance down at him and catch his gaze. His eyes are the darkest blue I've ever seen–nearly black. I tremble but turn my spine to steel despite the liquid heat starting to snake down my back and into the pit of my stomach. This is the closest we've been since the library before everything went to hell.

"Unfortunately, budgetary constraints prevent the administration from giving their poorly paid tenured faculty access to healing drafts unless we go to the clinic." He presses a length of thick gauze to my leg and looks back up at me. "But I'm guessing that's the last place you want to go right now."

Tears fill my eyes again before I rein myself back in. I chew the inside of my cheek, refusing to look at him again. "I don't want to go anywhere."

"Okay. Don't." There's a level of warmth in his voice that instantly brings me out of my head and into the library. His hand steadies my leg, but his touch winds through me, causing my heart rate to quicken. I ignore it because I have to. I can't think about... everything that happened, the things I accused him of, what I said and did. What he said, which was true.

What I've done. Tonight. Minutes ago, and the unraveling happening while I just ran.

He spends several minutes doctoring the wound and then moves on to wiping away every trace of blood. I barely move. I keep my mind locked on the present, refusing to go over what happened, but it's impossible. Just the thought of my great-grandparents causes fresh waves of tears to boil to the surface, and by the time Alex is done, my face is glazed, and my eyes are most definitely bloodshot, but he doesn't say a thing about it.

He's watching me closely, though. While I bleed blood through the bandage he just wrapped around my leg, he bleeds an aura of thick, unshakeable, but silent, concern. He rises, looks me over, those eyes so blue it's like looking into the deepest, most turbulent depths of the ocean, and reaches for me, cupping my cheek.

When he brushes my tears away with his thumb, I cave.

The silent whimpers turn to a rush of choking sobs I desperately try to bite back, but it's useless. I'm a mess. A blubbering, uncontrollable mess.

He remains there, sitting next to me on the bed, his thumb stroking my cheek while I come completely undone at the seams.

"What happened?"

He could ask me a million different questions–like how I not only disappeared into mist under his line of sight but reappeared less than an hour later in his condo. He could ask why I came here, of all places, but I don't have an answer to that other than I wasn't in control.

He smooths his hand down my arm to my wrist, which is bare, the missing weight of my bracelet another reminder of what I've done.

"I killed someone," I whisper, and his eyes meet mine again and hold.

"Was it justified?"

Was it? Can I honestly say I did the right thing?

"Yeah," I whisper after a moment, and he nods like this is just another conversation that normal, rational people have.

"It wasn't your first time, was it?"

I shake my head. I don't know how he can tell. He just nods. His eyes are so soft, so warm as he wipes my tears away, then he lifts me up and scoots me over onto his pillow. He turns off the light on his way out of the room, taking the wastebasket with him. I curl into myself, my tears less of a torrent and more a dripping faucet as they soak into his sheets, and watch his shadow break up the light spilling from the hallway. I listen to the scrape of glass and the swish of a broom. My eyes grow heavy, but my mind won't stop. I should get up. I should leave. I'm in a sweater and my underwear, but I can walk to my condo. It's only across the hall. No one would see.

"Do you want to talk about it?" The mattress sags when he sits on the edge, his hand a solid weight against my hip.

I curl into the touch, nuzzling his pillow to dry my tears, and shake my head.

"Okay."

"I'm sorry."

"You have nothing to apologize for." He cuts me off.

"I think I do." I finally look at him. "You know I do."

"Everything you said to me in my office was correct. You were right. You can't apologize for that."

"I–"

He leans down and presses a kiss to my temple, lingering there for several seconds, his lips just brushing my skin, my hair. I close my eyes, letting the sensation ripple through me, wondering again why something that feels so right also feels so wrong.

"You scared me," he admits in a whisper. "When you disappeared like that. I knew something was wrong. You left your phone behind. It's on a charger and has been buzzing every three minutes."

"I should have told you what I could do."

"It wasn't that. I've learned to expect the unexpected with you. It was your face. You looked–" He cuts himself off when I start to tremble again and rises enough to look down at me, smoothing his hand down my thigh. He reaches further down and fists a blanket he draped over the corner of the bed and pulls it over my bare legs. The sudden absence of his touch leaves me shockingly cold. "That look on your face made me want to do very bad things to whoever you were talking to on the phone."

"My dad." I take a breath, and it's much needed. My lungs allow an extra pinch of air, and my mind begins to clear, my thoughts untangling.

"Maybe not, then."

I laugh, and he smiles, pleased, I think, to hear that sound instead of the constant whimpering.

"Whatever happened is over now. It's late."

"I should go home."

"I'd like you to stay." There's a command in his voice that cuts through the steady, gentle hum I'm used to. "Please."

"The fact I'm bleeding isn't bothering you?"

"It'll bother me a lot more knowing you're hurt and out of my sight."

"You have no reason to be this nice to me, not after what I said to you."

"You meant what you said, and you were right," he reiterates, but he pulls the blanket up to my shoulders, expertly tucking me in. He leans down one last time to press his next words into my hair, and if I were able to bend, I'd be on my knees again. "So did I."

27

YOU ALL ALONG

Skye

I SLEEP THROUGH THE NIGHT AND WAKE TO THE GRAINY RED NUMBERS on the clock on Alex's bedside reading 8:43 A.M.

I don't normally sleep this late. I'm usually in my office by now, or in one of the lecture halls or research centers, but right now, I'm curled under a thick blanket that smells like Alex, resting my head on his pillow, watching the minutes tick by on his clock.

When I slide out of his bed, the door to his bedroom is ajar, but not by much. I realize with a small squeak that I'm in my underwear and the sweater I wore yesterday, but in the same instant, I notice the sweatpants and sweatshirt resting on the edge of the bed, neatly folded, with a new, sticky bandage for my knee on top.

So, this all really happened. It wasn't a bad dream.

I killed my great-grandfather. My beloved great-grandmother is dead. I lost my bracelet, am now a murderer, all things considered, and crash-landed in Alex's condo when he had no idea I could spirit across an entire kingdom without so much as lifting a finger.

And I was bleeding. Heavily. In the presence of a vampire.

I absolutely swim in the oversized hoodie. I roll up the waistband of the sweatpants and glance at myself in the mirror hanging over his dresser. I look like someone chewed me up and spit me out, but it doesn't matter, does it? I can't stay long. I need to go back. I need to go to Maatua, or Moonrise, where my dad is at the moment, and… I don't know. I don't actually know what needs to come next.

I step into the kitchen. Alex is leaning against the kitchen island with his laptop open, papers scattered across the smooth granite surface. He straightens, eyeing me with interest and a brush of concern, then looks back down at his computer with a sigh. "Hungry?" he asks.

"No. Not at all."

He types something out at a great rate of speed before shutting the laptop and pivoting to face me, his arms crossed over his chest.

I hesitate before asking, "What?"

"Where are you going?"

"Home. I suppose. I didn't mean to come here."

"I'd like for you to stay. For a while, at least."

"Why, Alex?" My voice cracks, but his eyes hold mine with an intensity strong enough to make the distance between us feel heavy and unbearable.

"Because something serious happened to you last night, and you came here–to me."

"You're not responsible for me."

"What happened?" His tone leaves no room for argument.

When I sink onto the couch, he turns to the stove and sets a kettle on a burner. I don't say a word until he places a cup of tea with milk and a whole hell of a lot of sugar on the coffee table in front of me, and even then, I can't find the words to explain. I'm startled by the scrape of a chair being dragged across the floor and look up as he comes to a stop, straddling one of the bar stools, his eyes firmly fixed on mine.

I swallow past that annoying, lingering, unbreakable knot in my throat and instantly feel like I'm being interrogated. Maybe I am.

"I should go to my office."

"There's no point. The entire campus is locked down, remember? No classes, lectures, or lab access for a week, at least."

I exhale, nostrils flaring. He arches a brow in challenge. He motions to the tea. I lift it, holding it between my hands to warm my aching, chilled fingers. "I can essentially teleport anywhere I want."

"I noticed."

I bite back a rather colorful retort in response to his entirely dry tone. "I got a call from my dad. My great-grandma was.... She hadn't been feeling well recently, I guess, and never recovered. She died." I can't bring myself to meet his eyes. I take a sip of tea instead.

"You mentioned you killed someone."

"Alex... I don't know how to explain this to you." Grief tangles in my chest.

"I want you to try."

"Why? Why does it matter? Why do you even care?"

"Is it not obvious?" he asks, his voice strained. "Or do I need to spell this out for you in mathematical terms?"

"Can you?" I'm half joking. Goddess, if he could actually do that? Turn emotions and feelings into an equation I can easily understand and decipher? Everything would finally make sense. When he only fixes me with an expectant look, I cave, curling inward around my mug of tea. "I can do things with my powers, but you already know that. I can see thoughts, memories, desires...." I hold his gaze, wishing he could just look into my head and pull the truth from within like I can. Sniffling, I continue, "My great-grandfather is special, like me. His powers were gifted, however. At least, that's what we think, and my great-grandmother was normal. A shifter who lived a long, beautiful life. She died, and my great-grandpa couldn't go with her." Tears fill my eyes, but they don't fall this time. "He couldn't go. He didn't want to live without her but couldn't leave our realm without help, and my dad... I think he refused him, but I... I did it. I pulled his life-line from the tapestry, cut it to length with hers, and they died together. But it wasn't his time. I forced it. I went against the Goddess's plan and–" I bury my face in my hands.

Alex is suddenly in front of me, taking the mug off my lap and setting it on the table. I sense his proximity before he kneels, moving my hands away from my face.

"I know you can't possibly understand," I mumble, searching his eyes. "I know it sounds insane."

"You did what you thought was right."

"It was what he wanted, and he knew I'd do it."

"And then you came here?"

I nod.

He nods as well, like all of this makes sense to him. "You didn't murder him, Skye. What you did was merciful. It was right."

"But I might as well have killed him in cold blood, just like the last time."

My fingers are chilled to the bone as a childhood memory sweeps through me. I can smell the familiar air of that townhouse in Moonrise like I'm there, and Alex's couch is my childhood bed. His voice, calm and soothing, is replaced by Mom's screams of pain and the crunching echo of a fist meeting her chest and stomach over and over again.

"I wanted him to stop hurting her," I say, but my voice is cold and distant. "So I stopped him."

Alex stares at me, not understanding. Maybe he doesn't understand any of this. Maybe this is useless, and I'm just a murderous freak of nature—like I've believed myself to be all my life.

"Show me," Alex says under his breath.

"What?"

He takes my hand and slowly rests the tip of my fingers against his cheek. "Show me."

"I could hurt you."

"You won't. Do it." He grips my fingers.

I take a breath and let go. My powers are unrestrained for the first time in many, many years. Since I was a little girl, actually. When I still had the freedom to dream—or have vivid, terrifying nightmares and prophecies that rendered me speechless.

Using my gifts like this is like stepping into a movie of my memories. It's one-sided, of course. My perspective of events that I was too young to understand. I let him see it all, showing him things I can't put into words. That day, when I was seven or so, when my dad sat in the backyard of that townhouse and taught me how to use my powers to pick out the agates in that big bucket of rockets I used to hide behind the tree. I didn't know him as my dad. I just knew my mom was happier around him and felt safe with him, and that made me trust him right away. My child-brain wanted my mom to feel safe and happy, and Blake made her feel that. I liked him. I wanted him to stay and play with me.

My thoughts move to the day I threw coins in that fountain in the temple that no longer exists, while my parents reunited after seven years apart. I show him the lake in Moonrise, and the sun glimmering on the rocks on the beach, my old room, the bed where I killed a man with my mind and nearly killed myself in the process.

And when I show him that memory, his grip tightens on my fingers, and I feel the tension in my chest loosen for the first time in… weeks. Maybe years. Maybe for the first time in my entire life.

My mind drifts, on its own accord, like pages being flipped in a book. Suddenly, we're in the recent past, in Maatua. Rain is thundering across the roof while my great-grandfather looks me in the eyes and tells me to do it, and I do.

I flinch, but Alex grips my hand in solidarity, in a silent command to continue.

I could show him my entire life. It's possible. I could just let my memories flow like opening a tap. But my memories scatter, the more present ones slipping out of reach. He catches glimpses of himself through my point of view–pieces of my thoughts when I'd found out he was a vampire, my overwhelming and incessant desire to be bitten, and how I still haven't quite come to terms with why I want it so badly. My confusion. Our emotionally charged fight in his office after Laney was murdered. The fact that I'm teetering on the edge of what I feel like is oblivion when it comes to him. How I want him. Not like we are, but more. Something big and stupid and real–because he's the only person I've ever known who sees me behind my tangled thoughts that don't match my facial expressions. He's the only person who gets it.

He said it. I didn't want to believe him. So I shoved him as far away as I could.

There was one person who got me, especially when I was young. My parents don't count. Sure, my dad knew me like the back of his hand because he and I are one and the same, but Posey got it. I would beg and plead to be allowed to go visit her in Veiled Valley. Alex sees this new line of thought and the memories it brings up–me, in the dark, gothic castle babysitting their eldest son, Fennec, Fen for short, when their second son was born. Me, sitting in Posey's alchemy room, talking about my first crushes and new friends while she made new charms for the bracelet I just lost.

"It stops me from dreaming like I used to," I admit, testing the new charms against the weight of the old ones.

Posey purses her lips, eyeing me like she can see right into my mind, and gosh, I wish she could. "You're confident now in your training and powers to not wear it anymore, if you want. You're fifteen, Skye. I made this for you when you were only nine. You don't need it. It's a crutch, but you're stronger than that now."

Another memory bursts through, popping the image like a bubble, and suddenly, I'm in the observatory, as a child, sitting in those familiar scratchy chairs, but I'm not looking up at the simulated stars and planets.

I've always wondered why I used to have visions about that place. I'd come to the conclusion that it was just visions of my future. That's the easy answer, isn't it?

"I'm going to cure her," he says, clutching his brand new science kit like it's the most beautiful, most prized possession he has.

I look at the boy from my memories and see him clearly for the first time.

I tear my hand away from Alex's face and stare at him. He slowly opens his eyes, taking a ragged, heavy breath before meeting my startled gaze.

"You," I choke out, confused, alarmed, I think, at this strange connection. "You've–how–"

"I don't know," he says quietly, but he doesn't seem shocked at all.

"You knew? You–you remembered me?"

"I knew who you were the moment I got a good look at you at that party at the beginning of the semester."

I rise, and he follows, towering over me. "Why didn't you say anything?"

"What could I have said? That I used to have weird dreams as a little boy about a shifter girl? That I woke up one day, and those dreams stopped? You were a figment of my imagination, Skye, until a few weeks ago."

And look at us now. Somewhere, in the aether, our tethers have crossed. Him, a vampire. And me...

I rise on my toes and press my lips to his. He tugs me close, a silent, unwavering confirmation that he's been waiting for this moment, his lips parting to breathe my name.

28

I DON'T LIKE TO SHARE

Skye

ALEX MOVES US AWAY FROM THE COUCH, TAKING TWO STEPS TO THE SIDE and pressing me against the smooth plaster wall. I breathe in his scent, closing my eyes against the sensation of his hands closing around my hips, his body flush to mine. It's like the library but... *better*. We're *alone*. There're no wandering eyes, no whisper-hissed lead up to this–to *this*. His lips part over mine before he leans in to kiss me like this is the first time all over again.

I make an involuntary sound–a moan, a noise I doubt I've ever made, and Alex sighs into the kiss, turning it from exploratory and measured to something wild and more passionate than anything I've ever experienced before.

His hands travel up the curve of my waist until he clutches my ribs, his thumbs resting precariously near the slope of my breasts, which ache with an intensity I'm not prepared for in the slightest. I feel deliciously heavy. I feel... warm and out of control in a way that would normally have me spiraling, but now?

He pulls away ever so slightly, panting a breath as our eyes meet in a silent question.

"Don't stop," I whisper, desperation lining each syllable.

I wait for his argument, for his infuriatingly rational mind to take over and ruin this for both of us. He leans in, the tip of his nose brushing mine while his hands travel upward, slowly taking me in by touch, and it's impossibly intimate being mapped by him.

I understand how his mind works, which is why I think this has been so fucking difficult. We're the same. Every move, every step, every decision we make, no matter how small or tedious, is a grand production–something calculated and meticulous.

I want to just let go for once. I don't want to think anymore. I don't want to see. I just want him in a dark room, guided by touch and feel.

That's all I want. It's what I need.

His lips press to mine in a strangled kind of kiss, like he's slowly losing himself, and when our eyes meet again, I witness his mask slip. His heated gaze sears mine from the inside out. Molten heat licks down my spine and spreads like wildfire over my skin when he inhales and braces one hand against the wall beside my head, the other dragging down my waist again.

"We're on dangerous ground," he murmurs, his voice low and deep, followed by a breathy sigh and the scrape of his fangs against the top of my ear.

"I know," I jab back. "You've said it before. You're a vampire. You could kill me. I get it. You've made your point. Now, I'm going to make mine."

His mouth tics into a wry smile that turns to a grimace within a second.

I rise on my toes and drag my tongue across the column of his throat before biting down–not hard enough to break the skin, but enough to leave a bruise, enough that he can feel it.

Shifters bite, too. A lot. My wolf whines with excitement and heat. Alex presses me hard against the wall, his grip on my hips hard. "What do you think you're doing, wolf?"

"I'll do it again," I warn, but he kisses me, and I giggle against his mouth as he picks me up and carries me into his bedroom.

It's only when he tosses me unceremoniously onto his bed that my nerves begin to creep in. He slowly takes off his shirt. His muscles ripple–tight and roping–with every move he makes. His black hair is ruffled, his cheeks flushed a deep, ruddy red, and his eyes?

They burn the brightest blue... for me.

I slip off my shirt–his sweatshirt. I'm not wearing anything beneath but panties. My fingers catch on the fabric, however, and I squeeze, trying to banish the memory from, Goddess, several years ago, out of my head.

He leans forward and braces his hands on either side of my feet at the end of the mattress, bowing his head and taking a breath. When he meets my eyes again, it's clear as crystal that he has sensed my hesitation–whether it's the jumping, erratic beating of my heart or the way I'm pulling inward–however vampires do it.

"Have you ever done this before?"

"I'm twenty-eight–"

"It doesn't matter. You don't strike me as someone who casually has sex."

"Is that what we're doing?"

He narrows his eyes. "Skye."

I roll my lower lip between my teeth. His eyes roam over my face and dip down, his jaw tightening when his gaze hones in on my breasts, and that deep, unsatisfiable hunger returns, painting his face in shadow against the bright burn of his blue eyes. He's sharper than I've ever seen him, like everything that makes him a vampire is now on display. I can see how he's dangerous. His otherworldly speed and strength. The power of his jaw. His fangs.

He's a killer.

But he's mine.

"I have a thing about... things that I think belong to me," I try to explain.

"Like your precious rocks? I've noticed."

"Wh–wait a minute. I very kindly allowed you to look at them."

"That's what I mean." He smiles softly. "The look on your face when I stepped closer to examine the rock you were holding in your office made it clear you're exceptionally territorial, even for a shifter."

"I think it goes beyond that in this case."

"What are you trying to tell me, Skye?"

"It's stupid."

"I doubt it."

I crumple the sweatshirt in my hands but feel surprisingly warm despite being mostly naked. I can feel his gaze everywhere, like he's drinking me down, memorizing the soft curves of my body and new angles no one else has seen.

"Every time I like someone, which is hard for me… well, the last time I slept with someone? He found his mate right after. And it wasn't the first time something like this has happened. I kiss someone, and they find their mate. I have a crush and suddenly…"

"I'm a vampire. We don't have mates."

A ripple of relief skitters through me. I meet his eyes, feeling suddenly bashful. "Are you sure?"

"You think I'm going to sleep with you and change my mind?" His shock, and, if I'm being honest, disgusted expression makes me feel almost like I'm being scolded. "Skye. I've wanted you for a very long time."

"But I have this thing, this matchmaking ability. That–I don't have a mate in my tether," I try to explain, but my thoughts jumble. I could show him? No, that's ridiculous. "I don't have a fated mate. For whatever reason, as far as I've been able to see in the tapestry. You know, the stars? The prophecies…. I don't have one, but everyone else does, and I have this uncanny ability when it comes to falling for someone and them being led right to their person, and it's never me. And I don't want to share you with anyone else." My yelp of surprise swallows my words. Alex has me by the ankles, dragging me down the mattress and pinning me with my arms over my head.

"I thought I made it clear what happens when a vampire feeds on a shifter, but I think something might have been lost in translation."

"You speak perfect–" The air leaves my lungs in a whoosh. I draw my thighs up, Alex resting between my legs while leaning over me with an elbow braced on the mattress. His other hand holds my head to the side, giving him access to my neck, where his tongue sweeps and circles over a very specific spot, and an even more specific bruise still painting my skin slightly yellow.

"I told you we couldn't do this again because I was sure I could remain neutral about my feelings for you," he says against my skin. "I was lying to myself and to you." He bites down–hard–hard enough I nearly screech in a strange, mangled sense of pleasure and pain. I writhe under him, but he holds me steady against the bed, forcing me to submit, and I love it.

He takes pull after pull until I am nothing but a puddle of sensation, my body loosening with each slow thump of my heart. He grinds against me, our hips flush, and I feel his cock pressed hard against my center through his pants.

"I think about you all the time," he says, then licks the wound clean. "Not just your blood. You. All of you. Your voice haunts my dreams. I can hear your heartbeat across campus. Watching you lecture, enthusiastic about everything? It's my undoing. I want you. This isn't natural for either of us. We're different, Skye, but fuck, I would do anything to be inside of you right now. The rest can wait."

He's right.

The next few seconds are a blur of the rest of our clothing falling off our bodies. As inexperienced as I am, every touch, every frantic, heated kiss feels utterly, overwhelmingly natural, like this moment was written in the stars, and maybe it was.

I know what this is, and it has very little to do with us. I want him. He wants me. Our wires are crossed, and our minds are out of sorts after several hellish days of death and grief. But we have each other right now.

That's all I need.

I think it's all he wants.

Just me. Like this. His arm wrapped around my waist and hauling me to the center of his bed. His mouth pressing kisses down the flat of my stomach to the juncture of my thighs. His tongue parting my folds and his hands spreading my thighs apart while I cry out his name. I arch off the bed with every suck, lick, and gentle bite, and he groans into the sensation of me coming unglued in his hands.

"I'm going to bite you again," he warns, his voice low and gravelly with desire, and he bites down on my inner thigh, his finger still inside me, his thumb drawing slow circles over my clit, and it's... magical. He bites me again and again, awakening a primal, starving beast inside of me. My wolf is just as surprised as I am by how insanely perfect this is–him and me. Me and a vampire.

"Vampires bite for fun, don't they?" I ask with a breathy laugh when he finally comes up for air, his lips slightly reddened and swollen.

He chuckles low, pressing kisses up my belly and over my breasts, pausing to lick and suck my nipples until I'm falling back into his trance again, my eyes heavy with a pleasure I didn't know was possible. He hovers over me, our bodies flush, his cock pressed to my lower belly–rock hard and hot. His body radiates warmth, I think, because of me, like I bring him back to life in a strange way.

"We do bite for fun. It can be a teasing or loving gesture, a lot like shifters nipping each other while in wolf form." He nips my shoulder for emphasis, and I smile until my cheeks hurt. "You're not much of a biter, though, I think."

"I bit you earlier," I argue. He nudges my thighs apart.

"I hardly call that a bite. You should practice."

He holds my gaze. Seconds pass with us just looking at each other. I think he might be hesitating. Changing his mind. Maybe vampires can have mates, and he's sensing it now–and it's not me.

But he slowly presses a kiss to my lips, lingering there, sharing a breath as he eases his cock through my entrance. It's a tight fit. Almost too tight. I gasp in a breath, and he closes his eyes, cursing quietly, overwhelming me with his touch and weight.

"You're mine now," he says, his voice distant and dream-like. "I don't like to share either."

29

I CAN NEVER GO BACK

Alex

13 Years Ago...

EMMA GRABS MY TREMBLING HANDS, TURNING THEM OVER TO CHECK for injuries I already know aren't there. Beyond the blood-splattered stone walls, another battle rages, an endless swarm of bodies against the glow of torches and bonfires dappled over the countryside.

Red velvet and tarnished armor scatter at my feet while my cousin sucks in a breath, her ocean blue eyes meeting mine. "What have you done?"

"Go to the nearest clinic outpost and find a way home to Crimson Peak," I urge, my voice trembling. Below, at our feet, dark, almost black blood pools around my shoes, spreading toward Emma's boots. Tangles of platinum hair float in a crimson current.

"Alex–"

"Go. Now." I grip her shoulders, squeezing tight, leaving bloody prints on her healer uniform.

"Alex? Alex, what have you done!" Emma sobs as I push her out of the puddle of blood, her boots leaving sticky tracks across uneven cobblestone. An ancient temple in horrendous disrepair rises around us, blocking the rain and the chaos beyond the shattered stained-glass windows.

"Don't look. Don't look at her, Emma. Please. Go. I am begging you to go."

"Oh, my gods. Oh, my gods! Alex!" Her wail of despair slices through me like a knife. I gather her to my chest, shushing her, begging her to keep quiet. A shadow darkens the doorframe, and Drake, her twin brother, steps in out of the downpour, blood dripping from his armor. His mouth is stained black, fangs on full display.

"What–" His eyes lock on the body behind us and widen. "Alex!"

"Get her out of here!" I shove Emma into his arms. They stumble back, but Drake whirls on me, grabbing me by the shoulder and tossing me into the wall. Chipped stone bounces down from the ceiling, scattering around the body–the headless body–painting the room red.

"Tell me," he pants, delirious, "exactly what happened."

"No. You have to get out of here before anyone sees us." He slams me against the wall again, and I grunt, wincing as bright pain laces through my battered torso.

"He's hurt, Drake!" Emma cries out, but Drake's eyes are glued to mine. He's so like his dad–my uncle Michael. It's amazing, honestly, how shifter sensibilities can bleed through overwhelmingly vampiric-leaning genetics when hybrid blood is involved. Drake bares his fangs at me, but his face–his warmth–the glossy, heated death in his eyes? It's all shifter.

"She had to die."

"Not by your hand," Drake argues.

"I had no choice."

"Emma, leave!" Drake barks, but Emma whimpers, shaking her head. "EMMA! Go!"

"I won't!"

Drake clutches my throat to keep me still and snarls at his twin, who bawls, torn between keeping her eyes on me versus her brother.

"Please go," I beg her, tears welling in my own eyes. "Please."

"No! We all have—we all need to leave! Together!"

"There's nowhere to go, Emma!" Drake's frantic, struggling to catch his breath. "Queen Matilda's army has the village surrounded."

"I can get out." I clutch his fingers, which are digging into my throat to the point my words come out as a scratchy, breathless grimace. "I'll run, and you'll take her head. Her army will back down when they realize their leader is dead. It's over, Drake."

"Her son is still alive," Drake argues. "Kai is worse than Queen Matilda ever was!"

"This was her last stand. Her people are disillusioned. You know it's true. Your father was—he's coming to your aid by morning. The witches are arriving any minute to help. This is your chance to be—to be a fucking hero. Take her head!"

Drake holds my gaze. A decade of war-torn memories flood between us. Two kids—we were two scruffy boys with scraped knees and a propensity for being exceedingly naughty. We grew up together, attached at the hip, like our fathers had. He was the closest thing to a brother I'd ever have. One day, we were ten years old playing war games, imagining what it would be like to be soldiers and heroes, and the next, we were training for a moment exactly like this.

It wasn't enough.

"Go north to Starlit Tundra," Drake says after a long, heavy pause.

Emma shrieks the word, "No!" but her voice is lost to the pounding in my temples and the warmth spreading from several stab wounds on my abdomen.

"Keep going north, past their settlements, until you can't go any further."

"What's past Starlit Tundra?" I ask weakly, and Drake… smiles.

Gods, in another life, had we not been princes, the heirs to our fathers' kingdoms, we would have been explorers. We would have been the ones to discover the fabled lands of the ancient fae gods and their proteges—the Goddess's own people the shifters here talk about so often. Like the golden woman that his mother, Faye, and his shifter grandmother, Emory, told us stories about. The people who could heal my mother. The people who could stop tyrants like Queen Matilda with a single twist of their wrists.

"I don't know, but you can find out."

"Don't!" Emma screams, but Drake lets me go, and I slip into the darkness, holding my stomach to keep my entrails from falling out of my shirt, and I run.

ALEX

THE PRESENT...

I NEVER ALLOWED MYSELF TO HAVE ANYTHING THAT WOULD KEEP ME shackled to one place. Not until I finished my PhD, and a prestigious postdoctoral position made me forget who I was. It was easy to forget my past and true identity. I was blinded by knowledge not yet available in my world. By science. By drills and beakers and miles and miles of glacier blue ice. Nothing else mattered for an entire decade. I ate, slept, and bled my research. I let it consume me until I was a shell of the man I was when I ended a bloody war with my bare hands and made it impossible for me to ever return home again as long as the son of the monster I killed walked free in our world. Hunting me.

Then I saw Skye for the first time, and she forced me to remember. She forced me to remember all of it. Which is why I tried so damned hard to keep her at arm's length. Falling for someone? It was out of the question.

But I'm a scientist. A fucking biologist. I know better than to assume things like attraction and desire are within my control.

This is so much more than that.

She cups my cheek, her eyes hazy with starlight. "Where'd you go?"

"I'm here," I whisper and kiss her again, like I've wanted to kiss her for weeks now, putting every ounce of feeling and energy I have between us.

Skye's body is a masterpiece of the Goddess's design. She's all soft curves and warm, peachy skin that tastes divine on my tongue. Her dark hair frames her face like a halo, reflecting soft lamplight like burnt gold and the deepest, heaviest wine.

Her lips part in a breathy moan. I'm barely inside her but already riding the edge of something powerful and overwhelming I've denied myself time and time again. Her inner walls quiver, squeezing in rhythmic waves that force me to brace a hand on the bed and slow down before I ruin this moment for both of us, ending it far too soon.

She mouths my name, her eyes open to slits bright with desire. Beautiful. A miracle of science and nature. She is what I was looking for all this time, isn't she?

Her fingers dig into my sides. I stroke deep, watching her, noticing the little line between her brows that forms when she concentrates on the new sensations building inside of her. It strikes me then that she's only done this once. Just once. I shove aside the acute feeling of jealousy that ripples through at the thought of anyone else, especially someone who couldn't even come close to worshipping her like she deserves, seeing and touching her like this, and thrust.

She gasps, drawing her legs up and locking her ankles at the base of my spine.

"Like this?" I draw the words over her cheek and thrust in deep again, the bed frame rattling against the wall, and she sighs sharply, arching her neck.

I can't help it. She shivers, gripping my arms, while I nuzzle her neck and inhale. She smells like the deepest vanilla and amber, like everything soft I want to fall into and never resurface, but it's her blood that drives me insane.

"Take more," she begs, drawing scratch marks down my back with her nails. "Please, take more."

I bite down on that little cleft between her neck and shoulder and suck deeply. She gasps, muttering something whiny and unintelligible, but cants her hips against mine, meeting me thrust for thrust, slow and deep, stroke for stroke.

I can taste the adrenaline surging through her. Her pleasure makes her blood rich and heady in a way that doesn't seem real. She's delicious. I'm obsessed. I can't get enough. I'll never get enough.

The bed creaks and shutters beneath us. Her pussy tightens, spasming, and I let go of her neck to curse and growl wicked, utterly deranged things in her ear as she comes multiple times. It's crazy. We're both insane. This can't continue, but I'd rather die than ever give her up.

So I won't, even if the conversation we have next is going to gut me.

I pull out, spilling onto her lower belly, barely making it in time. She's limp beneath me, her skin damp with sweat and pink from exertion. I press my forehead to hers, breathless, riding faint waves of pleasure still surging through my body, but when I open my eyes, she's looking up at me with that questioning expression that pulls me back to the present instantly.

"Vampires and shifters can… procreate."

"Ah," she says with a sleepy smile. "I was wondering."

"And I don't taste a single shred of contraceptive tonics in your blood."

"You can really tell?"

"I doubt I'd be able to differentiate between tonics, but you taste incredible."

Her eyes light with curiosity, and I'm hard again. I'm out of my mind when I press inside of her once more. Her lips part, and she exhales slowly, sinking into a shared sensation of awe. She's swollen and likely sore, so I'm gentle, taking my sweet time, reveling in the feeling of her and the little sounds she makes.

It's almost an hour later, our bodies spent and slack on my bed, which is a tangle of sheets, when she lifts her cheek from my chest and looks up at me, her violet eyes dimmer than usual. "I have to go back to my family, don't I?"

I brush my fingers through her hair lazily. "Yeah. You should."

She lies back down with a soft huff, her body curled against mine while starlight dances over the ceiling. Wind funnels against the windows, sending flurries of ice crystals shattering over the glass, but inside, it's silent. So quiet and warm I can hear her heart beating, and my body hasn't been this relaxed in a very long time.

I lean over and brush a kiss over her forehead. "I can talk to the university president for you."

"About what?"

"Bereavement leave, of course."

"Oh. Right."

"And us." I lean out of the way, allowing her to look up at me again. "Because people are going to find out about us, and I'd like to get ahead of any rumors."

She peers at me skeptically, the furrow between her brows deepening. "You being a vampire and me being a mystic?"

"No," I laugh. "Us. Whatever this becomes. The university has strict rules about relationships between employees, so while you're gone, I'll make sure everything is settled before you return. Plus, my secret is still safe. I've only told you and… Toby."

She jumps up, turning to face me. "You told Toby?!"

3 O

FACE THE MUSIC

Skye

AN HOUR LATER, IN THE HAZY, BLUE GLOW OF MORNING, THE STARS ARE still on full display like always, but at their dimmest now. Alex follows me across the hallway to my condo. The university is at a standstill, and the tension pours through the thick concrete walls. I'm used to silence, but this is something else entirely.

"Can you water my plants while I'm gone?" I ask with a touch of hesitation, looking up at him through my lashes while he leads the way to the loft where I mentioned I keep a suitcase. I watch his shoulder shrug through his soft gray shirt. His hair is mussed from lying in bed with me for the better part of an hour, and he radiates a new kind of warmth that's hard to put into words.

Alex is perplexing, but I knew that. Now, however? After being in the throes of passion with him? Having him touch me?

It's almost like his mind is split into factions all the time—hyper-focused on preservation. Now, he's not wearing his usual masks. He's looser, freer, and shockingly gentle.

It's almost too much for me to process after everything that's happened.

"Of course, unless you think Abby will be territorial." He drags the suitcase out from under the futon propped on the far side of the lofted second bedroom/office space I haven't used since moving in.

Before we came here to pack a few outfits and whatever I'll need to face my family after killing my great-grandfather, he told me the damning news that he told Toby the truth. He told Toby he is a vampire, and apparently, that came on the heels of both him and Toby witnessing me disappear into the aether. A double whammy of epic proportions.

"I haven't talked to her," I answer, turning on my heel to follow him back downstairs like the lost puppy I feel like at the moment. Thankfully, he's moving with confidence, carrying the heavy suitcase like it weighs little more than a feather, like he knows what drawers my shirts and underwear are in and how many socks I should pack for what I assume will be a week or more away. Like he's already memorized me and my space.

It's comforting. I imagine this is what Dad feels like with Mom. Having someone who knows you so well and can anticipate your needs without voicing them? It has to be rare, doesn't it?

"I can sense your mind moving a thousand miles an hour," he says over his shoulder with a wry smile. "What are you thinking about, Dr. Abbot?"

He sets the suitcase on the bed. I busy my hands by grabbing random clothing items and tossing them inside while he leans a shoulder on the wall and crosses his arms to watch.

"We had sex."

"We did."

"And… now you're helping me pack… for a trip back home to face my family. And I'm the reason we lost both great-grandparents in one go."

He tilts his head to the side. "I thought we worked through that."

"I don't know what I'm supposed to say to any of them, especially my father and great-uncle."

He rolls his lower lip between his teeth, his gaze grazing the side of my neck. I shiver under the weight of his attention.

"And, your student was murdered, and now the university is locked down pending a thorough investigation–"

"Skye?"

"And we had sex. And Toby knows that you're a vampire, and I'm– I'm something that disappears into thin air and–"

"Hey!"

"And you want to tell the president we're together so we don't get in trouble."

He kicks off the wall and takes me by the shoulders. "Look at me."

I can barely bring myself to look him in the eyes, but I try. He exhales deeply when I glance away again, frustrated.

"Does it bother you that I'd like to clear things up with the administration about us?"

"It just doesn't feel that pressing, given everything else we have on our shoulders."

"I want this as clear as I can get it. I have not allowed myself the simple pleasure of being with someone in over ten years. Even before that, it was damn near impossible. The thought hasn't once crossed my mind, but now there's you."

I slowly look up at him.

"We're being very stupid, Skye," he continues, and I bite back a laugh because he's so right. Gods. He's never been more correct about anything, I'm afraid. "But I've decided something."

"Oh, yeah?" My voice trembles just a touch.

"I'd like to try, at least. I'd like to try this with you."

"And what does that look like for us?"

He lets go of my shoulders and takes the stack of clothing from my hands, arranging it neatly in the suitcase while pondering his answer. "I want you." He braces his hands on the suitcase to close it, leaning his weight against it. "I want to explore that... often." He grits his teeth, and I realize he's never done this before. He might be... more inexperienced in matters of love than I am.

"Alex?"

"Yeah?"

"Do you want to be my boyfriend or something?" Goddess, how old are we?

"Very much so," he says, clearing his throat and throwing me a slightly incredulous look, but I laugh until tears well in my eyes, and he takes my face between his hands and kisses me. "I hate the way that sounds, but I don't know what else to call this. But I have to mention the fact that I am on limited time here in Lunaria. I have another decade until I need to weigh my options."

"Why? You're on track to be the dean of your department." The answer strikes me in the chest. "Oh. Right. You don't age."

"Right." He lets me go and bends to zip my suitcase. "Among other things."

"You need to repeat how we're incompatible. I'm more concerned that you're feeling like this under duress."

"Duress?"

"We've had a terrible few days," I gut out, more forcefully than I meant it to sound. "I just mean... I'm a mess, and you have the weight of Laney's death on your shoulders, and possibly another vampire here killing people."

"All of those things are for me to handle, and I am. How I feel about you has nothing to do with that. That's a totally separate feeling I'm still working through."

"And Toby–"

"Toby didn't have much to say about me being a vampire. He was more concerned about the fact that I was actively trying to talk myself out of letting myself have something that was mine. Something good and natural. You." He scrubs his hand over his jaw. "Why is it so hard to explain this?"

"Because we're scientists, and love is the one thing that defies all natural law?"

We stare at each other for a moment, and the tension fizzles, floating away on a phantom breeze. His smile is small and boyish–slightly cocky–like that explanation is exactly what he's feeling. I know because I feel the same.

I want things to make sense. I want to see it in front of me and in writing. Feelings, on the other hand, go against my nature. His, too, I suppose.

But I already know that's a bald-faced lie.

He's a vampire. A creature of feeling and instinct. I'm a mystic. A creature of visions and prophecy. We've both spent our entire lives fighting those senses.

"When I come back, we need to have a conversation about the fact that you were in my dreams when I was a girl. I need to explore that more."

"Why?" he asks, genuinely curious.

"Because dreams aren't random," I say with certainty, gripping the suitcase handle. I could use a shower and a cup of coffee, but I already know that the more time I spend here with him, the less confidence I'll have to face my family and deal with the motions coming next. A gathering. A funeral. The conversations that must be had. Me, who's never truly felt like I fit in, now likely the family pariah if anyone else gets the notion I was the one who took Isaac's life.

Alex sits on the edge of my bed, leaning back, casually watching me as I adjust my sweatshirt collar, my fingertips brushing over the spot on my neck he's particularly obsessed with, and I catch his smile.

"I was more gentle this time," he says.

"What are you going to do when it comes to blood while I'm gone?"

"I've gone weeks without it before, Skye. You don't have to worry about me."

"I will. You know I will. You could come with me?" The panic in my voice is palpable.

"I can't. The sun is too bright there."

"Oh, right." I look down at my hands and curl my fingers on my free hand into a fist, shoving it into my pocket.

He rises and walks to me, taking me in his arms, making me feel whole and small—making my world smaller for a moment.

He doesn't ask how I'm able to jump through realms and land

wherever I wish. He simply tucks my hair behind my ears and steps back, his arms crossed over his broad chest, and nods.

And I force myself to let go and just do it.

The world swirls with fractals of light before a new room comes into focus. Sunlight pours through large windows, highlighting a sunken living space and wall-to-wall fireplace. I let go of my suitcase, which tips to the side with a pop, the zipper, which was on its last leg anyway, cracking open.

Footsteps sound on the other side of a long, plastered wall, and then Mom is standing in the opening leading to the kitchen and dining room, her hands curled around a coffee mug. I glance down at my watch. It's not even 7:00 in the morning here.

She takes a breath and motions for me to follow her into the kitchen, but I stop under the archway.

Three more sets of eyes take me in.

Maeve rises from her chair at the dining room table with coffee in hand and arches her brow at me before glancing at Mom with a knowing expression that cuts me to my core. I wait for her to say that they all know I killed Isaac.

Fallon, with her golden-brown hair and the sea-green eyes she shares with her mother and younger sister, Naomi, who is sitting beside her at the table, ends up being the first to speak, and it's not what I expected.

"Well, you've arrived just in time," she says with a bite in her voice, which elicits a glare from her mother.

I accept a cup of coffee from Mom, who looks weary and uncomfortable as she looks at Fallon.

"Have arrangements been made for the funerals?" I quietly ask, but tension fills the room like poisonous gas just waiting for a spark.

"Not yet, but your grandparents are working on it. We'll all be traveling to Crescent Falls soon. Your dad is still in Maatua making arrangements for their bodies."

"Oh," I reply, glancing around the room at Maeve and her daughters. "Then what–"

"Fallon has been proposed to." Naomi chuckles, and Fallon rolls her eyes while Maeve looks... murderous.

Mom squeezes my upper arm as I stare at my cousin. Fallon is only twenty-one, barely in her majority power-wise, which is a thing for witches, especially Firestone witches like her.

"And I've accepted," Fallon says flatly, flipping her hair over her shoulder.

"You have not, and will not, accept," Maeve says sharply over Naomi's chuckles.

"What have I missed?" I ask the room and then settle my gaze on my mom, who sighs, looking like she's been refereeing the three Firestone women all morning.

I catch Fallon's gaze, noticing the faint swirls of power behind her eyes. She looks totally, completely resigned. Her mind is made up.

31

HER LIPS ARE SEALED

Skye

FALLON CLOSES HER BEDROOM DOOR WITH A SOFT CLICK AND GLIDES across the room to shut the curtains. She moves with the practiced grace of the princess she is–Maeve's heir who will one day be Queen of Eastonia–and she looks like it, walks, and talks like it as well.

But I know Fallon better than most. She's an enigma–soft and stoic on the outside, but on the inside?

She's the most animated, opinionated woman I've ever known.

"You cannot tell that bitch Naomi I'm telling you this."

"Your sister Naomi?" I arch a brow, chuckling, and she rolls her eyes to the gilded ceiling.

"We've been on the outs recently."

"Over what?" I sink onto the edge of her rather regal bed. I've always liked Fallon. She's six years younger than me but an old soul at heart, and for a while, it was just the three of us–her, Kieran, and me. We also grew up in Moonrise together, and that gave us a rather close bond. She was incredibly angry when I announced I'd be staying in Lunaria for the foreseeable future.

"You've missed so much, Skye." She pinches the bridge of her nose and faces me, her lavender gown fluttering around her ankles. She's like something out of a children's book. Beautiful, with thick, golden brown hair and delicate features against a backdrop of almost golden skin. She looks rather like the fae that occasionally visit Moonrise–striking and ethereal–and Naomi is the same, but darker, with dark brown hair and porcelain skin inherited from Maeve and Ella.

Fallon looks like her father, Soren.

"She keeps taking my things without asking." Fallon rests on her vanity stool, her posture still impeccable. "And... she's taking Mom and Dad's side."

"On this asinine proposal? I have to agree, Fallon. Just because you're a princess, it doesn't mean you still have to play the marriage game. You're a Firestone, too, for Goddess' sake. You'll rule Eastonia one day, and whoever you marry won't even hold a title."

"This is the first time in over two decades that an emissary from KiloKilo has reached out to anyone in the Allied Kingdoms."

I shift my weight, crossing my legs. "Essentially demanding you marry one of their princes, or else they wage war? That is insanity!"

"They won't." She rises again, pacing, tapping her freshly manicured nails on her arm. It's a warm, early winter day. Sunlight bakes the room, casting her in a halo of golden light. "They would be the insane ones. Your grandfather's army in Crescent Falls is already enough to cover that threat, let alone my mother's forces in Eastonia. The Alpha Kings of Celestoria and Lunaria would involve themselves like they always do. Hell, I'm sure Pantharas would heed a call to aid if asked nicely."

I'm speechless. "What exactly has happened since this summer?" It is always like this when I return to Moonrise, to my family and the drama that constantly seems to ensnare us. It's quiet in Lunaria. My whole life there is just my research. Ice. Textbooks. *Alex.*

I take a breath, reining myself back in after his memory attempts to sear me from the inside out. Fallon, however, notices my slight cringe and glides closer. "What exactly have you been up to in Lunaria? I've heard rumors."

"Oh? Of what?" Surely she can't know about Alex. I haven't told a soul.

"Well, Aunt Misty said she caught a male scent on your clothes the day Maddy and Isaac died."

I lick my lips, narrowing my eyes at my cousin–several times removed, I believe, but still. "That was her concern?"

She flashes a *very* rehearsed princess smile. "Well, it definitely took the pressure off my shoulders when it came to my engagement for a moment, and may have hidden the fact that you gave Isaac what he asked for in the end when no one else would."

The temperature in the room drops by thirty degrees at least. I don't ask how she knows. I don't have to. Fallon has always had an uncanny ability to manipulate answers out of everyone. It's not a magic trick or a stretch of her highly trained powers, either. It's her. Fallon has been, and will always be, able to get away with anything.

And right now, she's doing her best to back me into a corner so I'll tell her the truth before she starts picking apart my facial expressions and body language.

The good thing about Fallon, however, is that she can actually keep a secret.

"Do you want the truth, or will that ruin the game you're playing with the family right now?"

"I'm not playing games. The decision of whether or not I accept a proposal from KiloKilo's royal family is my choice and mine alone. No one in our family or any royal administration has set foot in that kingdom since my aunt Brie washed up there decades ago. We don't know if they're a real threat or not, but if they are, we're going in blind, and I don't like that." She crosses her arms under her chest and lifts a brow in challenge.

I have nothing to argue against there. "They're wizards."

"I'm aware."

"They may be looking at this... union... for their own gain when it comes to you marrying and producing heirs for their bloodlines."

"Obviously."

"And you're all right with it?"

"Of course not, but look at me." She shrugs, tapping her fingers on her forearms. Little sparks of crimson and amber light snake around her pointed fingernails. "It's a smart move on their part. I also find it highly advantageous. Naomi and I are powerful in our own rights, of course, but then you have Sterling... who can't do shit other than shift. Imagine a child of both a Firestone and a wizard, whatever they officially call themselves bloodlines."

"Are you on the outs with all of your siblings?" There are only three of them, despite Maeve's efforts to have as many daughters as possible toward the Firestone repopulation effort. I have vivid memories of my cousin Sterling's birth, however. He's only sixteen now, the youngest of the trio, but when Mom took me to visit Maeve and the new baby, Maeve told her that her Firestone ancestors made it clear to her that she only needed two girls and that Sterling was a gift–something both she and Soren wanted desperately.

I, of course, spent several years poring over the idea that external forces other than our Goddess were at play but found no concrete evidence either way, which was infuriating and frustrating, but I digress.

"Sterling is my favorite as it stands," she concludes, picking an invisible thread from her dress before crossing her arms tight again. "But whatever. I find this entire proposal-nonsense anything but. Look at the political climate as it stands. Your great-grandparents were the last true tie to Maatua's royal family, and the relationship with them has shifted greatly over the years. The generational gap is widening between the current players in power and the group that started all of this."

"Isla and Maddox?"

"Yes," she says, sniffing indignantly. "Maatua knows KiloKilo is a threat but uses Maddox's seemingly close relationship with their Grand Wizard at the time as a safety net that's no longer there, but they can't see that. I can. Plainly. KiloKilo's territory is massive, and Maatua is right there next to it, locked out by that pesky veil. And, what's just past Maatua?"

"Crescent Falls and Veiled Valley, I know."

She shakes her head, growing more frustrated by the moment. "I have an opportunity to see inside and get a feel for whether or not these people can be trusted and whether we should flex our powers as a family again and deal with it, once and for all."

"By marrying a stranger?"

"Is that so bad?" She's dead serious right now. I want to scoff, to tell her she's being insane, but I think I might have fallen in love with someone recently, and ever since then, everything I thought I knew about the world makes less sense. "Anyway. Enough about me. What exactly are you up to in Lunaria?"

"You know what I do for a living."

"I do. Seeing as your research into our solar system and beyond has greatly benefited our church and the mystics who think you're the second coming of the Goddess, I guess I don't need a run-down. But you're seeing someone?"

Here we go. "I am."

"Is he as brilliant and boring as you?"

I frown at her, but she's beaming, mischief shining behind those incredible sea-glass eyes. "He is as boring as he is brilliant, yes."

"I thought so. Oh, the aunts had a field day over the prospect of you finally finding someone." She crosses the room to toy with the bottles of perfumes and tonics on her vanity. "But he's not a shifter, is he?"

My heart falls into my stomach as intensely as a car wreck. "How–"

"Don't play dumb with me, Skye. I'm not going to tell anyone. I will enjoy, however, being the one who knows this juicy secret while everyone else spends the next twenty years guessing." Another radiant smile. She's so good at this. Goddess, she will be the queen everyone either loves or fears one day. As it stands, Maeve is more feared by other kings than anything–and otherwise worshipped by her people. But she's a young queen, and the first full-blooded Firestone to hold the title in over three-thousand years. It's all still new, which means Fallon has an unbearable amount of pressure on her shoulders already, and that has given her an unnatural ability to get her way.

"I don't think I have twenty years with him," I reply, curling my knees against my chest, sunlight playing over my toes. The castle all around us buzzes with energy while the royal family, and mine, prepares to travel to Crescent Falls by train. Some royal promenade in honor of Maddy and Isaac.

"Oh, so it's just casual? That's disappointing." Fallon runs a comb through her already perfect curls but catches my gaze in the vanity mirror's reflection and slowly turns to face me. "Or is it something else?"

"Do you remember Misty talking about the war and how she went through that portal?"

"Of course. That's a famous family story. What about it?"

"Well, the description of the people she saw—the women?"

"A shifter and what our beloved ancient Arthur believes is a mythical beast called a… vampire?" She arches her brows.

"Yeah."

"Yeah… what?"

"They're not so mythical."

Her spine straightens vertebra by vertebra. "Tell me more."

"You cannot say a word to anyone."

"Who would I tell?"

"It doesn't matter. It's for his safety."

"Interesting," she muses, tilting her head as she inspects my expression from across the room. "You actually like this man, don't you?"

"I do, but it's complicated. We haven't had a lot of time to discuss things between us, but it's clear we have feelings for each other, and biology may get in the way." I take the deepest breath and spill my entire heart to the only person in the Allied Kingdoms who knows how to keep her lips sealed.

Fallon's expression holds nothing back. Shock, confusion, suspicion, and awe. Those emotions tangle over her features until she's bent at the waist with her chin resting on her fist and hasn't blinked in over a minute.

"Has he told you why he had to leave his kingdom?"

"Kind of? I guess…. He killed someone important–a queen, I believe? He told me in such a rush."

"And you haven't just looked into his head yet?"

"No–I can't. It's not like looking into a witch's or shifter's head. It's totally different."

"Do you think he's somehow responsible for the murders in Aurorium? Skye, if he is–"

"He's not."

"But you said he killed someone important. That there was some kind of war going on where he's from. Is he being hunted?"

The idea of that spirals through me, slicing me open. "He's been in Lunaria for a decade. It seems improbable."

"Yet, he's so sure his kind has no idea our allied kingdoms exist?"

I nod, but Fallon leans back, and she does not look convinced.

"You can't say anything."

"I won't, but I want something in return."

"What? Anything."

"You won't help prevent me from going to KiloKilo when it's time."

32

RED-EYED MONSTER

Alex

Skye has been gone for four days when I knock on the door to President Alloway's office. Her voice is pinched when she mutters, "Come in," but her eyes light up the second I open the door and step inside.

"Dr. Scarlett. I wasn't expecting you, but I'm happy to see you." She rises and motions for me to sit in one of the armchairs in front of her desk.

I shake my head. "I won't be here long."

"I've been meaning to reach out," she says, easing back into her chair while I lean a shoulder on her office door to close it, remaining there, taking in the slate gray walls dappled with diplomas, certifications, and pictures. She tucks her bright white, stick straight hair behind her ears and clears her throat, closing her laptop. "Dean Kanten hasn't been responding thoroughly to my inquiries into the biology department and how he plans to move forward, safety-wise, after Laney's death."

"That does not surprise me."

She blinks and then motions again for me to sit down. This time, I accept the invitation, realizing that the one thing I came here to talk to her about just grew by leagues. I'm barely in the seat before she asks, "How are things in biology?"

"I can only speak for my department."

She waves a hand in dismissal. "I know that's not the case. Now that the warriors from Aurorium are starting to go back to their territory, and things have settled enough for student spaces to reopen, and people can mingle…." She meets my eyes with a sharply knowing look. "I have it on good authority from your colleagues that you and Kanten have a tense relationship."

I lean back in my seat. "That's not far from the truth."

"Then what is the truth?"

I glance at the same floor-to-ceiling windows I have in my own office. Dr. Alloway has an impressive view of campus, which is lit up like a star. "Despite his numerous awards, and his extensive background in the biological sciences…" I meet her gaze again, "I find him to be an arrogant, irresponsible scientist and a worse administrator."

A wistful smile touches the corners of her mouth. "Can you elaborate?"

"Is there a reason you're asking me about Dr. Kanten?"

"Isn't that the reason you're here?"

"I was actually hoping to talk to someone from campus resources, but most of the administrators are still locked out of their offices, and I was sent here instead."

She purses her lips and sighs heavily, twisting a pen between her fingers. "I'm only asking because I'm obligated to ensure the safety of our faculty and students. Several of your colleagues mentioned the tension between you and Dr. Kanten but wouldn't go into detail, citing how you tend to keep your life exceedingly private, as well as your research. Your lab, as well, is an exclusive place."

"Not exclusive enough for Dr. Kanten to completely ignore every email and maintenance request for the past four years." I lean forward, resting my elbows on my knees. My phone buzzes silently in my pocket, alerting me to a text, likely from Skye, who's been sending me updates the past few days–pictures of Moonrise, the train she just boarded, which she'll be traveling on for the next two days on her way to Crescent Falls. Meanwhile, I send her pictures of the plants in her office, pictures of watering her plants as proof I'm not neglecting them, and pictures of her precious rocks. I smile at the thought of her, then notice the slight tilt of Dr. Alloway's head. "Dean Kanten and I have been at odds for as long as I can remember. It's personal. He took issue with the research I chose to write my thesis on when I was finishing my PhD."

"Because it contrasted with his own research?"

"It devalued his published research, yes."

She takes a deep breath, letting it out with a whoosh. "I actually remember that."

"Then you'll remember the ethics committee got involved."

She nods, flexing her fingers before continuing to fiddle with her pen. "He's a difficult man to work with."

"He's purposefully ignoring me and my lab, and it has nothing to do with what exists below the ice. It's personal. He doesn't like me and has his own bias when it comes to me, my research, and the way I go about things, but that should have no bearing on the safety of my lab."

She looks down at her hands.

I continue, "Our sensors need to be replaced. Desperately. For years. We work closely with the engineering department, as you know, and they've been helping us fix the sensors, but repeated repairs have worn them down, and we can't trust the readings. A cave-in would be catastrophic, and something we have the technology to avoid, but as it stands, Kanten won't sign off." I don't say it's about the price, but I can see the truth settle in her eyes.

"I'll sign off on new sensors."

I nod, murmuring, "Thank you." I know I could go into detail about my issues with the dean, but that's not why I'm here, and I have a rather busy afternoon.

Alloway doesn't seem to care as she rises and paces to the window overlooking campus. She's essentially the Alpha here–the queen. "He didn't even know Laney personally, and she was a star student within the biology department."

"I know. I was the one who called her parents after finding out he'd alerted them about her death via email."

Alloway turns to face me. "I can assure you, the board is aware that Kanten isn't doing his job appropriately, and there's movement on that front to possibly replace him within the next year." I nod again, closing my eyes to hold back the chuckle threatening to break the dam of curses and raw rage I want to let out, but then she says, "And you're a front runner when it comes to who will head the biology department."

"No, thank you," I say without even needing to think it through.

This shocks Alloway, who looks confused and slightly alarmed. "You'd be dean–"

I rise, tucking my hands into my pockets. "I understand. However, I have no interest in any position other than where I am now. I enjoy being out in the field, in my lab, and with my students." She parts her lips to argue, but I press on, continuing, "And I didn't come here to talk about Kanten or my career trajectory."

She purses her lips, a deep line between her brows telling me exactly how she's feeling–annoyed. Likely frustrated and wondering why anyone would turn down the idea of moving up in academia. "Then why were you wanting to speak to campus resources? I assumed it was because of Kanten."

"I am in a relationship with a colleague and need to alert the administration."

"Oh." The furrow between her brows deepens. "May I ask who?"

Here we go. "Dr. Skye Abbot."

"Oh," she murmurs again, pinching the bridge of her nose. "Well, now, this all makes sense."

"I don't know what you mean."

She walks back to her desk and sits, opening her laptop and clicking a few keys. "I'll ensure Maisie is aware and will email you the paperwork you both need to sign." A knock sounds on her door, and she invites the person in–a board member, which is effectively my dismissal, but I sense something unsaid–something that shines through the way her heart began to beat with more fervor when I said Skye's name, and I don't like that.

I explain as much to Toby, two hours later, while walking briskly through Aurorium, bundled against the elements and washed in ever-present neon light.

"Alloway's always been kind of weird," he says with a shrug, the words leaving his tongue in thick puffs of mist. "Like she's had a stick up her ass since the moment she was born."

"I don't think it had anything to do with her personality," I argue, stepping out of the way of a trio of wolves pulling a sled weighed down by crates. "I'm under the impression she thinks my relationship with Skye is somehow influencing my decision to not pursue the position of dean when she cans Kanten."

"Why would it? Skye is a tenured professor now. She can stay here forever with a nice paycheck if she wants to. It's not like you can follow her anywhere sunny–" I grab his arm and pull him to a rough stop. Toby chuckles, shaking me off. "Sorry man, but I had to. You gave me a wealth of things to give you shit about when you finally admitted you're not just an anti-social dork but a vamp–"

"Don't say it out loud," I hiss. Another group of shifters pass in their wolf forms, eyeing us with interest before slinking into the neon glare bleeding onto the icy street.

"All right, all right," he gripes, tilting his head toward the shadow of a large box-like structure at the very end of the block. It's a warehouse, technically, and serves as a shipping hub for the territory, but also a bulk store. It's also where we get most of our supplies for the lab. "So, do you, like, want me to grab you some extra blood samples? Or should I stop in at the butcher's? What's your flavor? Reindeer? Just a bucket of blood or what?"

"I'm going to fucking kill you."

He laughs heartily and turns toward the warehouse, waving me off. "I'll be about ten minutes. I'll meet you back out here."

I huff a breath, watching his form fade into the shadows, and turn toward the post office. The bundle slung over my shoulder weighs against my back in a way it shouldn't, based on its contents. I step into the fluorescent warmth of the snug mail room and go through the motions of choosing a box that fits, buying a shipping label, and answering the endless questions of the mail tech in regard to shipping batteries and biological material. This bundle is none of those.

I stood outside Laney's dorm room yesterday while her roommates were let back in for the first time after her murder. Watching two twenty-something young women bleakly pack up Laney's things, tears streaming down their cheeks, had enlightened me to who Laney was. She wasn't just a mousey, shy lab tech. She was a friend. A daughter. A kid with a whole future ahead of her that was stolen with very little to show for it.

I slide the box of her personal belongings across the counter and watch the mail tech carry it into the back, which feels like closing the chapter on Laney's life in a way I don't know how to process.

I step back out into the frigid darkness and start walking back to the warehouse, but I'm not alone.

Across the street, a plume of cigarette smoke catches my attention, and I stop when a figure comes into focus under the glare of a streetlight. Hooded, with his face cast in shadow, he could easily pass as a local—someone out on an evening stroll and a vice.

But this man is standing far too still.

Instinct swallows my rational mind in one bite.

He takes another slow drag of his cigarette and then flicks it onto the ice, slowly crushing it with his boot, and tilts his head into the light.

Red eyes confirm what I've been battling with over Laney's murder and the previous murders. Of course, the bio-markers in the case I worked for the Beta of Aurorium didn't align with any genetic profiles on hand. They wouldn't have because I've never given blood here, and up until recently, I was the only vampire in Lunaria.

"Prince Alex." Kai smiles, fangs on full display. "It's been a long time, hasn't it?"

I step off the curb, walking determinedly in his direction, not a single thought in my mind other than my fangs slashing across his neck, like it would be that easy. He grins, backing into the darkness, his voice reaching me even when he falls out of sight, "What a life you've built on lies. Does she know who you really are? Or will I be the one to tell her all your dirty little secrets before I drain her to nothing and turn her into what you despise the most?"

I snarl and lurch into the darkness, sprinting after the blur of shadow weaving between buildings. Kai turns a sharp corner, sliding, his cloak billowing out behind him, carrying the scent of cigarettes.

I slide around the same corner, but the thick tread of my boots slows me down significantly, and when the next alley comes into view, nothing's left of him but scattered newspapers and several knocked over garbage cans.

I bend at the waist, panting, resting my hands on my knees while my lungs expand and sharply contract. I'm so out of practice. I've been cosplaying as a shifter and a wizard for so long. I've let my previous skill set fall by the wayside. I've forgotten why I'm here.

"Fuck," I rasp, straightening, trying to catch his scent, but he's long gone.

33

THAT CAN NEVER HAPPEN

Skye

I'VE BEEN IN THE SOUTHERN ALLIED KINGDOMS—MOSTLY MOONRISE—
for a little over a week but haven't faced my father yet. I anticipated
that. I knew he'd be busy helping make arrangements for Isaac and
Maddy with my grandpa Sydney. What I didn't anticipate is this.

Ryatt stares at me from across the coffee table in the castle in
Crescent Falls. He's dressed in his usual black but looks like a modern
man in a finely fitted black suit and tie compared to his cape and
rugged dark ensembles I'm used to seeing him wear in Eastonia. He
hasn't blinked in what I'm sure is several minutes. His acute, quick-
silver stare bores holes in my reserve, but I refuse to be the one to
fold and start the conversation he wants to have.

After several days of travel on the royal train, forced to witness the
epic fights between Fallon, Naomi, and Maeve, I could sit here in
silence and play this game with him for hours.

Family members, both closely and distantly related, filter in and
out of the room, but no one pays us any mind. I'm sure my dad will be

arriving soon. He's at the temple currently helping prepare for the public funeral taking place this evening.

The private affair for family and close friends is in an hour, here at the castle.

I fold my intertwined fingers over my kneecap and tilt my head while peering at my… great-great uncle? I've lost the lines of connection somewhere in the aether. It doesn't matter, though. His genetics run deep and strong in Maeve's line, with Sterling being an absolute spitting image of his great-grandfather to the point I often confuse the rare pictures of Ryatt in his early twenties with Sterling. Sterling, who is currently hovering in the archway that leads to the private drawing room on the second floor, watching our staring-contest with interest, isn't a Shadowsynger—not like Aris and his sons, at least. Some shadow magic curls between his fingers, but it's the fire in his mismatched eyes that has made me wonder what exactly he'll be when he's old enough to shift, which could be any day now if he's an early wolf like a lot of the men in our family.

Still, he narrows his silver-blue eyes on Ryatt and then glances at me, arching a brow as the mind-link connects between us.

"*Need assistance?*" he asks.

I shake my head, and Ryatt turns his head, noticing Sterling lingering, and glares. He ducks out of the room and into the shadows without a second's hesitation.

Ryatt slowly looks back at me.

My phone buzzes in my purse, like it has been doing all morning, but I've been too busy with family to check. I missed a call from Alex last night, too, which is really throwing off my senses. Irritated, I lean back against the cushions and cross my arms beneath my chest. "Mind-link? Or should we do this out loud for everyone to hear?"

Ryatt rises, his voice booming through my head. "Follow me."

"Fine," I grumble out loud and collect my belongings. I follow him through the castle, which is absolutely buzzing with lifted conversation. The air is scented with rose petal tea—Maddy's favorite, and no one but me and Ryatt is wearing black. That's because Maddy specifically stated that when she died, she wanted it to be a party where people laughed, smiled, and hugged–not wailed and cried until their cheeks burned.

I suppose we get a pass as the black sheep–or wolves–of the family.

I nearly trip over three of Josie's golden-haired children as they speed down a staircase leading to the fourth floor, not a single tear in sight.

Maddy would be delighted.

"This is Isaac's worst nightmare," Ryatt says, closing us into Ella's old painting studio. Cobwebs hang heavy from the rafters, shimmering with dust, which glimmers in rays of sunlight peeking through cracks in the boarded-up windows, but my eyes light from within, turning the otherwise dark room into shades of deep violet and silver.

Ryatt takes in the room, running his fingertips over the ridge of a severely aged canvas, tucks his hands behind his back, and faces me. "How did you do it?"

I decide not to dance around the subject. "I cut his thread in the tapestry to match Maddy's."

"Was it that easy?"

"He was a very old man, Uncle Ryatt. You can imagine how thin the threads become when they're no longer weaving and knitting into the... grand scheme of things. He wasn't an active player in the Goddess's game anymore."

He searches my eyes for understanding, I presume. I'm sure the average person wouldn't be able to even remotely understand what I just said, but he does, in his own way.

He's Isaac's age, but the Goddess isn't done with him yet. I'm sure he can feel it, which is why I keep that to myself.

"He didn't feel any pain," I add, and Ryatt nods.

"I'm sure the pain of losing Maddy and living on without her would have been worse than death."

"Then you understand why he asked me to do it? I wouldn't have just killed him if it hadn't been what he wanted."

"I know."

"Then why stand there and glare at me?"

"Because I'm trying to understand what makes you so different from your father, let alone the rest of our family." He paces to what's left of the windows, prodding the graying wood keeping the room dry and in darkness. "Blake is extraordinarily powerful, but you haven't shown the same signs he did when he was young. Still, I'd be willing to bet that you're closely aligned with his level of power."

I shuffle from foot to foot. "If you're wondering why Dad didn't do what Isaac wanted, you'll have to take that up with him."

"I have." Ryatt leans his shoulder on the wall and fixes me with a rather serious look. "And there's something that needs to be discussed after the funeral."

Unease skitters through me like the mice that now inhabit the room. "What do you mean?"

"It's about your future and how that plays into what the mystics have seen since Isaac's death."

"What are you—"

"There you are!" Misty steps into the room, disrupting decades' worth of dust in her wake. "You know the floorboards are thin enough to hear you walking around and murmuring? The kids are now convinced there's a ghost up here." I hold Ryatt's gaze. Misty quiets, cutting herself off abruptly. "Am I interrupting something? Sarah's about to start the funeral. Everyone's gathering in the ball-room." Ryatt's nostrils flare, but he turns and leaves the room, his shoulders rigid with tension. Misty frowns after him but turns to me. "What happened?"

"I'm not sure," I murmur, catching her eyes. Then, I bow my head and quickly step around her to join the family in saying goodbye.

After this, I can go back to Lunaria. I can continue on with my life and my research. I can pick up where I left off with Alex, and while sitting in a chair between my mother and Grammy Leona, watching Dad, who immediately picks me out of the crowd and gives me a withdrawn look that skitters up my spine and blooms into unease, I think about him. Alex. Not my grandparents. Not the slideshow of pictures being presented for close friends and family who gathered here today. Just him.

I wonder if we'll have a chance to sip coffee in the morning together like the intimate picture of Maddy and Isaac, so young, with Maddy pregnant with my grandpa and great-uncle Ryan, her hand resting on her belly. But of course, we won't. Alex doesn't do coffee because he's a vampire and drinks blood, and also when we had sex, he made it sound like–

"Skye?"

I blink, and the numerous chairs around me are totally empty. Voices drift from the garden, where early winter light spills through the grand doors leading to the perfectly manicured rose garden, where guests are now gathered.

Dad sits beside me while I straighten and look around. How long was I trapped in my head?

"Were you having a vision? I noticed you're no longer wearing your bracelet."

I blink several times to wet my eyes after so long spent staring off into space. "No, I wasn't. I was just–I lost track of the moment. I've had a lot on my mind."

Silence threatens to settle between us like we let it settle in the two weeks since their deaths, give or take a day or two. I've never gone this long without speaking to him since I was a child, and it feels strange and unnatural.

I've also never lied to my dad.

I have to start.

"I don't think what you did was wrong," he says, admitting defeat, which I know is hard for him. "I reacted the way I did because I worried about how you'd feel after the fact."

"Why didn't you do it? He asked you. I saw it. He showed me everything while Maddy was dying."

"Because he's my grandfather, and the idea of–" He bites down on his lip and turns his head to look at the small shadow edging into the ballroom. Mom gives him a tight, but knowing, smile, nodding at him discreetly to continue... like she knows he's been walking on eggshells around this conversation.

I feel almost bad for her, given that she's mates with the most stubborn man in the Allied Kingdoms, who also has an inability to express his emotions, and their daughter is exactly like him.

"I felt sad that they died, but I didn't feel like what I did was unforgivable, if that's what you're worried about. I've been fine."

I can feel him staring at me. I finally meet his eyes–identical to mine. Swirling with the same power.

"Has your...." He looks away, his cheek going a deep, rosy red. He clears his throat and looks like he wants to crawl out of his own skin when he asks weakly, "Has your boyfriend been supportive?"

"My boy–Dad!"

"It's all anyone can talk about."

"Who told you?"

"Misty caught a male scent on your clothes." He grits his teeth like this is the most uncomfortable thing he's ever had to do–and this man has been tortured, nearly killed several times, and essentially abandoned his family... twice.

But he knows nothing else because Fallon kept her word, like I knew she would.

"I'm twenty-eight years old, Dad."

"I am aware."

"I also don't have a mate in my tether, which you know."

He rolls his eyes to the ceiling. "It can easily be wrong."

"You know that's not true. Anyway, yes, I am seeing someone, and he's... he's a good *man*." I cringe at the last word. Dad looks at me, scanning the pained expression taking ownership of my face. Before he can pick me apart, I go into as much detail as I possibly can about Alex. How he's a scientist, a biologist, a paleomicrobiologist at that. What he's studying currently and his research into the Goddess particle. I even tell Dad about how Alex thinks I'm made of it–the same exotic matter I've been chasing in the heavens, trying to map. But the more I say, the more I realize that... Dad will never meet Alex.

Because Alex can't come to a place like this.

That truth sinks into me like an anchor, fixing me to the chair.

"Your mother and I look forward to meeting him," he says, but it's clear he's not looking forward to the idea of any man being within five feet of me.

He'd be losing his shit if he knew what Alex is.

Which is why he never can.

But… I'd have to choose between them, wouldn't I?

Not if I stayed in Lunaria forever. Not if Alex remained, somehow, tucked away somewhere safe where he'd never age while I turned into a wiry old woman that he had to push around in a wheelchair.

"Skye, you're doing it again. What are you seeing?"

I think I might actually be having a vision now because my thoughts tangle, those screeching voices ripping through my head despite my attempts to keep them subdued. It's so easy to stay in control when I'm with Alex or researching. My mind is a single track—not outside noise. But here? With hundreds of tethers now dancing in my line of sight and the tapestry fading into… white curtains lifted in a smooth breeze. Sunlight—so much of it. A bundle in my arms. A baby's cry, and my mom's hand squeezing mine.

The sound of ice crackling overwhelms what Mom whispers to me, and the vision fades before it even begins, turning to the violent blue of the deepest tunnels in Alex's labs, and the sensors that… don't work.

I gasp as the vision screams to a stop in a shatter of ice. Dad grabs my shoulders. I can feel his powers trying to press past the wards I've been trained to keep up since I was only a little girl.

"I have to go!" I shout, my voice trembling. I shove him off and let my powers rip through me like a rogue wave, praying I'm wrong.

I'm rarely ever wrong.

34

COLLAPSE

Alex

"WELL, SHIT," MARK, THE ENGINEERING DEPARTMENT HEAD GRUMBLES, crouching to get a better view. He braces his hands on his hips while huddled around the same screen I'm sharing with Toby. He's been knocking his head on the ceiling of this tunnel all evening, but that has more to do with his height and less to do with the already overly cramped quarters we're sharing. He's from the Deadlands and built like it. Burly and broad, he stands several inches taller than me, and I'm taller than most men on campus, but he has at least sixty pounds or more on me, and it shows. They breed them big in the Deadlands, supposedly. Toby's words; not mine.

"Shit," Toby parrots, shaking his head as the drill several hundred feet below us whirls and kicks up liquid sediment.

"I wasn't expecting a water pocket." I curse under my breath, rolling my neck to try to alleviate some of the tension. We've been at it all day long. Drilling, drilling, and drilling some more–trying to secure a perimeter around the fossil we found weeks ago and finally got the extra funding we needed in order to explore it. I was correct, as was Abby, who's currently up in the lab watching the footage on a similar screen and feeding us the data we need to determine just how far we've gone and need to go. But now?

I look up at the sensors on the walls. Only a few are blinking green while the rest remain totally dormant, which shouldn't be the case.

Toby just works his jaw, grimacing. "Did you feel that?"

"Feel what?" I motion for Mark to adjust the drill arm slightly to the left before turning it off. The drill will spin for several more minutes before winding to a stop, but this is as far as we're getting today.

"My ears popped."

I look up at the sensors again. Still green. I don't think I trust them. What I do trust is the data pouring in from up in the lab, and Toby's unfortunately right. "We're done here for now. The pressure is dipping to unsustainable levels–" An earsplitting crack rips over our heads.

Mark goes very still and then looks up, flakes of ice falling onto his lashes. I take a breath, trying to calm myself, and tip my head up.

It's a hairline, but it's there–a crack that splits the low ceiling of the ice tunnel in half directly above our heads. Spiderweb-like fractures spread around its main channel, but then it stops, and a low rumbling vibration echoes toward us in every direction.

"We gotta get out of here," Mark says, rising as much as he can, a wall of bright yellow nylon. "I don't think that's because of the drill, though. That was an earthquake."

"He's right," Toby confirms, motioning to Abby's continuous data. "We–"

Another ear-splitting roar shatters Toby's voice. The tunnel shakes violently, rolling like a wave. The walls of the tunnels splinter and crack off in small chunks. Mark grabs Toby by the hood of his parka and throws him toward the dark entrance of the tunnel, and I'm right behind them, snatching what insanely expensive equipment I can reach off the floor.

Other researchers sprint into focus, moving like quick shadows out of the other narrow tunnels leading to the main channels, which are wider and more secure with their metal bearings and archways. I'm jostled from every direction while I count heads and shout orders to evacuate, silently cursing the sensors and the fact that I had a conversation about this very thing happening only days ago with the university president.

I'm standing in place when the last of the researchers and lab assistants who signed in to use the tunnels tonight make it into the main channel and run toward the lab entrance, which is just ahead, maybe a hundred yards or so away and around a sharp turn. The channel empties, but then, I turn back into the splintering blue-hued darkness.

Red eyes light from within the shadows, the outline of a sharp, pale jaw on full display.

I blink, and the eyes are gone—a trick of the mind... I think. My senses aren't nearly as sharp as they could be because I've been pretending to be something I'm not for so long. Still, I hesitate. My instincts to preserve the lives of everyone in my lab feud with the possibility of Kai being here, in the lab, moving like the snake he is through the crumbling tunnels—helpless. If he's here and he dies under the ice... problem solved.

But that goes against the person I've been for the last decade. What if my mind is playing tricks on me, and there's a lab assistant somewhere in the darkness, frightened and lost? No—no, that's impossible. I've trained everyone who's ever stepped foot in the lab to evacuate the moment something goes awry.

The sudden screech of the emergency siren jolts me to awareness, but my instincts still prickle, begging me to at least do a round to make sure.

"ALEX!" Toby shouts, skidding to a stop around the corner. "What the fuck are you doing? You need to get out of here!"

"There's someone else down here," I shout back, my heart racing. Based on how I feel at this moment, I doubt I'm wrong. Someone else is down here. I can feel their presence all around me, watching, lying in wait. For help? Maybe.

"Don't! ALEX!" The ceiling above us cracks violently as the ice rumbles again. Shards of glass-like ice tumble behind me. Below me, in the web of tunnels, they spread for at least a mile in every direction, I hear the telltale popping sounds of collapse. The ice beneath my feet is growing thinner by the second.

"Alex! For fuck's sake!" Toby bellows.

I'm wrong. There's no one else here. Just me being a fucking dumbass. Skye would never forgive me if I died here.

I turn toward Toby's voice. "I'm coming. Make sure everyone is getting out of the lab. I want groups of six in the elevators–"

The ice floor beneath my feet caves in. I can't even save myself.

The last thing I hear over the shattering ice is a thick laugh somewhere in the darkness, and I swear on whatever gods still listen, that I see… red.

SKYE

MY POWERS SURGE BUT FEEL SLOPPY AND UNEVEN. I HIT THE GROUND on my knees, my condo in The Pillars coming into focus before my powers reel back into my body. The room spins. The voices of the stars scream through my ears in their unintelligible songs, but then it's quiet, but not… totally.

A strange humming sound erupts through my ears. It grows louder with each rapid beat of my thundering heart. It's an alarm. In fact, my living room is pulsating with red light. I try to stand, but my body refuses to listen, my limbs like Jell-O. I pushed myself too far this time, I fear. I curl my nearly frozen fingers into fists and give myself approximately three seconds to regain my composure before pushing upright. I sway, stumbling into the kitchen, and catch myself on the wall near my door. My coat is still hanging on the hook. I pull it on, trying to calm the voices screeching in warning, realizing too late that years spent ignoring my powers and focusing too heavily on the hows and whats of who I am and why the stars play such a huge role in our magic made my senses weak and my powers overwhelming to the point that my training feels obsolete. I've been stupid. Pretending for so long I'm something I'm not. I chased a future meant for a person with divine gifts, and now I'm paying the price... because something is terribly wrong, I could have–should have–been able to sense it long before it happened.

I'm barely down the hallway in The Pillars when I reach a crowd of faculty and professors standing outside one of the exits to the greater campus. Everyone is dressed for bed and ruffled–some donning bathrobes and slippers. It is well into the middle of the night here, which makes sense. I always forget about the time difference.

I scrub my hand over my tingling face while trying to side-step through the crowd, but I'm stopped by a hand on my wrist.

Dr. Gerralde stands beside his mate, a tiny woman in her early sixties or so in a bonnet and rollers, blinking blearily up at me. I've met Agatha a few times, but I don't know her as well as I know Dr. Gerralde.

"I didn't realize you were back," he says, tugging me closer while the crowd swells.

"I got back a few hours ago," I lie, rising on my toes to look out over the heads swarming the exit, which is closed despite several attempts to open it using badges. "What's going on?"

"I have no idea," he answers honestly, his voice heavy with exhaustion, like the alarm pulled him from a deep sleep. "We're supposed to evacuate to the commons if this alarm goes off, but we're locked in, apparently."

"Do you feel that?" I ask, motioning to the floor and walls, which feel like they're vibrating slightly.

Dr. Gerralde shakes his head, but then the doors open wide, and the crowd moves with a quickness only possible when self-preservation is in play, and he lets me go to help his wife move through the exit without getting trampled.

I'm jostled but stand in place, closing my eyes to try to separate the movement of the crowd and the vibration of the skybridge.

It's... not the crowd causing the shaking. A jolt spreads across the skybridge in a wave. I open my eyes and watch the floor-to-ceiling windows. They flex slightly and bounce each time the wave expands and returns.

"Oh, my Goddess," I whisper and zip my jacket to my chin, rational thought leaving my mind entirely.

Somehow, I end up in the commons–the wide, open section of campus several stories above the ice that connects to places like the library, cafeteria, and commissary, among other student-leaning spaces.

Everyone is talking over each other while waiting for the president to make her grand appearance. I track familiar faces but can't find Toby or Abby, and I definitely left my purse on the floor where I landed only twenty minutes ago, so I don't have my phone.

"The dorms are being evacuated, too," someone to my right says over the constant murmurs.

"Why?" another voice asks, nervous.

"You didn't hear? That lab–the one under the ice–there was a collapse."

My heart leaps into my throat.

"Are you serious? Oh, my Goddess! Is the entire campus about to fall under the ice? What do we do?"

"Apparently, the engineering team said it's stable enough, but the lab is gone."

Gone. The word ricochets through my head like a death knell. I crouch, hugging my knees, trying and failing to catch my breath while reaching for what little powers I have at the moment. I have to find them. Alex is always in his lab. Toby is usually right there with him. And Abby?

I squeeze my eyes shut for several seconds in thought. My powers are dim. Any stretch to try to scry for their locations would send me into an immediate power depletion, and I'll be more useless than I am now in that situation.

When a thundering of new footsteps signifies the arrival of every single student who lives in the dorms under the ice, I make my move, rising and walking through the increasingly frantic crowd until I'm able to slip into one of the elevators just vacated by the horde.

The alarms sound, but I bypass the security in the elevator with my badge, thanking the stars it worked, and then I'm dropping down into the ice.

I try to steady myself, pull myself back together. I don the same mask I've been wearing for years. When the elevator doors open, I step out into a chaotic mess of maintenance workers and what looks like the entire engineering department and their devices. They're running around like mice, yelling at each other.

"Dr. Abbot! You cannot be down here!" One of them shouts at me from down the hallway. "We've had a collapse. This entire section of campus has been evacuated until we confirm stability–"

"It's stable, for Goddess' sake," I shout over my shoulder, moving briskly down the hallway against the constant wave of red light pouring from the alarms.

"We don't know that yet–"

"I'm a physicist!" I pause and turn toward the trio of alarmed men rushing in my direction to stop me. My hand braces on the wide double doors leading to the biology department's lower offices, classrooms, and labs that aren't housed in their dedicated tower above us. "I know what I'm doing." I push through the door, not knowing what I'm doing, but thankful to have a working knowledge of mass to understand that the likelihood of the entire campus collapsing is so slim it's almost laughable.

Still, the air changes the second I breach the biology department's underground territory. Sniffles and muted sobs reach me over the hum of the alarm, and when I turn a corner, there they are.

A sea of neon yellow.

But someone is missing.

I think I already knew that, though.

3 5

CRUSHED

Skye

Abby catches me from across the length of the hallway. Her dark eyes widen, her platinum hair pulled back from her flushed face as she rises from a crouch and shoves her way in my direction. I have only a handful of seconds to collect myself before we collide. She wraps her arms around my waist and squeezes so tight I lose the ability to breathe for a moment.

"What are you doing here?" she says into my coat, her voice muffled by the fabric. "I thought you were in Moonrise for another week?"

"Tell me everything."

"Everyone needs to move now!" someone shouts at the end of the hallway, and I realize it's Toby directing traffic as lab assistants and postdocs lift themselves up from the floor where they've been trying to catch their breath. Abby pulls me to the side so we're flush against the wall, and people can pass by. There're more people than usual, I think, especially for this time of night.

Toby notices me, and his expression shatters. I realize in that moment, based on the glint in his eyes, that I'm right.

Alex isn't here.

He's down there.

Right below our feet and several hundred meters of ice.

"How?" I ask, my voice cracking with emotion.

Abby continues to clutch me like her life depends on it, and I'm convinced she's the only reason I'm upright.

"We're not sure what started it. Abby picked up earthquake behavior, but that's common on the ice regardless of drilling," Toby begins.

"That's what we were doing tonight. Drilling. Everyone was in the lab—every postdoc, every assistant we could find. This has been a long time coming and an entire production," Abby continues.

"A carefully choreographed dance," Toby confirms, widening his stance. A door at the end of the hallway I know leads to the upper levels of the lab—the elevator shaft and locker rooms—opens, revealing a group of maintenance workers. They pay us no mind as they pass, but Toby looks at the door, taking a deep, resigned breath. "Alex has been planning this for weeks, down to the last detail. The engineers, too. It's been his main focus since Abby confirmed the fossil. Nothing should have gone wrong. We had postdocs in every single tunnel taking data to ensure we weren't risking a collapse while drilling that section. All day, everything was fine. No cracks. No pressure changes. Then, an hour ago, we hit a water pocket unexpectedly. That doesn't necessarily mean anything. It shouldn't have meant anything. We hit pockets like that all the time when we drill, but the pressure changed, and... cracks began to form."

"But the timeline aligns with the data I have and the small cluster of earthquakes," Abby says, "which weren't strong enough to cause damage like this. It doesn't make sense."

I shake my head. The ins and outs of this procedure and this lab are totally out of my wheelhouse.

"The sensors weren't working properly, but we knew that going in, which is why we had teams taking data from every tunnel while we worked ours. The collapse... it doesn't make sense data-wise.

Something catastrophic would have had to cause it–an explosion or a major earthquake. We were being so careful."

Abby reaches out to squeeze Toby's arm. "I took my laptop out of the lab when we evacuated. All the data's still there. We'll find out what really happened."

Toby looks down at his boots. "Alex isn't answering his phone."

"Well, he's below–" I try to say, but he interrupts.

"I'm not sure he is. He was the last to leave the tunnels. We both were. We did a headcount while in the main channel, which is far more secure than the lower tunnels. We were safe enough for the moment to do it, but I walked around the corner to the entrance of the lab and he didn't follow. I went back, shouted for him, and he answered that he thought someone was still down there and I–I couldn't see how. I kept telling him to come back, and he said he was coming, I heard him running, and then everything just... fell in. The channel started to crumble. I ran, and I was sure he was right beside me. We got into the elevator with the last of the people evacuating, and I was sure he was on it. I saw him, for fuck's sake."

I straighten. "You saw him?"

"He's the only one who wears dark clothing down there. He had his hat pulled down, his hand over his face like he was trying to collect himself."

Something ugly twists in my lower belly. "How do you know it was him?"

"Because he was standing so still. You know, how Alex does. He barely moves."

Abby looks wildly between us, sensing there's something off about it.

"But when we all gathered out here and made sure everyone was accounted for, I couldn't find him. He won't answer his phone. Seeing you, I figured maybe he knew you were back and went to make sure you knew he was okay." Toby looks at me like I'm about to confirm his friend is alive, and when I exhale, my eyes filling with tears, his expression crumbles.

"Oh, my Goddess. He's still down there, isn't he?"

"Fuck," I whisper, sniffling. "Who else...? How...? What's happening now?"

"The maintenance office sent a team down into the lab. The main lab is fine–messy and not stable, but fine. The tunnels are gone, essentially, but they didn't search anything. We were sure everyone got out," Abby tells me and then says weakly, "The engineering department has body temperature scanners they can drop down into the tunnels, don't they? They're strong enough to pick up heat pockets from the surface of the ice down at least half a mile. We can find him that way, right?"

Toby and I look at each other. Alex mentioned Toby knows the truth.

Abby does not.

"That won't work, Abs," Toby says in defeat.

"If he's dead, it hasn't been for long. We can find him! If he's hurt–"

"Alex... doesn't have a body temperature that can be picked up by those scanners," I say, barely loud enough to be overheard.

Abby looks so confused, and it breaks my heart that she's been left in the dark. She might not forgive me for this, or anything that comes after, because I have one choice, and I have to make it quickly.

"Is there someone private we can talk?" I ask Toby.

ABBY CACKLES UNTIL TEARS STREAM DOWN HER FACE. "THAT'S NOT funny, Toby."

I pull a pair of yellow thermals over my camisole and discreetly slip into the thermal leggings Toby provided.

"I'm telling you the truth."

"Alex is not a... whatever you said."

"You know what I said. He's a vampire, Abby."

"They're not real. They don't exist!"

"They do," I say, draping my discarded clothing over a chair in the conference room we're hiding out in against the constant clang of footsteps and tools while maintenance ensures the campus is secure and not falling into the ice. "And Toby's right. Alex is a vampire."

Abby laughs cynically but glares at us both. "So, what? He's a dead man walking? He drinks the blood of innocents?"

"Not really," Toby says, but his voice falters.

I clear my throat while zipping up the thickly insulated overalls that Toby snuck out of the locker room and fix Abby with a serious look that has her straightening her back. "Alex is a born vampire, which is very similar to a shifter or witch. His differences are plenty, but they mostly have to do with his longer than normal lifespan and his biological needs–such as blood. You're right about that. However, he's not a monster from our childhood fairytales, Abby. This is who he is. He's a vampire, but he's also Toby's friend, and my–"

Abby shakes her head, looking stricken. "I knew you were sleeping with him."

"I'm not going into this with you now. We have no time to waste."

"You're wasting your time, Skye. You're not going to be able to gain access to the tunnels. I'll get you into the lab."

"I don't need your help like you think I do," I gut out, frustrated with the zipper on the parka that's the same color as the sun on the hottest day in Maatua. It's blindingly yellow. It would be so easy to find Alex if he were wearing the same thing. I choke back my misplaced anger at him and slip into heavily treaded boots and gloves and then pull a beanie over my hair, turning to my friends.

I take two steps to close the distance between us. "Don't be afraid," I whisper. "This will only hurt a little bit."

"What?" Toby says, but I slam my hands on his forehead and Abby's simultaneously, tearing into their minds as carefully as I can, but I'm running out of time to save him.

Usually, I wouldn't need to do this. I could simply... reach out to Alex through the aether, letting the stars guide my way, but scrying is not my strong suit and never has been. My grandma Sarah is a master at it, but I never developed as strong a pull toward that skill as she has. I have to go backward to find Alex, so I do, poring through Abby and Toby's memories of the last hour until Abby grabs her laptop and leaps into the elevator, and Toby calls out to Alex to hurry.

I catch a glimpse of Alex in that single memory–barely a second where he's in Toby's direct line of sight, and do something I'm not sure will work.

I grab onto Alex in that memory. He's nothing but his voice for several seconds before my powers, dimmed to the point of pain, find something interesting.

A single thread in our tapestry that weaves through several different lifelines. He has affected so many lives in a positive way that he's here, in my visions, the last ten years of his efforts forever cemented in the stars. I could follow each crossing of threads, I'm sure. Maybe one day I will, and I'll be able to tell him how much good he's given my world and my kingdom.

But not now.

Because I found his tether.

I grab it, letting his memories wash over me. He was sure someone was in the tunnel behind him. Red eyes. A familiar presence he couldn't shake. He thought he was going insane, was debating his options, fighting his own instincts, and then the floor gave way beneath him.

A shadow leapt over him at the last second, running to safety. He saw it but barely. He was already falling, crashing, *crushed.*

But alive. I can feel him now. I know where he is.

I yank out of Toby's head. Abby falls in a heap to the floor beside him, her eyes open but rolled back in her head. She's still breathing, thank the Goddess, and Toby falls against the wall and slides down to rest behind her, groaning and gripping his temples. I toss my badge in his lap. He's barely lucid, but he's awake enough to hear me when I command, "Meet me in my condo in twenty minutes."

The words are barely out when my powers erupt and suck me into depths so deep it's suddenly impossible to breathe. It's thick in the aether between realms. Sometimes, it's a vat of nothing–inky black nothing that swells and constricts when I travel through it–but sometimes, it's starlight, like now, that streaks and shifts until I've found my destination.

Maybe I'm insane. Actually, I know I am, because where I'm going is where Alex is currently stuck and fighting for his life over a thousand feet below the surface of the lab, but if I can just… touch him?

I can get us out of here.

The darkness doesn't fade. I have no way of knowing I've reached my destination until I feel my back being shredded by jagged ice. Condensation drips from what used to be a tunnel, based on how smooth the wall feels. I blink several times, willing my happily lazy and dormant wolf to wake up enough to help me in the dark, and she does after some prodding. My eyesight shifts, and a collapsed tunnel spreads out around me, piles of ice blocking each end of the tunnel. Alex lies on his stomach, face down and silent, a block of ice crushing his legs.

He's not moving.

That doesn't mean anything to me.

I leap toward him, grabbing his arm, my powers screaming to stop and wait, but I can't. Dark, black blood coats the floor where he fell so hard it knocked him unconscious. He's been bleeding out slowly.

But it's very hard to kill a vampire.

"Hold on." I croak and scream in pain as my ragged, overworked powers surge and carry us both… home.

I hope.

SOMEONE ELSE'S TURN

Skye

I crash into my condo with a crack that echoes through the space, rattling the potted plants along the window where the skyline is nothing but starlight, and the ever-present aurora dancing almost as if to mock me. Tonight, it's crimson, just like the red glare of the alarm still painting my condo in red light, but thankfully, the sound of the alarm is off, or maybe I've tuned it out.

I gasp several breaths. Icy pain jets up and down my spine. I'm depleted, for sure. It's been decades since I've felt this kind of cold, and I live in the coldest place in our world.

But the body beneath mine is warm. Just a little bit warm.

"Alex?" I rasp, grabbing his face between my gloved hands. He's impossibly bruised. His hair is frozen in odd angles, but his skin is soft and only slightly gray from the cold.

When he doesn't answer me, I press my gloved hand to his chest, waiting seconds to feel the rise and fall. His heart already beats so slowly, but now it only flickers every minute or so, like he's in the deepest kind of sleep. I frantically rip at the torn fabric of his jacket and press my ear to his chest over his thermals, listening closely, whispering small prayers that overwhelm the sound of my door opening and closing and twin footsteps rushing toward us.

"Skye? How–" Abby rushes to my side in shock, but Toby quickly ushers her out of the way and kneels on Alex's other side, turning his head.

"I think one, if not both, of his legs are broken," I say, noticing the blood seeping into the carpet. "He's hurt."

"We're gonna help him," he says sternly, gripping my hand. "Okay? It's gonna be fine, but what the fuck was that back in the conference room?"

I recoil at his tone, and even Abby is looking at me like I just turned into a monster right before their eyes. "I'm sorry. I'm a mystic. I don't know–I don't know how else to explain. I'm sorry."

Abby shakes her head and looks down at Alex, then me, squinting at what I'm sure are ice crystals clinging to my cheeks. I'm shivering violently, and I think she realizes it's not from being in the tunnels. "What's wrong with you?"

"I–if I deplete my powers to a certain point, my body is–is programmed to sh-shut itself down to maintain–maintain my heart rate. It's called a depletion event. It's very common in–"

"Witches, I know," she says under her breath. She takes a deep gulp of air and braces her hands on her hips. "Okay. This is insane. Is everyone in agreement that this is completely insane? I feel like I'm owed a major apology from all three of you right now, which is the only reason why I'm going to help."

I wince, but she continues, "I'm going down to the clinic. Toby, give me your badge. I'm guessing everyone is still evacuated to the commons, and I need to be able to get into the clinic and the storage room without a fuss."

"Do not get caught," he warns, handing her the badge in question. She rolls her eyes at him.

"What do you need? Healing tonics, for sure. Bandages. What else?" She looks at me sharply, obviously so beyond livid my frozen skin begins the thaw under the scorch of her glare. "What do *you* need, Skye?"

"I'll be fine soon."

"That's another lie. *What do you need?*"

I nod, hating this, wishing I knew what to say, how to grovel at her feet for forgiveness for years of lies. "Healing tonics are fine. I just need rest, and then I can heal his wounds."

Silence rushes between our sorry group.

"You can do that?" Toby asks.

"Kind of," I admit, meeting his eyes. I've never felt worse in my life than I do now, and it's entirely my fault.

Abby growls something under her breath and leaves in a rush, slamming the door shut behind her.

We spend the next ten minutes trying to keep Alex alive, but he doesn't so much as flinch against our poking and prodding. He's getting colder, too, and I eventually regain enough strength to help Toby get Alex out of his torn lab clothing and down to just his thermals.

Toby covers him with a thick blanket. "There isn't much we can do for him now. Not until Abby gets back. Do you think healing tonics are going to work on him, anyway?"

"I don't know. I hope they do. I think he needs… blood." I meet his eyes. "First and foremost." I start shrugging out of my parka, but he stops me with a hand pressed to my chest.

"Not you."

"He's fed off me before."

Toby grits his teeth. I wonder if Alex told him that, but based on his face, no. "You're barely able to hold yourself upright. It can't be you. Fuck, okay, get me a knife."

"No!"

"Skye, look at me. You've done enough. You got him back. He was going to die down there. It could have been days or weeks until the tunnels were settled enough to get a rescue team down there, and it would have been far too late. You saved him. I've got it from here."

My body refuses to move. He sighs deeply and runs his fingers through his hair.

"He can feed off other people, right? It doesn't have to be just you, or is that… vampire cheating?"

"I don't know how that works!"

"Okay, then let me do this. Go warm up. Take a bath or something. You're gray."

My lower lip trembles as I slowly slide away from them on my knees. It takes me several attempts to rise and surrender, but when I do, the entire weight of the situation settles on my shoulders. I run a shower as hot as I can handle. I strip out of my thermals and step inside the porcelain box, sliding down the wall while being beaten by water that feels like little needles on my frozen skin. My body steams, but the heat wraps me in a warm embrace, and soon, I'm sitting near the drain, my cheek against the wall, my eyes open but reeling over visions I siphoned from Alex's head. He mentioned the likelihood that someone was hunting him, and now it's clear to me, at least, that that's the case.

Could someone–another vampire–especially someone not familiar with the university or his lab–cause a tunnel collapse like that? Was it premeditated?

Just like Laney's murder?

Also, why am I feeling so… territorial over the idea of Toby giving Alex the blood he needs? It should be me. *Only me.*

An entire half hour creeps by. The endless supply of hot water blurs the time. I only step out and towel off when my fingers turn to prunes, and when I emerge, dressed in thick flannel pajamas and slippers I brought into the bathroom with me, my wet hair twisted in a towel, Toby is resting against the side of the couch with a bandage roped around the palm of his hand, and several empty healing tonics are scattered across the floor.

Alex is no longer on the ground.

"I dragged him onto your bed," he says with a shrug. "You're right. His legs are pretty fucked up, but after a few shots of my pristine, shifter, Alpha blood, he stopped bleeding and warmed up a bit."

I bend to pick up the tonic vials. "How many did you give him?"

"Four or five."

I stare at him in shock, but he shrugs again.

"What's the worst that can happen?"

"That was far too much." I look at the bloodstain on the floor with a sigh. "Where's Abby?"

"She went to clean up our mess," he replies, stretching his legs out in front of him. "I mentioned I couldn't find Alex before you showed up. She's making sure you and Alex have alibis if anyone questions that."

"She hates me."

"She doesn't hate you. You know how she can be."

"I've been lying to her for so long."

"About what? Having the power to teleport?" He chuckles. "She'll get over it. It was a rough night for everyone. Especially you."

He meets my gaze. I feel him reaching out with an invisible hand. I know what he wants to ask before the words can materialize on his tongue.

"I like Alex a lot. I've known he's a vampire for a while now, before you did. It hasn't changed anything between us. But he's... he's in danger now, I think. I don't think the collapse was a freak accident or anything your team did. Alex is so careful. If he thought for a second that anyone was in danger, he would have gotten everyone out with time to spare. The collapse might not have even happened."

"I know."

"I think someone did this on purpose."

Toby looks down at his hands. "I have my suspicions, too."

I edge toward him. "What can we do? I can–I should get my family involved."

"Don't," he warns but then calms, adding, "Talk to Alex first. I'm going to stay here, on the couch, if that's cool with you. I doubt Abby wants me in our apartment right now anyway, and I know Alex and I are going to have hell to pay tomorrow when we explain what happened. I want to be here when he wakes up so we can get a story lined up."

"Okay." I walk into the kitchen on unsteady feet, my powers still pulsating and settling while they're coming back to life. My wolf is in a tizzy, however, when I glance at my open bedroom door and the heap of shadows on my bed. I pull a few cleaning supplies from a kitchen cabinet, dead set on cleaning the stain on the carpet but abandon the task.

Toby groans as he lifts himself up onto the couch and lies back. He shuts his eyes and immediately falls asleep.

The rest can wait, but this can't.

I silently edge into my bedroom. Alex looks peaceful in a dead way, which is definitely unnerving and would be slightly frightening if I didn't know him well. I sit next to him on the bed and take his hand.

"I'm so sorry, and you're going to hate this, but I'm involved now. Whatever you were trying to shield me from has caught up to us, and you almost died today. I might die right now trying to mend your wounds," I murmur, looking down at his legs. Toby cut his thermals off at the knees, giving me a clear view of the swollen, bruised skin and dried blood. The healing tonics must have had some effect because Toby was right—the gashes on his calves and ankles are closed, but the tonics only went so far.

My powers grumble when I flex my fingers. I've never done this before, but I know my dad can do it, and I really don't want to have to call him and ask if he'll help. I'm sure I have a hundred missed calls from my family in Moonrise after my abrupt departure. I'd rather not dig myself a deeper grave than I already have, not yet.

As someone who adores the sciences, I've taken enough entry-level biology and anatomy classes to be able to guess my way through Alex's biology and anatomy, so I rest my hand on his right leg, imagining his bones and muscles. The tissue and fascia holding him together. The veins and arteries. The singular cells. I imagine knitting them back together just so—all better.

I'm not sure if my powers do anything, but when I open my eyes again, curling my achingly chilled fingers into fists, his bruises are less severe, and his legs aren't nearly as swollen and painful to look at.

I sneak under the covers and roll to face him, propping my chin on his shoulder, and spend the next hour looking out the window watching the aurora dance against a field of stars.

I wonder what that vision earlier was trying to show me—the one about curtains and a baby. A future I'm not sure Alex is in, but for now, he's here, and as I close my eyes and drift into a shallow sleep, I know he'll be here when I wake up.

3 7

ALL THE LIES

Alex

Skye is pressed to my chest when I open my eyes. I stroke my fingers down her spine while staring aimlessly at the ceiling. She has to leave today for the funeral and to spend some time with her family. I already put in her bereavement leave, not that it matters. The campus is shut down as it stands. I doubt I'll be able to access the lab.

I jolt, gripping the fabric of Skye's flannel pajamas at the base of her spine. She flinches but settles back into sleep with the deepest, most exhausted sigh I've ever heard, and I glance at the clock on her bedside table. It's early morning.

We spent the night at my place. I don't remember coming here....

I slide away from her, careful not to wake her, and reality hits me the second I glance down at my thermal pants, which are hacked off at the knee.

I was in the lab last night. We were drilling, finally bringing what should have gone down as a successful production to fruition after weeks of preparation and careful planning.

It all went to hell, and I was buried under the ice.

I whirl back to Skye, who has dark circles under her eyes, and her fingertips, now clutching the pillow I just vacated, are tinged blue.

"Hey!" Toby hisses from the door, which is open just a crack, just enough for me to see his bared teeth and wild eyes.

"What the fuck?"

He shushes me and slowly opens the door. "I have coffee going. Do not wake her up. I'm shocked she even agreed to go to bed."

"What happened, Toby?" I step into the hallway, pulling the door closed behind us. He waves a hand toward a stack of clothing on the kitchen counter. It's from my condo, which he has the code to, but still. "How long have I been out?"

"Maybe four hours?"

Relief washes through me, numbing some of my sharper senses that are currently going haywire. Toby tries to pour another cup of coffee, but the pot is empty, nothing but smooth black droplets that he frowns at, and meets my eyes. "Shit. You don't actually drink coffee, do you?"

"I honestly don't mind it," I admit.

"Take a shower, and I'll make another pot. We have some shit to discuss."

I turn back to the hallway, but my gaze catches on Skye's door. "What did she do?"

"We have time—"

"Please. I need to know."

"She got you out of the tunnels. Used her magic or whatever. I'll go into detail once you're out of those blood-soaked clothes. I already spent an hour scrubbing her carpet free of your blood. I'd rather not ruin her couch."

Twenty minutes later, just past 7:00 in the morning, I'm pacing the room while Toby pours himself what I think might be his fifth cup of coffee in the time span of an hour, and I'm listening to him explain what happened after the tunnel collapse.

"I called her yesterday. The funeral was yesterday. She didn't say she was coming back," I argue when he mentions Skye suddenly showed up outside of the lower levels of the biology department shortly after the collapse happened, and the evacuation of campus began.

"She's got a weird thing going on," he says, motioning to his head. "She made me get a bunch of gear from the locker room while I argued with Abby about how you're a vampire, which she now knows, by the way. I was distracted by my mate, and Skye took advantage of that. One second, I catch her pulling on a beanie, and the next moment, she's in my head, looking for you. It was the strangest, most painful thing I've ever experienced."

"She's a mystic."

"She said as much, but aren't they supposed to, like, read prophecies and shit? She was *in my head*!"

"She's a little different."

"You don't say?" He laughs and promptly burns his mouth on his coffee. "She knew where to find you. She told us to meet her here in twenty minutes. Abby passed out. I was hanging on by a thread but managed to get us here in fifteen minutes, and she was already here—with you."

I scrub my hand over my face. "She spirited to me and brought us here the same way."

He blinks several times and cocks his head. "She what?"

"She can travel from one place to another by breaking herself apart on a molecular level."

"I'm being serious."

"So am I."

He's stunned into silence, blinking slowly like an owl. "I don't get it."

"A few weeks ago, when she accidentally came in contact with Stardust, and I told you she was hungover... I lied. Her reaction to Stardust was unlike anything I've ever seen, and I'd know, because you were hooked on it our junior year."

"I was not."

I fix him with a sharp look.

"Okay, fine. A little bit."

"She," I cut in, "is made of it. It's naturally in her blood. The synthetic variant riled her senses, made her powers... act funny. But–" I step toward him, my hands outstretched in surrender. "Stardust is meteors, right? Ground up with synthetics strong enough to deliver it into the bloodstream for the thrill. Skye is made of the same thing. It's something she naturally produces."

"She's a meteor?"

I heave an annoyed breath. "It's her magic. It comes from somewhere else."

He nods like he understands some of this nonsense. Because to scientists like us, this is exactly what nonsense sounds like. "The realm of the gods is a real thing then, isn't it? It would align with her current research into far-off star systems."

"It doesn't matter because it's not something I'm ever going to be able to reproduce. I got a blood sample from her. Laney–Laney processed it for me, and I've pored over that same slide over and over again. I've tasted her, for fuck's sake, and her blood doesn't give me a high. It's... normal. Beautiful but not.... Her magic isn't carried in her blood, but it's there in the sample. I just can't access it. She... has to give it away."

"You're talking about the Goddess particle, aren't you?" Toby straightens and sets his coffee mug on the kitchen island.

"Of course I am. It's the one thing I've dedicated my research to for my entire career. It's what I've been praying we'll find traces of in those fossils and artifacts. But I can't harness it. I can't reproduce it. Skye is the Goddess particle, and she's–mine. I can't use her. I won't."

"She healed you."

"What?"

"Your legs were broken. Like, crushed." He leans his hip on the counter and folds his arms across his chest. "I gave you five healing tonics, and that stopped the bleeding. Then, I gave you a little bit of my blood."

"You what?"

He holds up his hand, rotating his palm so I can see the bandage. "Don't worry, man," he says with a smirk. "I just sliced myself open and dropped some blood into your mouth. It wasn't intimate or anything."

"Do not—"

"Do that again? You were dying, and Skye was the same color as the walls. She looked like she was dying and started pulling off her clothes to offer you what little life she had left on a silver platter. I sent her to bed. You're welcome."

"Do you see now why I've—"

"Why you kept her at arm's length? Yeah, trust me. After last night, I get it. Who else knows what she is and what she can do?"

"Her being a mystic is common knowledge, given who her father is."

"We suspect the tunnel collapse wasn't a random event, and the data Abby collected proves it," he guts out, his eyes holding intensely on mine.

I brace a hand on the wall and turn my face toward the window, closing my eyes.

Toby continues, "You told me you thought someone was still in the main channel. I think you were right. There was someone there, someone who wasn't part of the lab. Someone who shouldn't have been there. Someone that I—I thought was you when I got on the elevator with the last of the lab assistants, and then he disappeared when we got to the surface."

"Toby?"

"You need to be honest with me, man. I need you to trust me with this. You told me you were a vampire, and what did I do? I fucking shrugged, asked if you can still eat steak or just suck them dry, right? I don't fucking care, but I care about this. Abby is involved now. Skye is heavily involved. Our women. My mate and your—well, knowing Skye for as long as I have, if she's even remotely interested in you, it's a big fucking deal to her."

I shake my head, but Toby crosses the room, dead set on cornering me.

"I've known you for a decade. I've known you, this version of you, and I like you. I don't want you to get hurt again. Last night fucking sucked, and I know, for a fact, we're going to be running around with our heads cut off today trying to make sense of what the university expects us to do now that millions of dollars and ten years of research are gone in a matter of seconds."

"I'm a prince, Toby," I cut in, turning to meet his gaze. "My parents are king and queen of a kingdom with predominantly vampire populations thousands upon thousands of miles from here, over the north pole. I was twenty when I left. I wandered for three years before I stumbled into Lunaria, half dead, and lied my way into getting admission to the university."

Toby doesn't move. He doesn't so much as breathe, just stares, his cheeks stained a soft pink with emotion he refuses to voice, let alone show.

"There was a war. It dragged on for nine years, and I put an end to it."

"How?"

"I killed a rival queen of an enemy kingdom. I had her cornered by some miracle–showed up at the right place at the right time–and she was alone. I had one shot to just end it, and I did, but she had a son my age. A real fucking piece of work. He was the one leading her armies against my parents' kingdom and doing everything in his power to turn the public against my mother."

Toby's shoulders slump just a touch, his body adjusting to the torrent of information moving between us–my life's story, now his to know.

"My mother isn't like me. She's a turned vampire, and Queen Matilda started campaigning for a true vampire empire where born vampires rule and turned vampires go back to being the slaves they were originally created to be, in her opinion. Shifters, too. She said they were meant for food and shouldn't have their own kingdoms and territories, so she targeted them first, her armies, led by her son, raiding entire packs and sucking them dry. The shifters barely had a leg in the fight. My uncle Michael, a hybrid, got involved, so my father got involved. I was a kid. I was a kid hearing that Queen Matilda's war was being waged against my mother, who was turned against her will hundreds of years ago by vampires like me. I enlisted as soon as I was old enough to fight and had been wielding blades and honing my skills long before that. I stepped onto the battlefield at sixteen and saw the worst of the world for those three years. I trained in apothecary medicine just to save what mortal lives I could when the witches and shifters joined the fight, but we kept losing, and then–then I had her, and she was right there, and I didn't think. I didn't think I'd never be able to go home and see my parents again. I just killed her, and her son vowed to spend the rest of his immortal life hunting me down, and now he has."

"You think he's here?"

I push off the wall, pacing past Toby. "He's been here. He's been killing again. And he'll target Skye to get to me, just like he used Laney to get my attention."

I look up from my pacing and find Skye huddled in the archway leading to her bedroom, her weary eyes locked on my face.

38

ANOTHER BODY

Skye

Alex holds my gaze for several seconds. Two weeks of separation and the gravity of the last six hours crush the space between us, turning the rest of the world to nothing but static noise. He runs his fingers through his damp hair and nods to himself like he's just made an executive decision.

Toby lingers just within view—waiting for the same thing I am.

Direction. Any kind of direction about how to move forward... for him. As a team. His friends. Me... whatever I am to him.

"Meet me in my office in an hour. If anyone asks, I'm going through the data about the collapse," he tells Toby, who takes the command as the dismissal it is, and within the space of two thundering heartbeats, we're alone.

"I wasn't going to let you die," I say, closing my arms around my middle, preparing for a fight. "I couldn't. Not when I have the ability to... be anywhere, at any time. I found you."

"I knew you'd come. I could feel you there, just like when I was a kid, and you found me in my dreams."

I suck in a breath, my emotions tangled, and he moves toward me slowly, each step calculated and careful, like he's worried about me turning and sprinting away. Like this situation is enough to finally scare me into seeing him as a monster and not the man I… love.

He takes my shoulders, his hands stroking down my arms. Into my hair, he says, "I'm sorry. I'm so sorry for everything. I wanted to keep you in the dark about Prince Kai. Being a vampire was already a mark against me."

I press my face into the crook of his shoulder, breathing him in. "What happens now?"

"The lab is likely destroyed, is it not?"

I nod.

He sighs, his body closing around mine. He braces a hand against the wall at my back and leans his weight into mine like I'm the only thing keeping him anchored and calm, and maybe I am, because he relaxes when I wrap my arms around his middle and sink into his touch. "Dealing with the university after this will be the least of my worries."

"But your research?"

"It'll take another decade to rebuild the tunnels in a new location, if we're lucky and find the funding within the next year or so. It's over. And I… need to start making plans."

I lean back to look up at him, noticing the pained expression casting shadows across his face.

"You're leaving, aren't you?"

"Not yet, but it's something I have to consider."

"No–no, you can't. This isn't over. I can–I can find this guy. I found you by scrying. I can do the same for him. It's not that hard."

"You're freezing," he says, shaking his head. "I can sense how weak you are."

"I'll be fine in a few days. Don't jump to any conclusions yet."

He steps away from me and leans his weight on the far wall, the snug hallway feeling suddenly like an ocean has opened up between us.

"I can't continue this dance, Skye."

"Then end it with him. Kill him if you must."

"I mean with us." He looks directly at me, bright blue eyes shining in the dim light filtering down the hallway from the living room. "I put you in a horrible position yesterday. I almost died, had my life's work crumble in a matter of seconds, and my only thought in my last seconds was you. Being with you. A far-fetched future with you, where we lived together doing what we loved–being scientists. It's all I cared about in the end, and I'm at a crossroads now. I don't want to keep running. Part of me wants to go home, if I'm being totally honest. I want to see my family again. I have to go home because I am the prince and heir of my parents' kingdom, and one day, centuries from now, I'll have to be who I was born to be, but as long as Kai is in the picture, I can't return. And now, there's you."

He pushes off the wall, looking so determined that it sends a skitter down my spine.

"There isn't a world where you and I make sense. A world where we end up together peacefully, and you're not in Lunaria permanently, are you?"

I flinch, looking down at my toes.

Alex nods, taking a huge breath. "Why didn't you say anything?"

"About the fact that the mystics foretold me rising to power within their ranks? Because it doesn't matter. It's my decision."

"The university gave you tenure knowing you had maybe five years here before you were called back to Moonrise."

"How did you find out?"

"Alloway," he says, closing his eyes for a moment. "I had a conversation with her when you were in Moonrise about our relationship. It was brief, but when I mentioned your name, she acted like my rejection of the position of dean of the biology department seemed to make perfect sense to her all of the sudden."

I blink, furrowing my brows up at him. "She offered you the position of dean?"

"And she thought I wouldn't take it because you have a time limit on how long you can be a physicist."

I've never told anyone about the prophecies the mystics foretold about me. My dad technically leads their church, if that's even the right name for it. They consider him a king, but my journey into my power majority shifted things in the timeline, and more and more, they lean toward my leadership. It's me, according to those strange women in their crystal masks and white robes, who pulls the strings in our universe. Me, who speaks as the mouthpiece of the Goddess, and the stars who do Her bidding.

Me, who will one day have to return to that spooky orrery and be the goddess they intend for me to be.

"I didn't think it mattered," I tell him. "It didn't matter until you."

"Neither of us can stay in Lunaria," he says almost absently, like it was an internal thought not meant for my ears.

"We're still in control of our futures. I'm in control of mine. I have the choice. What I want to be, and who I want to be with, has always been my decision. I want love like my parents have. I hate that I don't have a mate in my tether, but I have you, Alex. I get to choose you."

"And you will sacrifice so much by doing so."

"Because I'll get old, and you won't? Because we can only live in Lunaria? In secret?"

"Because I can't give you the kind of life you deserve."

"And what do I deserve? What do you want, Alex? Because you tell me what I want so easily!"

"I would love, more than anything, to marry you. To make you my wife. To take you home and introduce you to my parents–who would love you, my mother especially. I want to be the father of your future children, but hybrids are so rare, and a hybrid pregnancy is incredibly risky. I could get everything I want and still lose you," he rasps, fire in his eyes so deeply rooted it's been burning since he was a child.

"Do you know what I want?" I ask, stepping toward him, closing the distance between us again. "You. Just a shot at being with you, however that looks. Do you think just… deciding to go for this is the hardest thing we'll have to do? We've both been pretending to be people we're not for a decade at least, Alex. I'm tired of it. Aren't you?" I look down at my hands and then hold them up for him to see. Violet starlight swirls between my fingertips. "I wore that bracelet practically my entire life. It was a safety net for the power I was afraid to stretch. I love physics. I love my weird brain. That will always be a part of who I am, but I met you, and that challenged everything I thought I knew, and when I had a vision that something was wrong, and it led me here, to you? That's all the confirmation I needed to know that you and I were meant to meet. That we had dreams of the same place, of each other as children, for a reason. I'm done fighting it and trying to rationalize it. I'm done looking for answers in equations I'll never figure out. There's no reason for this other than fate."

He holds my gaze, so still. So different from me in so many ways. I can barely keep my hands from fidgeting–always moving. He reaches out and takes my fingers, curling his hand over mine. My light shines through the gaps in our joined fingers before settling.

"I want to help you be able to go home again. I want you to see your parents again, and the last thing I want you to do is worry about me, because I think I might be in love with you," I admit.

"You think?"

"I haven't–I might have tried my hand at... writing a formula about... laws of attraction and risk, but..."

I look up, and he's right in front of me. I can hear his heart beating faster than ever before, and for a moment, he's like me. All flesh and heat. All feeling and instinct.

Maybe we're not so different.

His kiss sweeps me off my feet and officially ends our suffering, answering every question we have thoroughly and neatly, leaving no room for interpretation.

He picks me up and carries me into my bedroom, kicking the door closed behind us. It's fast and messy the way we take our clothes off and fall into bed together. Alex whispers promises on my skin that sink and spread like golden tattoos–similar, I imagine, to what a mate bond snapping into place would feel like. He nudges my legs apart and sinks through my folds in a single thrust. I gasp, arching my neck back, panting as he grinds his hips against mine again and again until we're both crying out.

But just as my body succumbs to release, and pleasure rolls through me, I open my eyes to his.

"I love you," he says against my lips and kisses me so tenderly it untangles something long knotted in my brain. Something I'm not sure was in the stars for me.

Now, I understand it—why my dad did everything he had to do, even when my mom kept him at arm's length for so long. And if there's one thing my dad and I have in common, it's being extraordinarily territorial over what we believe belongs to us. He has my mom.

I have my rocks... and Alex.

And Kai, whoever the fuck he is, has hell to pay, because I will find that bastard if it's the last thing I do.

I LEAN MY WEIGHT AGAINST THE WALL IN ALEX'S OFFICE, FLIPPING through a binder of scribbles I found on his bookshelf. He's enraptured by a conversation with Toby, who has been going over the data in the lab just before the accident.

Abby isn't here, and I know the only reason I'm here is because facing her wrath is the last thing I want to do. Knowing Abby as long as I have, I've come to the conclusion that it's better to let her work things out on her own and calm down before trying to apologize to her.

She does, unfortunately, live for dramatics, and today has been dramatic enough.

A sharp knock sounds on Alex's office door.

"Come in," he says gruffly and looks up just as President Alloway and several board members walk in, their faces washed in emotions I struggle to understand. Concern, for sure. Losing the lab is a financial hit to the university, but no one got hurt.

"I'm glad to see you're in one piece, Dr. Scarlett," Alloway says tersely, but she's wringing her hands.

"We're going over the data right now about the collapse and the events leading up to it—" Toby begins, but Alex slowly rises, sensing the same kind of tension I can feel flooding the room like poisonous gas.

"A rescue team has just returned from what remains of the lab."

Toby arches a brow. "Why?"

She produces a piece of paper–a printed email. I try to discreetly catch a glimpse, but Alex takes it, scanning the contents, his eyes narrowing.

"Dr. Kanten emailed me yesterday saying he was going to your lab last night to check on the sensor issue himself after I brought it up," she says pointedly, fuming. "He never returned from your lab, Dr. Scarlett."

"He was never in the lab," Alex says slowly, shaking his head. "We had over forty people in the lab last night for a drilling operation, and he was not part of it. I kept a list of everyone who enters and exits my lab for safety reasons–"

"Be that as it may, a rescue team was sent down this morning and recovered his body."

"What?" Toby and Alex ask in unison, and I'm frozen in place.

Alloway steels her expression and says, "The authorities in Aurorium are now involved. Dr. Kanten was murdered." Her eyes land on Alex's face, full of suspicion.

3 9

SCRYING SHAME

Skye

ALEX SHUTS THE DOOR OF HIS CONDO WITH A CRACK THAT ECHOES FROM one end of the space to the other. I turn in a circle, tapping my chin in thought as he moves aimlessly through the kitchen, opening and shutting cabinets like the answer to this mess will be found on a shelf between pieces of glassware he never uses.

"Obviously, it was Kai," I say, and Alex braces his hands on the counter.

"I find it hard to believe that Kanten was in the lab at all."

"So this other vampire killed him and took him there!"

"No, Skye, not with all the maintenance workers around securing that section of campus."

"Then he was in the lab, and so was Kai, while you were drilling. Abby's data points toward tampering. What did Toby say in your office? Explosives?"

"We would have heard it." He smooths his hands over the counter. "Skye?"

"Yeah?"

"I need you to consider something."

My stomach drops to my toes. I already know what he's going to ask before his lips part. "No. I'm not going back to Moonrise. Don't argue with me about it, either."

He gives me a look from under the cover of his dark, thick eyelashes. "Kai did this, which means he's on campus, which means he knows exactly where I am and who I'm with."

"Then why hasn't he made a move on you here yet?"

"Because he's fucking with me and my job, trying to force me out of the shadows. I could have killed him, I suppose, a decade ago. The fact that he's been able to hunt me down makes me believe he lost his kingdom after I killed his mother and has ample time on his hands to drag this out and hurt me where it will have the most effect."

"Then you ignore it for now. You didn't kill your dean. You know that. Toby was with you until the last second."

"He will come after you. That's a given."

I edge toward him, feeling shockingly light despite the circumstances. I've never had the opportunity to really dig deep into my power profile, even after an extended period without wearing my bracelet, but now, I feel amazing–like the stars at my fingertips are mine for the taking.

"Please don't worry about me. Honestly, if he came to us, it would make this far easier, but I have a feeling he's going to keep his distance for a while if you're right, and he's doing all of this to mess with you." I sidle up to his side. "Let him come. Alloway might be the bigger fight."

"She does have grounds to believe I had a hand in his death. My disdain was unfortunately documented."

"It means nothing," I try to assure him, but I'm also internally reckoning with what the next few days will look like.

But days pass, and the campus's electric pulse returns like nothing happened–just like after Laney's death. I get it, I guess. Academia and the thrill of the chase of academic prowess suck everyone here into its orbit, making everything else matter far less than I suppose it should.

Alex, however, is either totally unreachable or standing mere feet away from me at all times. It's a strange dance, and his frustration and unease send my senses into a riot I haven't been able to calm.

Midterms are a shitshow, to put it lightly. The biology department, especially Alex's students, take over one of the random bubble labs on the surface of the ice and try to salvage what little research they can during the next two weeks, but it seems fruitless. His lab is roped off, and his badge no longer works to access it, but the university seems keen to sweep the entire situation under the rug.

Even Dr. Kanten's death has been kept quiet, with the general consensus being that the man went on extended leave. Only the board and the heads of Alex's department are allowed to know the truth until the Alpha of Aurorium's authorities finish their investigation.

I lecture like usual, and Alex is always there, sitting in the back of either the lecture hall or the observatory. I go to his lectures to ease his mind about my whereabouts, and while he's otherwise indisposed, Toby has been tasked with ensuring the vampire who has a bounty on my head, according to Alex, can't get me alone.

Abby came around about three weeks after the lab collapsed. At first, she dodged my calls and attempts to apologize and clear the air, but she soon grew bored and moved on to new drama, like how rumors have started to fly about me and Alex. Also, her curiosity about whether or not Alex has similar anatomy to a male shifter, or if his body is different in places I'm sure he'd like to remain private, got the best of her, and when Solstice Break began, we were back to our usual routines together–grocery shopping at the commissary, drinking coffee in the commons, and whisper-fighting in the library.

But the current of unease runs thick, even now, weeks after the lab collapse and the murder of the biology department's dean. It weighs on Alex, especially now that Kai has seemingly disappeared.

Maybe it's over.

Or, maybe it's just beginning.

Alex moves behind me in his bathroom, pulling on a sweatshirt over his thermals. His hair is still wet from the shower, and my body is still pink and covered in his bites when he reaches past me to grab his watch off the counter. He takes up so much space in my head, just like he takes up so much space in this bathroom, which is now also full of my favorite "can't live without" toiletries. We bump into each other when I open the cabinet behind the mirror to find my toothbrush.

"I can go back to my place, you know. I was given a rather nice condo only a few doors down."

"I have some guys coming today to move your mattress here and to get rid of mine," he says, pressing a kiss to my temple, and my argument is effectively moot.

Moving in together wasn't a conversation we had in earnest. It happened naturally, over the course of several stressful weeks where we sought shelter from our situation and campus politics in each other's arms, which meant I started spending more and more time here. It started slowly with my toothbrush getting its own spot, then some clothes, then a few of my favorite rocks and crystals found homes on his windowsills.

Then Solstice rolled around, and I didn't travel home for the holiday. Alex brought my plants over, which we decorated with ornaments and string lights. It was a strange but comforting glimpse into a future I'm not sure either of us think will actually happen, but we did it, and made that memory ours, even if the world still feels like it's on the verge of caving in.

But that two-week-long bubble of delusion popped when the spring semester started. Alex began to loosen up his concern over me. Kai hasn't made any appearances, and no one else has died... so life moved on. The board announced Kanten's untimely death but left out the details of the murder that we're also still in the dark about. I don't know how he died. Even Toby and Alex aren't aware of the details, and Alloway's hope of Alex becoming dean was quashed in one formal meeting with her and the board, where he pretty much said he'd rather run naked across the ice field until he reached the border of Crescent Falls than be the dean.

Alloway didn't like that very much.

Meanwhile, I spent my time researching the stars and mapping the heavens… and moving more and more of my things into Alex's condo until my home was nothing more than a shell of stale air and plaster walls.

It feels right lying next to him in bed, even though he rarely needs to sleep. It's a comfort I find hard to explain.

I know two things for certain now. The first being that Alex and I were meant to cross paths. There's so much about him that aligns with me and who I am. He makes me feel fuller than I ever have and calms my mind to the point that the constant chatter of the stars drowns out, and I can function like a normal being again.

The second thing I know for certain is that scrying isn't as easy as my dad and grandma make it sound… and doing it in secret is damn near impossible with a vampire boyfriend hovering over my every move.

"What's up with that bowl in the kitchen?" Alex asks around his toothbrush while I braid my hair.

"Oh, it's just a salad bowl," I lie. I don't like lying to him at all, but desperate times call for desperate measures, I suppose. "Abby found it in that antique shop in Aurorium."

"Your rocks would look nice in it," he muses, distracted. He got an email this morning that the Beta of Aurorium wants to see him, so he set up a meeting in the little city across the ice. I can tell he doesn't want to go, and we both know, but haven't voiced, that this has everything to do with the investigation into Kanten's death.

The collapse was eventually ruled a freak accident, even though Abby's data says otherwise. The four of us thought maybe it was for the best and have been living in this bubble of delusion for far too long now. I woke up this morning after a series of dreams that made me break out in a cold sweat. Visions danced behind my closed eyelids for hours that I couldn't decipher, which makes me believe something's coming, but it's something I can stop.

If I scry.

And find that fang-toothed bastard before he can hurt Alex any further.

I follow Alex out of the steamy bathroom, watching as he pulls on his coat and slides into boots. He grabs a bag off the counter and slings it over his shoulder–dressed for not only the weather but an entire day in Aurorium. I saw his list of errands. I saw the texts from Toby, who's likely on his way to the subway station right now to meet him, so they can go together.

Abby is likely hiding out at the entrance of The Pillars, waiting for Alex to leave so we can enact our plan.

I suppose not being typical mates means I can get away with stuff like this.

"If anything happens," he says, hesitating by the door, "please–"

"I'm going to be fine. Everything is totally fine, Alex. I'm safe. I'm just hanging out today." I hate this. Goddess, I hate lying to him! "Abby's going to come over later, and we're going to make popcorn and watch that show she loves."

"The dating show?"

I nod, and he continues to hesitate. I can see the gears turning behind his eyes–trying to come up with excuses to stay here and ignore the Beta's summons.

"If you don't go, the Beta will come here and cause a ruckus."

"You're right. I know," he breathes, annoyed. "All right. I'll be back this evening."

"I know you will. And I'll be here. I promise." I resist the urge to cross my fingers behind my back. He slips through the door. I start a timer on my phone for exactly three minutes and pace back and forth around the kitchen island. The timer dings, and I move.

"Abby?" I hang the upper half of my body beyond the entrance of The Pillars into the corridor leading to the center of campus.

Abby pops up from behind a trash can, looking frazzled and slightly red in the face. "I almost got caught. Almost. Goddess, he walked right past me and stopped."

"We have maybe four hours to do this."

"Is that a long time or a short time?" she asks nervously, but I grab her wrist and pull her into the hallway, where we rush past other doors and Solstice decorations people have failed to take down, which grinds Alex's gears in a way I find hilarious, but I digress.

Closed inside Alex's condo once again, I turn to Abby, who pulls several containers of table salt out of her backpack and sets them on the counter beside the bowl. "Is this safe?"

"No," I admit, and it's the most honest thing I've said all day. "Are you ready?"

LET'S MAKE A DEAL

Skye

ABBY CRUNCHES INTO A CANDY BAR WHILE I DUMP COPIOUS AMOUNTS of salt into a bowl. "Why salt water?"

"It needs to mimic the water the mystics use in Moonrise to scry, but I don't have access to the water sources that run between Maatua, Veiled Valley, and Moonrise here, so I'm going to try this instead. I've read that salt acts as a conduit for energy and might keep bad things from interfering in the connection." I glance at her, and she grimaces, stuffing the rest of the chocolate into her mouth.

I'm grimacing, too, because for whatever reason, the smell of chocolate and peanut butter is making my head spin in a bad way. I shove my sudden nausea aside, chalk it up to nerves, and pour a pitcher of tap water into the bowl.

"Can I ask you something before we get started?"

"Of course." I mix the concoction briskly until every salt crystal dissolves.

"Why do you study astrophysics when you can just, I don't know, see everything anyway?"

I get what she means. It's a good question, but I have an answer. "I get visions. That's part of being a mystic. Mystics are trained to read the stars through an orrery, or like this, by scrying, but having the power to do so doesn't mean it's accurate. I can pull prophecies from the stars but only if I can see the stars, and the positioning is correct, and there's a lot of factors at play—time of year, light, weather, the moon cycle, which means prophecies are never totally accurate. So I study the sky. I've made maps that the witches and mystics now use in their magic, and it's been successful. If a witch, like your mother, used lunar magic, she would need an accurate sense of the stars' positions and an exact reading on the moon cycle for spells to be foolproof. Before, that was nearly impossible—an act of sheer luck—but now, I have maps and formulas available because I did the work." I rest my hands on either side of the bowl. "Scrying is entirely different, though."

"How so?"

"I have to have something to latch onto—a memory or a physical object—something tangible." I take a deep breath. "That's why I need you."

"Because you still haven't told Alex you're doing this?"

I close my eyes for a moment. "He's dealing with so much already. We don't know where this other vampire is, and the university effectively covered up the tampering in the lab that caused the collapse and the dean's death."

She rolls her eyes. "Good riddance."

"Anyway," I push on, bracing my elbows on the counter. "I just want to be sure Kai is gone and not a problem anymore. For Alex's sake, so we can all move on."

"Is this going to hurt?" she asks, skeptically.

I grit my teeth, glancing at her. "Maybe a little?"

"Skye, I only agreed to this because you said I could handle it."

"You can because you're a hybrid. Witches are a lot heartier when it comes to being used for magical purposes like this." I reach across the counter and take her hand. "Are you ready?"

She doesn't even have time to nod before I dive into her head.

Abby is easy to maneuver through. She doesn't have secrets to guard and wears her opinions and thoughts on her sleeve, so when I travel back to the day of the collapse, it's all there for me to pick through in startling focus. She was in the main part of the lab the entire time. I only catch glimpses of Alex before he went into the tunnels with Toby. I bypass hours of relative calm, and the lab begins to shatter. Abby herded everyone in the main room out through the elevator and went back for her laptop, where the data, she noticed, was off in a way that made her wonder if the collapse wasn't natural–and then her thoughts get tangled because she was confused. Then, Toby was there, and Alex wasn't.

I see the moment Toby guides her into the elevator and tries to go back for Alex. Another man in a dark parka like Alex wears in the lab hurries onto the elevator with them, which is cramped with other researchers. Toby looks relieved because... he thinks it's Alex.

But it wasn't.

"I have him," I whisper and let go of her hand while wrapping my powers around that one specific moment where she glanced at the stranger before looking away.

Abby gasps and grabs her head, but I'm already gripping the bowl. I lower my face to the water, which ripples against a current of my own design. The tip of my nose touches the surface, and the water illuminates with violet light speckled with stars, and I open my eyes.

The room fades. I'm ripped into a void of darkness. Images flash in tangles of color that remind me of being in Alex's head, and right now, I wish I'd practiced on him, just once, because now I have to fight to turn these streaks of memories into images instead of color.

My powers thrum through my veins in a way I've never experienced before. I feel hot and heavy as I push and shove against the streaks of color and light, but finally, like bursting a bubble, I'm through. Images expand in rapid succession. Memories of Aurorium, of seeing me, of wondering what type of exotic creature I am. Memories of slaying a man in the terminal out of sheer bloodlust and nearly getting caught. Memories of catching sight of Alex for the first time after a decade of hunting him.

My heart beats out of rhythm while the memories flip like pages in a novel.

Kai took the train to campus the night I met him in the terminal with Abby. He watched me until the train sped out of sight. He remembered my scent, kept note of it, while he snuck around campus for days undetected. He watched me and Alex in the library. He saw Alex kiss me.

He saw that Alex had something that couldn't be replaced.

He watched Alex like a hawk then, following him on and off campus while forming a plan that would hurt him the most, noticing that Alex's vampiric senses had weakened after being out of use for so long. But, he couldn't access the lab, which he believed would be exactly where he could make the biggest mess and fuck with Alex's head the most, so he did the next best thing.

He killed a local wolf–a woman–outside of Aurorium out of need. He wanted to be strong to enact his plan. He snuck back onto campus and watched Alex and Laney conversing in Alex's office. He watched me walk in, and followed Laney, making a mental map of her routine.

Then, he made his move and cornered her in the clinic. He made it messy. Made it hurt. Told her it was Alex's fault she was dying this way. He almost decided to turn her, but he was starving after so long on the ice and killed her almost by accident.

And then he–

An image cuts through his memories. My body jerks, and somewhere in the aether, I hear Abby calling out my name, panicked.

I'm in an ice cave, somewhere deep on the ice field, miles away from Aurorium. I'm in his head. I can feel new thoughts. This is the present in his mind. I'm seeing through his eyes.

Abby calls out my name again, but it's lost in the groan of an unforgiving wind beating down on the only shelter Kai could find, and he's spent weeks here, starving.

He got hurt that day in the lab when he finally gained access with the help of the dean, whom he killed in the tunnel after tampering with a drill that should have been offline. The drill went haywire, cracking a pocket that sent tremors through the lab, causing the collapse. The dean fought back when he was killing him, though. He stabbed Kai several times, and without blood and adequate shelter, on top of the unforgiving cold, healing has been slow.

But there's something with him in the cave. Something dark and bloody. An animal, perhaps. Dead and small. Not enough, but it will do for now.

"I can feel you in my head, witch," he rasps.

I'm yanked free of his mind against my will by a vision that clouds everything else. Abby screams my name, but my body hits the floor, and I have a brief moment of clarity, my eyes on the ceiling of Alex's kitchen, before I'm dragged into the vision. The stars scream in warning. My powers stretch to their limit, and then, it's quiet.

The glare of the lights in Aurorium distorts the vision. Alex is talking to a man I don't recognize at first, but I realize I'm intimately familiar with now.

"You've lost me everything. My kingdom. My armies. I should kill you now, but I'm enjoying this game."

"Stay away from her."

"I will make you a deal, bastard prince. Her life for yours–for eternity."

"SKYE!" Abby grabs my cheeks, slapping me for several seconds. The vision, however, doesn't let up, but shifts, and I'm in… Maatua? But a part of Maatua I've never seen. It's paradise, but in a strangely unnerving way.

Fallon grabs the hand of a man with dark hair and sun-tanned skin. They're fighting–passionately, and he pulls her into a grand, almost Gothic estate, slamming the door behind them. The vision pans out like I'm airborne, giving me a glimpse of a wide swath of islands and coves–and then, a heavy, crushing sensation embraces me–squeezing the life out of me.

"Wake up! This is freaking me out!" Abby cries, shaking me violently.

I open my eyes, panting, and look wildly around before she comes into focus.

"What the fuck? What the actual fuck, Skye?" she screeches,

pulling me upright. "Your nose and ears are bleeding! Are you okay? Is that supposed to happen?"

"I think–it got a little out of hand," I admit, but a wave of nausea rips through me. I throw up directly onto the floor beside us. Abby grabs my hair while I retch, shivering, unable to stop.

"Is that supposed to happen?" she asks.

"No," I reply weakly, dizzy, feeling like I haven't slept in weeks for some reason. "I haven't been feeling well. It's been stressful–but I found him. He's out on the ice but coming back to Aurorium. He'll intercept Alex and try to force him to make a deal…."

"Are you sick? Can I take you to the clinic, please?"

"I'm fine," I choke out, but I feel like I'm going to throw up again. This time, I make it to the bathroom, at least, but Abby babies me into bed, where she sits beside me and fiddles with my fingers.

"Can I ask you something again?" she asks nervously, and I nod, my head throbbing. "Are you fucking pregnant, Skye?"

"No–no, of course not, Abby. That's–Alex said it's really rare–"

"Have you been doing anything to stop it from happening?"

"Uh… I don't think so? I can't have this conversation right now. I just pushed myself too far, and my powers hurt–"

"You smell pregnant," she hisses, clutching my hand.

I sit up and look into her eyes. "What?"

"I can smell it on you. My mom's a midwife, remember? I practically grew up in her practice. I'd recognize this scent anywhere. Shifters can sense that. Hell, I bet if Alex were a shifter, he would have noticed this right away."

"I am not pregnant."

"You are," she says sternly, looking suddenly panicked. "I'd bet my life on it."

41

POSITIVE

Alex

THE BETA OF AURORIUM LEVELS ME WITH A LOOK FROM ONE END OF A long, wooden table. The packhouse in the city is one of the only buildings that isn't drenched in artificial neon light. A massive stone fireplace heats a wide, open room decorated rustically with animal hides and leather galore.

It would be comforting in a shifter-like way if not for my current situation.

The Beta flings a file toward me and folds his hands on the table surface.

"I'm sure you're aware of the situation at the university," I say, opening the file. "My lab is completely demolished. I can't run–" I stop my voice in its tracks. The pictures on the top of the stack of paperwork in the file are of Laney and Dean Kanten. Laney in shambles. Dean Kanten in one piece, but pale, his body sunken in and distorted but in a way I find grossly familiar despite the wreckage of the ice tunnel he was found in after an extensive search.

"I've spoken to the university about you, Dr. Scarlett. I was told you had a tumultuous personal relationship with Dr. Kanten."

"You were misinformed. I didn't have a personal relationship with Dr. Kanten."

"Professionally, then."

I heave a breath and close the file. "Is there a reason you asked me to come to Aurorium today, or is this an interrogation?"

"My Alpha has tasked me with continuing the investigation into four murders we now believe are connected, and you were the last person to see the young student from the university alive—"

"Laney."

"Laney," he says with a tinge of annoyance. "And your relationship with Dr. Kanten leaves room for interpretation."

"I didn't like the man, and that's as far as it goes."

"Did you kill him?"

I narrow my eyes into a fierce glare. "No, but I haven't mourned him, either. I know what you're going to ask, so this is it; Dr. Kanten made it impossible for my lab to have the safety measures required to keep the lab running safely and efficiently. His disdain for me was a direct result of years of academic and professional competition between us, but it was entirely one-sided. He had a vendetta against me. I simply wanted functioning sensors in my lab that would have prevented the level of collapse we dealt with several weeks ago. Killing him wouldn't have solved my problem."

"But you wanted his position as dean," he argues.

I bark a laugh. "If you actually talked to the president of the university, you would know I've turned down several offers to be dean of the biology department. As it stands, I'm not even in the running because I pulled myself from consideration. The board is in the process of choosing Kanten's successor as we speak."

The Beta frowns but doesn't look convinced. The door to the meeting room opens, and several warriors waltz in to walk me out, marking the end of the conversation, but the tight feeling in my chest doesn't leave.

I'm supposed to meet Toby at a bar a few streets over before we head back to campus. I've been slowly restocking the make-shift, surface-level lab whenever I'm not lecturing, but the last few weeks have made it clear that my run at Lunaria University might be coming to an end.

I have Skye to think about, and that's why, when a man steps out of the shadows at the end of the street ahead of me, I decide enough is enough.

Kai's eyes are the color of polished embers but glow a deep red when he lifts his hood ever so slightly into the glare of a streetlight.

I stop in the dead center of the street. He turns and walks calmly between two buildings, and I follow, keeping a cautious distance between us, but my fangs lengthen, and blood thrums with every step I take.

I lose sight of him in the alley, but not for long.

"Prince Alex," he says from the darkness of the loading dock tucked between a trio of towering buildings. We're in the shadows here, clustered away from the populated streets and icy thoroughfares just beyond the reach of the ever-present darkness.

"How do you expect this to end?" I ask sharply, putting ten yards of distance between us, not that it matters. We could be at each other's throats in a matter of seconds–in the span of a single breath.

"That depends on how easy you want to make this for the both of us."

"What do you want, Kai?"

He chuckles bitterly, stepping closer but stops, tattered boots sliding over the ice. "You've changed."

"How so?"

"Look at you–all sleek and fancy in your modern fare while your own people–"

"I know, without a shadow of a doubt, that the only reason you'd dare to be here is because there's nothing left for you back in Red River. Am I wrong?"

Hatred flares behind his eyes. "Who is to blame for that? You are the reason my armies fell. You are the reason I was pushed out of my own kingdom, and my mother's throne was toppled–"

"I freed an entire kingdom of slaves the second Queen Matilda's head hit the cobblestone."

"And for what? Petty name-calling? Ha!" His snarl is bloody. "My mother was a true vampire. High-bred. High-born. True vampire blood blessed by generations of blood-born ancestors. You, prince, are scum."

"You forget I am also a blood-born vampire."

"But the woman you call mother is not. An undead witch parading as queen of Scarlet Thunder? That is the reason there was a war. King Michael and Queen Faye acted only because their precious shifter populations were threatened by the prowess of the blood-born armies—a worthy cause, something my mother anticipated. But your whore of a father and fraud of a mother joined the fight because—"

"Because your mother threatened my mother's life," I snarl.

"You aren't the true prince. They can never give their kingdom a true heir, and my mother made that clear to the masses."

"Did your mother ever tell you that she was the one who gave me to Emelda?"

Kai blinks, his furious expression wavering.

"Well, I suppose we learn something new every day—"

"Shut up, you weak, disgusting excuse for a man. I've been hunting you for almost a decade. I figured you died, just like everyone else thought. Your parents, on the other hand, have never given up hope, but it was you who won the honors of that war. You're a legend now. A god among beasts that now roam freely across my lands. Shifters and witches alike—the lot of them. Free. Free to interbreed with vampires as they wish and tarnish bloodlines."

"You're disgusting."

"And I was not shocked when I found you shacked up here, pretending to be someone and something you're not, lusting after a hybrid, by the scent of her."

My nostrils flare when he licks his lips. "Delicious, that one. I can only imagine what she tastes like."

"Never speak a word of her again."

"I came here to drag you back. I want you alive, Prince Alex, because if I bring you home… imagine the shock and the turning of tables in my favor when the public finds out the fallen prince they worshipped for ending the war has been alive this whole time and hiding like a coward."

"I built a life I wouldn't have been able to have back home."

"I know why you're really here," he whispers, laughing under his breath. "Oh, Alex. How they talk about you like you were some miracle worker. Your apothecary advances across all genera. Brilliant, they call you. But you, based on your, what do you call it? A laboratory? All your shiny instruments and machinery…. You aren't really masquerading as a scientist in search of the unexplainable. You are looking for a cure."

I bristle, and he grins like a cat.

"All this talk about my mother's grand plans of a pure vampire race, and you are trying to find a way to turn your mother into the same thing–to cure her of the torment of being turned. What's the reason, Prince Alex? Was it clear to you as it was clear to my mother that you'd never rule, and your parents would need an actual born heir in your place?" When I say nothing, he continues with a smirk. "I suppose your silence is answer enough."

"What do you want from me, Kai?"

"I've already told you. You're coming with me. I want you alive to witness the downfall of your family in my wake when your secrets come to light."

"I have no secrets, and I won't come with you. War against my family all you want, but you're banished and washed up, no longer in power."

"I will continue to make your life here hell."

"You can try."

"She's next. You think a woman as smart as her will stick around when you're forced into hiding again? Where will you run this time, Alex? What ends of the world can you possibly run to? I will find you everywhere. I will hunt you for centuries. I will kill everyone you hold dear, just like I killed your precious protege. You're weak now.

You've gone so long without having to be who you really are. I could kill you now."

"Try."

He laughs, his face tilting to the faint light of a flickering street lamp. His gauntness is answer enough.

"You're barely surviving here. I have time to make a decision."

"And I have time to kill the woman you love. Maybe I'll even keep her for a while for my own entertainment."

I snarl and lunge, but he disappears in a blur of movement, skirting around me so quickly I lose sight of him before the trash in his wake has fallen back to the ground.

I immediately go back to campus, texting Toby my plans to skip the bar while I ride the train, my heart hammering. Time moves at a crawl. I should have tried to kill him then, but there has to be a better way, and that solution stares me in the face while I hesitate outside the door of my condo.

I do need to go home, eventually. I need to see my family again. I need to bring this fucker to justice and end this cleanly, but that means… years away from Skye–and an uncertain future ahead.

It means ending things with Skye, the woman I love. The woman… I would travel thousands upon thousands of miles in order to keep her safe.

I probably can't kill Kai on my own. He's powerful, even as hungry and defeated as he is right now. His skill in battle is legendary, and he will make good on the many threats he threw my way tonight.

Which is why I will go with him. At least until we're far enough away from Lunaria that I can kill him in his sleep.

"Skye?" I call out, closing the door behind me. It's unnaturally quiet and dark in the condo, and for a moment, I panic, imagining her blood painting the walls of the bedroom as I race down the hallway.

I throw the door open and find her in one piece, sitting on the edge of the bed.

"Hey. Hey, Skye? Are you all right?"

I kneel in front of her. She has her hands balled in her lap, clutching something small.

"Skye?"

She looks up at me when I smooth her hair behind her ears.

Then, she unravels her fingers.

A pregnancy test sits in her palms. I see the result. It's a glaring positive that hits me in the gut.

"I went to the clinic with Abby," she says quietly, stricken, I think, with the same kind of shock ripping through my system. "I'm already two months along. I had no idea. The first time we ever–Alex, I don't know what to do."

All plans to leave exit my brain.

I have to kill Kai.

Right now.

As soon as fucking possible.

42

A MISCALCULATION

Skye

ALEX TAKES MY TREMBLING HANDS. "EVERYTHING IS GOING TO BE okay."

"How?" My heart races. Guilt and uncertainty tangle into a ball of yarn in my brain that I'll never be able to unwind. "You don't–you can't possibly want this. Especially not now."

"I do, and we're going to figure it out. I'm more concerned about the fact that you're about to go through a hybrid pregnancy." He sits beside me on the bed, smoothing his hand down my back. "My great aunt Emory," he explains, taking a deep breath. "She was a shifter, similar to you. Full shifter, though, and her pregnancy with my uncle Michael was… terrible."

"How so?"

"I don't have all the details given that this story was told to me as a teenager–something meant to keep me from pursuing shifters for their own safety, I suppose." He grits his teeth, but I feel oddly light.

"Were you a major flirt or something?"

"No." He laughs, winding his arm around my back and tugging me close. "I was not. If anything, I was awkward and terrified of women. My cousin Drake was the worst offender, but we were often grouped together for conversations like that."

I lean into his side, smiling at the idea of Alex, now a world-renowned biologist and a man who oozes confidence, being what I imagine as a lanky, socially awkward teenage boy.

"Vampire pregnancies are an ordeal. The babies take a lot of energy, and most vampire women close themselves away for months with the care of physicians–especially in the early days. Emory struggled immensely."

"I've been feeling unwell for a while."

"I've noticed. I thought it was stress."

"So did I," I admit. "I'm sorry I didn't voice it."

"I should have picked up on it."

"How could you have? With everything else we've been dealing with? It's not your fault."

"It feels like my fault," he says, swallowing hard. "And I've fed from you recently. I should have sensed it. Fuck, Skye, I'm sorry."

"Don't be."

He turns me to face him, pulling me onto his lap. His hands rest on either side of my face, and his expression turns so serious he could slice through me with his gaze like butter against a heated knife. "You're going to be very sick for a while. I'm shocked you're not bedridden now, given how far along you are, but I promise you, Skye, that I'm going to do everything in my power to keep you safe. I love you. I am in love with you, and I have been since the moment I saw you. You are mine, and I will protect you and this baby."

"What are you planning?"

"I will protect you," he reiterates, and I have an overwhelming sense that something else happened that he's not telling me. Did he talk to Kai, like I saw?

"Is this about Kai?"

"This is about us." He leans forward, resting his forehead against mine. "The university isn't going to be kind about this. You're going to need an extended leave of absence. They're already aware of our relationship, but things need to change now–quickly."

I lean back, not sure I like the urgency in his tone. He's... afraid of something.

And then it hits me.

"They'll push me out of my position?"

"Yes, and I already have strikes against me with Alloway. The Beta of Aurorium is acting like I'm a suspect in the murders."

"What are you suggesting we do?"

"Get married. Immediately. Tonight, if we can. I know the temple in Aurorium is always open–"

"You can't–you can't actually want this! You're a prince, Alex. Aren't there rules for you about this?"

"I haven't been the Prince of Scarlet Thunder in thirteen years, Skye. That doesn't matter now."

"You don't want to marry me."

"I do. Fuck, I do. I want you protected–both of you. I want to marry you because I want to be able to call you my wife but also because, if anything happens to me, everything I have is yours. I don't have much, but it's enough to keep you and the baby going for a while. But I need you to listen to me now. You know the university is going to do what it can to push you out of your position once they know."

My stomach curls. I feel heavily nauseous again but push it down. He's right. I've had female colleagues who straight-up disappeared after announcing their pregnancies and showed up in industry positions in various cities across the Allied Kingdoms. The campus here isn't conducive to family life, and that's apparent at every turn. Most professors and faculty with families live in Aurorium and commute to work, but housing there is hard to find.

And my time here is limited anyway. Alex found that out recently.

His time here is limited as well.

"We have to consider you going back to Moonrise, at least for the duration of the pregnancy."

I hate that he's right.

Going home means telling my family the truth.

"I'll marry you, but only because I want to. Because I love you, and I want us to be together, whatever that looks like. And I will marry you tonight because I know you're plotting something you're not telling me about, and you're nervous about it."

"Skye–"

"I can look into your head and find it–unless you want to tell me?" I hold his gaze.

"Kai made himself known tonight. Threatened me. Threatened us."

"And what are we going to do about it?"

"I'm going to handle it," he says sternly, but I don't like the look in his eyes.

I don't like it even when we're standing outside the temple in Aurorium with a marriage certificate in our hands, our signatures still wet. Abby and Toby tagged along as witnesses, and while the moment we stood in front of a rather confused priestess felt like we were exactly where we were meant to be, Alex seemed off–distracted, his expression painted in shadows of determination and promises of death.

Because Kai is here, in the city, somewhere.

The next morning, Alex slides out of bed and leaves, murmuring something about needing to meet Toby in the lab and then settle our issues with the university. He kisses me, tells me to rest, that he has this, and he will make everything right for us.

And I know he will.

But I can't sit around while he carries the burden of our uncertain future on his shoulders.

I move through the winding skybridges of the campus I thought felt like home once. Maybe it did at one point. Now, I feel suddenly suffocated within its walls, choked to death by social restraints that I'm afraid will haunt me and Alex for the rest of our lives.

I step into the observatory. It's empty, just like I hoped it would be. I toy with my phone, tempted to call my parents, wondering how angry they'll be to learn their daughter is pregnant and had a shotgun wedding and the ink on the license is barely dry, but that's not what I'm worried about.

Alex is a being of calculated risk. He knows exactly the best course of action in any situation. He wanted to marry me to keep me and the baby safe. I understand that part. But he failed to voice that the real reason he wanted us attached from a legal standpoint is because he's planning on killing Kai—and believes he'll die in the effort.

I married him because now he'll have the safety and protection of the royal family of the Allied Kingdoms, no matter what.

Because he's not going to kill Kai.

I am.

I close my eyes and let my powers flare.

I've found Kai once before. He might be a beast of pure death, but he's a stupid one. His mind is open and mine for the taking. He has no training in mental wards because he's never needed it until now. My hatred of him, a stranger, runs so deep, I could find him anywhere. My hatred of him for what he's done to Alex, for what his mother did to Alex, his family, and his kingdom, is the reason the entire brunt of my powers funnel and hone in on his location.

The silence in the observatory explodes into murmurs. I finally allow myself to be the mystic I know I can be, letting go of my restraints, and fold the stars into a weapon of my own design.

Kai is in the city, smoking a cigarette, watching the entrance of a grocery store. He watches a mother juggle shopping bags while two young children slide on the ice on either side of her. I dive into the vision, into his mind, peeling back layers of emotionally driven sparks of color to decipher his inner thoughts. He thinks she'd be an easy target. Her man is likely at work or hunting out on the ice. He can subdue her quickly. He can easily subdue a child. He'd be well fed.

"Can you feel me?" I ask him, grinning around the feeling of him jolting into awareness at my intrusion. *"I found you."*

If I were more powerful, I could undo his mind from dozens of miles away, but I'm not. I just get glimpses from here. I need to touch him to take him apart.

"I'm coming for you," I whisper into his head. He snuffs out his cigarette, smiling wickedly.

"It's been so long since I've tasted a witch. Do your worst. I'll be waiting."

He turns into a shadow between two buildings. I let the connection drop. I have what I need. I can scry from anywhere to find him now.

I rise and move through the campus, jogging, my heart hammering. I have to do this quickly. I want to finish this before Alex and I have to face the consequences of our rushed actions. I want to free Alex of the burden he's carried for almost half his life. He wants to protect me. I want to return the favor, which means bending myself into a being of death once again.

I've killed before out of hatred. I've ripped a mind apart. I've never forgotten how it feels.

I still have the keys to the old apartment I shared with Abby. I slip inside and find her sitting on the couch with her laptop propped open. Her lips part in shock when she sees me.

"Skye? Are you okay?"

My voice doesn't sound like my own when I reply, "I need to borrow some clothes."

"What's going on?" She rises slowly, setting her laptop down. "You don't look well."

"I need you to do something for me," I tell her, swallowing against a sharp knot forming in my throat. A sob, I think, because the truth of what I'm about to do is now striking me directly in the chest. "If Alex asks where I am, tell him I've gone out on the ice."

"What?"

"Tell him I'm sorry, but if we're going to have a shot at the life we both want together, I have to do this. It's all for him." I lick my lips. "And… tell him not to worry. I've done this before."

"Skye?" She rushes me, but I hold out a hand. My fingers brush her collarbone, and that's all it takes to subdue her. My powers flare through her head, forcing her to sleep. She slumps, and I catch her, lowering her back down onto the couch.

I can only hope Kai is the same—only much deader.

I put on her bright yellow thermals and equally obnoxious yellow parka. I slip into her best winter boots with pointed spikes. Then, I let my powers surge, and her apartment shifts form, fading in and out until the warm, sterile air turns to bitter cold wind and a landscape of pure ice.

Kai turns to face me, red eyes shining like dying stars. His fangs, twice as long as Alex's, fully expand.

It was… almost too easy.

Somewhere in the aether, I catch glimpses of Abby waking up and crawling on her hands and knees to the coffee table where she left her phone. She calls Toby, barely able to speak, but begs him to find Alex. She tells him I'm in trouble, that I've gone out onto the ice.

The visions fade. I look around while Kai approaches me, drinking me in with his cold-blooded eyes. The campus is only ten miles away. Alex is fast. He can cover that distance in minutes.

I have minutes to finish this.

I turn back to Kai.

But I miscalculated.

Alex was right when he told me Kai was powerful. He was right when he told me vampires could outrun me in a breath.

Kai has me on the ground in a single second, and before I can even touch him, his fangs sink into the base of my throat–and rip.

43

OUT OF OPTIONS

Alex

THERE IS NOTHING IN MY HEAD BUT RED VIOLENCE AS I SPRINT OUT onto the ice. Students out for a stroll in their wolf forms dart away, but I'm a blur of motion. I'll pay dearly for this. I can't return to campus, that's for sure. The ever-present darkness is my only cover. I have no idea where I'm going, but forward is my only option. Forward, forward, running miles in minutes I'm not sure I have. I'm a fucking idiot. I underestimated her. I think I underestimated her love for me, if I'm being totally, brutally honest with myself. Skye protected my secrets with her entire soul. I should have seen it in her eyes when she began to notice something was gravely wrong when I asked her to marry me. I should have seen it in her eyes when I left her this morning.

She knew Kai tried making a deal with me. She's so powerful. She might have had a shot at fixing this for both of us if Kai wasn't like me—but worse.

Wind rips over the ice, nearly knocking me on my side, but I keep going, ignoring the warning bells skittering through my tangled mind. My wife is out here. The woman carrying my child. The woman I love. I won't stop. I've run further and longer than this before.

The wind changes direction, carrying the heavy scent of blood that is all too familiar, and I feel my body curling into a version of myself I haven't felt in many, many years. My brain shuts down entirely. The Alex I was before–the scientist, the man with diplomas hanging on the gray slate walls of his office–fades, replaced by the monster I was born to be. My fangs elongate, slicing my lips open, but I don't feel it. My mouth is already soaked with my own black, undead blood when I see yellow on the ice. Bright, neon yellow that settles in my bones and explodes into rage I feel in my soul.

A dark shadow curls over Skye, trembling and grunting with each gulp of her blood he takes. I scream with fury. My mind shuts off entirely. I am nothing but moving parts propelled by instinct, and that instinct is to kill.

I collide with the other vampire, rolling over the ice. We're dragged to a stop by the wind, but I have him pinned to the ground in a split second. Kai's fangs are jagged, one tip missing. He hisses and fights my weight, but I rip his tattered coat open wide and slice through his chest with my fangs.

His screech of pain is lost in the wind.

He grabs my hat and yanks it free, clawing at my hair, ripping open my scalp with his elongated nails. He yanks my mouth free from his chest and rolls us across the ice, but I fight, focusing on the reason we're here. I need to kill him. That's the only thought in my mind. Killing another vampire royal is almost impossible. I have no weapons. I am untrained in comparison to him, but it doesn't show. He tries to bite through my parka and gets a mouthful of goose down, choking on it. I shove him off and lunge, tossing us further and further away from the bundle of yellow and red in my peripheral vision.

"You're done," I rasp, biting down on his neck, trying to tear him open. "This is over. I win. I win, you fucking monster. Red River is dead."

But he—his blood—tastes like... Skye.

"She was worth it. Now I know why you wanted to keep her for yourself so badly," he chokes out and uses my moment of clarity to push me off.

I stumble to my feet, frantic, my eyes locked on the body a hundred or so yards away. Skye lies motionless on the ice, the yellow parka she stole from Abby stained with so much blood it's almost impossible to tell its color anymore.

I look at Kai, who scrambles to his feet, his hand pressed to his neck. Black blood oozes between his fingers. His mouth, however, is coated with her red blood.

I imagine my mother, her dark eyes and calm voice. I think of my father and his sarcastic drawl. I think of Drake and Emma—the last moment I saw them. Emma's tears and Drake's determination to ensure I had a chance to run.

All for this. I ran for this. For her. For a life with her.

Kai snickers. I slowly look from Skye to him.

It's impossible to kill a vampire. I told her that. She tried anyway because she's a better person than I am. I would have run. I would have taken her to the ends of the earth to try to keep her safe. I would have hidden her and subjected her to a life like mine—lonely, away from her family and friends.

She is a better person than I. A braver person.

I snap. It happens quickly. My mind and body separate again, and before my rational brain has a chance to catch up with what I'm doing, I have Kai on the ground. He's surprised as well, his eyes wide and open, a glint of fear behind those orbs of red. I doubt he's ever been afraid before.

I don't have a single thing to say to him.

"Alex!" Skye cries out. I'm not sure if it's actually her calling out for me or a memory, but it's the reason I grip his mouth with both hands, his fangs sinking into my flesh, and rip his jaw to pieces. He can't even scream.

Blood gushes, spraying me in a torrent. Her blood. The blood he drained from her. He was going to kill her, draining her to the last drop. He was going to take her from me as punishment for my actions against his mother.

I scream into the feeling of his skull caving in under my wrath.

And then the ice is quiet. The wind howls in the distance, carrying the last notes of Kai's life.

I rise, shaking, the puncture wounds on my hands healing so quickly I don't even feel any pain. I turn to the body across the ice. Skye. My wife. My mate, if I could choose.

———

SKYE

ALEX SLIDES ON HIS KNEES ACROSS THE ICE. THE SCENT OF BLOOD flooding off his clothes is sharp, fresh, just like the cracking sound of a jaw being broken apart that still echoes through my mind, blurring my senses to highlight only one sensation–his hands on my broken skin. Warm and damp, they close around my cheeks, then lower, to the gaping wound where my throat should be.

The sky dances with stars beyond his silhouette while he whispers what we already know we don't have time to accomplish. We're so far away from campus and the clinic, where it's unlikely they'd be able to save my life as it stands. In any other circumstance, I'd be bleeding out, a lost cause. Dead on arrival.

I have no blood left to bleed.

"Skye?" His voice is impossibly broken as he lowers his face to mine, pressing his hand against my throat like he can stop whatever blood loss is left. I'm limp, barely able to lift my arms to clutch his blood-soaked jacket, curling my numb, trembling fingers into the soft cotton spilling from the torn seams.

Frigid air bites his exposed skin as much as it's sinking its teeth into mine.

I want to tell him to go back, to leave me, but it's fruitless. Alex will never leave me. He's made that perfectly clear at every turn. I am his. He is mine. This isn't a mate bond. It's bigger than that. Our threads weren't woven together from the moment of our first breaths. There is no single star of fate shining down on us as death sweeps over the ice, creeping toward me like a long-taloned shadow, waiting in silence to strike.

We wrote this. Willed it into existence with every breath, every word. In every stolen moment of silence, locked in each other's arms. In every promise, every laugh, and breathy sigh.

If I had a mate, it would be him.

If I could choose, I'd choose him. Over and over again. Forever.

And for that, I'm so sorry.

He has… centuries to live.

I have… seconds.

I'm not ready.

"I'm going to get you out of here. It's going to be okay. I promise. Look at me, Skye. I've got you. You're going to wake up, and everything is going to be okay, and I'll be there, waiting for you. Just keep–" His voice breaks with a sob that strikes me in the heart, forcing it to beat once more. "Keep looking at me. Please. Don't close your eyes. I'm here. Look at the stars, Skye, aren't they beautiful? I can see the Cerridwen Galaxy, just like you said. I get it now. I understand." He presses his lips to mine and cries out in utter despair. It's gut-wrenching. My fingers twitch. I want to make it better for him. Isn't that what we do for each other? Make it better? Make it tolerable?

"I love you. Don't leave me." He shakes me violently, and I don't feel a thing, because I'm already gone, aren't I?

Above me, the tapestry is a hazy stream of flickering lights against the stars. I count the threads, following the lifelines of those I love, finding mine… breaking. Splintering into pieces, carried away on a soft, phantom breeze, piece by piece, atom by atom. Me–and our baby. Our miracle. Both threads just… fading.

I know what he's thinking. It's already shining in his eyes. He doesn't need to voice it–an option he wishes he had. Kill me. Make it quick. Painless. Then drag me somewhere underground until I rise again–made in his image. He's thinking about it, struggling with trying it, even though we both know it wouldn't work, praying that it might, because I'm already leaving him. He'll lose both of us that way. I'd never be the same. He'd never forgive himself. But it doesn't matter anyway. I am a mystic, but I'm also a wolf shifter. Wolf shifters can't be turned. We both know it. My fingers slacken, beginning to slip from the fabric of his parka. He has mere seconds to decide to try it.

And I already know he won't because he's a good man, but he'll live the rest of his long life wondering what it would have been like if he'd made the selfish decision to try to turn me into something like him, but colder, deader.

Like his mother.

His gutted, sharp cry of anguish follows another violent shake, like he's trying to jolt me back to life.

My heart beats once, then twice, before the tapestry slowly begins to fade.

He's out of options and out of time.

I have one option. Just one.

"Forgive me," I whisper with my dying breath. "Do not let go of me."

I clutch his parka with the last of my strength and let my severely diminished powers warm my broken body until the ice beneath us cracks and sizzles. The stars fade to black. The world around us ceases to exist. It's a violent journey. Too sharp. Too bouncy and uneven, unlike anything I've ever done before, but it's my remaining powers dictating our path, and I have no choice but to let go and let them lead the way.

Hazy, rainy sunlight fills the space behind my eyelids. I open my eyes to slits—to Alex, groggy, bearing his weight against my upper arms to keep me pinned to the floor, which is no longer a sheet of unforgivingly cold ice.

It's carpet.

A hazy figure in black shoots up from behind a desk made of shadowed glass.

"Forgive me," I mouth when Alex opens his eyes, startled and confused. Behind him, papers lift and twist to the floor in the wake of the man leaping over his desk and racing toward us.

I know what this looks like. Alex is pinning me to the ground. I'm missing my throat. We're both covered in blood–so much blood, and it's mostly mine.

None of it is Alex's blood.

Yet.

This was my only option. I'm not done here. I want a life with him, whatever that looks like. I have to at least try.

"Forgive me," I mouth again, my eyes slipping closed to the moment Dad's powers erupt, and Alex is torn from my body and is lost in a shower of glass as his body shatters through one of Dad's bookshelves, and then my eyes fill with red before the light fades entirely.

44

MURDERING MONSTER

BLAKE

THE MAN FALLS TO THE GROUND IN A FLURRY OF GOOSE DOWN, BLACK nylon, and a shower of glass at the very second royal warriors burst through my office door.

I can't breathe. My lungs strain against the torrent of panic driving every move I make as I whirl to the warriors storming the room and shout for them to subdue the stranger, but I can't hear my own voice over the rapid thunder of my heartbeat in my ears.

My *daughter* is lying lifeless on the carpet of my office. The same office she grew up in, spent entire days rolling my crystal spheres across the carpet and racing around on Soren's shoulders. I see her like that now—a child.

Rage storms my senses. My roar of fury threatens to splinter the windows as my knees hit the ground by her head. I reach down, trying to gather what's left of her in my arms.

Kenna bursts into the room, breathless, her silver eyes wide and frantic as she reaches my side.

"HELP!" I shout, clutching Skye to my chest. "Kenna!"

"Lay her down!" Kenna is white as a ghost, paler even than her clinic robes and apron. Several of her assistants rush in after her, all witches, all in the same white robes that match the pallor of their cheeks when they see her, my child, in tatters. "What happened?" Kenna rushes out, turning frantic eyes on mine.

I can only shake my head and look in the direction of the unfamiliar man currently being dragged to his feet and pinned to the wall by four of Maeve's guards.

The second Skye's burst of magic erupted through my office at the palace, I knew something was wrong. I sent out an alert through the mind-link before she'd even come into view, and when she did, and I saw all that blood... and her throat... and him....

I snarl involuntarily, gripping Skye's practically lifeless body. Kenna shakes my arm, sinking her nails through the fabric of my shirt. "Let her go. I need some space. Look at me, Blake. Look–look at me!"

All I see is red. Red blood. Red rage knocking me sideways and turning me inside out. This is *my baby*. I saw her come into the world and take her first breath.

That rage turns to a twisting, gnawing kind of anguish that makes me want to tear the world to shreds, and I can't fight it.

"Look at me. I've got her. You need to back away before you kill everyone in the room." Kenna grips my arm again, squeezing.

The man being held against the wall suddenly comes to with a groan and jerks against the hold of the guards, who shove him against the wall with force in return. His eyes open to slits, then wider, a startling, deep blue, and lock on mine.

Seconds move like hours. His eyes widen in recognition, and he begins to frantically jerk against the hold of the warriors, snarling and hissing with fury, then stills when he sees Skye on the ground.

His eyes soften. His expression goes slack. The fury and confusion behind his expression shatters into... something I don't understand. Not at first.

Kenna smooths her hand over Skye's chest before she reaches for her ravaged throat, her healing powers drifting over Skye's skin. I already know it's not going to be enough to save her life.

"I can keep her heart beating, but she needs to be moved down to the clinic and stabilized as soon as possible. Lucy, call down to the clinic and have an operating room prepped immediately," Kenna rushes out, and more witches circle around us carrying supplies and towels to sop up the blood that isn't soaking into the carpet.

Because there isn't any. It's gone. Almost all of it.

I'm still looking at the man. At his grimace of concern. At his pointed *fangs*.

"You fucking monster!" I snarl, and all hell breaks loose.

Shouts of alarm echo around the room, but I have a one-track mind when my fingers curl around his throat and squeeze, all of my strength locked on keeping him pinned to the wall where my bookshelves used to be. I don't remember moving. I have no memory of letting my daughter go and slamming into him so hard that his eyes momentarily roll back in his head, but I did, and now he's coming back to reality, and his eyes aren't on mine.

He takes a strained breath, his gaze honed on my daughter. Skye's legs twitch. It's the only part of her within view as the healers kneel all around her, but when Skye lets out a tangled breath and groans, then screams in panic and pain, he jerks again, desperate, his eyes widening.

"Skye? Skye, honey, it's me, it's Kenna! You're safe! Look at me, sweetheart, it's me. I'm not going to hurt you."

Skye is panicking, trying to fight against the hold of the nurses.

"Skye, you need to calm down. You're very hurt. Look at me, Skye. You need to stay as still as possible. We're doing everything we can."

My daughter whimpers, jerks, then goes quiet. The tension in the room crackles for several seconds before she comes to again and rushes out a pained breath.

"Calm down, honey. You have to calm down." Kenna looks wildly at her assistants. "We need to move her, now!"

The man tries to break out of my hold, his eyes desperate, locked on Skye.

I shove him again. "Don't fucking look at her!"

"She's not lucid," Kenna explains to her assistants. "She's hurting badly. Is the operating room ready? We need to go. I don't have time to wait–"

Skye's scream of pain and fear explodes around the room. Even I'm temporarily useless against the sound. It burrows into my chest, erupting into a sharp, aching kind of worry only a parent can feel, but I hold fast to the monster that did this to her.

"What the fuck is going on?" Maeve shouts from the doorway, Soren catching her arm before she can enter, but her arrival is lost in the first word Skye manages to say.

"A-Alex?"

"I'm here. Skye, don't–don't try to talk," the man, Alex, apparently, says on a strained breath. Instinctually, I tighten my grip on his throat, and he grunts, unable to take a deeper breath. He doesn't even look at me nor fight it. He's looking at her. He's not even blinking.

Skye cries out in pain again, and the witches start moving, preparing to allow the guards to pick her up, but when her face comes into view... she's looking right at this bastard, her eyes still cloudy with the death that came so close to claiming her.

Alex stops trying to get out from beneath my hold. He relaxes, his eyes suddenly glossy with relief and... this doesn't make any sense. He did this to her. He's covered in her blood–I can smell it. He's drenched in *all* of her blood.

I shove him hard, and he gasps at the sensation of my forearm pressed sharply against his ribs.

"Dad!" Skye cries out, but her voice is muffled by another cry of pain that slices through the air and threatens to bring me to my knees.

I don't bother to ask him who he is.

I grip his face, my fingers digging into his forehead, and when he shouts in agony, Skye screams, "DAD! DON'T!"

I'm swept into his mind–carefully, thoughtfully, deciding it will be better in the long run, when he's in a cell beneath Maeve's palace, if his mind stays in one piece, but I know what I'm looking for... and find it.

Him, on the ice, hunting. Hunting for her. He's desperate, sprinting into the darkness, then slows when he sees her.

Broken.

He falls to his knees, unable to remain upright, then sees the shadow unlatching itself from my daughter's neck, and Alex's mind goes a sharp, brutal red. Everything beyond that is a deadly kind of rage. No imagery, just feeling. He killed something out there, brutally, showing not a single ounce of thought or mercy. He didn't think twice about it either, like he was driven by instinct, and that instinct was to kill.

And it wasn't Skye. It was *for* her.

I pull myself out of his mind, swaying, bracing my hand against the wall by his head.

Maeve is at my side, gripping my arm, shouting at me, but I can't hear a word she's saying.

I open my eyes and look right at Alex.

He won't look at me. Even in a haze of my powers, he's looking at Skye, watching as guards carefully pick her up to carry her down to the clinic.

"Call her mother," I tell Maeve groggily, panting. "Tell her to go to the clinic."

"What the fuck? Blake, this is my castle, you fucking prick. What happened? Who is...? Who are you?" She snarls, turning her anger on Alex, who's watching in panic as Skye fades from view, and the chaos in the room settles like the shimmering glass covering the carpet.

I grip Alex's shirt and drag him off the wall, tossing him into one of the armchairs in front of my desk. He tries to rise, but I motion for him to stop, holding his gaze.

"Sit down, and tell me everything."

"I want to go with her," he says bitterly, flashing his teeth, those fangs.

"*Sit. Down.*"

He doesn't move. He's eyeing the door, his hands clenched into fists at his sides. When his upper lip pulls over his teeth again, Maeve's lips pop open for several seconds before she shuts them tight and shoves past me to the stationary phone on my desk, which she fists, frantically dialing a number.

"Don't get up," I command, softer this time.

"I want–"

"I take it this isn't the monster that did that to her?" Maeve cuts in, staring at me expectantly.

"No. This is the boyfriend–"

"Husband," Alex corrects with force.

Maeve and I stare at him. I'm not sure what this feeling is, but it's new. I'm not sure I like it.

"She's my wife." The feeling shining behind his eyes is something I know all too well, however, and it guts me. For a split second, I imagine the moment I found Marianna in her old townhouse, guarding the stairwell, battered and broken. I imagine those days spent in the clinic, thinking I was losing her to a curse.

I see that same kind of despair in Alex's eyes now.

"Sit," I say a third time, adding, "Please."

Soren snorts a laugh from the far side of the room. "I've never heard you say that before."

"I didn't realize you were still here–"

"Misty? Listen, I need you in Moonrise right now. Yes. Yes–It is an emergency, yes. Bring Sydney. Cole, too, probably. Who am I kidding? Bring the whole fucking cavalry." Maeve hangs up the phone and turns her attention to Alex, who isn't sitting and looks like he's about to make a run for it. "You'll get lost immediately. Don't even try."

"Where is she?" he pants, wincing as the clouds part, and sunlight streams through the windows. I watch him with overt curiosity. I don't even bother to hide it.

Soren paces into view, frowning at Alex, then me and his mate. Then, he makes a show of closing every curtain until Alex hisses out a breath in pain and shakily sinks into an armchair and hangs his head in his hands.

"Marianna is on her way to the clinic," Maeve says in a near whisper and leans her thigh against the side of my desk, arms crossed neatly under her chest. "She asked why I was the one mind-linking with her and not you."

"I'll handle it after I've handled this."

"Ryatt is on his way."

I close my eyes for a moment, mouthing a silent curse.

"Arthur, too."

"Goddess-damnit, Maeve."

She shrugs, totally unperturbed. "We have a *vampire* in Eastonia. And, apparently, he's your new son-in-law."

Alex looks up at us, pale, like the past hour drained him of life, if that's even possible for his kind.

"She's pregnant," he says quietly, but the statement explodes through the room. Soren whips around, and Maeve braces a hand on the desk.

"What?" The word leaves my lips before my brain finishes registering the news.

Alex's eyes meet mine and hold. "She's *pregnant*."

45

MEETING THE FAMILY

Alex

Blake looks at me for a long, long time. His stare is exactly like Skye's–unyielding, expectant, and unnaturally violet. She wasn't wrong about that.

I'm the one who breaks from his gaze to look down at my filthy hands. They're caked in Kai's and Skye's blood. It doesn't feel like enough. Ripping him into sections before tearing his head clean off his shoulders doesn't feel like enough.

I curl my hands into fists.

The woman, the queen, which is the only person she can be, cautiously moves around the desk in my direction. "Skye's pregnant?" She's just as beautiful as Skye described, with thick, dark brown hair and sea-green eyes that swirl with power I can taste. The other man, the one who kindly shut the curtains to shield me from the spray of sunlight ghosting through the clouds, does not move to stop the woman who is, obviously, based on their mingled scents, his mate.

She is in charge.

But she's not nearly as powerful as Skye's father. That's really, really fucking clear.

Blake motions for Maeve to stop, and she does, but she looks overtly annoyed that her body bent to his will. She folds her arms over her chest and tsks, checking her watch. Waiting. For what? I have no worldly idea.

"You're the father, I assume?" Blake asks coldly, and I suppose I deserve the ice in his tone. Skye warned me it could come to this, that our secrets could reach the surface before we settled on a plan. We talked about these things in quiet moments in each other's arms over the past few months. We thought we had time. We were so stupid. So naive. I thought she was safe.

"I am."

The door to the room rips off its hinges. A gust of violent wind explodes, sucking the air from the room.

I'm ripped from the chair and tossed so violently across the room by an unseen force that my vision goes startlingly black. Sharp, lifted voices screech, then shut out, leaving me in a veil of utter silence. A void. The black holes Skye talks about to put me to sleep at night.

A real, deep, kind of sleep.

———

"You have no right to keep him here, chained up, like some kind of prisoner!"

"This is on Maeve's orders, not mine."

"He is Skye's *husband!*"

"We know nothing. Ryatt nearly killed him, and Skye is—Skye can't explain. Not yet." A small, female voice cracks somewhere nearby, but everything is dark and fluid. I try to open my eyes, but they're heavy, maybe broken. I don't know.

"Marianna already called the university. Skye wasn't lecturing. An extended leave of absence was just put in for her *two days ago*. She didn't say anything to us about it."

Voices drift in and out, and I'm trapped, unable to move.

"If he's the Alex Scarlett they mentioned, he's technically missing, according to the university."

"You're telling me this—this thing is a… what did you say it was?"

"A paleomicrobiologist."

"Whatever that is."

"Ryan, please, you're not helping the situation."

"That's an advanced field of study," says a calmer, drier male voice. Someone steps toward me—a man, a shifter based on his scent, but my senses are flooded by the alarm bells pinging through my skull. A steady hand presses on my shoulder, then fingers press against the side of my neck, feeling for a pulse. "I have a colleague who occasionally holds guest lectures at LU. Alex Scarlett is renowned not only at LU but abroad. If this man is him, he's a genius. A leader in his field."

"Cole—"

Dad? No. No, Skye has an uncle named Cole. I know that. I remember that. She told me all about these people. I…. Where is she? What have they done to her? How's the baby?

"He's also a *vampire.*"

"He's Skye's husband. Is anyone listening to me?" The pitched female voice floods the room, and she's furious. She'll tell me what I need to know if I can just… *wake up.*

I open my eyes to slits, and it takes all of my strength. Dim light blurs my vision. Shadows dance all around me as a red velvet room slowly comes into view. My fingers twitch, and the shadows part, followed by a flurry of movement as a fresh shadow falls over my body.

I close my eyes just as an older woman with thick, curly dark hair and shocking silver eyes takes up the sliver of my hazy field of vision.

"Good morning," she says softly, kindly. "You can open your eyes. There's no sun in here. You're safe."

"Don't talk to him like that," a deep male voice rumbles, followed by a sharp swat and a grunt. "Kenna, just be careful, please."

"I need everyone in the room to shut the fuck up," Kenna says sharply, I think, and suddenly her hands are on either side of my face.

I open my eyes at her touch, and she smiles down at me. It takes all of my strength to fight my natural tendency to bare my teeth and hiss. I'm sure everyone here, the group of seven or so people staring at me like I'm some lab experiment, would love that.

"My wife?" I croak, and Kenna's eyes soften further. She purses her lips into a sympathetic smile before turning her head and shooting daggers at two men—twins, I believe, and close to her own age—standing only a few feet away, tucked in the shadows of a regally decorated bedroom.

I'm in a bed, lying on top of ornate satin sheets, and I am, in fact, in chains.

"Skye is recovering. She's going to be all right," Kenna says after a moment, and another woman steps up beside her, golden blonde hair glistening in the faint light of a lamp on a nearby bedside table. She looks oddly familiar, but I can't place why. "And the baby, too. It's going to be a while until she wakes up. We're keeping her asleep as long as we can. She's very weak."

"What's your name?" the new woman asks, and Kenna moves her touch downward to my chest, which feels oddly warm and prickly.

"Alexander—Alex Scarlett. Doctor… Alex… ander… Scarlett."

"There's no rush." Kenna moves her hands over my stomach, and the heat becomes unbearable. I wince, and the chains binding my wrists and ankles rattle when I try to curl inward. "I'm sorry. I'm just making sure my idiot father didn't maim you beyond repair. You've responded to our healing methods quite nicely, though."

"Where is my wife?" I rasp, my vision blurry. "I want to see her. Now."

The blonde woman is staring down at me so intently it's like she's looking into my mind. She might be. All of these people have powers in some way, right?

"We should bring them together," she says to Kenna. "I think it would be best for both of them—"

"He is not going within an inch of my granddaughter until this is sorted," snarls one of the twins, the leaner one, who steps out of the shadows, and… yeah. That's him. Alpha King Sydney. It has to be. Skye described him to a T, and he fits her description perfectly.

"You are all acting insane!" the blonde woman shouts, and I cringe as the sound reverberates through my skull.

A bickering match ensues, and after what feels like an eternity, the women successfully shove the men out into a hallway that spills golden light into my prison, leaving only two men left.

If I can call the second man that.

He's extraordinarily small, strange-looking–ancient and wiry. He says nothing from his perch on a stool in the corner of the room but scribbles notes in a leather-bound journal like his life depends on it, peering at me over the rims of his half-moon spectacles.

The other man... I recognize his kind instantly.

"We've never formally met, but I've heard about you. I'm Cole. I'm a physician out of Crescent Falls. This is my wife, Misty. She's Skye's great aunt." He steps forward and places his hand on the blonde woman's shoulder, and the sour look on her face shifts, calming. Mates, most definitely.

Cole has dark gray eyes, but they're normal, not swirling with power or an unnatural shade. He's just... a shifter. Good. That's good.

"I want to see her," I manage to say, but it hurts. Everything hurts.

"Soon. She's doing well, okay?" Misty, the blonde woman, clears her throat and nods like she's trying to make herself believe it. "Look, this is not a good situation. Skye nearly died. It's a miracle she made it, and Blake, her father, you met him–" She hesitates and licks her lips, glancing up at Cole. "He says he... saw what happened. Looked into your head?"

I nod, and she continues, "Who did this to her?"

"He's dead." I close my eyes for a moment, wincing against the warmth of what I believe are Kenna's powers sinking into my skin, my bones. "It doesn't matter now."

"You're sure? Maeve can send–"

"I tore him apart. He's dead. There's nothing left of him. I made sure of it."

The room falls into silence, leaving only the scratchy scribbling of the tiny man's pen. It's loud enough to make my temples throb.

Kenna clears her throat and sits on the edge of the bed, and that's when I notice there's a third man in the room. He only steps out of the shadows to make his presence well and intensely known when his mate, Kenna herself, curls her fingers around my calf in a touch that would be comforting if the man wasn't looking at me like I'll be signing my death warrant if I make any sudden movements.

"There's a lot we need to know," Kenna says, eyeing her mate as he approaches.

"It can wait," Misty says, shaking her head.

"Maeve needs to know," Kenna cuts in, closing her eyes for a moment before looking down at me. "If we let you go, let you out of these chains, will you… try anything?"

I bite back a deranged laugh. I feel like all of my ribs have been broken and rearranged. I'm exhausted. My head is killing me. I want nothing more than to fix this, though. I should have ended this a decade ago.

"I just want to see her. I need to see her. The only thing you'll risk by letting me loose is me running through that door into the sun I know is there."

"What will happen in the sun?" Misty asks, more curious than anything.

I turn my gaze to hers. Gods, I know her. I've heard her described, at least. Why? "I burn. It won't kill me, but it hurts like fucking hell, and I'd rather avoid it."

Misty eyes me for a moment before nodding at Kenna, who turns to her mate expectantly and holds out her hand for a key.

Everyone steps away from the bed as I'm freed by the tall, blond man who looks like he'd love more than anything to pull my fangs from my mouth with a rusty pair of pliers.

I lie there for a moment, twisting my wrists and ankles until my body awakens, and memories of the ice come hurdling back to me in flashes of red blood and nylon yellow. Skye's dark hair splayed and frozen in a puddle of her own blood. Everything we dreamed of, the ridiculous, far-fetched life we tried to build crumbling like sand through my fingers.

"My name is Prince Kieran Alexander of Scarlett Thunder," I rasp, taking the deepest breath I can against the pull and pinch of what must be freshly healed cracks in my ribs. "I go by Alex. My father is King Cole Alexander. Ten years ago, I killed the Queen of Crimson River. Last night, I killed her son." I turn to look at the shocked group of shifters and gods or goddesses, whatever they are. "There is no one coming for me."

JUST WAKE UP

Skye

I'M DEAD. I MUST BE BECAUSE I OPEN MY EYES TO GRAINY SUNLIGHT highlighting a room I'd be able to see fully in the dark. I know this shallow, cream-colored carpet. I know there's a bright purple nail polish stain in the corner of the walk-in closet on the far side of the room, hidden beneath a stack of boxes. I doubt my parents know it's there.

There're three windows along the wall–circular and wide. My grandma Leona fussed so much over the fact that Dad designed windows no one could make curtains for, and by some miracle, she managed it herself. But the curtains in my childhood bedroom aren't... familiar. They're different. Thick and black, they block out the majority of the light, only letting fractals of what I believe is the sunset through.

Am I in hell? Is this what it looks like? Being thrust back into my awkward teenage years? I fist the comforter–velvet corduroy–my favorite.

I turn my head away from the strip of light flickering over the room and watch speckles play across the smooth, limestone-washed plaster walls. Scuff marks and nail holes pepper them from years of wear and tear. I lived an entire life in this room. Grew from a little girl to a woman.

And now, apparently, I'll spend eternity here.

"It's a valid question," says a deep but dry male voice that sends prickles of familiarity washing over my skin. "I don't have an answer to it. It was something we often discussed, however."

"Moonrise doesn't have a biology program. I mean, it does, but not like in Crescent Falls or Lunaria. Tarsian University is the closest you'd get to the level of tech you have back in Aurorium." Dad's voice effectively wakes me from the deepest, limpest stupor I've ever experienced. I jerk into awareness. The room spins.

"This conversation is premature." Alex. That's—that's Alex's voice just beyond the door. "I have to return to Lunaria. There's no way around it."

"She cannot travel."

"She won't," he replies briskly, but his tone? I imagine him pulling his lower lip between his teeth like he always does when he's mulling something over in his mind. "She can't risk it, but I have to face the tribunal. The Alpha of Aurorium would like my head on a spike."

"He'd have to catch you first." Uncle Soren's words are broken by chuckles.

I… must be dead. I have to be, because if I'm not, Alex, my vampire husband, is standing in the hallway outside of my childhood bedroom laughing with my father, the scariest man in existence, and Soren, who backs Dad up on everything.

Heavy footsteps break the soft, easy laughter, and I recognize the voice of my great-great-uncle Ryatt. Oh, my Goddess. He's here, too? "Any progress?"

"She woke up briefly this morning," Dad replies.

"Posey and Aris just arrived. They're at the castle as it stands, but Posey has been biting her nails to the quick waiting to see her."

"Did they bring the kids?" Soren asks, and Ryatt mumbles something I can't catch, and then footsteps are edging away from the door, fading with every passing second.

"*Wait,*" I whisper, but the word is a jumble of sound like I haven't used my voice in weeks.

The light fades, and the house falls into silence. It's heavy, like the Goddess is lowering a thick, weighted blanket over my room as the sun sets, and I drift on a current of starlight, snug and settled between realms.

"HER FINGERS ARE STIFF," POSEY SAYS, HER VOICE PULLING ME BACK into the present, but the room is a wash of bright sunlight, and a cool, late winter breeze lifts the thick curtains I can only see because they're the darkest items in the room. Everything else is hazy–blurred beyond belief. I'm not sure my eyes are even open. Posey bends and flexes my fingers, her powers warming my skin like she can feel my– what's it called? Resonance–right. That's what alchemists call magic like mine. I wonder if she realizes I have literal stardust in my body– that I'm made of it. Made of the... same stars I... study....

"I DON'T HAVE A CHOICE IN THE MATTER." ALEX'S VOICE IS SO CLOSE, I swear, if I opened my eyes, he'd be right here beside me. "I've been in contact with the university president. I'm being called back. The Alpha of Aurorium is demanding it."

"You have the support of the royal family. It's my decision, actually. The Alpha of Aurorium can get fucked, for all I care."

"Maeve," Soren growls in warning.

Open your eyes. Please. Just open them. Wake up. Wake up!

"Last I checked, I was still the Firestone Queen, and Lunaria has long been an ally. Unless that's changed, it's my decision! He has immunity."

"They believe I am responsible for the murders that took place,"

Alex says dryly, so casually, like he's spent ages in the presence of my loudest, most opinionated family members while I've been... here. Trapped in my own body.

"The university doesn't think that," Mom says sharply, tsking. "And what of the Alpha King of Lunaria? What does he have to say?"

"Nothing. He hasn't said anything." Maeve chuckles under her breath like this entire situation—whatever it is—has been the most amusing thing that's happened in a very long time.

"He's terrified of her. That's why. The Alpha King of Lunaria will not force her hand—or Alex's." It's Dad this time.

Oh, Goddess, I need to wake up. Where am I? Is this a dream, too? It has to be because Alex and I—we hadn't decided yet. We were still deciding how to do this, taking it one day at a time so we didn't lose our minds and then...

Kai.

Oh. *Oh.*

I reach into the darkness, feeling for... anything, anyone. A shuffling ensues, and the bed dips, because I'm horizontal. I'm in bed. My bed. My bed in Moonrise. My bed in my childhood bedroom. It isn't a dream.

None of this is a dream.

"Skye, don't move," Alex says as other voices rise and tangle around him, but in my mind, I'm back on the ice, facing Kai, thinking it's our way out.

"Skye, please don't spit this out—"

Something bitter and slippery slides to the back of my tongue, and I gag, choking on the liquid as my throat refuses to work.

"You have to try. You can do it. You've done it before," Dad's voice rings out. I feel his hand on my arm, tight, fingers expanding and squeezing my bare skin. "You can do this. I know it hurts. Just try."

"Someone call Misty and see if she can get back here as soon as possible," Maeve says, but her voice is further away, lost in the shuffle.

I swallow. My throat burns like it's on fire. My chest convulses, and I jerk, crying out as bright, overwhelming pain tears across my neck.

"Good job. Good girl," Dad says weakly before cursing under his breath and letting me go, but his presence is replaced by someone else.

Cool hands grip my upper arms, turning me onto my back. An icy, deliciously clean scent wraps itself around my senses and tugs, forcing me to submit, to remember.

"How much longer do we have to do this to her?" Alex asks bitterly, each word clipped with frustration. His touch starts to fade. My body numbs. My arms and legs grow heavy, and my heart rate slows to the point that I feel myself drifting... off... again.... *No. No, no I will not... fall... asleep again... Stop. Wake up. WAKE UP!*

The scream that sears the room from top to bottom is a sound I've never heard before. It hurts. It stings my throat and bursts my eardrums. A screech echoes somewhere in the distance, followed instantly by a strange stillness that traps me in an unwanted embrace. I can't move. I can't see. I can't feel.

But someone is here with me. In my head. Gripping my powers and twisting them into submission until I fold, slipping back into the void.

"The baby is due this summer, if my calculations are correct," Kenna says, her voice whispering through my mind, reeling me back to the surface. "Late spring if it's early. Early babies are so common in this family. They just can't wait to get here and meet all of us."

Mom exhales deeply, nearer, like she's standing right beside me. "And the baby's healthy?"

"As far as I can tell. It would help if anyone, including me, had any knowledge about vampire babies, but we only have Alex, and he's... well, going through a lot."

Mom exhales again, and my body slips to the side as the bed dips from her weight. My eyes strain against the darkness, then a pinch of light, filtering through my eyelids. I can feel the comforter again. I flex my fingers under the blanket, the soft fibers playing over my skin.

"Maeve has made it clear he's not going back to Lunaria until the Alpha drops the case. The university has already done a thorough investigation, and he's innocent. That's clear. It's all for show now."

"Misty wants to talk to him."

"I know. Blake said as much."

"I'm worried about it. I don't think–I really don't think she should. It took years for her to get over the war, and still. I can't believe she wants to revisit it."

"Do you believe she met Alex's family, like she thinks?"

"He told Soren he recognized her somehow. Not like he'd seen her, but heard about her. I was sure he was confusing her with Isla, but based on his story, I think there's a high probability that she did, in fact, see his aunts and his cousin that day, when she went into another realm–"

"He–she went–further–" I gasp against the pain of my voice leaving my throat. I'm not sure why my powers tangle, giving me a vision of Misty during that terrible war. Her going through that portal, seeing two women like I'm now seeing them, the memory of that moment written in the stars doing their best to wake me up.

Mom gasps, her hands finding mine under the covers and gripping them tightly. I open my eyes to slits, the room coming into startling focus, much more detailed than before. Kenna hovers over me, her face twisted in concentration.

"She–saw the future—that day–but they're real–" The sentence turns to a whimper. I taste blood. My eyes burn from lack of use and fill with tears I can't blink back.

"Take it slow, sweetheart," Kenna urges, glancing at Mom.

Mom shakes her head. "No more tonics. Please. Alex made us promise. Blake is in agreement."

Kenna bites her lower lip and sighs. "Fine, but you know how I feel about it."

"Alex?" I mouth, sucking in a breath that hurts so fucking much. "Where is he?"

"Shhh, honey, please," Mom begs, smoothing my hair away from my face. "Don't talk. We'll fetch him."

"I'll get him right now."

A crack echoes through the room. I turn my head toward the door. A shadow fills the doorframe.

Alex steps into the lamp light radiating from my bedside table. Reality slams into me, knocking the air from my lungs. This is real. He's real.

I slowly, carefully, lift a hand to my neck, my fingertips dusting over thick bandages. Memories of the ice come sprinting back to the forefront of my mind. Bloody, terrifying memories.

"Stop," Alex says, arriving at my side at the speed of light. He kneels at my bedside, grabbing my hand before I rip the bandage to pieces.

"How–long–" I whisper, and his eyes glisten.

He looks up at Mom and Kenna, shaking his head in disbelief. "She's awake? This is her? She's lucid now?"

Mom nods but seems just as shocked and uneasy as he is.

"How long?" I repeat, my voice is like gravel.

"Three weeks," he says, closing his hands around mine and bowing his head. "Oh, gods. Fuck. Okay. Okay."

I missed all of it. Him meeting my parents. Their shock. The fights I was sure would ensue. I am, honestly, a bit disappointed.

"What happened?" I ask, and Alex looks up from our joined hands, resting his chin against my fingers. He looks like hell. Tired. Stressed. The works. But his features aren't sunken, and he has a warm glow to him that he only gets after he's been… thoroughly fed.

Jealously like I've never experienced soars through me, waking up the rest of my body in an instant.

"You've missed quite a bit," Kenna says with an annoyed huff, looking at my mom. "She really needs to be resting. Sleeping. Preferably not talking."

"Tell me everything," I urge. Alex's face is blurred by my tears. "I want to know."

He smiles and then laughs, shaking his head with a deep, broken sigh, but... his eyes are bright, locked on mine, and shining with knowing.

"You're the same. Persistent. Always with the fucking questions even after almost dying."

"She did die," Kenna huffs. "Several times!"

"I missed you," Alex says and leans toward me, pressing a kiss to my forehead. "It's over now. You're safe. It's all over."

4 7

THREE WEEKS

Skye

It is not, in fact, all over.

"What?" I croak while Mom aggressively fluffs my pillows and settles me upright in my bed. I was right–I'm in my old room in my parents' house in Moonrise. Thick, impenetrable curtains hang from my windows, blocking out ninety percent of the sunlight, only allowing strips that Alex seems to walk through without any issues. I don't remember anything, save for the first moments of the attack and glimmers of hazy images of my dad's office before it all grows black and blurry.

"The Alpha of Aurorium wants someone to take the fall for the murders," Maeve, who spirited into the room ten minutes ago, explains with overt annoyance. She's perched on the edge of my bed, dressed casually in a dark red sweater and matching pants, with her extraordinarily thick brown hair piled messily on top of her head.

Kenna left the room twenty minutes ago. To do what, I have no idea, but Alex remains, pacing and tapping his fingertips on his chin

371

while watching every breath I take like this is all he's done for what I now know has been weeks.

Three weeks. Three entire weeks I've been kept asleep. Three weeks of the family coming to terms with him and me. Three weeks of Maeve and my dad negotiating with the authorities in Lunaria. Three weeks of Alex in this room, watching me like a hawk.

I still struggle to swallow and speak, my throat unnaturally tight and raw. My skin screams with a blistering kind of itchiness that's driving me absolutely insane. I should be healed completely by now, shouldn't I?

"The Alpha of Aurorium can suck my–" Alex begins to say, which is so out of character for him, but I suppose he gets a pass.

"Anyway," Mom barks, throwing an extremely shady glare at Alex, who is unaffected as always, and turns to me and smiles. "Alex is fine. The Alpha King of Lunaria already handled it. Alex is a free man." Mom rolls her neck. "And also no longer works for the university."

I glance at my husband, who catches my gaze, conveying a silent message that it's unfortunately not as uncomplicated as Mom's making it sound.

Maeve, however, leans over to pat my thigh. "You really scared us. I'll never forgive you." Her cat-like smile burrows into my heart and warms through my blood, making me feel a bit less groggy.

Still, I'm dying here. I want to scratch my throat so badly, but Mom keeps batting my hands away, tsking and forcing them back under the covers.

"Why–" I wince, desperate to clear my throat but finding it impossible. "My throat?"

Alex smooths a hand over his face, growing more and more agitated as the seconds pass. Maeve notices and rises, clicking her tongue at Mom, who glances between Alex and me. I can tell she's internally fretting over me but sucks in a breath and resigns herself, following Maeve out the door.

They leave the door open.

He stares at the open door, blinking a few times, then grumbles under his breath and strides across the carpet, closing it against the quiet voices drifting in from the hallway.

"Lock it," I whisper, grimacing as the words burn over my tongue.

He does, and he turns and leans his weight against it, fixing me with an exhausted, overwhelmed look.

My lips part to ask a million questions, but he cuts in, "Don't. Don't try to talk. You're not completely healed yet."

"Why not?"

He sighs, scrubbing his palms over his eyes like he hasn't had a chance to close them in the weeks we've been here. He steps forward and sits on the end of the bed, taking a moment to make himself comfortable, and replies, "Because Kenna, Cole, and Misty couldn't heal you entirely. They were worried about you losing your ability to speak, so it's been slow." He leans toward me, his hands resting on either side of my thighs, closing me in against the bed. "You've been kept asleep, in a stupor, while you heal as slowly as possible. But now that you're awake, I understand that Misty is going to return to finish the job."

I reach up to try to scratch the bandages, but he stops me, gripping my fingers, then toys with them like he hasn't... touched me in so long.

He scooches closer, his eyes, so blue, locked on mine like he's silently asking permission to lie with me, and I wholeheartedly allow it, and within seconds I'm tucked in the crook of his shoulder, my cheek flush with his chest. Alex relaxes against my weight with the deepest sigh. It vibrates through his chest, and he slumps, resting his chin on the top of my head.

Then, after making me promise I won't speak, he tells me everything.

ALEX

Three Weeks Ago...

. . .

I can't avoid the sunlight here. My skin prickles, but I ignore it, following Kenna down a long, narrow hallway in a building situated on the side of the palace that's apparently open to the public. Healers in starched uniforms step out of rooms, pushing carts. Babies fuss, and voices murmur through open doors. Windows at either end of the hallway spill warm winter light tinged with silver as snow dances in a dizzying haze, which is my only salvation from the sun's effects.

She turns a sharp corner, glancing over her shoulder to make sure I'm still behind her, and hurries up a staircase. I press myself to the wall to allow a trio of healers to walk past us, then follow, my heart rate creeping upward with each passing second.

I was told, when I was finally freed from the chains and allowed out of that room, that Skye was stable but still in terrible shape. After a lengthy conversation and assurances that, unlike shifter males, who are notoriously territorial and will kill before asking questions when it comes to their mates, vampires tend to be a little more... level-headed in situations like this, Kenna agreed to take me to see Skye.

Another hallway comes into view, shorter and more private than the last. There's a single door at the end of the hall, which stands ajar, soft voices trickling into the void of cream-colored walls and perfectly waxed tiles.

Kenna disappears into the room. I follow but halt in the doorway.

Several sets of eyes lock on my face. Spines straighten. The tension skyrockets.

But there she is. Fast asleep. Bandages thicker than my forearm wrapped around her neck and chest, bare save for a blanket covering the parts of her body that are only mine to see. I close my eyes for several seconds, bracing myself on the doorframe, and then a presence steps to my side, quietly encouraging me to come closer.

I open my eyes to Blake, her father, who looks so beaten by grief that it momentarily catches me off guard. The same powers, the same particles of stardust, swirl in his eyes as the ones I see in Skye's.

The rest of the people in the room fade into obscurity as Blake guides me to her bedside. Marianna, her mother, who looks so much like Skye it hurts, rises from the chair next to the bed, and I drop into it, bracing my elbows on the mattress and leaning forward to take one of Skye's limp hands.

I tell them everything. My entire life. I tell them about my kind, my parents, significant moments of my childhood, and the bloody wars that raged between the time I was ten to twenty, when I put an end to it. At least, I hope I did.

I tell them about killing the queen of a rival kingdom and the fallout that followed. I tell them about the three years I spent on the run, pushed further and further away from home until I was so lost, so desperately deep in the aether between our kingdoms, that it was unlikely I'd ever find my way back, and how I kept going. I tell them the things Skye already knows—my background, how I was able to enroll as a student at the University of Lunaria, how I deserved to be there and proved it time and time again.

Then, I tell them about the past month.

"I made a deal with him," I say, looking up from Skye's hand to meet Blake's eyes. "He was going to keep killing. He was targeting Skye, and I promised I'd leave with him and go back to where I came from if he left her out of it."

"I'm guessing she didn't take that well?" Blake asks flatly, and there's nothing more I can do but nod.

"During that time, things were moving quickly between us. We moved in together. Only she, and two of our friends, knew what I am, but the university president became aware of our relationship and urged us to do things cleanly. We were... working through the reality of our relationship. Skye doesn't care that I'm a vampire, that I'll outlive her by centuries, that the likelihood of having children was almost impossible, something she voiced that she wanted, and I wasn't sure I could give her."

Marianna rests her hand on my shoulder. Blake watches the movement, but I can already feel him in my head, quietly, painlessly confirming the details of my story. It feels so different compared to Skye's clumsy, painful explorations.

"Then she found out she was pregnant. It was a shock for both of us. She was so sick, and I was at a loss about how to help her, and then Kai made himself known. He threatened us." I look up at the faces in the room. Her parents, Misty, and another man–an older man with dark hair and eyes like polished silver. The tattoos on his fingers ripple when he grips the back of a chair housing a regal older woman with dark brown hair and sea-green eyes.

"I wanted Skye to return here, to her family. She was going to need all the help she could get during the pregnancy. She needs the best healers. Healers we didn't have access to in Lunaria. The University is so medical. Nothing we had access to could account for the fact she's–" I look at Misty with a sudden urgency.

"The baby is okay. But this has been hard on both of them. They're not in the clear yet, but as it stands, she's all right. They both are," Misty confirms, but her expression is grim.

"This baby is a hybrid. Half shifter, half vampire… and possibly a mystic, like her." I squeeze Skye's hand. "They didn't deserve this."

"What happened in Aurorium?" the silver-eyed man asks, and I look up at him. Ryatt. He has to be the Shadowsynger. He's a legend– a god, all things considered.

Blake rolls his shoulders. I already know he's seen everything at this point.

"Kai threatened her life. He killed one of my students and two locals off campus. Then, he killed the dean of my department, a man I didn't get along with, which is why I was considered a suspect. He was willing to do much more, including making my lies public, which would not only risk Skye but myself, and I was the only thing standing between him and her. I was able to face Kai, and he made me a deal. I would go with him, and he would spare Skye's life. I had to consider it, but I wanted her protected before then, especially from university politics, and honestly, in the event I didn't return." I meet Blake's eyes. "We married in Aurorium, quietly. Skye took leave from her lectures so she could rest, and that gave me the opportunity to try to deal with Kai."

Blake leans back, glancing at Ryatt.

"You were going to kill him?" Ryatt asks.

"Of course."

"Then what happened?" Marianna asks weakly, but her eyes are on Skye.

I look at Blake, who stares down at his lap, a small, knowing smile touching his lips. "Skye doesn't like being told what to do," he says under his breath, "and took matters into her own hands."

48

——————

WRITTEN IN THE STARS

Skye

TWO MORE WEEKS PASS IN A BLUR. AT FIRST, IT SEEMED LIKE A HUNDRED years. I was constantly poked and prodded and wasn't deemed healed enough naturally to have Misty and Kenna step back in with their magic, but finally, the morning came when I managed to swallow without pain, and the rush to heal me completely returned with fervor. Misty arrived, working her magic, sewing me together from the inside out. Kenna managed the baby, keeping whoever this tiny person growing inside of me is safe, but I wasn't out of the woods yet.

The worst thing about this recovery was the sharp and violent return of my pregnancy symptoms. I traded being bedridden with a catastrophic injury for being bedridden with nausea so severe that I lost ten pounds in a matter of days. Alex was amazing through all of it, but I know conversations were being had in the background about the ability of me returning to Lunaria, because right now, it doesn't seem like an option.

And, this morning, the option to return to my research, and my tenured position, faded entirely.

379

Alex sits beside me on the couch downstairs in the sunken living room. A fire rages in the hearth, and it's another snowy, endless late winter night in Moonrise. We've been sitting in silence for ages, Alex's fingers intertwined with mine, but he hasn't been able to say what he needs to.

I know him. I know he's gone through every detail and planned every minute of the next several months. He's been doing that since we found out about the baby and explained how hellish this journey would be for me. He carries the weight of his guilt, and I hate that he can't feel happy about this yet because he's worried about me. About us. Me and our baby.

Now, he doesn't have a choice but to confront his feelings and our reality.

Dad paces in front of us, tapping his fingers on his arm. Maeve appears in a flurry of crimson starlight and glides in our direction, dressed casually compared to the regal gowns she favors during court appearances. A faded sweatshirt with a logo of a sports team Uncle Soren likes catches the light of the fire as she comes into view, looking gravely down at me and Alex, who rises and runs his fingers through his hair.

"This is what I've decided," she says with a soft, unsure sigh. I straighten as much as I can, resting my hands on the slight swell of my belly. "Skye, you need to stay here, at least until you're further along in your pregnancy and can cope with your symptoms. There's no help for you in Lunaria, but you have access to the best healers here and our family. I think it's the safest option." She gives me a pleading look.

I glance at Dad, then Alex, who are looking at each other instead of at me. I wonder if they have the ability to mind-link because I've caught them doing this several times over the past two weeks.

"Fine," I manage to say, my voice still slightly hoarse.

"You can stay here, at home, or at the palace in your own suite. Whatever you're most comfortable with," Maeve adds, giving me the saddest, knowing smile. "It might be easier having you in a suite at the palace because of the proximity to the clinic, since your father insisted on building this fortress in the middle of nowhere." She sweeps her arm across the living room and lets it fall to her side. "And… you."

Alex turns to look at her. I feel the air being sucked from the room with each second that passes.

She clears her throat, looks at Dad, and says, "Alex will return to his kingdom."

"What?" I blurt, trying to rise.

"It won't be forever," Maeve cuts in, but I'm already struggling to my feet, clutching the couch cushions for support.

"No, he's not going back!"

"Skye, please," Alex says under his breath as he turns to me, taking me by the elbow to guide me back onto the couch, but I clutch him like my life depends on it.

Dad's throat bobs, and he looks away, stricken, and I could scream.

"You're agreeing with this? You're going? It took you three years to find Lunaria! How long…? This can't…. No. No, you can't." I turn pleading eyes on Maeve and my dad. "No. Why? We're having a baby in six months!"

"I'll go with him," Dad says to Maeve, and the air is effectively sucked from the room.

"Blake," Maeve warns, but Dad purses his lips and nods, turning to face his cousin.

"She's right. It could take years, even with Evander's Ghost resources helping and all our transportation technology at his disposal. He's been gone for *thirteen years*. We'll be sending him into an uncertain political landscape."

Alex stills and watches my dad's mouth move, standing in shock.

"I could get us there in a few days, with stops along the way, places I've seen in his stored memories from his journey to Lunaria."

"You're talking about spiriting thousands upon thousands of miles away into a territory that has no working knowledge that we exist," Maeve says with heat, her eyes narrowing. "Think this through, Blake."

"Our only other option is sending Alex and several of our best men on a years-long journey away from their families. Plus...." He looks at me and exhales deeply before turning back to Maeve. "I need to be there as your emissary. You know this is the best course of action. I've traveled that far before. With the right herbs and specific stops, Alex can make the journey with me without issue. I'll take another Ghost warrior with me–possibly Zayn, if he's willing, which I believe he will be."

The mention of the stranger has an odd effect on Maeve, who turns wild eyes on my father. "Zayn is one of my best palace guards."

"And there's a reason you chose him specifically to guard Naomi and Fallon. I'll need him for a few months. That's all. I'll bring him back."

"You're serious about this?" Maeve steps toward him, toying with her sleeves. "Escorting Alex into vampire territory?"

"You were right when you mentioned they have no idea we exist. Acting as your emissary means I can scope the political landscape and ensure our reveal won't cause issues. Alex can see his family and decide the best course of action for him, Skye, and my grandchild while he's there."

My spine feels leaden as I watch the conversation. Is my dad... talking about me going to Scarlet Thunder with Alex in the future? He must be. He has to be.

"Alex is the heir apparent to his father, which means he's first in line to the throne, and if he's stepping back–"

"I get it," Maeve hisses, livid. "I just don't like it."

"Then you send him on a journey that will take years through terrible terrain with no guarantee he'll ever return, let alone in time to meet his child."

Alex looks between Maeve and Dad, his expression shockingly neutral. But I already know he's made up his mind.

"Dad, it's dangerous," I choke out, shaking my head. "A jump like that–especially multiple times–could kill him or both of you."

"We'll be fine. You jumped with Alex to Moonrise with barely a shred of your powers left, and he made it in one piece. Zayn, as well, has a unique power profile that will be useful to us."

"You'll owe me for taking my best guard with you on this asinine adventure," Maeve snaps.

Dad rolls his eyes to the ceiling and heaves a breath before looking directly at Alex. "Are you in agreement?"

"Yes," he says without skipping a beat.

"Then it's decided. We'll leave tonight. It's a full moon, which will make it easier on my powers. I'll have Kenna bring the herbs and potions we need to ready you for the journey."

I'm already up and moving through the house, my head spinning. My mind tumbles over the thought of what the next... several months will look like. Alone. Alex and my dad lost in the aether. All the things that could go wrong.

I open my bedroom door and swiftly close it behind me, my face cracking while I choke back a sob.

"I suppose the rumor that pregnancy hormones cause even the most straight-forward, level-headed women to go absolutely mad must be true."

I open my eyes to Fallon, who's casually sprawled on my bed in all of her finery–a pale pink gown of silk glimmering in soft lamplight that reflects off her jeweled fingers and polished nails.

She looks up from an old version of the *Physics Digest,* cocking her head to the side.

"What are you doing here?"

"Spying on my mom. What else?" She smiles wryly and rises, patting the bed. "Come sit with me."

I glide onto the mattress and lie down facing her. She strokes my hair like she has decades of wisdom in her twenty-two-year-old body, like her soul has been here far longer than her physical form. I'm sure that has something to do with being a Firestone, but I'll never know for sure.

"I'm not returning to Lunaria."

"I'm glad to hear it."

"My research into the heavens is over."

"Oh, please. Be serious, Skye. You'll continue your research at the

University of Moonrise, where you'll be surrounded by people like you—magical. Lunaria sounds boring as hell."

My answering smile is weak. I think I might be crying because Fallon swipes her thumb across my cheek.

"And you'll be safe here. You and the baby. You'll stay at the castle with me, right?"

"No." I shake my head. "Dad is going with Alex. I need to be here for my mom."

"Your mother has a rich and busy social life and dozens of close friends. She will be fine, but you could use a break and some pampering."

"Why are you being so nice to me?"

"Because," she says with a sigh, "I'm like you. People don't give me enough credit for how ridiculously intelligent and cunning I am. I see everything. I know everything. At least, I like to think so."

I pinch her hip, and she laughs.

"Anyway, I also don't believe I have a mate. I'm technically not a shifter, so why would I? But I know if I did find someone I loved, I would move mountains for them… if I could. But you can't move mountains for Alex right now. You made it possible for him to return to his family. You took away the one thing in his way of being free."

"I ruined our lives."

"Because he can't go back to Lunaria?" She rises, her eyes on the doorway behind me. "I don't think he cares to. I think he's exactly where he wants to be."

Fallon silently disappears in gentle, strobing light painted a soft crimson—almost pink. Flakes of stardust fall like glitter on my bed before dispersing.

I scrunch my face into my pillow. Alex rounds the bed, his tread heavier than usual like he, too, is weighed down by all of this. He sits on the edge of the bed and runs his hand up my leg, stopping at my thigh. "I'm going to come back."

"I know. But not for a long time."

"A few months, that's all. And while I'm gone, you can… get our life started."

I look up from my tear-stained pillow. "How can I? You can't live here in Moonrise! It's too sunny. You're the only vampire–"

"Then change that for me."

"What?"

He lies down beside me, nose to nose, and exhales deeply. "Change it for me. Use your powers to change those parts of me so we can have a real shot at a life together."

"I can't do that."

"I think you can. I've seen your blood sample, remember? I studied it. I obsessed over it. I found what I was looking for in your eyes, Skye. You have the power to change the world. You can also change me."

"Is that what you really want? It would take away parts of what makes you–you." I sigh, and he curls his arm around my waist, dragging me closer.

He nuzzles my neck in a way that makes my body flood with heat.

"I want to grow old with you. I want our son to have a childhood without restraints. I want you as my mate, and if that means I give up certain parts of myself, so be it. I just want to try. Look at me, Skye." I open my eyes to him, memorizing the deep, ocean blue. "I love you. Nothing else matters to me. I have to return to Scarlet Thunder for a while. That's all. And one day, when we're settled, I'll bring you there. Both of you, and I'll show you my world like you've shown me yours."

"Are you sure?"

"I've never been more sure of anything."

That statement means so much coming from someone deeply trained in the sciences, a vocation where everything is almost always up for debate.

"What if I ruin you forever?" I whisper, and he smiles, his fangs glinting in the lamplight.

"You won't."

He takes my hand and rests my fingers on his forehead.

49

NO LONGER A MONSTER

Skye

FIVE MONTHS LATER...

MY OFFICE AT THE UNIVERSITY OF MOONRISE IS IN A SPIRE overlooking the back half of the sprawling, ancient city of gold and the lake, which shines a deep turquoise in the mid-summer sun. I juggle several books as I move like a snail up another spiraling staircase, pausing several times to catch my breath and wave away the curious, concerned looks and pleas to help that my fellows throw in my direction. I'm due at the end of the week, and while joining the university as a fellow and researcher with plans to start lecturing again next year has been the best kind of distraction, this pregnancy has been awful, and I am so ready to be done.

It's been a marathon, and I'm not a runner by any means. Lately, I've been desperate to shift, but I'm too far along to risk that now. So, I walk around the lake. I hike up and down the staircases in the palace, where I've recently taken a suite at Kenna's urging because, according to her, I could give birth any day, and it feels like it.

But I refuse. I'll keep my thighs locked until Alex returns.

It's just… been so long.

"Hello?" I lean against the wall on the landing at the top of the staircase. My office is just down the hallway, and I have grand plans of sitting down and not moving again until the sun sets and I have to leave before I accidentally get locked in, which has happened a handful of times in the past few weeks. I'm doing anything I can to keep myself from thinking about Alex and my father. We haven't heard from them in months, which we anticipated. There's been no news, and Maeve keeps telling me that that's a good thing. Vampire armies haven't invaded Lunaria and the north territories of Celestoria, so whatever they're doing must be working.

I've tried to scry. I have every available mystic looking for them at the orrery to no avail.

I'm weak, and my powers are fully dedicated to keeping this giant hybrid baby healthy. So be it. I give up.

"Are you still at the campus?" Mom asks, her voice bright and excited through the speaker of my cell phone.

"Yeah. I have a few hours of work I'd like to do before I come over for dinner, if that's still the plan."

"You sound exhausted."

I look behind me at the stairs winding into oblivion. "Just getting my exercise."

"Kenna's been throwing a fit for the past week about your inability to follow her directions about rest, sweetheart. I know the university has been pressuring you to take leave. Why aren't you listening?"

"Because I can't–" I bite back my sharp tone and start over. "I just need something to do. I can't sit around doing nothing. I'll go crazy."

Mom sighs heavily. "I understand, but I've told you this before. Your father is the only person I trust to actually do what he says he'll do, no matter what. He came back to us once, Skye, and he'll do it again. With Alex in tow. I promise you that."

Music drifts down the hallway, carrying whispered voices. I squint in the direction of my office, finally catching my breath.

"I'll come to the palace for dinner, so you can just go home tonight and rest. We'll eat in your suite. It will be fun. Maeve and the girls are getting along right now, so it should be a quiet night."

"That sounds good, Mom," I say, and she tells me she loves me and to keep my chin up, but I'm heavily distracted by the music now, which sounds a lot like it's coming from my office.

I creep toward the door, juggling my books and shoulder bag, and turn the knob.

Confetti explodes through the air, and shouts of "Surprise!" nearly deafen me.

The air clears of multicolored paper, revealing the entire astronomy department crowded into my office, which is thankfully big enough to not only house a dozen people, but two tables full of food, and a table packed full of blue and pink presents.

"Oh, wow," I whisper, smiling widely while resting a hand beneath the massive swell of my belly to keep myself upright. "You didn't have to do this!"

"Well, you've insisted on working until the baby arrives, so it was the least we could do," says Chancellor Greta Fielding, taking the books from my hands and tucking them under her arm. "We're so excited for you, Skye."

I'm overwhelmed, to say the least. My desk chair has been transferred into a throne of pink and blue taffeta, and a sash is forced over my shoulders, stretched to its breaking point over the curve of my stomach.

"All of this and no crown?" I laugh, but I'm effectively shut up by a plate piled high with food. Someone brought a chocolate cake with black cherry icing, which is my favorite, and promised to send the leftovers to the palace, which means I now have plans for the rest of the evening... stuffing my face. I suppose I get a pass. I already weigh a thousand pounds and can barely fit through doorways without knocking my stomach on everything in my path, but this is fun. Laughter rings through the room while my colleagues tell stories about their own pregnancies, births, and experiences raising children. I'm the youngest by far but in good company because my department is mostly women–a sharp contrast to the mostly male-dominated physics department in Lunaria.

Halfway through my third slice of cake, I notice more people funneling into the office–which includes several heads of different departments and even the shifters who run the absolutely unreal advanced warrior training academy attached to the university. It's suddenly a huge party–full of sound and conversation that overlaps and pings from wall to wall.

I'm leaning into a conversation with two women from faculty administration when I feel a shift in the air.

My powers skitter then settle. The activity of the party seems to fade, like everyone is suddenly moving in slow motion. A man parts the crowd mingling near the doorway, stopping to bob his head in greeting to the men who turn to him. Dark hair–so black it's nearly blue–catches the summer sunlight streaming through the stained glass windows as he turns to face the room.

Ocean blue eyes scan the room before locking on mine.

"Alex?"

His smile is so bright, so unburdened and radiant. Several people turn to look at him, dropping mid-conversation as my husband moves across the room to me.

"This must be the husband," someone says in the background, but I'm wholly focused on escaping my chair, my body betraying me every step of the way.

Alex grabs my hands and eases me out of the chair. His eyes are wide and bright as he takes me in, shaking his head in muted shock, but then I'm crushed to his chest. He's warm.

"Gods, I missed you," he says into my hair and then leans back, caressing my face. "Look at you."

"How are you here?"

"I just got back." He presses his lips to mine, breathless. He's so warm. His skin has lost that pale vampire pallor over the past months. I take his hands, turning them over, tracing thin blue veins.

I look up into his eyes. "It worked."

He smiles, and… his fangs are still there.

"So, you must be Dr. Alex Scarlet," says Henry Alcot, another senior-level administrator at the university, who vigorously shakes Alex's hand and immediately drops into conversation about his availability to talk to a few of his friends in the apothecary sciences department.

I'm in a trance, however, my fingers intertwined with Alex's, as the party moves on. Before I know it, I'm walking across campus, arm in arm with Alex, shuffling in direct sunlight like this is what we've always been able to do together.

When I used my powers on him, I wasn't sure if it worked. Nothing seemed to happen. We spent that night tucked in my bed, whispering promises, dreaming of an unsure future where we could be together like this–out in the open and safe.

I let my powers travel through his biology, pinpointing his differences, moving and shifting parts of him to fit into a new biological design–something unique to him. If I did it right, I thought he might be able to tolerate sunlight, that his survival wouldn't just be based on his need for the blood of others. Selfishly, I didn't do away with that entirely because I like being bitten… but otherwise, I left him unchanged, until…

I did something I prayed he wouldn't regret asking me to do.

He left the next morning on a snowy winter day. I watched him and Dad get into a car with plans to go to the orrery, where Dad would perform the jump, and that was that.

But I had an hour alone with Alex that morning before the sun rose and painted the city of Moonrise with silver light. I asked him if he was sure he wanted to give this up–an eternal life. Immortality. Others in our history would have, and have done, terrible things to have it.

He kissed me and told me nothing in the world could change his mind.

So I made him a tether and fixed it to mine.

Mates of our own design–forcing the hand of the Goddess.

I made him mine as long as I live because, when it's my time to go, he'll come with me.

Then, he left, and I didn't know if I'd succeeded. Now, in the present, walking in the sunlight as the palace comes into startling focus, it's clear.

We did it.

We're free.

Alex walks me through a side door in the lower levels of the palace near the loading docks. No one pays us any mind, but his grip on my arm grows tighter with every step we take from campus to here, where he's pulling me into a small room near the massive palace kitchen. We didn't speak the entire walk. There was, I realize now, far too much to say and ask.

He caresses my face again, searching my eyes for the answers to what I know are millions of questions. How am I? How have I managed for so long without him? How can he possibly make this up to me?

I rise on my toes with effort and kiss him, clawing his shoulders to bring him to my level, and cry against his mouth–but finally, after months of torment and months before that living in uncertainty, he's here.

And he's home.

"How did it go?" I ask tearfully, breaking from the kiss.

He laughs against my mouth. "There's a million things I need to tell you," he says, pressing another kiss to my lips, "but there're also some people who would like to meet you. They're upstairs. Your mom told us you were on campus, but I couldn't wait to see you. I had to come."

"Who's upstairs?"

50

EPILOGUE

Alex

Toby braces his hands on either side of the bundle of blue fabric on my bed, tilting his head and squinting at the little fist reaching through the folds of a baby blanket. "Was he born with fangs?" He reaches like he's about to stick his filthy fingers in my son's mouth.

I swat his hand away. "No, of course not. He's a baby."

"Babies can have teeth. Don't–don't look at me like that, Alex. They can. Look it up. It's rather terrifying."

Lucan starts to whimper, flailing until he loosens the blanket. Toby winces and backs away, allowing me to scoop Luc up and tuck him in my arm, giving my friend a better view of the newborn who was born only two weeks ago.

"Wow. He looks like Skye."

"He does, doesn't he? That's exactly what I thought when I saw him for the first time." Actually, I was thinking a million things during a horrific twelve-hour labor that Skye breezed through while I crumbled, her face set in silent determination. I've truly never met another

393

woman like her. Once she sets her mind on something, it happens. It's the reason I'm here now, in our suite at the palace, with our friends and family gathering to meet our son. She set her mind on me once. I'm still not sure I deserve it.

"So is he a vampire or not?"

"It'll be a while before we know for sure. My Uncle Michael is here. He's a hybrid, too, but leans more toward his wolf shifter side, though. I think it's different person to person." Luc grabs my pinky. I jostle him a bit until he settles, which happens quickly. Since the moment he was born, quiet and honestly quite relaxed given the circumstances, he's been… easy going. He barely cries and is perfectly content resting between us in bed while we read books or in our arms on walks around the castle.

The door to our bedroom flies open, and Abby waltzes in, suntanned and bright-eyed, carrying the scent of ocean breezes and damp sand in her wake after several months in her new industry position in Maatua.

Toby arches a brow at Skye, who follows behind her.

"Gimme that baby!" Abby squeals and takes Lucan from my arms, inspecting him thoroughly before placing him on her chest and giving Toby incredible puppy-dog eyes. "I want one."

"I'll give you a baby," he says, his cheeks stained red.

I glance at Skye, who's trying to hide her smile. Abby whirls with Lucan in her arms and glides back to the door. "We're taking him upstairs," she tells Skye, squeezing her forearm. "So you can get some rest."

"You're stealing my baby again. We talked about this."

Abby grins and nuzzles Lucan. "I'll give him back, I promise!"

"She'll give him back," Toby echoes but winks at me. Skye steps to my side as we watch our friends leave our suite, closing us into a rare, private moment of quiet.

She turns to me and folds into my touch. I wrap my arms around her and rest my chin on the top of her head, taking a much needed deep breath.

I returned three weeks ago–in time to witness the birth of my son.

It was simultaneously the best and most stressful day of my life, but while Skye had her entire family rallying around her, I also had mine.

My mother and father, as well as my Uncle Michael, but more because he was beside himself with curiosity, came back with us, making the arduous jump from Scarlet Thunder to Moonrise, which took over a week with multiple stops, one of which was Lunaria and the university, where I quit on the spot, said goodbye to my postdocs, my colleagues, and my students, and haven't looked back.

But I had the opportunity to show my family what I'd built and why.

At least, I thought the diplomas hanging on my office walls and my extensive publications were my reason for everything–a future I wouldn't have had otherwise.

Skye's hair smells like vanilla and roses. Lucan has her impressive cheekbones and bright eyes, but his eyes don't swirl with violet light–yet. Our suite in the palace is temporary but feels like home. It smells like us. The sheets on our bed are soft, and sunlight paints our bedroom in shades of gold and butter yellow throughout the day. I spend my days sitting with my wife, with my son resting on my thighs while our family dotes on us.

Skye is my reason. The reason I put an end to a bloody war. The reason I ran. The reason I left everything I knew and loved behind. She's the reason I finally faced myself in the mirror and remembered who I was before.

"Should we join the rest of the family upstairs?" she asks, closing her eyes.

I tighten my grip on her waist, shaking my head. "They have what they really want. My mother and your mom are going to be busy for the next half hour trying to convince Abby to hand Lucan over."

Skye chuckles against my chest, but I can feel her exhaustion. Her muscles are tight despite how she slumps into my touch like she hasn't slept since Lucan was born, but not just because we have a newborn.

Later that evening, in the sitting room in our suite, surrounded by bright wallpaper and windows letting in a cool night breeze to break the relentless heat of the day–Skye wasn't lying when she said Moonrise is hotter than hell in the summer. Skye rests on a couch beside me with Lucan, fast asleep, tucked in the crook of her arm while Maeve and Blake converse with my father, Cole, on the far side of the room, just out of earshot. Uncle Michael is there as well, nodding alone while Maeve gives them her spiel, even if the setting and circumstances feel remarkably casual.

Deals are being made in the shadows. Treaties of peace, and honestly, secrecy, have been signed. While Scarlet Thunder, Crimson Peak, and the Allied Kingdoms will remain peaceful, they'll also remain separated... for now. There's no telling what the future will hold.

"How is our darling?"

My mother, Emelda, kneels at the foot of the couch beside Skye, who carefully turns Lucan to face his grandmother, who doesn't look a day over thirty even though she's well over two-hundred years old. Mom smiles, her eyes creasing, as she strokes her thumb over Lucan's cheek. "He's beautiful, just like you," she says with a teary smile, her eyes locked on Skye's face. My wife smiles shyly, and I notice her eyes dip momentarily to my mom's fangs.

"Mom, can I talk to you for a minute? Privately?"

She nods and rises, and I guide her into the study down the hallway leading to my family's bedroom, closing the door behind us with a soft click.

Her black hair ripples as she faces the window and the lake in the distance, which glimmers against a wash of golden city light. "I know what you want to talk about," she says in our native tongue, which feels so foreign after thirteen years of not hearing it. "You're staying here–forever."

"We'll visit. We've actually decided, with Blake's help, to make the journey in two months or so if Lucan's strong enough for it."

"You're meant to rule after your father," she says, turning to face me. "As his heir."

"It could be hundreds of years before an heir is needed. You know that."

"Our kingdom is stronger with you by our side. It's always been that way."

"My life is here, on that couch in the other room."

"I know." Her dark eyes meet mine. She shakes her head, curling her arms around her middle. "I can't...."

"Don't say it. It doesn't matter."

"It does matter."

"It doesn't. It never has."

"Drake told us everything, Alex. Everything you studied since you were a boy was to try to fix me! Because despite how we tried to shelter you from the truth and gravity of our situation, we couldn't. We love you. I love you. I love you now. Goddess, Alex, you were mine. My son. The one thing I wanted more than anything." Her eyes shine like starlight.

"I am, and will always be, your son. That isn't changing. But I cannot be the king of Scarlet Thunder."

"This is the life I wanted for you, Alex. I wanted you to fall in love. I wanted you to love someone as fiercely as I love your father, but–"

"But love is like looking into a mirror, and the reflection in front of you is all of the atrocities in our world? Trust me, I know. I think about Skye's safety every gods-damned day. I've been thinking about Lucan's future since the moment we found out he was on his way into the world."

"Skye isn't a vampire, Alex. One day, decades from now, she'll be gone."

"So will I."

"What?" Mom's lips part in shock, but the door to the study opens slowly with a creak, and Skye slips inside, carrying our son, cloaked in shadow.

I glance from her to Mom, raising my hands in surrender. "Skye is like her father, and she was what I was looking for in Lunaria. The Goddess Particle. The thing I thought could fix this for you, and not just for you–for Aunt Alma. For everyone like you both who were turned against your will."

"Alex, stop," Mom warns, but she notices Skye standing in the shadows and nods. "This is impossible."

"It's not. I'm still a vampire. I'll always be a vampire. That hasn't changed. But I can walk in the sunlight with my family. I can eat, for fuck's sake, without having to use my wife as a feeder."

"Alex." Mom shakes her head, but her eyes are locked on Skye's, a strange kind of hope glimmering there.

"She can work miracles. She is the Goddess Particle. She can heal you. Make you whole."

"I can turn you back into the witch you were or into a born vampire. It's your choice."

Mom is silent for several long, aching moments. She looks between us, wringing her hands, so I take them in mine, squeezing.

"You raised me as your own, and I love you. You will always be my mother. Always. But now, I have the opportunity to give you something for being the one to raise me into the man I am today. Let her help us."

Skye steps forward with Lucan resting in her arms, still fast asleep, but her eyes are glowing a soft violet now. Mom gasps.

"You could have a baby of your own. Dozens of them, if you wanted."

"Will it... will it hurt?"

"You won't feel a thing," Skye assures her and looks up at me for confirmation that this is about to happen.

It has to. That's the thing. In the end, Mom agrees, and I leave them in the study to have some privacy for Mom to ask her questions. I whisper to Dad to let him know where she is when he looks concerned that I've returned alone, with Lucan in my arms instead of with Skye, and he joins them, leaving me with Blake and Maeve.

"So it's settled," Maeve says, her arms crossed. "All is well with the vampires, and we can go back to our regularly scheduled programming."

"I'll be traveling with your parents back to Scarlet Thunder in two days, and when I return, I've set up a few meetings with the university

I'd like you to attend. My contacts there are interested in making your–"

The door to the suite bursts open with a crack that sends a shockwave through the entire regal apartment. Soren darkens the doorway, his face scrunched in a furious frown.

Blake arches a brow. Maeve scoffs, her voice pitched. "Did you just kick down the door?"

"Where is our daughter?"

"Which one?" she asks, concern turning her impeccably set features into disarray.

Soren hands her a piece of cardstock with an odd sheen that catches the overhead light and shimmers with what I can only describe as magic.

Skye and my parents step out of the study, interrupted by the commotion.

Maeve reads the letter, gasping, and her eyes fly to Soren's. She mouths *no*, but startles as the cardstock disintegrates in her hands, like it were meant to destroy itself the moment she read it.

"What was she thinking?" Maeve shouts and shoves past Soren. Her husband turns to follow.

Skye steps to my side and sighs at the door, which is hanging off its hinges. She takes my hand and squeezes. "So... still want to stay here in Moonrise? Or should we call this a wash and just move to Scarlet Thunder?"

51

FALLON'S STORY

FALLON

THE HUMID WEIGHT OF MID-SUMMER BEATS DOWN ON MY BROW AS I move through the garden, frowning at the twenty-foot wall shielding my view of the city of Moonrise–and the public's view of *me*. I crouch to pull a few weeds from the base of the hedgerow and dust my fingertips on the apron I stole off a hook in the servants' hall just off the garden, twisting the rough fabric between my fingertips. I rise and move on to the thickets of mustard greens, ignoring the tomatoes because their leaves make my fingers green and itchy, and all the while, a tall, aggravating, annoying, pointless shadow follows my progress.

I look up at the guard in royal garb–which includes a helmet and mask of iron–something I suppose was designed to look menacing, and it sure does. Sunlight glints off braids of iron and onyx covering his nose and mouth. His eyes are pools of the deepest black, even in direct light. His chest and arm guards are no different and likely weigh over a hundred pounds.

I guess that's nothing to a man his size.

"I know you're sweating to death in there," I chide, glaring up at the guard who's been my constant shadow the past two months, always lurking just within view wherever I am... including my suite, which really chaps my ass.

Publicly announcing my engagement to a, so far, unnamed prince of KiloKilo hasn't gone in my favor when it came to my parents, and now they believe that a spy from KiloKilo is going to snatch me in broad daylight while their kingdom calls it part of the contract, or however Mom worded it when we both spiraled into a screaming match that only ended after Dad hauled Mom over his shoulder and took her outside, and Sterling dragged me by my collar into the next room.

The guard says nothing to me. Nothing at all. Ever. He just stands there exuding male arrogance and duty.

"How much is my father paying you to stand here like an idiot all hours of the day?"

Nothing. Not even a flinch.

My gaze travels down his body, taking in his broad shoulders and chest and the slight taper of his waist. He crosses his arms over his chest, metal clanging, but I smirk, lingering on the thickness of his thighs in a fakely greedy fashion that's sure to make him uncomfortable enough to *leave me alone*.

But, alas, he remains there, only four feet away, watching me watch him with the same acute interest.

"Do you count how many steps I take in a day, too? How many times I run a brush through my hair? Oh, do you know what color my undergarments are today?"

Now, he turns to the side, looking out over the garden, where a small group of maids are bustling down a path away from us, carrying baskets of herbs and vegetables.

I follow his line of sight, which locks on one maid in particular. He goes as far as to turn his head ever so slightly to follow her before she falls out of sight again.

"Oh... so you have a crush?"

His head whips back in my direction.

I almost lurch out of my skin. I see him everywhere, all the time, but I've never seen him move that fast. Over the past six weeks or so, he's just been a column of armor in my peripheral vision, almost an appropriation in a gilded suit rather than someone with thoughts and feelings–let alone flesh. I almost ask if he's a vampire like Alex, which would explain the need for heavy, full-body armor at all times, I guess, but no. I can sense that he's not. He's a shifter male by his build, for sure, but there's something else about him that I suppose I still need to figure out.

"Well, that all but confirmed it," I mutter and rise, dusting my hands on the stolen apron. "Go chase her down and talk to her. I'm trapped within these walls, anyway. It's not like I can go anywhere." I raise my wrists to show him the golden bracelets inlaid with moonstones swirling with crimson powers. His icy black pools for eyes show no hint of thought or expression. Curiosity gets the best of me. I step toward him once, then twice, edging toward him like he's a feral, skittish animal, but he doesn't move away, not even when I'm standing mere inches from him, toe to toe with the 6'5" behemoth of a guard who towers over me by more than a foot. He angles his head down, looking directly at me while I skeptically peer up at him, then down at my bracelets, and raise my wrist so some of the crimson light shines over his helmet.

He tries to straighten in time to miss the glare of swirling light but not fast enough. His eyes illuminate, shining a deep, polished blue in the center but surrounded by the darkest brown, fanned by black lashes.

He steps away, grabbing my wrist, and turns me toward the house.

Outing *over*. Back to *timeout. Someone kill me.*

I shake out of his iron grip and frown up at him when he rests his fist against my lower back, barely touching me but touching me enough to silently command I move as directed. "I thought you'd be ugly, and that's why you wear that stupid mask. I know you're hot, too."

His fist tightens, gloved knuckles whispering against my spine.

"Temperature wise," I correct, rolling my eyes as the garden rolls into the south side of the castle, where the kitchen doors are open to let heat and steam escape. My hair curls violently in the humidity. Chefs and assistants rush around the kitchen preparing for dinner tonight, which seems odd given the level of production taking place.

It's only me and Sterling here currently. Mom is in Pantharas for another two weeks for a summit, and she took Naomi with her. Dad is in the Roguelands. Hell, even Skye and Alex are out of town to visit their friends in Lunaria with Lucan in tow, and Uncle Blake went with them, bringing Aunt Marianna, and so I'm... alone. Sterling doesn't necessarily count for company because he has his own thing going on, which includes *freedom*.

I slink through the castle, fuming, pulling the silken, capped sleeves of my shirt and matching skirt. I did, however, hang the apron up where it belonged unseen, but not so unseen... seeing as my ever-present shadow is still following me.

I glance over my shoulder at him. He keeps a roughly ten-foot distance between us–far enough away to give me a touch of space to decide where I want to go but close enough to jump into action should anything launch out of the shadows and take me captive.

Just as I turn the corner into the private western wing of the palace, which houses all the suites belonging to the family, I run into a familiar face.

Thank the Goddess.

I've never been more bored.

"Oh," Grandma Kenna says with a smile bright enough to light the night sky. "I was wondering where you went off to."

Regardless of feeling happy, she didn't leave me behind to go visit Uncle Aris and Aunt Posey, or whatever else she could be doing, like being down at the clinic, I reply, "Don't worry. My babysitter has been doing a fine job of ensuring I didn't climb over the exterior wall and make a break for it."

I whirl into a random open door that happens to be a seldom-used sitting room, but the doors to the balcony are open, as well as every single window, letting in a sweet, cool breeze brushing off the lake in the distance. I sigh and settle into the cool shadows before plopping down in a chair. Grandma Kenna follows me into the room, and so does… he.

Grandma gives him a small, flat smile as he closes the door behind him and settles into position. I roll my eyes back to the window with a huff.

"Oh, darling, it's temporary."

"I am being treated like a prisoner in my own home," I cut back, biting down on a snarl.

"And it's your own fault. You did exactly what your parents told you not to do. There is no engagement. There has been no contract or treaty of peace between the Allied Kingdoms and KiloKilo. In fact, they've sent their own forces into the sea beyond their veil, encroaching on Maatua's territory. Testing them."

"I am aware of the current political climate."

"Then, why were you so foolish, Fallon? You knew better than to force your parents' hand. Your mother's hand, especially." She throws her hands in the air in frustration. "You pick on her, you know. I watch you do it. You get under her skin on purpose."

I toy with the bracelets keeping my powers under lock and key–again, against my will–but it did seem like a better trade-off than being trapped in my room until my parents returned to the palace. "She makes it too easy sometimes."

"You," Grandma Kenna says under her breath, "are like her in so many ways it makes my head spin sometimes. Everyone says Naomi is her and Ella's spitting image, but while you didn't get her hot-headedness, you truly inherited her… insane skill of jumping to conclusions."

"I didn't jump to a conclusion. I made a decision that benefits the kingdom and solves a major issue in our relationship with a violent territory that proves every passing day that they can, and will, attack."

"The days of arranged marriages and breeders are over, Fallon. This is not your path."

"Then, we go to war with KiloKilo." I shrug, and for some reason, my babysitter shrugs his weight across the room, bowing his head ever so slightly like his helmet is weighing down his head. I hope it is.

I hope it hurts. "You read the proclamation. We have something of theirs, and they require something of ours."

"What the Grand Wizard required was *you*, and your mother said no. Whether we have something of theirs is entirely up for debate."

"And I said yes because, in the end, it's my decision. I am almost twenty-three years old. I am in my majority power-wise."

"Your parents are not going to serve you up on a silver platter to an enemy, no matter how advantageous–"

"They won't have to because I have already done it."

Grandma scrubs her face with her hand and fixes me with a sharp look.

I cross my legs and lean against the cushions, glancing at my babysitter again, and add, "But no one needs to worry about me falling into enemy hands because they'll have to get through him first." I twist a lock of my dark golden hair around my finger, letting the sarcastic remark settle.

Grandma Kenna looks at the guard with a sigh. "I have to agree that it's overkill. You can take off your helmet if you want, young man. It's ninety degrees. You must be dying in there."

He hesitates for a moment before reaching up, gloved hands with scaled armor catching the unforgiving sunlight, reflecting like fish scales as he slowly removes his helmet.

I sit back in shock as a young man with dark brown hair and a straight, sharp jaw appears, his hazel eyes scanning the room. His bronzed skin is glazed with sweat, and his cheeks are bright pink from the heat.

His eyes meet mine and narrow into the fiercest glare I've ever encountered.

I arch a brow. He mimics the motion.

"Well, I'm sure that's better. General Zayn won't allow anything to happen to you while your parents are away, and when they return, we can settle this issue diplomatically, *right?*" The last word is a warning, but I'm barely acknowledging Grandma Kenna anymore.

Nope. Just my rather handsome babysitter who's looking at me like he'd like nothing more than to dangle me over the balcony by my toes.

I roll my eyes to the ceiling with a huff. I can survive another two weeks under his constant watchful eye, can't I?

It is, to be fair, entirely my fault that I'm in this situation.

I wholeheartedly dug this grave myself.

ALSO BY BELLA MOONDRAGON

The Alpha King's Breeder series:
Bought by the Alpha: The Alpha King's Breeder Book 1 (free!)
Loved by the Alpha: The Alpha King's Breeder Book 2
Lost by the Alpha: The Alpha King's Breeder Book 3
Luna of the Alpha: The Alpha King's Breeder Book 4
Legacy of the Alpha: The Alpha Kings's Breeder Book 5
Daughter of the Alpha: The Alpha King's Breeder Book 6
Descendants of the Alpha: The Alpha King's Breeder Book 7
Shadow of the Alpha: The Alpha King's Breeder Book 8
Son of the Alpha: The Alpha King's Breeder Book 9
Spare of the Alpha: The Alpha King's Breeder Book 10
Claimed by the Alpha: The Alpha King's Breeder Book 11
Atonement for the Alpha King: The Alpha King's Breeder Book 12
Rejected by the Alpha: The Alpha King's Breeder Book 13
Abducted by the Alpha: The Alpha King's Breeder Book 14
Abandoned by the Alpha: The Alpha King's Breeder Book 15
Champion of the Alpha: The Alpha King's Breeder Book 16
Foxed by the Alpha: The Alpha King's Breeder Book 17
Mystic of the Alpha: The Alpha King's Breeder Book 18
The Alpha King's Breeder Books 1-3
Wolf Shifter Fairy Tale Retellings series
Beauty and the Alpha Beast: A Beauty and the Beast Retelling (free!)
Sleeping Beasty : A Sleeping Beauty Retelling
Tangling With the Alpha: A Rapunzel Retelling
Slipping Away From the Alpha: A Cinderella Retelling

Snow White and the Seven Rogues: A Snow White Retelling

The Luna's Vampire Prince series:

The Culling (free!)

The Kingdom

The Conquered

Pregnant With Four Alphas' Babies

Chosen As the Breeder (free!)

Mated to Four Alphas

Threats Against the Breeder

At War for the Breeder

The Stolen Breeder

Four Alphas, Four Babies

Becoming the Luna Queen

Descendants of the Breeder

Children of the Breeder

Desired by the Devil series

Whispers of the Devil (free!)

Banter of the Devil

Murmurs of the Devil

The Mafia Kings series

Indebted to the Mafia King (free!)

<u>Loved by the Mafia King</u>

Claimed by the Mafia King

Secrets of the Mafia King

Burned by the Mafia King

Kidnapped by the Mafia King

Dark Stalker Romance series

Tempted by Sin

Fated to Sin

Secret Billionaires series

Finding the Secret Billionaire by Olivia Bhelle Kildare

Falling for My Secret Billionaire by Bella Moondragon

Driven by the Secret Billionaire by ID Johnson

Wolf Shifter Alpha Kings series

Ravens and Ruins (free!)

Sundrops and Shadows

Snowflakes and Sabotage

Waves and Wickedness

Breezes and Bodies

The Vampire King's Feeder series

Claiming the Alpha's Daughter (free!)

Loving the Alpha's Daughter

Finding the Alpha's Daughter

Bewitching by the Alpha's Son

Writing as B. Moon

The Boy Who Died

Sign up for Bella's newsletter here.

Or get a free novella from The Alpha King's Breeder series when you sign up here:
The Beta and the Maid

Follow Bella on Facebook here.

Follow Bella on Bookbub here.